M000034849

See Glass

by

Ido Graf

This is a work of fiction. Names, characters, places and incidents are either the product of the author's imagination or are used fictitiously, and any resemblance to actual persons, living or dead, or to actual events, business establishments or locales is entirely coincidental.

Copyright © Ido Graf 2020

All rights reserved

Ido Graf has asserted his right under the Copyright, Designs and Patents Act 1988 to be identified as the author of this work.

Media Requests & Film Rights

All press enquiries or film rights requests relating to Ido's books should be directed to Ido Graf's publicist.

Any negotiations regarding the novels should be directed to his lawyers of choice in Washington D.C.

Please make any enquiries through the contact page.

https://www.idograf.com

ISBN: 978-1-9162140-1-9

CONTENTS

I dedicate this novel with the deepest love, affection and gratitude to:

My mother and to the memory of my father,

&

Our little darlings, Grace & Jude,

'And flights of Angels sing thee to thy rest.'

Mummy & Daddy

'Ignis aurum probat, miseria fortes viros.'

'Fire is the test of gold; adversity, of strong men.'

Lucius Annaeus Seneca

Roman dramatist, philosopher and politician (4 BC - 65 A.D.)

PROLOGUE

'One day can change your life! Have you ever heard that saying before?'

'This is my story of that one day.'

I WAS SITTING AT A SMALL, wooden table, having just ordered a glass of beer and a plate of calamari. It was a traditional, beachside restaurant and a common sight along much of the Mediterranean coastline. The exterior tables were artfully arranged on a dusty, concrete slab, with the restaurant itself, to the landward side. A low wall separated the beach from the seating area, though the floor merged into the sand of the beach where gaps for access occurred. The sun was, in part, shielded by a flat, reed matting roof. It looked as if it had been repaired, poorly, many years before and had not been touched since.

A warm breeze came off the sea, funnelled between the cliffs on either side of the scenic, Andalusian bay. The shifting wind intermittently masked the intoxicating smell of a large Bougainvillea, gone wild, which had lazily climbed up one of the restaurant's walls and had partially covered the reeds. Strands of vibrant, green leaves and masses of magenta flowers hung down through gaps, softly caressing unwary customers as they passed by, as they did from time to time.

Families were playing, swimming, tanning and laughing along the shoreline, mostly hidden behind windbreaks and beach umbrellas. Their chatter, carried on the wind, was quite discernible and predominantly Spanish, with a smattering of Portuguese from the few tourists. In the bay, many small boats, bobbed around as they were buffeted by the persistent waves.

In truth, it was a fairly typical scene, on a fairly typical day along the shoreline of the Andalusian Med. It was only later that I came to see that there was nothing at all typical about the events which unfolded, on that sun-drenched early afternoon.

As I enjoyed the warmth of the sun on my face, I watched lazily, as two seagulls flew in tandem, out towards the distant horizon, giving the occasional squawk as they battled against the breeze. They seemed to have no particular destination as they meandered into the distance, eventually disappearing from my view or maybe from my concentration. As the cooling, salt-laden wind gently brushed my skin, the effect, coupled with the repetitive sound of the waves, was sublime. With each cleansing gust, the troubles I had encountered in the preceding months, imperceptibly melted away and my spirits lifted, effortlessly. I had the almost physical sense of someone who has carried a heavy load for a long time only to feel it lifted from their back. And always, the constant noise of the incoming and receding water dragging sand and pebbles back and forth across the shore.

The table was covered with a sun-bleached, red and white Gingham cloth which was coarse to the touch. A straw basket, overloaded with fresh, roughly cut bread, lay in the centre of the table, along with two rustic, glass bottles, one of vinegar and one of an emerald coloured, olive oil. A small, empty plate lay to the side, a residue of oil the only remnant of its contents. I had eaten the offering of tapas with relish – large green olives stuffed with lemon and packed with flavour. A rapid movement drew my eye to the wall of the restaurant. A small lizard scuttled up the face, stopping to look about him before he darted off again with a great sense of purpose.

A sudden gust of wind angrily rustled the pages of the newspaper that I had been reading. It lay, discarded, on the ground beside me. The chattering pages reminded me of the headlines of 'El Mundo' which proclaimed the deaths of yet more prominent politicians and other notables.

3

Some were unexplained, and some appeared to be just coincidental. Russia and America, along with Europe and South America, had been rocked by many unexplained and unrelated, it seemed, events. Overall, it made for depressing reading, as if I weren't depressed enough already.

As I waited for the food and the beer, I began to pull at a piece of bread and to slowly eat. Over time, I found myself chewing in unison with the rhythm of the wind, almost hypnotically. It tasted as if it had just left the bakers oven. It had.

Sometime before, I had noticed an elegant yacht silently sailing into the bay. It shone brilliantly in the high sun. Initially, I had paid it just a passing notice; however, my eyes were drawn towards it once more.

The yachtsman eventually dropped anchor close to the shore, and the occupants began busying themselves on deck. The French tricolour which hung from the back of the yacht flapped violently. While I watched, a man, a woman and a young girl climbed over the side into the small, white dinghy which was in tow. As the man let slip the painter, a yellow Labrador jumped from the stern into the sea and made an enormous splash, to the happy excitement of the young child. I followed the little group as the man slowly, but deliberately, rowed them into shore. They were closely followed by the Lab, who seemed utterly at home in the sparkling water. Looking back now, I do not know why I was drawn to them ...but I was, helplessly.

At that point, I turned, hearing the waiter approach. He held a bottle of beer and a glass. The man carefully poured the drink, taking great care as if it were an ancient Claret, watching it lightly froth, as did I. Thanking him, I returned my gaze to the bay. By the time I had looked back towards the rowing boat, the woman and infant were struggling up the beach. They were laden down with towels, beach umbrellas and other 'necessities'. The man, some distance behind them, was pulling the dinghy up onto the sand, helped by the intermittent action of the relentless waves. He was strong and powerful, and he made swift work of it.

This little group, who had sailed into my world, increasingly held my attention, as I continued to watch them. I was a voyeuristic intruder in their lives and a voyeur by trade.

Having made the boat secure, the man walked over to his companions, who had by then claimed their area of golden sand as their own. Lying on their beach towels, under a large, red umbrella, he stood over them saying a few words. The Lab happily lumbered from the water, then shook the sea from his fur as he showered the group. The adults hardly noticed, but the happy, little girl let out a scream and then began to laugh once more.

The sailor had a strong face - hard. But when he looked at his companions, there was a clear impression of deep affection, a softening, which shone through. He lent down and, smiling, he ran his hand through the young girl's long, blond hair. Leaving them, he slowly began to walk up the beach. He was followed, briefly, by the Labrador who was wildly wagging his tail. However, the dog's pursuit did not last, and he eventually turned back and lay down under the umbrella beside the girl, exhausted from his swim. Suddenly at ease, he quickly dozed off, with a paw laying across the young girl's leg.

The man threaded his way through the sunbathers and up towards the restaurant. Some of the women on the beach threw him occasional, admiring glances, but he didn't seem to notice. Seeing me looking at him, he stared straight back, looking right through me. The kindness and love of a few moments before had gone. It had been replaced by a cold, steely, thoughtful expression. I held his gaze for a moment before looking away, but I still sensed him coming closer. I could feel him watching me. A sudden tingle of nerves raced along my spine, dancing to a tune I did not care for.

The restaurant was not large, and he sat one table away, facing me. We were the only people sitting outside. The waiter arrived, and the new customer ordered a drink, in fluent Spanish, 'Pastis, por favor.'

He did not look Spanish, more North European. The Spanish he spoke was from the Americas and most certainly not Castilian. I could see from the corner of my eye that, like me, he had begun to eat the bread that the waiter had just left for him in a small basket. He ignored the glazed, blue dish of tapas – boquerones fritos, fried anchovies. With each piece of bread that he took, he lightly drizzled it with olive oil from the bottle on his table. The breeze began to pick up, and I was glad, as it had become too hot, and the smell of the salt was quite cathartic. I could feel beads of sweat on my forehead, which I had not noticed before. I took a gulp of beer and quickly glanced over at my fellow diner, as the returning waiter gave him a glass of Pernod and a small, clay jug of water. It was then, as he picked up the pitcher and methodically poured water into the Pastis watching as it clouded, that I noticed a faded tattoo on his left forearm. It was not clear, as his heavy tan helped to obscure it partially, but I recognised it immediately. It was the badge of the French Foreign Legion.

I called over to him, 'A moi la Légion!' and gave a smile.

It was a traditional call for assistance from fellow Legionnaires. He suddenly looked directly at me, his expression surprised and serious. Seeing my smile, his face, which had been tense, relaxed. Following my gaze, he looked down at the tattoo on his forearm.

Looking back, expressionless, he said in fluent, but harsh French, with a heavy accent, 'Vous êtes un legionnaire?' I replied, 'J'étais,' and I pulled the short sleeve of my blue, seersucker shirt up to reveal the same image on my bicep - my past, our connection.

I said, in what I took to be his native tongue, 'You are English, no?'

He replied, 'No, American, but I lived in England for a time.'

'American - that explains the Spanish.'

He stared at me, no longer cold; instead, the man appeared more questioning. Seeming more at ease, he replied, 'Yes and no. One of my grand-mothers was Mexican, and I grew up with it. I like to speak Spanish when I can, as it reminds me of her ...' pausing for a moment, a shadow seemed to pass over him, before he continued, 'you're German or Austrian ...or maybe Swiss?'

'German originally, from Munich to be pre-cise, but I live in Paris now. Or at least I did.'

There was a pause, 'Did?' Adam, for that, was his name, said firmly.

'Yes, I lost my job three weeks ago. *They* had to make cuts, *they* are downsizing ...the internet has been a blessing and a curse. I'm an investi-gative reporter ...well, I was a reporter. I'm now a cut, a bad news story,' I said, giving as hearty a smile as I could muster.

'Are you down here drowning your sorrows?' he said enquiringly.

'No, not really. We ...my family and I already had this holiday booked before the firm let me go. So, we just thought that we would come any-way and use the time to think about the future. However, my wife and my daughter seem much more interested in shopping rather than plan-ning. So, I thought I would contemplate alone.'

I smiled back at him, but he just looked right through me. He was, to my mind a little strange, not antagonistic, but distant – maybe troubled and he seemed to be continually examining and assessing. I felt slightly uneasy with him. It was not an unfriendly stare, more an observing look. He did not seem to be a bad man, just preoccupied ...strong-willed certainly. His hair was dark, and though his skin was tanned; it did not look like his natural colouring. He was dressed in loose, blue canvas shorts and an open-necked short-sleeved shirt of pale, cream linen. His shoes were Docksides, blue with a white sole; they were faded and well-worn, as was the rest of his garb.

He took a sip of his drink, savoured it and then asked me, 'Have you any idea what you will do?'

As he said it, he slowly glanced back towards the young woman and the child who had accompanied him. The woman had remained on her beach towel, while the little girl played in the surf with the Lab.

As he looked, I followed his eyes, and I said, 'I'm not sure, it's not so easy now. I have responsibilities, and I'm older. Who wants an old Legionnaire, who thinks he can write?'

The man's silence demanded a better answer.

He turned back to look at me once more, again I followed his lead and giving a half-smile I said, 'I don't know ...there are a few opportunities in Africa, in mining with some old friends from the regiment. But the parts of Africa available to me would be difficult for my wife and Élodie, my daughter. The ones on offer are not the safest countries in the region. My wife wants me to write a book about my 'wild' adventures in the Legion, but it's been done before. Who knows! What about you?'

He returned his gaze to the woman and child. Then he said, 'We've been travelling for a while, sailing around the Med. We are heading to Malta now ...and then maybe some island hopping around Greece.'

'Sounds like a great life! What do you do for a living?'

He instantly turned and looked straight at me, and after a short silence he said, 'I'm in security ...a private client.'

His gaze was suddenly intense, almost threatening. I sensed that I had asked the wrong question.

The man had said 'client', but I wondered if he meant 'clients', the young woman and child. Though, something did not work with that scenario. The way he looked at the pair was too familiar, too intimate for a bodyguard. He clearly did not want to elaborate, so I let it go. After all, I was not on the payroll anymore ...I had no more stories I needed to tell.

'Papa!' I turned my head to see my daughter running towards me with outstretched arms, and then we hugged before she quickly kissed me on both cheeks. Her mother was following behind at a short distance.

I looked back to the former Legionnaire who was now looking and smiling, and I said, 'Please let me introduce you to my daughter, Élodie and here is my beautiful wife, Claudine.'

As my wife glided in, with a shopping bag in one hand, he smiled and said to them, 'Hello, I'm Adam, a friend from the Legion.'

'Hello Adam,' they said almost in unison and with wonderfully musical French accents.

Adam's senses were overcome, as the gusting air was suddenly alive with the scent of Coco Mademoiselle by Chanel.

Élodie turned to me and said, 'Papa, I have just seen a beautiful dress. But it is ...' she glanced furtively at her mother, 'too expensive.'

As I glanced at Élodie, I saw my wife look past me and towards Adam smiling and raising her eyes to the heavens in gentle mockery.

Élodie gazed up into my eyes and smiled sweetly. I asked, 'How much was it?'

'Fifty euros, Papa!' she said sheepishly.

I peered into her happy face and did not have the heart to deny it. Smiling, I said, 'I'm sure you would look very elegant in it. Maybe Maman could bring you back to the shop?'

'Papa!' she cried out in joy and turned to her mother, who displayed a mock frown, before melting into a broad smile.

Looking at Adam and then at me, she scolded, 'So Legionnaires are tough?'

Adam said, smiling, 'But we are only ex-Legionnaires!'

Élodie ran to her mother and held her hand, tugging gently but firmly on it, 'Maman, can we get it now? Pleaasseee!' and with that, she happily led her mother away, skipping as she ran.

As they disappeared from the restaurant,

Claudine looked back and called, 'Wonderful to meet you, Adam,' and then she was gone.

Adam said, 'You have a lovely family.'

'Thank you ...yes, I am truly blessed.'

Adam was quiet for a while, and I left him to his thoughts. The waiter delivered my calamari with a whole, fresh lemon which had been roughly quartered. It was an enormous plate of food. As the waiter departed once more, I asked Adam if he would like to share some with me, but he just smiled and declined.

I asked what regiment he had been in and he replied, 'The *2e REP, 4e CIE.*'

The Régiment étranger de parachutistes and the 4th Company were specialist snipers and demolition experts. They were a real hard bunch, even for the Legion.

'One of the tough guys, hey! So, what was your role?'

'I was a sniper ...' he said.

He was silent for a moment looking at his glass, and then he continued, 'It ran in the blood. I had been a U.S. Marine Scout Sniper, so it was a no brainer when I enlisted in the Legion.'

I could not help but think that that was not all he had been.

I hadn't known many Americans in the Legion, and I asked him why he had chosen to join up, and he said, 'I wanted to learn French and to experience the life there, in France. I felt I owed the French people something and helping to defend their country seemed ...appropriate.'

'What for their gift to the U.S. of the Statue of Liberty?' I mocked.

He was thoughtful and silent for a moment and then said, 'My mother and her parents had been given refuge in the 1940s by a kindly French family in the Haute-Savoie. My family were Jewish. The Legion seemed as good a way as any to repay the debt to the French people!'

'How about you?' he countered.

'Ha, I wish I knew,' I said, as I methodically ate my food, 'I expect it was a yearning for adventure more than anything, but I'm happy I joined up ...the Legion was good to me.'

I lazily squeezed lemon juice onto the calamari and ate some more. When I looked up at Adam, I found that he was staring at me once again, but this time with a poker face.

'I don't know your name?' he asked.

'Franck,' I replied. It was the name I had taken when I had joined the Legion and not my given name.

We spoke at length about our time in the Legion and the comrades we had met. Though we had served at different periods, there were Legionnaires whom we had both known.

After some time, he again fell into a thoughtful silence, as I finished my calamari. Relaxing, I eased back into the chair, finishing my beer off swiftly.

'That book you mentioned,' there was a silence, and then he said, 'I know of a story that you may wish to write about. And who better to tell it than a Legionnaire?'

'I'm only an ex-Legionnaire!' I smiled.

Though he also smiled, he said nothing. It was my turn to stare, and I said, 'You've intrigued me now?'

I extended my outstretched hand towards his table and asked, 'Do you mind if I join you?'

Moving his breadbasket to the side, he invitingly pushed the chair opposite him away from the table with his foot. I quickly joined him and calling to the waiter, I ordered another round of drinks. The journalist inside me had been awakened from its enforced hibernation.

We waited in silence until the waiter had fulfilled the order, which only served to heighten my anticipation. Adam poured water from the jug into the new glass of Pernod and took a long sip of the Pastis, again savoured it and then began to recount his tale.

As he spoke, I said nothing. I did not drink my beer or eat from the basket of bread and nor did I look away. He spoke fluidly and sometimes wistfully as if the words came from a well-remembered memory. I had served in the Legion for five years, and I had met some very colourful characters, some of whom I had wished that I had never met. Most had a story to tell, some strange, some deadly, some false, though I had come to appreciate that many of the tales were true.

When Adam had finished, I took a long sip of my drink. I then asked, 'Did this actually happen?'

He made no answer. Picking up his glass, he

finished the last of his Pernod. Standing up, he left a pile of coins on the table and then went to leave, looking back at me, he smiled, saying only, 'Au revoir, mon ami et bonne chance,' and then he was gone.

I watched him, in utter incredulity, as he walked back across the beach to his companions. He walked tall and steady despite the soft sand, and once again, the women looked and once again, he did not appear to notice. After twenty minutes, he and his party packed up and went back to the shoreline. He moved the boat into the surf, and as it rocked in the waves, he helped, first the girl and then the woman on board. He pushed the dinghy into deeper water. Then Adam climbed aboard setting off for the yacht, his paddles enthusiastically digging into the waves. As before, he was followed by the ever-industrious dog.

Relentlessly toiling through the waves, they made fast the dinghy with the painter and climbed aboard the boat. The Lab came alongside the stern and Adam's two powerful arms dropped down to scoop him up, wriggling and wet, into the cockpit – I thought for a moment that I had caught sight of the tattoo once more, but in reality, the distance was too far. The sea was stippled with whitecaps and occasional sheets of spray and looked destined to become even more animated. Adam pulled the anchor up, and as they got underway, the yacht turned in the waves, and I saw its name, 'See Glass'.

I was perplexed – 'sea glass' was the name

given to the glass that came from discarded bottles which were broken and tumbled by the motion of the sea over time to resemble translucent pebbles, but which still retained their original brilliant blues, greens and other assorted colours.

Either the yacht's name was incorrectly spelt, '*See*' instead of '*Sea*', or it seemed to have no discernible meaning. I thought about it, wondering if it alluded to a sailor seeing a sea as flat as glass, but it still seemed wrong.

'What could it be?'

Momentarily the yachtsman turned back to look at me, but that was the last I ever saw of him. I lifted my glass in a toast saying softly, 'Au revoir, mon ami et bonne chance à vous.'

Suddenly, I was distracted. I looked down, hypnotically, at the pages of 'El Mundo' as they flapped violently in a directionless breeze.

Transfixed, my eyes bore through the moving pages and burrowed deep into the recesses of my thoughts, 'Could it really be true?'

I grabbed my tattered notebook from my pocket and slid the small pencil out of its spine. Momentarily, I stared into the distance as I gathered my thoughts and then I began to write furiously.

I have tried to fully recall the events of that day and the story he imparted. Adam was the name he gave me, but I doubt that it was the real one which he went by. He did not ask me to change names, places or any dates. I suspect he had done so already.

Many of those who were involved in this matter are now dead or have disappeared. Of those who live, only one wants the story to see the light of day.

What follows is a faithful recollection of what I was told. As to its truth ...that is for you to decide?

CHAPTER ONE

AN ACRID SMELL OF SMOKE and burning rubber filled the air while the falling ash gave the appearance of a winter snow scene. The moustachioed man had a look of utter despair as he surveyed the desolation before him. He stood, melancholic, amid bomb craters and rubble with no structure around him untouched by shrapnel or bullets. Piles of shattered brick and glass lay strewn everywhere, and great tangles of re-enforcing wire hung helplessly in mid-air, violently torn from the concrete which had once encased it.

The relentless sound of shellfire was deafening, and with the passage of time was clearly coming closer. He saw, a little way off, assortments of terrified civilians and motley bands of dishevelled troops running in all directions. Then he noticed a small group of French SS volunteers from the 33rd Waffen Grenadier Division of the SS Charlemagne. They had emerged from an alley and were heading towards the area of the Brandenburg Gate. The troops appeared determined and even now, invincible. The tired man felt a sudden sense of pride at seeing them, as they reminded him of how unified the world could have become under the National Socialists.

Darkness was beginning to fall, but the flaming vehicles and the ruined buildings gave an unearthly feeling to the ugly scene

Nearby, an army truck sat on the road looking as if it had been deftly parked close to the kerb. It had no wheels, and all the windows had been blown out. Its bonnet was twisted, and most of the bodywork was peppered with shrapnel damage, giving it the look of Swiss cheese. The back of the vehicle was empty and in part, heavily charred. A young man hung lazily from the driver's side door. He wore a filthy blood-spattered uniform which bore the insignia of a Panzergrenadier. One arm and half of his head were missing. What remained of his face seemed quite serene to the moustachioed man who gazed at him, trancelike.

Suddenly an SS-Oberführer burst out of a heavy metal door set into a long concrete wall. He headed past the two SS sentries who stood guard and ran over to the man, wrenching him from his thoughts.

'Herr Reichsführer, the vehicle will be here momentarily.'

The man turned around and looked, unspeaking, at the SS officer.

The SS-Oberführer said once again, more nervously this time, 'Herr Reichsführer, we should leave as soon as possible, once it arrives.'

The man, Heinrich Himmler, looked at him and then turned back to stare at the dead soldier in the truck.

'How could it have come to this?' he thought to himself, 'we were invincible!'

Inwardly he thought that this was now the taste of defeat.

The officer stepped forward and stretching his arm out in an outwardly respectful, encouraging gesture, he again bade Himmler ahead. Carefully, but determinedly, he gradually led Heinrich Himmler towards what remained of Voss Strasse. Himmler would never again see Adolf Hitler or the Führerbunker or even Berlin for that matter.

As they left the grounds, the Reichsführer looked back towards the bunker and the surrounding buildings, which would soon become the tomb of so many in the coming days. He departed with a growing sense of relief. Himmler thought of his last talk with Hitler only moments before. It was Adolf's birthday, but nobody felt like celebrating. It had been a sombre and distressing meeting. Hitler had placed his hand gently on Himmler's shoulder as he departed. Himmler felt that that final touch had been the saddest moment of his life.

Continuing, the two men picked their way

through the knot of contorted steel, rubble and the occasional dead body. Ahead of them, they saw their Kübelwagen, waiting in the middle of the road, its engine still running. The SS driver had remained at the wheel, while an SS-Untersturmführer stood guard beside the open passenger door. That junior officer held a Maschinenpistole 40 firmly in his hands, and he had three stick grenades pushed casually under his belt. The soldier had the look of a killer, and he scanned the area as if he expected to kill again.

Himmler climbed into the vehicle, followed by the two officers. Before the doors had fully closed, the driver screeched away repeatedly swerving to avoid the debris on the road.

The SS-Oberführer shouted at the driver to make his way out of the city as best he could and then to head north. The man did not need to be told twice.

The ride was extremely uncomfortable as the vehicle constantly lurched and then bumped over the rubble. Himmler hardly noticed this as he looked out at the scene of devastation all around him. His skin looked grey, and he had aged by ten years in the last few months. The supreme confidence of previous years had been replaced with concern and fear. But still, there was his inner belief that he would rise again if only he could survive.

He had been one of the most feared men in Nazi Germany, but now it was him who was scared.

He turned to SS-Oberführer Gartmann and said in a tired, hushed voice, 'Once we are away from 'this place', I need to get to Lübeck. Arrange a meeting with Count Folke Bernadotte. I will propose that he act as a go-between with the British, the Americans and me. I intend to offer an alliance between them and the German Army to exterminate the Soviet menace permanently.'

'Certainly, Herr Reichsführer!' Gartmann snapped enthusiastically.

He turned to look out of the side window. An almost imperceptible change occurred in his eyes. After years of unswerving loyalty, Gartmann had, over the last six months, begun to lose respect for the Reichsführer.

Though still wary of Himmler's diminishing power, Gartmann secretly believed that the alliance was the fanciful dream of a man who had lost all touch with reality.

He knew the fate that awaited many within the ranks of the SS would be unpleasant and final once the allies, or worse the partisans, had captured them.

He thought to himself, 'Herr Reichsführer, you will soon be dead and yet, I will live. It will not be you who is the next Fuhrer in our glorious Fourth Reich!' Then he smiled and said cryptically, 'Soon the Spider's work will be done!'

The meeting at the Swedish consulate on the 23rd of April did not give, as Gartmann expected, the desired result for Himmler and his offer was rejected.

Once this final throw of the dice was lost,

Himmler, Gartmann and a small group of companions headed for the coast to rendezvous with a U-boat which would take them to South America and to safety.

Coming to the village of 'Neuhaus an der Oste', Gartmann suggested that they split up to better evade capture. The SS-Oberführer had pre-arranged the beach rendezvous point with the U-boat captain and subsequently passed on the location to Himmler and the others in the party. After that, they broke up into smaller groups.

Gartmann headed off with a young and enthusiastic SS-Hauptsturmführer. Within an hour, Gartmann had killed the junior officer, stabbing him from behind straight through the heart, just before throwing his body into a ditch. There would be no witnesses to what was to occur.

Gartmann knew, now, that he would be the only person waiting on the beach for the inflatable to pick him up and to make the transfer to the U-Boat. He had purposefully given the others a false rendezvous point forty miles further along the coast. He figured the further they had to travel, the more chance they would have of getting caught. Gartmann wanted Himmler apprehended, executed and out of the way.

Several hours later he stood among the sand dunes, alone in the darkness. Oddly, he was enjoying the fine drizzle that fell on his face. Gartmann knew that before he felt the warmth of the Americas, he would probably not see the outside of the submarine for several months. This was his farewell to Germany, for the time being. He pulled a gold lighter and a tatty cigarette packet from the pocket of his greatcoat. The SS man had chosen a very remote spot for the pick-up, but even so he still cautiously looked about before he lit up. He kept the flame of the lighter burning after he had the cigarette alight and once, he had taken a long, satisfying drag. Illuminated in the glow, he held up, admiringly, the green packet of Eckstein No5s, his favourite brand. Gartmann took another deep lungful of the spicy, unfiltered smoke, held it and then slowly exhaled, letting the lighter flame extinguish as he did so. He felt a growing sense of relief, warmth and comfort.

He had arrived at the coast nearly two hours early. But with each passing minute, he initially became more anxious and then increasingly worried.

The rendezvous had been set for 11.15 p.m. Gartmann looked at his watch and read 11.40 p.m. Several times, his heart skipped a beat as he thought he heard a noise in the dunes. The Luger which he had previously stuffed in an inside pocket of his heavy woollen coat was held ready in his hand. It took enormous self-control to keep a grip on himself and to decide that the wind and his imagination were playing tricks on him. He could not stop imagining a vivid scene in which he was swinging at the end of a rope beside Himmler.

He felt sick to his stomach.

'Had the U-boat been sunk?'

'Had Himmler found out?'

'Was it a trap?'

He was about to light his fourth cigarette when a silhouette on the horizon far out across the waves caught his eye.

Seeing a sudden beam of light, three flashes, out to sea, he signalled the sailors in response with his lighter flame. His heart began to beat faster, and his whole body erupted in a sigh of relief. He felt an uncontrollable elation. As the submariners came ashore in their inflatable, he headed out to meet them and trudging through the sand he smiled and said softly to himself, 'Auf Wiedersehen Herr Himmler. I hope you enjoy the drop!' Gartmann purposefully left out Himmler's rank as a final and intensely pleasurable insult.

Fate, however, had other plans for Herr Himmler. He would never face a hangman's noose. Within a month he was dead, 'apparently' by his own hand while in custody.

Gartmann climbed into the rubber craft, making it clear that he would now be the only passenger. After battling back through the waves, he was welcomed on to the U-Boat by a nervous Leutnant zur See. The man continuously scanned the area for allied shipping or planes. After stowing the inflatable, the crew and Gartmann disappeared into the hull.

Almost as soon as the last hatch was sealed, the U-Boat slipped below the surface. 'Der

Schatten', 'the shadow' went with it, a very relieved and happy man.

CHAPTER TWO

I N THE FAR CORNER OF the kitchen, on a heavy rug, lay a large yellow Labrador. He was not sleeping, but he looked as if he could have been asleep. His eyes were half-hooded, still watching with a certain lazy, furtive intensity. The subject of the dog's curiosity stood by the counter. The Lab watched as a man wielded a knife swiftly and with the natural control of an expert. He was slicing garlic, releasing its powerful odour as he did so. The man was slicing it wafer-thin, on a thick, wooden cutting board. To the back of the board, lay a tomato, a courgette and several mushrooms. All were sliced in the same precise manner, and all stood in neat order, like soldiers on a parade ground.

To the left of the man, the last remnants of dried spaghetti were sinking into a pot of rapidly boiling water. He finished slicing the garlic and

27

left it where it lay. Putting the knife neatly on the worktop, he grabbed a large bottle of olive oil from the rear of the counter. Pulling out the cork, he poured a few drops into a pan, replaced the cork and then the bottle. As he did so, still watched by the Labrador, his mobile phone began to ring.

The man opened a leather pouch on his belt and removed the device. Looking at the caller's ID and pressing answer, he held it to his ear and said nothing. The caller spoke only one word, 'Red,' which had been pre-arranged long before. The voice was that of an old man, and that old man sounded scared.

He, in turn, replied, also with only one word, 'Blue,' and as he did so, his countenance changed. Gone was the relaxed face, to be replaced by that of a man who sensed great danger.

He killed the call and the gas on the cooker. Swiftly turning towards the exterior kitchen door and looking back at the dog, he said, 'Kaiser, stay.'

He grabbed a tweed hunting jacket from the back of a chair and from a shelf above the door he took a pistol, a Glock model 17, in a black nylon shoulder holster. Adam quickly pulled the shoulder holster on, over his tan, moleskin shirt, followed by the tweed jacket. Grasping three more clips of bullets from the same shelf he opened the door, dropping the clips into the large left-hand pocket of his coat.

He slammed the door shut and running across the part-cobbled courtyard, jumped into the driver's seat of the long-wheelbase Land Rover. The air felt cold, and the wind was wild, as autumn was just settling in. Adam raced away, turning his lights on as his wheels, desperate for traction, peppered the countryside with gravel and mud. He drove around the side of the farmhouse and passed the farmer's barns which concealed the house from the track. Driving the quarter mile along the rough lane through fields of sugar beet, Adam slid to a halt at the metalled road. His route clear, he screeched away from Sloe Farm, driving at an unsafe speed for two miles twisting and turning through the erratic, hedgerow lined route.

Reaching the crossroads near his destination, where he would usually turn right, he carried straight on. After two-hundred yards, on the gradually descending road, he turned off left into an old bridleway and shortly afterwards, killed the lights and then the engine. Adam jumped out of the Land Rover and ran back the way he had come, feeling his heart pounding as he did so. Quickly crossing the metalled road, he climbed through a gap in the hedgerow on the other side and into the field beyond. He did not feel the hawthorn, blackthorn and dog rose as their spikes and thorns violently scratched his hands and face. Adam knelt silently at the edge of the recently ploughed field, listening and watching ahead. Only rooks, unsettled by the increasing wind, cawed loudly. All before him seemed as it should have been, though he knew it could not be. Directly across the field and making its southern boundary, was a long stone wall. Within its perimeter, partially hidden by large oak and beech trees, there lay an old Georgian manor house, Rook Hall. Intermittently, he caught the smell of the smoke from one of its chimneys, which carried on the wind.

He did not wish to approach the house by crossing the field directly as there was a full moon, and he would have been highly visible. He wondered if others, as yet unknown, had chosen this night for that very reason. Instead, he weaved his way along the hedge in parallel with the house and following the line of the road's gradual descent. On reaching the corner, he dropped down a shallow bank to the edge of a small brook that formed the eastern side of the field. He followed this for two-hundred yards, hidden by the bank, and at the end, he climbed up the incline and into the small wood that bordered the property.

As the crows were already making much noise among the swaying trees, his appearance made little impact. At the lip of the bank, he waited once more and watched and listened. Again, nothing seemed out of place, though he could sense that something was very wrong – he could almost taste it.

Adam was close to the long wall. It was made of limestone and was light in colour. He saw, thirty yards away, an untidy clump of ivy which had slowly climbed the wall over the years. He had meant to have it removed, but now it would be of use to him, and so he crawled on his belly towards the base of it. The cold earth against his hands and face went unnoticed. Adam used the spread of its dark green, waxy leaves to disguise his profile against the stonework and its thick upright, woody stems for support. Scaling the eight-foot wall, he still used the ivy at the top as cover as he carefully viewed the grounds. Everything was quiet. Adam could see the side profile of the house in full and a fair proportion of the rear facade. Still, the only sound emanated from the crows and the wind and now his intense suppressed breathing and pounding heart. The smell of the wood smoke from the chimney had become much more noticeable. In times gone by, it would have been a welcoming smell on a cold evening, but no more. He believed that it would be coming from one of the ground floor fires, probably the study. Adam waited for a minute and then nimbly slid over the wall, scuffing his hands on the rough-hewn rock and gently dropping to the ground.

As he landed, there was a faint, almost unheard crunch of dead leaves. Seamlessly he pulled his gun from its holster. He felt more at ease now, less vulnerable. Once more, he waited for a moment and then began to gently creep along the edge of the wall, always remaining in its shadow. Adam wanted a better view of the front of the house and a fuller view of the grounds. Then he saw it. He wished he had not.

Near the base of a large beech tree, among the wildly, dancing leaves, lay a dark, unmoving mound. Adam knew what it meant. He crawled towards the dark shape and saw the face of his friend and colleague, gradually revealed. Luke lay there, unmoving, on his back with arms outstretched. He was dead. Two bullet wounds were visible in his chest and a third, slightly off centre, through his forehead. His rifle, still in his hand, looked unfired and on checking Luke's Ruger MP9 pistol, it was in place in his chest holster, again unused. He did not have a chance; he wouldn't have even known what had hit him. Luke was a big man, six-foot-three and solidly built, with skin of the darkest, ebony black. He lay near the perimeter wall, close to the gravel drive, which extended between the house and the front gates. Adam had met Luke in the Legion many years before. He put his hand on Luke's shoulder and squeezed a final farewell to that fine Djiboutian. Throughout, he continued to scan the grounds, looking, smelling and listening for anything unusual, anything deadly.

Adam made his way back to the shadow of the wall and crawled towards the front of the property. Using tree trunks as cover, he edged his way further into the grounds. He could then get a better view of the main facade of the building. The upper floors were in darkness, but much of the ground floor was fully lit. The large, oak, entrance door was wide open, and the steps leading up to it were bathed in yellow light emanating from the hall.

It was then that he saw Franco. He wore smart country clothing, like the other guard, and was also powerfully built. He lay on his side close to one of the stone pillars which flanked the steps. He must have been using them for cover when he too was killed. Bullet marks riddled the stone steps on the right-hand side, just as they did with Franco. He had numerous bullet wounds in his body and one on his cheek, just below the right eye socket. Staring at the dark sky as if in wonder, a tear of blood slipping from the unnatural hole in his face. Adam held his stare for a moment as he looked at Franco, who had been a constant in his life since basic training in Castelnaudary, in southern France. There were few Sicilians in the Legion and so, he had enjoyed a kind of celebrity status, often hinting at a dark past. Franco's weapons lay beside him. Adam checked them. Both barrels of the shotgun had been fired. Unlike most of its kind, this one was loaded with lethal solid slug shot which could have taken down a bull. His automatic pistol was still in his right hand, gripped tightly. It too had been fired, judging by the litter of shell casings that surrounded him. They had guarded Oscar, or as we had referred to him, the Major.

Adam surveyed the area of the gardens around him. He felt a sick sensation in his stomach, his heart pumping as the adrenaline surged through his body. Adam sensed that the welcoming light of the house did not offer any welcome at all, it held only danger and death. Equally, he knew that he had to enter the house, like a moth to a flame. Adam looked at the front door and the empty hall beyond.

'Was it a trap or the remains of a hasty departure?' he wondered.

Adam crept back towards the boundary wall, keeping to the shadows of the trees and the bushes. Using the wall to cover his blindside, he edged his way around the house to the back door. He saw no visible signs of forced entry. Adam scanned all of the windows and doors for any watching eyes but saw none.

Quickly crossing the garden, he headed for a section of the house wall that had no overlooking windows. He crouched down near a metal plate that butted up against the brickwork, towards the back of the Hall. This was unused now but, long ago, had been the chute for the delivery of coal. To the unknowing observer, it had been welded shut to prevent entry by unwanted intruders. However, under a loose brick to the side of it, a small metal leaver released the metal plate together with the frame that it sat in. He quietly pulled it back and slipped into the chute below. Adam braced himself against the walls by exerting counter pressure with his legs and his back, just as he had been taught in the US Marines when climbing a 'chimney'. It referred to a cleft in a rock face with vertical sides which were predominantly parallel. While he hung in space, his body tense from the effort, Adam lowered the metal cover back into its slot before hearing it lock into place. Gently releasing the pressure on his legs and back, he slid down the chute, gun at the ready, until he could step out into the former coal cellar. It had not been used for many years and was, typically, quite damp.

The Hall now used an oil-fired central heating system, which had been fitted in the 1960s. The open fires were mainly for aesthetics and occasional enjoyment and also served as a backup. They were no longer fed with coal but burnt wooden logs instead. It was inky dark, and Adam grabbed a small Maglite that he carried in a pouch on his belt. He scanned the room with the torch and found it to be, as he expected, empty.

Climbing the worn, brick stairs on the far side, he slipped some keys out of his pocket and after listening for any noise, he quietly unlocked the door. Slowly turning the handle, Adam opened it, with light flooding in, just enough to see the view of the hall passage and to listen for any unexpected sounds. As he did so, he caught the faintest of traces of perfume in the air. The firelight from the study gave an unearthly, flickering illumination to the silent hallway. Adam opened the door fully, and slipping into the passage, closed it behind him. Rather than going to the study first, he methodically checked each of the ground floor rooms, gun held at the ready, starting with the kitchen. Finding nothing, except the awful mess caused by a hasty search, he crossed the hallway and quickly entered the study with his gun held steady, ready to fire.

The room was as he had always known it. But besides the mahogany pedestal desk lying unnaturally, outstretched on a Persian rug, was the Major. He was on his back. Oscar had three random bullet wounds to the chest and one through his neck. The expression on his face, with its staring eyes, was one of horror. Adam, after the scene in the grounds, had expected such a scenario. But what he did not expect, was to find Oscar partially dressed in the faded uniform of an SS officer. Lying near Oscar's lifeless hand was a pistol, a Luger from the WW2 period. Adam checked it and found that it had been fired recently. He saw several shell casings lying nearby. He briefly turned and saw two bullet holes. One in the door frame, near where the handle would have been, and a second, a foot higher, was buried deep in the wall. The trickle of blood from the hole in Oscar's neck had begun to dry. Carved deeply into his forehead, was the double Sig rune, in its Armanen form - SS. The callousness of this act, while he lay dying or dead, was appalling. Oscar appeared to have had his civilian clothes removed after he had been killed and he had been roughly dressed in the uniform. The collar patches had been ripped off as were the medals and these lay part-smouldering in the fire where they had been cast away. Adam exited the study, leaving the front door open, and slowly began to climb the stairs.

He checked each room, on the upper floor, in turn, and found nothing untoward. Then as he crossed the landing preparing to descend the stairs once more, he heard a faint noise like a child whimpering. He walked back towards the master bedroom and then re-entered it. Adam had checked the room previously and knew that no one was there. He remembered back to one of his earliest times at the Hall when the Major had shown him a secret hideaway, a priest hole. The elderly man had been 'to the manner born', and he had much enjoyed giving a guided tour of his historic country pile. Oscar had explained that during the persecution of Catholics, in Elizabethan times, priests had been hidden in such secret rooms inside large walls or within chimneys in homes of wealthy aristocrats. The façade of the house was that of a Georgian building, having been remodelled in the early 1800s. However, the actual structure of the house dated, in part, back to the fourteenth century and had, since then, been repeatedly altered, as tastes had changed.

Adam walked over to the oak, half panelling beside the chimney breast looking for the way to open the secret door. The whimpering had abruptly subsided. He had seen Oscar's hand go to the corner of the panel but had not clearly seen what action had opened it.

Adam ran his hand over the wood, pushing and pressing the various parts. Unexpectedly, one wooden component gave way under pressure and the whole panel door popped open. There was a sudden, shrieking whimper from inside and as his torch shone into the small compartment, he saw Rebecca, Oscar's granddaughter. She looked terrified at the sight of him and of the gun, which was levelled at her. She cowered uselessly, behind the Louis Vuitton handbag that she held. He dropped the gun to his side and turned the torch, so that it illuminated his face, to allow her to recognise him.

He said softly, 'It's me, Adam, your grandfather's assistant. Don't worry, I'm going to help you.'

She looked at him with eyes that were wet, red and very scared, and he saw her mind slowly beginning to take it in. He had not seen Rebecca for many years, though he remembered her well. The face he now observed in the shadows of the small room was of a petrified woman. Her face was streaked with makeup from the tears, but, regardless of that, she was still strikingly beautiful.

Rebecca's grandfather had often spoken of her and with great affection. He had told Adam everything, even that she had been named after his beloved childhood Nanny who had died in America, shortly after the war. She and her family, along with many other Jewish families, had been helped to escape the Nazi's atrocities by the work of his parents and other like-minded souls.

The SS Major's aristocratic family had clandestinely worked against the Nazis. They had spirited many Jews away, making good their escape into Sweden and Switzerland. Others still were conveyed through France and on to Spain and Portugal before they made their way to the USA or England. The family had given practical and financial assistance to the escapees. Adam knew only too well, the significant risks which they had endured. His own grandparents on his mother's side had been helped to escape the Nazi purges from the, as it was then, East Prussian town of Stolp, now the Polish, Slupsk.

Rebecca hadn't seen him since she was at school ten years before, but the face had stayed in her mind, and with his kind words, she began to slowly relax and then to collapse into tears. Rebecca watched him with some interest and curiosity, with her mind wandering away from the dangers below.

Adam asked her to try to be quiet and to explain to him what had happened. Then he turned suddenly, as before she could respond, they both heard an almost imperceptible noise in the depths of the house. It was a noise that was wrong, very wrong, indeed. He turned back to Rebecca and held his finger to his mouth to indicate that she must be quiet, and with that, he entered the priest hole pulling the door shut behind him. In the enclosed space, the smell of perfume was more profound, intoxicating ... Chanel No 5 he thought to himself.

Adam knew that it would give them away eventually.

CHAPTER THREE

Harz Mountains, Northern Germany

IT WAS DARK IN THE vast expanse of woodland. The rains that had persisted during the day had now subsided.

The terrain was higher, deep in the forest and the beech woods that dominated in the lower climbs had gradually diminished. It was spruce that was pre-eminent at altitude, though lone rowans, birch and willows clung on to their patches of earth with surprising vigour among the boulders and various rock formations. Boggy areas were reasonably common among the trees and were populated by many plant species such as sphagnum, cowberry, blueberry and bog-rosemary.

The forest was eerie at night, gone were the occasional walkers and hunters of the day. The spruce trees were still laden with moisture from the rains, and the multitude of drips falling to the forest floor gave up a rhythmic, other-worldly sound and an enchanting scent. Far away, the staccato call of a Tengmalm's owl, increasing in volume from start to finish, was slowly becoming less discernible.

In a clearing, close to a forest track stood an old hunting lodge. It was built on a low stone wall surmounted by horizontal, squared-off logs which formed the main structure. Lime green, wooden shutters stood open on many of the windows and on all the downstairs ones. The roof was covered in cedar shingles and had a very steep pitch on it, presumably for shedding snow more readily during the winter months.

A lynx silently appeared from the under-growth on the edge of the clearing, gliding along the face of the property and past the stone steps that led to the front door. It paid no attention to the building and noiselessly disappeared down the track. Some, as yet unknowing creature would die that night.

Above the wooden door, at the top of the steps, there hung an enormous pair of mouflon horns. The smell of wood smoke was heavy in the air, occasionally masking the aromas of the forest.

Through one of the windows could be seen a large room with a group of men, both standing and sitting. There were five of them. Lying, un-caringly, on the floor were three German Short Haired Pointers each mottled in liver brown and white. They slept near the fire, exhausted from their days hunting. Around the walls of the room were hung horns, antlers and stuffed heads of red deer, roe deer, wild boar and wild sheep - the mouflon.

A log fire raged aggressively in the hearth of the rough stone chimney breast as a tall, fair-haired man, of maybe thirty years old, entered the room. He turned to an elderly gentleman who sat in a heavily worn, leather chair and said, 'Herr Müller, I have news from England.'

'Well!' Herr Müller said as he unhurriedly placed the glass of Jägermeister on the arm of the chair, his expression glacial.

The younger man, who paid no notice to the others in the room and who appeared to be standing to attention, then said hesitantly, 'It has almost gone exactly to plan, sir. Except that he is dead.'

'What!' the older man screamed as the ice in his glass rattled violently, 'I gave express instructions that he was to be taken alive. What have they done?' Müller cried in despair.

'Herr Müller,' the young man, who looked extremely nervous, continued, 'they said that they had tried to take him alive, but he had a gun and had made it impossible to capture him. They did say that there was someone else there, apart from the guards, and that person is still alive and may yet be of use.'

'Who Karl?' the seated man yelled.

The dogs remained asleep, all except one who rolled his head around to look at the source of the unwanted disturbance. Seeing that it was unimportant to him, he returned to his rest, letting his eyes slowly close once more. As the other men in the room listened intently, the young man, Karl, said, 'A woman arrived a short while before they ...,' he hesitated, 'commenced matters. They said he greeted her very fondly. Possibly the granddaughter?'

'Where is she now?' Herr Müller said, his anger hardly subsiding.

Karl looked apprehensive when he said, 'They searched the house but could not find her. They said she must still be in there, in hiding. They left the house and cut the phone lines and have retreated a little distance away from the grounds. They are hoping she will come out when she feels that it is safe, and they will take her then.'

The old man looked perplexed and said, 'What if she has a mobile phone? She may summon the police or *other* help.'

Karl said, 'They will deal with whoever comes to her aid once she has revealed herself.'

He had added emphasis to the words 'deal with' giving it a sense of menace. Herr Müller clearly understood his meaning, and for once, a distasteful smile appeared across his face.

Herr Müller asked, 'Did they find it?'

'No sir, but they are certain that they will.'

'They had better be certain,' Herr Müller said in a soft voice, though his face had turned ominously dark.

With that, Müller waved Karl away.

Once the door had shut, he turned to the others in the room and said, 'There can be *NO* further mistakes with this matter. It is of the utmost importance to us. The clock has begun to tick!'

All of those in the room solemnly nodded their agreement but remained silent.

In a dark corner of the room, a lone woman stood, ignored, watching the proceedings. She was noticeably apart from the others. The woman was short and stick thin and had severely bleached, cropped hair. She was not physically unattractive, but the set of her jaw, her pursed lips and the cruel look in her eyes made her utterly undesirable. The woman's face had shown no emotion during the evening, except once. At the mention of the girl, an almost imperceptible smile appeared and then disappeared as quickly as it had come.

Nobody, even Müller, acknowledged her existence. Nobody, even Müller, liked her. They all knew, however, that she was loyal to the cause and in her own way, useful, so they tolerated her.

They never used her first name and only ever addressed her, when they had to speak to her, as Frau Vogt. Nobody knew if she was a Frau or a Fraülein, but they all independently thought that Fraülein, Miss, was far too sweet to use in her case.

CHAPTER FOUR

Rook Hall, Shropshire, England

ADAM HAD AN ALMOST uncontrollable desire for retribution, which he wished to mete out to the perpetrators of the killings. But he knew that these were professionals and though he might kill some of them, his survival could not be assured. This did not concern him. He had debts of loyalty to repay. However, he was confident that if he died, Rebecca's death would be inevitable, and he had an overriding duty to her. In the dark of the priest hole, he could sense her terror, and he noticed that she was trembling violently.

While Adam considered his options, Rebecca said, 'Is grandfather safe?'

He turned to her and touching her hand gently, he lied, 'Yes, he is fine, but we need to leave, and then I will return.' Adam did not want to tell her at that point that the Major was dead, fearing that she might utterly break down, thereby completely giving their hiding place away.

'There is a tunnel that leads to the outside from here. Grandfather told me of it when I was a young girl. He said it had not been used for centuries and that I should not go into it unless there was an extreme emergency. I never understood what he meant by that ...un ...until now.'

'Where is the entrance?'

'Here, behind me. This panel is actually another door,' and with that, Rebecca had turned and pressed the secret entrance on one side and in the light of his torch, Adam saw it slowly open, scraping violently against the rock wall as it did so.

Suddenly, they heard another sound, this time a loud creak coming from the main stairs. He turned the torch off in case any light shone through cracks in the panelling wall. The small space was engulfed in an overpowering, damp smell which emanated from the tunnel.

He whispered, 'It's fine, just move forward, quietly, into the tunnel and start to make your way along towards the exit. Take care. I'll turn the torch back on after a few paces, once I have shut the tunnel door behind me.'

They both had to crouch as the tunnel was not very tall, but it was well constructed with a stone floor and arching stone walls. As they left the priest hole, he shut the inner panel door softly, but not before he heard a sound in the bedroom. They made their way down, along the tunnel which descended at a steep rate through the interior of the wall of the old Hall, eventually, levelling out as it passed under the house, becoming damper as it did so.

With every step, Rebecca felt herself cringe with revulsion as her skin brushed past cobwebs in the half-light. They continued for a few hundred yards before they came to a dead-end, it appeared that there had been a cave-in caused by damage from tree roots which had sealed the tunnel. As Adam did not know how much more of the passageway had caved in, he decided to make their escape through the roof of the tunnel. He gave the torch to Rebecca and asked her to shine it upwards and forward. He took a large, black military knife from the poacher's pocket hidden within the inside of his coat and with that, he began to dislodge the loosely, remaining stones from the top of the arch. It was reasonably easy to work as the roots had done significant damage and gravity had also lent a helping hand. He left the stones and soil where they fell below the hole, as they would provide a makeshift plinth to climb upon.

After fifteen minutes, he saw a very faint glow of moonlight shining through the remaining soil and grassroots. He took the torch from Rebecca and turned it off. He then dug more cautiously and quietly as the soil and roots, in turn, gave way to grass. As he removed the turf ceiling, dead leaves fluttered down into the tunnel, and the light levels rose slightly once more. The silence of the tunnel was disturbed by the sound of rooks, the wind above and the ever-present rustling leaves. Eventually, the hole was large enough to slide through. Adam did not know what awaited him but, his lifelong motto *Audentes Fortuna adiuvat*, fortune favours the brave, dictated his actions.

Using the stone and soil pile for height and the tree roots above for grip he stealthily climbed up through the hole. He peered out, like a mole, listening and watching. They were approximately eighty yards outside the perimeter wall and were within the woods, near the brook. He waited for a short time, scanning the area for sounds or shapes that didn't quite fit, but there was nothing. Adam silently slithered out of the hole and lay still after having taken his pistol from its holster. Once more, happy that all was safe Adam dropped his arm into the hole and Rebecca took his hand in hers. As he gently lifted her upwards, she carefully scrambled her way out from the tunnel and following his lead, lay still beside him, her heart and lungs pounding violently. Again, waiting and once again being satisfied, he pointed her towards the brook, indicating that she should make her way swiftly, keeping close to the ground. She did as she was asked and then, hearing the stream bubbling ahead, she slipped down the embankment to its thin, gravel edge.

Moments later, Adam slid down beside her, and they rapidly made their way back along the bank to the edge of the field. They did not follow the hedge along the side of the road. Instead, they traced the brook under the roadway through a low, brick, arching bridge, which was hardly discernible from above. Once safely on the other side they followed the hedge line up to the bridleway and returned to the Land Rover. As Rebecca sat beside him, he gently placed his hand on her arm to comfort her, hoping that she could try to be sanguine, given the awful situation. She glanced over, though her expression did not change.

Adam did not reverse out on to the country road, instead preferring to cautiously follow the track slowly to its end where it once more met a distant tarmac road. He then turned on his lights.

CHAPTER FIVE

Harz Mountains, Northern Germany

THE FIVE MEN WERE STILL, as they had been, standing and sitting around the front room of the hunting lodge set deep in the forest. Unseen, Frau Vogt, though nobody really cared, had not moved. The warm, ethereal glow from the windows seemed at odds with the darkness and the damp of the surrounding trees. The warmth was not indicative of the mood within the room. Herr Müller sat fixated on the hearth, a dark, pensive look on his face, lost in his thoughts. The other four men were much younger than him and aged between thirty and forty-five. None talked, but each held a glass, one drank Jägermeister, like Müller. The others drank Lagavulin, a single malt whiskey from Islay in the Hebrides, off the west coast of Scotland. Frau Vogt did not drink.

One of the whiskey drinkers, Rolf, stood by

the window looking into the forest at nothing, in particular, just the shadows and the blackness. He savoured the peaty, iodine taste of the drink as he waited for news from England. They all waited, while the three dogs slept on.

Suddenly, the lone sound of the crackling fire was disturbed by the pounding of running feet in the hall and then the noise of the door bursting open. All three of the dogs sat up and watched the unfolding scene, mesmerised, sniffing the air expectantly.

'Herr Müller, they are in the building. They saw movement from within.'

'The girl?'

'No, Kaspar said it was a man. Shortly before this, they heard a vehicle drive down a nearby road, and they went to investigate. Klaus found it parked a little way down a farmer's track. The engine was still warm, but there was nobody there. He attached a tracking device, as it seemed out of place.'

'Good! It may be a farmer, but it is dark there now, and it does appear to be very odd. It may be someone '*of interest*' ...where are they now?'

Karl said, 'Kaspar and Stefan have entered the Hall again and are searching for them.'

'No! Make sure that they retreat to the perimeter and wait. I do not want to alert this man. Send Klaus and Heinz to track the movements of that car. Make sure they stay out of sight and warn them to use their car lights sparingly. If it is our man, he will be watching for them.'

'Yes, sir!'

'And Karl,' Herr Müller said more softly, 'get me, La Araña!'

'Yes, sir!' Karl said once again.

CHAPTER SIX

Sloe Farm, Herefordshire, England

ADAM DROVE, IN SILENCE, for over four miles through twisting country lanes and took a circuitous route to ensure that they were not followed. The pace was swift but not dangerously so. Despite Adam's best endeavours, he did not see Klaus and Heinz as they kept pace in the black Volvo XC90. The tracker allowed them to hold well back out of sight and anyway, they were exceptionally good at their job. Rebecca was lost in her thoughts, while Adam was lost in concentration, with one eye on the road in front and one in his rear-view mirror. A more direct route would have been faster but, he thought may have been inviting trouble. Passing through the medieval market town of Ludlow, he carried on for several miles before turning off the main road on to a narrow side road.

After a quarter of a mile, Adam slowed the car as he approached an old, oak, five-bar gate at the side of the road. It had been pushed open some years before and had then been left. Now, near-collapse, it was partially hidden by grass, nettles and brambles. He retraced his journey of earlier, along the rough, dirt route towards the farmer's barns. Halfway across the field, three red-legged partridge, startled by the car's headlights burst from the cover of the sugar beet. They ran ahead of the vehicle on the track, repeatedly screeching in a low *'tchree-agh'* call. The relentless Land Rover forced them into flight, and after a sudden burst of flapping wings, they settled into a long, flat glide. The occupants of the car hardly noticed as the feathered escadrille banked across the field disappearing, abruptly into a wood nearby.

The vehicle slowly crawled down the pot-holed lane, eventually turning in, behind the large wooden barn that was filled with bales of hay. They came to a stop in the courtyard, and Rebecca looked at the quaint, Victorian, red brick farmhouse that had previously been obscured. The other side of the cobblestoned yard was faced with small, disused farm buildings and stables looking as if they were from the same era. They were in a poor state of repair and looked quite tired.

Adam led Rebecca into the house. They were greeted by Kaiser, who did not just wag his tail, but his whole body too. She smiled at the exuberant dog and crouched to vigorously stroke him, forgetting momentarily of the evening's horrific events. Adam offered her a drink, and she asked for a G & T. She was utterly dishevelled, with mud on her shoes, stockings and hands and leaves and twigs on her coat and in her hair.

He pointed her to the downstairs toilet only to see her return ten minutes later looking much more respectable and he noted, strikingly pretty. She slid into a large antique chair in the lounge while Kaiser lay down at her feet, one paw resting across the arch of her foot. Rebecca rhythmically inhaled the enticing smell of the chair's leather cover, finding it oddly calming.

Adam took a bottle of Plymouth Gin, from an Edwardian mahogany sideboard, where it stood sentinel with various other bottles of spirits. From a shelf above, he grabbed a heavy crystal tumbler. Adam walked through to the kitchen, and Rebecca could hear him opening the fridge and dropping some ice into the glass.

Many of these older houses in Britain had a serving hatch, and Sloe Farm was no exception. It was a small opening in the wall between the kitchen and the dining room where food and cutlery could readily be passed from one to the other. Over time the dining room had become the lounge, and the serving hatch had become redundant. It was by then partially obscured by books and ornaments, though it still allowed some access. Adam leant down to call through the opening to Rebecca to ask if she wanted something to eat. As he did so, Adam saw Rebecca surreptitiously glance at the door to the kitchen as she also slipped her phone from her bag. Adam said nothing but continued to watch. He saw her type a text and send it. It was very quickly responded to, and he saw her read it. She then glanced over at the door again as she turned her phone off and quickly slid it into her bag.

Adam looked away, deep in thought and continued his preparations.

When he returned, she saw a slice of lime had been neatly slipped onto the rim of the tumbler. Kaiser's eyes and ears had maintained close surveillance of the events. Adam poured a shot of gin into the glass, followed by the full contents of a small bottle of Fever-Tree Indian tonic water, making the ice cubes dance loudly. Adam was silent, deep in his thoughts, trying to make sense of the events of earlier. He had been very generous with the gin, as he felt it would do her good. He passed the glass to her and allowed her to drink a large mouthful before he spoke.

'Rebecca,' he said softly, 'please, could you try to relay for me, your memories of tonight at the Hall?'

She looked at him, teary-eyed, 'Who are you? What are you? What is happening? I mean, I know you work for grandfather, but why was he so angry and scared?'

He could sense that she had the edge of hysteria in her voice, which was completely understandable.

Adam was silent. Then he looked at her and said, 'You will remember me from your younger days before your parents died. I was introduced to you by your grandfather as a gamekeeper and an Estate Manager. It was not my actual position. My comrades and I were asked, by your grandfather, to act as security guards, posing as gamekeepers and groundsmen. I was also his friend.'

'I should have known! He never seemed to organise any shoots when I was there, and I couldn't understand why there were so many of you. I thought he just enjoyed the company. But why would he lie to me?'

'He did not wish to, but he did so to protect you. The Major ...uh ...Oscar loved you very much.'

'Major ... loved ...?' Rebecca said with an air of desperation and stunned shock.

Adam looked deep into her eyes and with a heavy heart, said, 'Please forgive me, Rebecca, but your grandfather is dead.'

She broke into uncontrollable tears, and her face fell into her hands, to hide her grief. Kaiser stood up on all fours and began to gently nuzzle her. He got no reaction, so he continued his efforts, while Adam looked on feeling a deep sense of shame. Then, after a few minutes, her hands parted, and she cradled the dogs face against hers. Continuing to slowly stroke the dog and to gently cry, she said, 'You lied to me too!'

The words cut like a knife. Adam had failed in his duty tonight, and now these sad, soft words felt like a killer blow.

'Please forgive me. I had no other option. If

you had lost control at the Hall, then we would have been in the gravest of danger.'

She suddenly cried out, 'Saving your own skin!'

He said nothing to that, but she could see by the darkening sadness of his face that she had gone too far. Her words had been uttered in anger, and she knew they were cruel and unfair. He had risked his life to help and to protect her.

'Please, Rebecca, could you recount what has happened tonight?'

She looked at him, disconsolate.

'Take your time I know it has been difficult for you,' he continued.

Rebecca's eyes began to well up with tears as she said, 'I am sorry ...but I can't tell you much ...I arrived in the late afternoon, and as I pulled into the drive, I saw Franco just inside the gate – he just seemed to be walking alongside the front wall, quite casually. Then as I parked in front of the house, the big African guy is it Luke, came out of the grounds and asked if I would like a hand with my luggage. I had quite a few bags, you see. He has always been such a gentleman. I told him that it would be kind of him, and he explained to me that my grandfather was in his study and to go ahead. He then dropped the bags in my room.'

'Did either of them seem concerned or anxious?'

'No, not at all. In fact, Franco winked at me and gave me a wave. He's such a flirt! They just seemed normal - friendly.'

'And did you see anything on the road or else-where that concerned you or anything unusual ...parked cars, walkers, shooting parties or such like?'

'No, nothing ...but I wasn't really looking. I was just glad to be coming home after so long away.'

'Are they alright?' she asked.

He ignored the question and said, 'When did you realise things were unusual?'

She wished she had not asked about Luke and Franco and a sudden chill ran through her body.

'I ...I suppose it was when grandfather was listening to me chattering on about all that is going on in my life ...just nonsense really. There was the sound of a car passing by the front gates. It was hardly noticeable, but it seemed to slow down a touch as it passed the Hall and then it picked up speed a little, after passing. I wouldn't have thought anything of it, but it seemed to make grandfather ...a little uneasy. After that, he only half-listened to me and kept looking out of the window. I also saw Franco walking back towards the Hall, but I thought it was odd as he was walking backwards, and he was looking to-wards the road.'

She began weeping, and he walked over to her and placed his hand on her shoulder, saying, 'Please go on.'

She looked up at him and then looking away, went on, 'Grandfather asked me if I remembered the hidden room and passage, he had shown me as a child. He said that I was to go there and that

I was not to come out or make any sound until he came for me. Grandfather looked truly worried and was very insistent. I began to ask what was wrong, and he suddenly lost his temper. He shouted at me and told me to go there immediately. I was completely shocked. He had never raised his voice to me in the past. I ran from the room, and as I began to climb the stairs, he came out of the study and called after me. He apologised and told me that he loved me. That is the last time that I saw him.'

Before she could cry again, Adam asked, 'Did you see or hear anything else?'

'Ye ...Yes, as I got to the top of the stairs, I heard some shots. I don't think it was a shotgun ...more a rifle, I think. I looked back to the hallway, but grandfather was gone. I ran to the priest hole and shut myself in. I hid in the darkness, and then there was silence for about fifteen or more minutes before a terrible racket started. Guns were being fired constantly for quite a while, lots of them and then it was silent again. I don't know how long it was after that, but I then heard a few shots close together. They sounded like they came from inside the house. I was petrified. I heard men speaking ...shouting really, downstairs and then it sounded as if there were lots of people moving around the house quite quickly. Next, I sensed them coming upstairs. There was an awful commotion, and it sounded like they were searching for something. I heard a lot of doors, drawers and cupboards being quickly opened and the sound of things being thrown all over the place. Then I heard one man shout back down the stairs saying, 'I can't find it or her! I was so scared, Adam.'

'Were they his *exact* words?'

'Yes. But it was strange,' Rebecca continued.

'Why?' Adam asked.

'Well ...he was speaking in German!'

Adam knew that she had studied German and French at school. He was lost in thought, his brow deeply furrowed.

'Why was that?' she said.

He stared directly into her eyes and saying nothing for a moment, he said, 'Rebecca, what do you know of your grandfather's past? Tell me everything!'

She took a sip of the drink, seeking solace from its timelessness.

'Grandfather ...he was ...' as she began to speak, she felt a choking in her throat, 'born in the southeast of Switzerland in the Graubünden Canton. He spoke Romansh obviously, but also some French, a little German, fluent Italian and English. He didn't often talk about his family as it must have been painful for him. Just before the war, his family moved to Italy as his father was looking for work and better prospects. Near the end of the war, they were travelling in a train north, back to Switzerland. They were trying to escape the fighting. The train was attacked by American fighter planes, as it had German troops on board. All his family were killed, and he was injured in the leg jumping from the train. When the British soldiers came, he was treated by their doctors, and they found that he was useful to them, as he spoke so many languages. He translated for the army for a year and then they helped him to come to England where he started various businesses and eventually, he retired, as he became extraordinarily successful.'

Adam said bluntly, 'Most of that is untrue. I am sorry, but your grandfather told you these stories to protect you.'

Rebecca stared at him in horror, and before she could answer, he said, 'Your grandfather actually came from an aristocratic family, Prussian. The area is now part of Poland but was previously part of Germany. He joined the army before the war started and entered a Cavalry regiment, as was the tradition in his family. Talented, he rose rapidly through the ranks. The Major was brave and swift promotion was possible for a gallant man such as him, due to the terrible attrition rate of officers. He then transferred towards the end of the war into the SS.'

'The SS!' she cried, almost stupefied. She knew little of the SS, but what she did know was utterly vile.

'Yes,' Adam said.

She put her head in her hands and began to weep again.

Adam put his hand on her head and slowly stroked her hair, saying, 'They were strange times, and you should be careful not to judge him too readily. You do not know everything there is to know.'

She wondered what he meant by this cryptic assertion.

He put his hand in his coat pocket and pulled out a small, sealed package. The paper wrapping had yellowed with age, and it had, Rebecca, written on the outside.

Adam handed it to her and said, 'Your grandfather gave this to me some years ago, to be given to you if he died.'

She snatched the parcel from his hand, throwing it to the floor, 'More lies!'

Adam leant down and picked it up, replacing it in his pocket.

CHAPTER SEVEN

La Araña', Buenos Aires, Argentina

IN A LEAFY AVENIDA, IN the suburbs of Buenos Aires a phone rang at the main reception desk of a small office of an international logistics company. It was called 'La Araña', 'the Spider'. The receptionist had been painting the nails of her left hand in a vulgar, tarty red enjoying the fumes that the cheap liquid gave off. Answering the call, she said lazily, 'Si!'

Karl, irritated with her tone, barked, 'I have Herr Müller on the phone!'

In rusty German, the receptionist said smartly, 'Jawohl! Einen ...einen Moment ...bitte!'

The Argentinian promptly put the call through to another room, further along, the central hall. The Director of the firm, Herr Schwartz, answered curtly, 'Schwartz!'

'Herr Schwartz, ich habe einen Anruf von Herrn Müller,' the receptionist said shakily and without waiting for an answer, transferred the call.

Hearing the change on the line, Herr Schwartz said in the most charming of voices, and quite unlike him, 'My dear Müller, how are you?' he leant back in his chair and looked out across the rooftops, interspersed with trees. He considered the tranquillity of the scene in the early evening light, glad to be speaking his native German once more.

Herr Müller said, 'Manfred, I have wonderful news! We are on the trail of the gold ...the Spider's Web gold! ...after all these years of searching ...it is within our grasp!'

The line was silent, Herr Schwartz's gaze sightlessly bore into the middle-distance through his window, as he tried to grasp the enormity of what was occurring.

Das Spinnennetz, the Spider's Web, was the Third Reich's last throw of the dice, as the walls crumbled around them in early-1945. The gold, which they spoke of, was to be retrieved from the mysterious Castle Zbiroh and transported to the northern coast of Germany, to then be taken by U-boat to the port of Buenos Aires, Argentina. However, it had never left on its journey.

In Argentina, the bullion was to have been invested in many diverse and unrelated businesses around the world. It was believed that Himmler wished for it to be managed by the shadowy individual, Herr Schwartz. The Spider's Web dossier gave Schwartz his final orders, together with a list of influential individuals and families who were Nazi sympathisers, mainly of German extraction, who were spread across the globe. They were ordered to cloak their German ancestry and to hide their Nazi sympathies. They were to further infiltrate the higher levels of politics, banking and the security services of their respective countries. They would work in secrecy and without knowledge of each other, save for intermittent contact with the arachnid at the centre of the Web, Herr Schwartz. He would guide their career paths, with his team, as necessary and assist them where possible either financially, or through the use of other members of the Spider's Web.

Only many years later, when the time was right, would these diverse individuals and families be made aware of each of the others who also formed strands of the Spider's Web. Then, the masterplan, which had been hatched in the dying embers of Berlin more than half a century before, would begin the countdown - to the Fourth and Final Reich. The world domination that Hitler and the Nazis had always desired. The 'apparent', disparate parts of the Spider's Web working covertly and in total unison.

The individuals had infiltrated the left-wing, right-wing and liberal organisations of many powerful countries. Some had retained but played down their German heritage. In contrast, others had tried to re-write history claiming other countries for their ancestry to prevent, even the slightest suspicion of any fascist sympathies or other murky past.

Herr Schwartz had not received the gold or the full list of sympathisers in 1945 as expected. However, he had enough information to compile a list of specific influential individuals, who he could use to start the process. That and 'donations' from various former Nazis and Nazi groups in the late 1940s and the '50s gave him the basis for his organisation and his life's work.

'Manfred are you there ...?' asked Herr Müller.

'Yes ...yes, I am here ...I just cannot believe it!'

Manfred slowly ran his hand back and forth over his desktop, as if he was trying to dust it with an imaginary cloth. He continued, 'Herr Müller, how certain are you that you can retrieve our gold?'

'Nothing will stop me now!' answered Herr Müller in the most sinister of voices, which had the sound of a wild animal's growl.

'And the list? What about the list?'

'I am less certain of that, but I feel that it may well lay with the gold,' Müller said.

'That would be perfect. If not ...then no matter! Once the process starts with those people we have already assembled, then the others will begin to emerge from the shadows.'

Herr Müller continued determinedly, 'You must not fail! Accelerate the preparations now. We are at the very birth of the Fourth Reich. All the personnel are in place across the globe, and the gold will be the fuel with which we will propel ourselves into total power. No one will stop us this time!'

Schwartz paused for a moment and then said

in a virtually soundless voice as he began to almost taste victory, 'We will then wreak a terrible vengeance on those people and their descendants who stole our birthright in 1945!'

CHAPTER EIGHT

THE PHONE RANG WITH A soft echo, in the vast room, within the walls of the Kremlin. It lay on the desk of the private office in the official residence of, Viktor Ivanov, the President of the Russian Federation. It was not the only handset before him, but its number was the sole one which was known to one man and one man alone. Only Ivanov knew who the caller was, Herr Schwartz.

The President was engaged in negotiations with an admiral, two generals and various politburo officials concerning recent difficulties in the Black Sea region. He heard the phone ring but made no attempt to answer it or even to acknowledge it. He did, however, promptly wrap the meeting up, ushering the bemused participants out, with little ceremony. As they departed, they left their stench of cheap aftershave hanging in the air. The odour was so strong that he could taste it.

They had not gone long when rather than picking up the desk phone he took a mobile phone from his pocket and pressed a saved speed dial number. The phone was encrypted, and this was a call that had to be completely private.

The phone rang in Buenos Aires, and Herr Schwartz answered immediately. 'Viktor!' He said, 'Our time has now come! You have always known that you are part of something much greater. Now that greatness can be revealed. There are others like you, many who are also in positions of great power, all over the world and they work towards the same goal, the same ideals. You must begin to destroy our enemies within your government and others in a position to deter you. It is not enough to just remove or kill them, they also need to be discredited. Your work must start immediately, using only those whom you feel you can rely on. I will send you, shortly, the names of those who you can trust implicitly within your country, they are already part of the Spiders Web. What you do now, in these next few days and months will lay the foundation of our Fourth Reich. For the moment, I cannot tell you of all of those other Kameraden, around the world who form the Spider's Web, save for one name.'

Schwartz, silent for a moment, continued, 'It is, Carl Brown, the President of the United States of America.'

'What!' Ivanov barked and then after a

moment's silence, said, 'How ...how could it be ...?'

'There will be many surprises for you, such as this, over the coming months, my friend. You will work closely with him, though, no hint of your close relationship should be evident, not yet. You must give the appearance for now, that there is possibly even a certain animosity or even distrust between you. Only when we are ready to strike, will we show our true allegiance. I will contact you again soon, Viktor. Heil Hitler!'

Ivanov replied, 'I understand. Heil Hitler!'

No pleasantries passed between them, and Viktor heard the line go dead.

Slowly dropping the phone to his side, Ivanov looked through the window at nothing in particular, in a state of near disbelief. After what seemed an age, he began to smile, saying quietly to himself, 'It has begun.'

CHAPTER NINE

Collections Department, Mossad headquarters, Tel Aviv, Israel

THE MAN, IN HIS EARLY thirties, knocked on the door. He was slim, had an olive complexion and lightly thinning, black hair. He was smartly attired in a cream suit, black shoes and an open neck, lilac shirt.

A booming, hollow voice growled from the other side, 'Enter!'

He opened the door and, shutting it behind him, walked to the front of the desk, standing loosely to attention. He did not speak.

The older man who sat behind the table was reading a document, which he held in both hands. He had not looked up when his visitor entered. He liked to make them wait.

After a moment, and without putting the document down, he queried, 'Well?'

The younger man said, 'Sir, we have had a

message from the Embassy in Bern. There has been some unusual activity in Germany, in the Harz.'

He left it at that. Two could play the power game.

'Well, Daniel! What is it?' the seated man barked, unexpectedly turning his penetrating gaze on the young operative, who suddenly looked decidedly uneasy.

'The agents who have been monitoring the hunting lodge have noticed a lot more activity there, over the previous two weeks. Then last week, a group of six of their men left on a plane from Berlin to Manchester. Our London office was notified, and they sent two agents to track them.'

'Why was I not informed of this before!' the older man hollered.

Daniel, who could sense a slight, uncontrollable tremor building in intensity in his left leg, said, 'The Controller in Bern did not feel that it was sufficient to...'

The older man cut him short, saying harshly, 'He did, did he? Well, what has happened to change his view?'

'Er ...earlier this week the Germans travelled south-west towards Wales. They stayed in a hotel, 'The Feathers', in a place called Ludlow, a town in Shropshire, and then this afternoon they headed out towards a large house, which stands alone in the countryside. Our agents followed them. Since then, the Germans set up surveillance on the building, which is called Rook Hall.

Sometime later they launched an attack on the property. A woman had arrived shortly before the assault, though our agents did not actually see her leave. Two Germans are now in pursuit of a car with a man and a woman who seem to have escaped from the Hall.'

Daniel, stopping uncontrollably to swallow the saliva which had been building up in his mouth continued, slightly stuttering as he did so, 'Our a ...agents saw at least three people eliminated at the house, and they are now tracking the Germans.'

'What on earth is going on? I should have been told of this before!'

'Um ...Yes ...Well ...'

'Get Bern on the phone for me! ...Now!' he shrieked.

'Yes, sir!' Daniel whimpered. Shaken and more than a little relieved to be going, he left the room immediately.

Ariel Mandler, for that, was the seated man's name, remained, while he waited, staring at the wall in deep contemplation. His hands gripped the arms of the chair with a much higher intensity than was normal for him. He had to look at a wall as there were no windows in his office. His brow was deeply furrowed, and he had the look of a man who was trying to solve a puzzle which had no solution.

He processed what little information he had been given thus far, trying to understand the actions of the Germans.

'Why Shropshire? Why such a large team?

Who could live at Rook Hall? Why did the Germans want to kill them? Did they actually kill who they were after?'

Mandler knew Shropshire, though not well, from his time in their London office, where he was stationed as a young agent. It was a sleepy part of England, in what was called the Welsh Marches along the border with Wales. It was pretty, quiet and filled with historic towns and villages. It was certainly not, he thought, a hot-bed of international intrigue or neo-Nazi activity, at least - until now.

The phone rang, and he slowly and deliberately picked it up, saying, 'Mandler!'

'Good evening sir,' the voice responded.

'That's where you are wrong, Ezra. It is not a good evening, is it! Give me the facts and then give me your take on them!'

Ezra cleared his throat uneasily and said, 'Our agents in Germany noticed some unusually increased comings and goings at the hunting lodge in the Harz. We have tried to unscramble the electronic traffic but have not been able to yet. Then about a week ago, a visitor arrived. The agents had not seen him before, but they took photographs of the unknown person, and our men then tracked him back to Berlin after he left. The individual was taken to and from the lodge by one of Müller's men. We now know that the visitor is a senior member of the British Foreign Office working in the Embassy. It seemed clear to our agents that it was not an official visit. On reaching the outskirts of Berlin, he got out of the car in a side street and then took a bus back to the Embassy.'

'What are his duties there?' Mandler snapped.

'His official title is *liaison officer*, but we believe he may be attached to MI6. We are having him checked out.'

'MI6! What is he up to?' Mandler paused and then said, 'I smell a rat!'

'We are not sure, but after his visit, the tempo at the lodge increased. Whatever he had to say to them, it now appears that it was important. It was soon after this that Müller's team left for England. I understand from Daniel that he has updated you on events in Shropshire?'

'Updated me! Yes, he has updated me!' Ariel boomed, 'I hope for your sake, that it is not too late!'

Ariel could sense fear in the silence at the end of the phone,

'Well, what do you think is going on?'

Ezra swallowed hard and said, 'I'm not sure. But one of the bodies in the house was that of an old man. He was the owner, who we now know to be a Swiss National, Oscar Accola. But I do not think he was always Swiss.'

'Why not?'

'We can find no records of him in Switzerland, before 1945. He just seemed to appear in England after the war having, it seems, come from Switzerland. We have not been able to find any trace of his background here, though he does have Swiss nationality. Also, when our agents found him, he was wearing the uniform of an SS - Sturmbannführer with the insignia ripped off and partially burnt.'

Ariel, stunned, said nothing. He just stared, speechless, at the wall. He had heard and seen many strange things in his career, but this was undoubtedly one of the most peculiar.

Ezra continued, 'Someone had also carved the SS sign into his forehead, we believe after he was dead.'

Ariel still said nothing. He was trying to make sense of the bizarre turn of events.

Mandler then said, 'It's possible that it is revenge ...of some sort, but it is a long time to wait to serve it up, on an old man. It may form part of the story, but there has to be something else. If they wanted to kill this *Accola* if that was even his name, then why continue to track these others. There must be something else, something fundamental to Müller and his neo-Nazis! I want this made a top priority. Strengthen the team in Germany and get four more men up to Shropshire from the London office to assist the others. We need to crack the Germans' communications as a priority, and therefore I'm going to send an electronics team to Germany. They will leave Tel Aviv tomorrow morning. Keep me updated with any developments – this time!'

As Ezra went to respond, he heard the phone on the other end being slammed down.

He breathed a gentle sigh of relief to be off the hook ...for the moment anyway, he thought. Ariel's final two words, Ezra thought, were a rebuke that might come back to haunt him.

Ariel pressed a button on his desk, and moments later, Daniel came in, without knocking on this occasion.

'I want a search made of the records. Top priority!'

'Yes, sir,' Daniel said.

'Get me a list of SS men who we understood were alive after the war, but who have not been accounted for since.

Pay particular attention to any officers - in particular, the rank of Sturmbannführer and anyone who made their escape through Switzerland or who had Swiss contacts. Make a second list of those who died before the end of 1945, but where no proof of death exists - this man may have been a slippery individual.'

Daniel barked, 'Yes, sir!' before turning and leaving the room.

What Mandler and his agents could not have known was that the man from the British Embassy had placed a call on a burner phone soon after he had arrived back in Berlin. The phone call was made to Sir Rupert Fitzgibbon, the Head of MI6. The conversation had been succinct, and on completing it, the Embassy man had furtively dropped the phone into a drain on the roadside. Fitzgibbon had been walking along London's Embankment when he had received the call. Stopping to speak to the liaison officer, he had leant against the Embankment wall, deep in thought. As the call finished, Sir Rupert looked across the Thames towards the Palace of Westminster, before breaking into a wide smile.

As he turned away looking quite chipper, his own burner phone, unseen, gently slipped from his hand and disappeared into the waters below as he headed back to work.

CHAPTER TEN

THE FOLLOWERS HAD TRACKED the Land Rover to its final stop. Seeing that it had left the public road, Klaus parked the Volvo in a farmer's field nearby, just inside the gate and hidden from view by the hedge.

Heinz took a Zeiss Victory, night vision device from the back of the car and Klaus grabbed a rifle - they both carried handguns, *de rigueur*. Klaus habitually used the gun for deer in the Harz forests, but now he was hunting another quarry, in another land. The weapon was a Russian made ORSIS T-5000 with a ten-round box magazine, a night scope and he had fitted it with a detachable bipod for better stability. His was made to order and was a left-handed version with a folding stock and the extended version for Magnum-class long-range cartridges. It was no ordinary hunter's rifle but more a precision sniper's rifle made by a small, private-ly owned factory in Moscow. Klaus favoured it, as its accuracy was superb, the only choice when he sought a kill.

They left the SUV and crossed the road into a neatly ploughed field, enjoying the smell of the recently turned earth.

Making their way along the hedges, they came to the copse that adjoined the sugar beet field. Both men moved to its edge and crouched down, and Heinz took the night vision device from his side pocket and began to view the collection of farm buildings in the distance. Occasionally, they caught the smell of coal smoke carried on the wind from one of the chimneys. The clari-ty of view was excellent, but the angle was not ideal. He could see the barns and the tail end of the Land Rover parked behind them in the courtyard, and although the outbuildings were in view, he could only partially see the house. He indicated to Klaus, with a hand signal, that he would need to move further along the border of the small wood and the field to get a better angle.

They had only gone ten feet when a terrifying noise signalled the angry and urgent flight of the three red-legged partridges being forced to leave their roost once more. They were not happy with this second disturbance, and they made sure that the two Germans knew, in no uncertain terms, of their displeasure. Klaus and Heinz had dropped to the floor at the sound of the birds. They watched in dismay as the partridges made their noisy departure, gliding across the sugar beet field and off into the darkness beyond.

Inside the house, Adam heard the commotion and immediately ran to the rear door of the farmhouse grabbing a pair of Bushnell Lynx night vision binoculars, on the way. He shouted to Rebecca to wait where she was. Adam burst through the passage at the back of the farmhouse and into the barn which faced the road. Climbing up the neatly stacked, bales of hay, Adam carefully positioned himself on top and then surveyed the landscape with the binoculars through the open sidewall of the building. Adam had remembered roughly where the three partridge, which he had disturbed, would have landed. After a swift recce of the road and field, he concentrated on the area around the copse. It may have been another group of birds, though the sound had appeared to emanate from the area where they would have come to roost. It could have been a fox or a badger that had startled the birds, but Adam had grown older and had stayed safe through being cautious.

He watched, and he waited, ...and he waited. There was no other noise save for a pheasant way off in the distance, making its haunting, evening call. Usually, he would have found it enchanting - now it was just an irrelevance. He continued to wait five minutes, ten minutes ...twenty-five minutes ...

Rebecca suddenly appeared at the base of the hay bales and whispered in a terrified voice, 'What is it?'

'I told you to wait ...it's probably nothing. I just want to make sure. I'll just be a little longer.'

With that, he returned to analysing the small wood. After thirty-five minutes, his efforts paid off. At first, he thought it was a trick of the eyes, as they were becoming tired. The movement was so small, but no, it was a definite movement. It was not the wind, as the bending of the grasses he observed was in a different direction from those on the edge of the thicket. He waited, and now he focused all his attention on that one point. Then he saw it, a large mass moving almost imperceptibly at ground level, a man crawling ... very slowly.

Then he saw another movement a few feet to the left, similar to the first. Still at least one hundred and fifty yards away and unawares that their cover was blown. He dropped gently to the brick floor next to Rebecca, and with his finger to his mouth, he indicated that she should remain silent. Grabbing her arm, he drew her through the small passage and back into the house.

Once inside, he said, 'We must leave right now. Just wait here!'

He raced upstairs, and after a few moments, he returned with a bag which he had left in the house pre-packed for such eventualities. He then went to a wooden cupboard and pulling the door ajar, he opened another hidden metal door behind it with a key from his pocket. It was full of weapons and ammunition. Grabbing a large canvas bag from the cupboard, he filled it with the contents and zipped it up.

Then he turned to Rebecca, who looked stunned by the ongoing events of the night, saying, 'OK, Let's go!'

He gave her the bag to carry, which he had taken from upstairs. She looked almost hysterical with fear, but she did as he asked, acting as an automaton.

Adam left the light on in the kitchen and, opening the door gently, he pulled the pistol from its holster and slipped into the courtyard.

He called back into the kitchen, 'Kaiser, close!' and with that, the dog, who at first had been fascinated by the strange events, but was by then utterly bemused, raced to Adam's side and lay down.

Adam dropped the bag by the side of the farmhouse and crouching low, he peered around the corner and with binoculars in his left hand and pistol in the right he surveyed the scene. There was no discernible change.

He turned to Rebecca and said, 'The car is unlocked, jump in the back behind the driver's seat, lie down in the footwell and shut the door after Kaiser jumps in.'

Kaiser's ears pricked up at the sound of his name.

'Go now!'

She raced to the car door as ordered and jumped in, throwing the bag she held into the opposite side. She heard fingers clicking behind her and the words, 'Kaiser inside!'

A moment later, the dog bounded onto the back seat and lay down, wagging his tail with an utter fury, tongue hanging out as he panted and observed all vigorously. This was an exhilarating day for Kaiser ...meeting new people, lots of rushing around and now a road trip. Rebecca, who did not share his satisfaction, leant over and gently pulled the door shut as Adam's door was opened and he jumped into the car throwing the bag of firearms into the passenger seat.

The keys had been left in the car, and Adam started it, simultaneously throwing it into gear. The wheels spun wildly before suddenly finding grip, spraying pebbles and muck into the air and against the wall of the farmhouse. The noise was deafening, disturbing a group of Jackdaws who added to the general commotion when they burst, screeching, from their roosts in one of the outbuildings.

Instead of heading back up the lane, Adam swerved around the side of the outbuildings racing down a rough track along the edge of the continuing sugar beet field. The farmers used it often but maintained it less frequently. He was now temporarily shielded from sight and from a shot by the farm buildings, but the ride was bumpy and wild. Klaus had locked the stock on his rifle at the sound of the car starting, splayed the legs of the bipod and made ready for a kill shot. He had expected the Land Rover to return up the track, but he readily saw that it had gone to the rear of the farm, as it re-appeared on the far side. His eye firmly at the scope, he began to track the path of the vehicle, gently putting tension on his trigger finger and trying to control his breathing.

Adam continued along the track heading through two old wooden gateposts, which made a break in a long hedge, though they held no gate.

It was a pressure shot for Klaus with a quick set up of this kit, a speeding target, moving wildly and a night shot, though the distance was well within the range of the ORSIS. Time was running out for Klaus. Heinz barked, 'Take the shot!'

Klaus ignored him; he did not need the added pressure. He held on, his finger tense. Then, body motionless, he finalised his aim, and with the slightest movement of his left index finger he loosed off the deadly .338 Lapua Magnum bullet from the chamber, his tensed body, checking the powerful recoil. The sound of the shot was deafening, and it echoed throughout the low valley.

As Adam passed through the wooden posts, the driver's side window shattered, and simultaneously a hole appeared in the windshield surrounded by small cracks. Rebecca and Adam were showered with broken glass, but Adam kept his foot to the floor as the Land Rover disappeared into a field of full-grown maize which shrouded the vehicle. Kaiser was now less than happy with the unfolding events. What had started as a glorious adventure, was now utterly unsatisfactory. Rebecca, for her part, was petrified. As they bounced around the back of the vehicle, Adam raced on. Adam had chosen his home carefully. He wanted to be hidden from passing traffic, and he also needed a second exit. His caution and planning had now proven its worth.

The track was narrow and leaves, and the occasional corn cob flew wildly through the open, shattered window. Once through the field, the route improved as it joined a bridleway which continued along a ridge for a further quarter mile. At the end of this, he skidded to a reduced pace, just before it led onto a public road. He had seen no car lights through the hedge that bordered it as he had approached. So, without entirely stopping, he slid the car onto the road and disappeared into the darkness.

CHAPTER ELEVEN

Harz Mountains, Northern Germany

HERR MÜLLER WAS TALKING to Rolf when Karl came into the room. His pace was slow but deliberate.

'Klaus and Heinz have found the girl. She was with one of the guards, they believe, at a farmhouse, a little distance from the Hall.'

'Was!' Müller questioned.

'Sir, they were spotted, and the man and woman have escaped through a back route. Klaus fired at the driver ...the man ...'

'Fired! I gave no orders to kill them. Those fools! Do they not understand what is at stake here?'

'Sir,' Karl said nervously, '...all is not lost. The window was shattered, but the man was unhurt, they believe. Though they have lost them, Kaspar and Stefan were on their way to the farmhouse having been called by Heinz. They must have passed near to the escape route taken by the man, and they have picked up their tracker again. They are following the couple now but at a distance. Klaus and Heinz are going to make their way to rendezvous with them.'

'Excellent! They must be taken alive. Warn our men that they must not lose them!'

It was said by Müller with a profoundly sinister inference.

'Yes, sir!' Karl, under no illusions, barked and left the room.

Herr Müller turned to the others in the room who had watched proceedings intently, as had the three dogs. 'After all these years of searching and waiting, we have our quarry in sight!' he gave a soft smile, but it was devoid of any sense of kindness.

All looked intently at Herr Müller, but no one responded.

Outside in the dark forest, the only noise amid the trees was the repetitive dripping from the canopy. Without a sound, the lynx reappeared from the undergrowth further down the track. Its pace slower now, its profile slightly larger having dined in the darkness of the night. It retraced its former route along the trail, via the edge of the clearing, gliding once more past the stone steps and the face of the property. As it had come, so it went, effortlessly disappearing into the shadows – the taste of blood still on its lips.

And still the lights shone brightly in the windows as the men waited.

CHAPTER TWELVE

La Araña', Buenos Aires, Argentina

HERR SCHWARTZ SAT AT HIS desk in the offices of 'La Araña', in Buenos Aires. The complex taste of coffee and leather from the Camacho Perfecto cigar he had just savoured was still fresh on his lips.

He picked up the handset and placed a call to a number in Moscow. The phone sounded for several minutes before he rang off. Moments later a call came in from a mobile phone in the Kremlin, 'Herr Schwartz, it's Viktor, I apologise for the delay in returning your call.'

Schwartz ignored the apology and launched in with, 'I have received reports that you are doing well in Russia.'

'Jawohl, Herr Schwartz, there have been many unfortunate deaths, suicides and arrests of individuals of 'questionable' loyalty,' Viktor said, smiling, 'our plans are progressing at an

increasing rate. Now the rest of them are too petrified to say anything – they all expect a knock
on the door imminently!'

'Gut, Viktor, sehr gut!'

'For some time,' Schwartz continued, 'our organisation has been sowing discontent in Europe,
the Middle East and North America. Through
our agents, we have used various initiatives to
ferment disquiet among the populations.'

'We have increased uncontrolled immigration, through the work of the leaders of many
of the world powers, but particularly the political leaders in, among others, Germany,
Scandinavia, France, America and the UK.'

Viktor said, almost unbelievingly, 'They all
work for us?'

'Yes, Viktor, many do,' Schwartz said smugly,
'Remember, we have had over half a century to
plan for this eventuality. The world thought that
they had killed us off, but we only went into the
background.'

'But why immigration, surely ...'

'After the war, the communist swine and lib-
erals destroyed our legacy and indoctrinated the
young with their lies. This scum has control of
the world banks and the media. Immigration
was the only way to increase hostility among the
world populace and to sow the seeds to bring
forth the rise of the National Socialists once
again.'

'I am at your service, sir,' Viktor said, pecu-
liarly coming to attention as he did so.

Schwartz carelessly watched the thin column

of smoke which trailed upwards from the remnants of his still smouldering cigar which lay in an onyx ashtray on his desk. He eagerly breathed in its aroma, like a connoisseur, before continuing, 'Soon there will be elections in Spain and in Sweden. Get your teams to infiltrate the media and popular culture in those countries and help to swing the votes to influence the elections. In Spain I want the next Prime Minister to be Adolfo de Guindos Paramo and Ingvar Reinfeldt in Sweden.'

Viktor blurted out, 'A liberal and a green!' he had spoken from the heart and before he had had time to think. Viktor had met Reinfeldt previously at a conference and knew of the Spaniard. What he knew he did not like. He despised them both. Suddenly beginning to perspire, Viktor continued, 'Ple ...Please forgive me, Herr Schwartz.'

Schwartz, uncharacteristically, laughed, 'Don't worry Viktor, they are Kameraden. There are many others.'

Viktor had little time to take this on board before Schwartz continued, 'You will continue your work in Russia, but now I want you to stir the pot in the east – the Baltic States, Ukraine, Poland and the others ...there is already disquiet. It shouldn't take much to light the fire. I also need you to work with our people in Europe and in particular with the American President, Carl Brown. Your agents and technical teams will infiltrate and monitor any organisation or person who threatens his tenure or our agenda.

Discredit them and destroy them. Continue to give no inkling that there is any friendship, or trust, between your two countries, not yet! You must ensure that Brown stays in power, at all cost!'

'Yes, sir!'

Schwartz continued, 'I have spoken to Brown in a similar vein. You will both be contacted by my team, here in Argentina, with details of the other members of Das Spinnennetz, whom you can rely on.'

Strangely, Viktor had become aware of tiny beads of sweat appearing on his upper lip.

'Heil Hitler!' Schwartz suddenly snapped.

'Heil Hitler!' Viktor replied as he heard the other phone being put down gently as the line went dead in Argentina.

Chapter Thirteen

Cleobury Mortimer, Shropshire, England

IT WAS TERRIBLY LOUD AND icily cold inside the Land Rover, with air rushing in through the side window opening and the shattered windscreen. Adam was driving at a frightening pace, as the car raced through the country roads.

After ten minutes, Rebecca, who could not contain herself anymore, shrieked to Adam, 'What is happening? Are we safe?'

He shouted back, 'Yes, all is going to be fine. Just stay down for a while longer.'

She turned to Kaiser who was bouncing, not so merrily, on the back seat as the wheels thundered down the road. Rebecca, put a hand up to his head and began to gently stroke his face to comfort him but also, in part, to comfort herself. The yellow lab wagged his tail feverishly in appreciation and made a brave effort to lick her face, which was not an easy thing to do, given the violent movements in the vehicle.

Then the car began to slow down quite dramatically and Rebecca, concerned with the change, looked up to ascertain the reason. As she did so, she saw a black and white road sign disappearing past the car. It said Cleobury Mortimer, which was a small town not far from Rook Hall. She knew it well, as she would often drink with friends at the 15th century Kings Arms pub. She had spent many enjoyable evenings there, long ago, sampling the local ale and warming herself near the grand, open log fire.

Adam drove at a moderate pace as he passed through the town. She could smell the wood smoke mixed with the penetrating smell of ale from the pub as they passed by, and she dreamt of happier days. Having gone through the centre, they came to the far outskirts of the town. Adam pulled off the main road and shot down a gravel drive that was lined with tightly clipped yew hedges. She could hear the crunching of the small stones diminishing under the tyres as the Land Rover slowly came to a halt. The building before them was set back from the road behind a Victorian terraced row. It too had the look of a Victorian-era property and was understated and quaint, in a very English manner. As Adam opened the driver's door, Rebecca heard the front door of the house opening in unison.

'Hello, Peter,' Adam called.

'Adam, I thought it was your Land Rover! This is an unexpected pleasure. What ...' he cut off mid-sentence, as he saw the bullet hole in the windscreen and Rebecca's tear-streaked face.

'Can we come in, Peter?'

'Yes, yes, ...of course come along inside. I've just made some mulled wine. That will warm you up on this blustery night,' Peter tried to look friendly and cheerful, but there was also a hint of concern in his face.

He was ex-SAS and would, on occasion, assist with guard duties, when they were short of manpower up at the Hall. In his spare time, he and Adam would often go hunting for deer.

Rebecca climbed out of the Land Rover as she saw the two friends shake hands. She called out to Kaiser to follow her, and he did so with little effort. The flustered lab raced across the gravel for a cuddle from Peter who had dropped to his haunches and was vigorously stroking the fur on his back. Kaiser was in the throes of utter ecstasy as Peter said, 'Hello Kaiser ...how's my little friend?'

As Rebecca approached, Adam said, 'Peter, let me introduce you to the Major's granddaughter, Rebecca.'

He slowly stood up, and with one hand still stroking the dog, he said, 'Hello, it's a pleasure to meet you finally – I've heard a lot about you over the years! Please do come in ...and you Kaiser, come along!'

Kaiser ran past Peter into the house and busied himself methodically exploring in the various rooms as if he was looking for a downed quail amongst the reeds. Then, Rebecca, followed by

Adam and finally Peter also entered. It was a well-maintained house, but it clearly lacked a woman's touch.

'Please sit down,' Peter insisted, and they both dropped down onto a long, leather Chesterfield settee which had been placed in front of a roaring, open coal fire.

Kaiser returned from his travels and lay down on the rug beside the hearth, enjoying the warmth and at last, the calm. He was absolutely shattered. Within a few moments, he appeared to be fast asleep.

Peter disappeared into the kitchen which lay to the back of the house and called out, 'Are you hungry? I have some game pie if you wish?'

Adam looked at Rebecca, who now appeared utterly bedraggled. He was sure that she had not eaten at the Hall and he had not eaten anything himself, since lunchtime. Adam spoke for both of them, 'Yes, that would be great!'

Just as Adam had finished speaking, Peter came back into the lounge saying, 'There you go,' he handed them each a glass of a steaming brew redolent of a winter's evenings with family, 'I'll just be a moment with the pie.'

Peter disappeared back into the kitchen, and Rebecca could hear him faintly singing to himself as he worked. Rebecca warmed her hands on the mulled wine and collected her thoughts as she watched the flickering flames. Neither Adam nor Rebecca said anything. Kaiser just slept on. Rebecca slowly sipped at her drink, relishing the smells of the exotic mix of red wine and spices and the happy memories it evoked of Christmases past.

Five minutes went by after which Peter returned with cutlery and some china. He gave one plate each to Rebecca and Adam, handing them a knife and fork at the same time. Each of the beautifully decorated pieces of china held a large portion of the pie, some mashed potato and a dollop of brown pickle.

'I thought you would prefer to stay in front of the fire rather than to sit at the table. I'm not one, myself, for formal dining,' Peter chuckled.

Rebecca smiled at him, saying, 'Yes, thank you.'

They put their glasses on the floor and readily ate the food.

After they had finished their meals, Peter took the empty plates and gave them both a top-up of mulled wine and then returned from the kitchen with a glass of his own.

'No rest for the wicked, hey!' he joked, as he sat into a large leather chair next to the settee.

Peter did not ask what had happened, preferring to let them speak at their own pace.

Adam looked over at him, saying, 'I'm sorry to burst in on you, but we've had trouble up at the Hall ...bad trouble.'

He continued in a subdued tone, 'Luke and Franco are dead ...and so is the Major.'

Adam struck a swift glance at Rebecca, who stared into the fire, trancelike.

'Do you know who ...'

Adam cut in, 'No, but they were professionals

...They may have been German. I need your help, Peter, if you can give it?'

'Certainly, what can I do?'

'We need to borrow your car as the Land Rover is too obvious now. I would be grateful if you could also look after Kaiser for me?'

'Well, that's nice and easy,' he laughed, 'certainly! And I am sure Kaiser will greatly enjoy his sleepover!'

The lab stayed lying down, eyes shut, snoring softly and yet his tail slowly wagged against the rug at the sound of his name.

'I'm not sure how long it will be, as it will be dependent on this.'

He pulled the sealed package from his pocket once more and turning to Rebecca said, 'I know this is all exceedingly difficult for you, but you must read the contents of this parcel. Your Grandfather said it was vital, and I believe it may explain, in part, the events of tonight.'

Rebecca took the package that he offered to her. She sat staring at the paper wrapping which had yellowed with age, and she read the words, *My Darling Rebecca*, back to herself several times as tears slid down her cheeks. She slowly ran her hands over the parcel, as if she was gently stroking it.

Adam spoke softly, 'Please Rebecca, we may be in grave danger, and our only chance could be held inside.'

She looked up at him, despondent and tearful, and he was suddenly taken by her striking beauty and purity, as he felt his heart miss a beat.

She turned her gaze back to the package and began, slowly and carefully, to peel away the wrapping. The three of them watched as she revealed several pages of typed paper and what looked like a small black notebook. Rebecca turned the items in her hand and then placed the journal, unopened, on her lap.

She held the loose pages and read them silently to herself. Once she had finished, she looked up at Adam with a face as white as marble and eyes that seemed transfixed in the distance far beyond him. She gently passed the pages to Adam, and he also read them silently.

As Adam read, Peter sipped at his drink and stared at the flickering flames of the fire.

4th May 1998
My Darling Rebecca
If you are reading this letter, then I will be gone from you. What I have to tell you, I fear, will come as a terrible shock. Much of what you have been informed about your past is a lie, but I beg you - believe me, that it was only ever done for your protection. I hope you will come to appreciate that, even if you cannot do so initially. I will recount my actual past, and the factors that motivated me and I would ask that you only judge me when you know all that I have to say.

My name was not previously Oscar Accola, though you only ever knew me as such, and

I was not Swiss. I was actually born into the Prussian aristocracy and was christened Otto von Freitann. I came from a long line of military people, and I joined the army as a young Cavalry officer, in 1938, just before the outbreak of war.

However, following the Blomberg–Fritsch Affair of 1938 the Wehrmacht was effectively subjugated to the will of Adolf Hitler. My family and I were vehemently opposed to Hitler and to the Nazi Party, as were many in our class.

It was clear that the Nazis wanted to weaken the Wehrmacht's aristocratic generals, thereby strengthening Himmler's Schutzstaffel, the SS. They began with the War Minister Marshal Werner von Blomberg who was ruined when the Nazis 'found', just after his wedding, that his new wife had a criminal record for prostitution. They forced him to resign.

They were emboldened by his removal, and they then turned their attentions on Werner von Fritsch, another aristocrat and the Commander-in-Chief of the Army.

In a plot, it was said, designed by Reinhard Heydrich, von Fritsch was accused of homosexuality by Himmler. The case was eventually proved to be false. The witness, Otto Schmidt, was found murdered once he withdrew the accusation against von Fritsch.

At that time, Hitler replaced many generals and ministers with Nazi sympathisers.

Eventually, Hitler took personal command of the armed forces relieving the subsequent

Commander-in-Chief, Walther von Brauchitsch, of his post. We were forced to personally swear an oath of allegiance to Hitler. Many of my colleagues and I in the German officer corps were angry with the unfolding events, but the Nazis had become too powerful and too dangerous to openly confront.

It was widely understood that following the coming war, the Nazis would then turn their attention on the aristocratic families. The latter would suffer the same terrible fate as that of the Jews and all the other poor unfortunates. I became interested in the Kreisau Circle. It was a group which was formed in 1940 by those brave souls opposed to Hitler. Many of them were from aristocratic backgrounds. However, I was asked not to join in with their activities and to have no further 'overt' contact with them. Instead, I was to turn my back on my Prussian past and to do my best to infiltrate the Nazi regime. I was to spy for the Kreisau Circle and to pass on any information that was of assistance to them.

I joined the Nazi party and began to associate with Nazis and to espouse the Nazi doctrines. I also stopped using the 'von', as part of my name, which demonstrated my noble ancestry. I eventually applied for a transfer from the Cavalry to the Waffen-SS. I was shunned by many of my friends and colleagues who saw this as a betrayal, not knowing my true motivations. Though my aristocratic background was frowned on by the Nazis, my war record *was exemplary. I rapidly progressed and was awarded the Knights Cross of the Iron Cross in 1941 while serving in the Balkans. Many of the sons of the nobility that I had grown up with were effectively being purged from the military, perishing at an increasing rate on the field of battle. It was believed that the Nazis were assigning the noble Junker class to perilous missions on the front line to increase their attrition rate. There was little that could be done as the climate of fear, intimidation and murder was all-pervasive.*

I was no different. Even though I had effectively renounced my past, I was still viewed with suspicion and was readily put forward in my unit for the most dangerous military manoeuvres. In one such battle, I received the Oak Leaves clasp while on operations in the Crimean Offensive of April 1944.

Following the assassination plot, by courageous von Stauffenberg, of 20 July 1944 when Adolf Hitler survived, many members of the Kreisau Circle were arrested, tortured and executed. I became very fearful for my life. Thousands more innocent people were killed in the aftermath, but I survived. Those few brave men who knew my secret took it with them to the grave.

In late '44 I was awarded the Swords clasp to the Knights Cross of the Iron Cross with Oak Leaves. During fighting in the Carpathian Mountains in what had once been South-eastern Czechoslovakia, I had been severely wounded

in the leg by a grenade. I was initially evacu-
ated to Castle Zbiroh to the west of Prague. It
was a magnificent chateau-style castle that lay,
amid the border of the vast Křivoklátské and
Brdy Forests of Western Bohemia, on a low
hilltop. It was labyrinthine and dated back, in
parts, to the 13th Century. In '43 some German
soldiers had had to divert to the castle for the
repair of their vehicle. By chance, the truck
was loaded with radio equipment which began
to act strangely, and its range became signifi-
cantly magnified. The rock formations that lay
under the castle, and in particular deposits of
Jasper, were found to be responsible.

On hearing of this phenomenon, the SS commandeered Zbiroh from the Wehrmacht, who
had been there since the beginning of the war.
The SS went on to use it as a secret listening
post and removed the castle from all maps.

Little did I know that fateful day, that after
I entered Zbiroh, the course of my life would be
altered forever.

I know that what you have now been told will
come as a devastating betrayal of your trust.
However, I have had to live a life in hiding since
the war as there are still powerful forces who
wanted to know the secret which I have kept.
They are ruthless individuals who will stop at
nothing.

Your parents did indeed die in a car crash.
However, it occurred while they were escaping
from neo-Nazis, who were trying to locate me.
Fortunately, you were not with them at that

time; otherwise, you would not have survived either. After that, I became even more cautious and made sure my tracks were covered, as best I could. I had hoped, over time that they had forgotten me, but the prize I hold is too great to pass over, and I fear that they will never rest.

I have enclosed a notebook which relates to the specific events that changed my path through life and put me in the sights of the SS. It will explain much that I know and which you do not. If I have been killed, then I fear that the only way to protect yourself is to find and expose this secret that has lain hidden for over half a century.

The map on the notebook's last page will direct you to a metal box and a book that I buried, in 1945, while I was being pursued by units of the army and the SS. I could not retrieve it before as it lay behind the Iron curtain for many years. Once the curtain was drawn open, I was too old and too wary to begin looking for it, and I preferred not to disturb the ghosts of the past.

The secrets inside are valuable to many, but most of all, to the neo-Nazis. I beg you, do not let it fall into their hands. You must take great care.

I hope you now understand some of my past and what has motivated me.

Please find it in your heart to forgive me.

Ich hab Dich lieb mein kleiner Schatz.

The letter was finished in blue, fountain pen ink, Your Grandfather, Otto.

'That answers why they spoke German! May I see the notebook?' Adam said.

Rebecca took it from her lap and without opening it, passed it to him.

Adam flicked through it and then turned to the back where he found the map. After a few moments, he said, 'Do you have your passport with you?'

Rebecca, who was still dazed, said, 'Uh ...yes ...yes, it is still in my handbag from my journey home. Why?'

'We need to find this briefcase before anyone else does!'

He turned to Peter and said, 'Can I just borrow your computer and your phone for a moment?'

'Sure, no problem,' he said as he pointed into the room next to the kitchen.

Adam disappeared inside, and Peter tried to make small talk with Rebecca, but she repeatedly seemed to become lost in thought and eventually, he let her be.

Kaiser still snored contentedly and Peter, glancing over at Rebecca, saw her eyes watching the resting dog as he noticed a gradual softening in her countenance. Rebecca concentrated on the dog's furry chest as it rose up and down almost effortlessly, wishing that she could be so carefree and at ease.

Thirty minutes later, Adam returned with some papers he had printed, and as he did so, he noticed Rebecca slip her phone into her pocket furtively. He turned to Peter, 'We will have to go now.'

'Sure,' Peter replied, 'here are the car keys.'

He threw them through the air to Adam, who caught them effortlessly and one-handed.

'Thanks, Peter, you're a real pal!' he said with conviction, staring directly at his hunting buddy.

Turning to Rebecca, Adam held out his open palm and said, 'Shall we go Rebecca?'

She looked at his hand and then into his eyes. She said nothing.

'Rebecca, we have no choice – we must go.'

She stood up slowly and turning to Peter; she said, 'You have been exceedingly kind to us, I will not forget it.'

'It's nothing. Don't even think about it. Well, I hope you have a successful trip.'

Adam passed her the notebook, and she placed it into her handbag, alongside the folded letter. She turned to leave and walked out into the darkness, as Adam opened the door for her. The night was getting colder, and there was a strong smell of wood smoke from the nearby chimneys. Ordinarily, she would have enjoyed this quintessentially English village scene, though now it made little impression on her.

Just to the left of the Land Rover stood a mud-spattered Audi A4 Quattro in an elegant shade of scuba blue. She made her way to the passenger door, accompanied by the crunching of the gravel. As Adam pressed the electronic key, the doors opened with a loud squawk, and the lights came on automatically.

He turned back, having passed through

the doorway, and shook Peter's hand saying, 'Cheers, I'll repay the favour one day!'

With his free hand, he passed the keys to the Land Rover over to Peter, saying, 'Stay!' to Kaiser who had made his way to the threshold and was looking longingly at Adam.

'Don't worry Adam, we'll have a ball,' Peter said, as he crouched down next to Kaiser and grinning, gave him a big hug which elicited a great deal of tail wagging and face licking.

Adam smiled and then slipped around the side of the Land Rover just in time to see Rebecca getting into the passenger seat of the Audi and pulling the door shut behind her. He opened the boot, threw his bag into the back, jumped into the driver's seat and started the car. Almost instantly the vehicle, under Adam's control, began to reverse, smoothly and swiftly holding its course across the noisy gravel and backing out, equidistant to the lines of yew hedges that bordered the drive. Rebecca saw Peter, Kaiser and the house gradually becoming increasingly more illuminated by the bright front halogen lights as the car retreated further away. Peter smiled and gave a wave as Kaiser panted, tongue out and wagged his whole tail and body vigorously.

As the car slid past the row of Victorian houses that partially shrouded the drive from the passers-by, Adam slowed and edged his way out onto the road. There was no traffic to be seen, and Adam rapidly reversed out and then, slamming into first gear, pressed the accelerator pedal steadily to the floor. The sound of gravel, which had been trapped in the car's tread, could be heard for some moments hitting the underside of the vehicle as centrifugal force and friction spun it away.

The Audi had immense pick-up, and Rebecca could feel her body being pressed, firmly, into the sumptuous, leather seat as they disappeared out of the village and into the countryside beyond.

She turned to Adam and said, 'There was something I forgot to tell you earlier.'

He glanced over to her questioningly and said, 'What was it?'

She replied softly, 'When those men were looking for me in the house, I heard one of them whispering to the other one. I was terribly scared as they must have been directly outside my hiding place. The man said that things would be very different in a month, regardless of whether they found what they were looking for or not. Then the other man quickly told him to shut up. He was furious.'

'Did they say anything else?' Adam questioned.

'Yes, but they moved away, and I couldn't make it out. I'm sorry!' Rebecca fell silent and looked utterly despondent.

Adam said nothing, though his mind was racing, 'What would happen a month from now to change things?' he pondered.

CHAPTER FOURTEEN

The Online Marketing Bureau, Saint Petersburg,
Russian Federation

VIKTOR HAD JUST PUT DOWN the phone. The call had come from Buenos Aires, from a colleague of Herr Schwartz. The enormity of the goal and the incredible planning were as nothing to the people involved. He could hardly believe some of the names that he had been given. People who, behind the facades, were secret National Socialists like him. He smiled and thought to himself, 'We cannot fail this time!'

He looked from his window at the walls of the Kremlin, lost in a trance for a few moments. Eventually, he turned back to the table and picked up his desk phone.

He rang through to a number in Saint Petersburg.

A softly spoken girl answered the call in a

sultry voice, 'Online Marketing Bureau, how can I help you?'

'It's Ivanov!' he said abruptly.

'Yes, sir,' she responded in a more officious tone, 'I'll put you through straight away.'

There was a click on the line just before the Director of the Bureau spoke, 'Sir, how can I help?'

The Online Marketing Bureau had been set up several years before by one of the Russian Oligarchs, Yevgeny Kerimov, who had prospered since the dissolution of the Soviet Union. He had also thrived due to the benevolence of Ivanov. The Bureau was innocuous, on the face of it - one of several such bodies in Russia, which assisted Russian companies with their online marketing strategy. Some were actually a front for covert hacking and trolls. The intent was to disrupt foreign businesses and government initiatives designed to assist competitors. There was an even darker side - helping the Russian State with anything it required to further Russian dominance.

'Ah, Yevgeny, my friend. I have some more work for you!'

'Anything, sir! You only have to ask!'

'Good, I need you to concentrate all of your efforts on a task which is of the utmost importance to Mother Russia.'

Ivanov continued, 'You will do your best to undermine and destroy anyone or any entity which tries to cause damage to the American President. It is a top priority.'

Long ago, Yevgeny had learnt not to question and not to try to understand Ivanov.

He replied, 'Certainly, sir!'

'I also want you to double your efforts in Europe. Ferment as much trouble as you can - immigration, the economies ...anything. Push the Far Right and destroy their detractors.'

'As you wish, sir!'

The phone line went dead, and Yevgeny stood for a moment, utterly perplexed. He still held the phone in his hand looking down at it with a look of concern etched across his face. Then he got to work.

Little did Yevgeny know that this had nothing to do with the best interests of Mother Russia, far from it!

CHAPTER FIFTEEN

Interpol headquarters, Quai Charles de Gaulle, Lyon, France

JULIETTE DUPONT KNOCKED ON her boss's door and without waiting for an answer, walked into the small office on the second floor of the International Police Organization, more commonly known as Interpol. As she entered a subtle wave of a rich and very feminine scent washed over the room. Juliette had been with the organisation for three years and had previously been with the Police Nationale in Paris for five years. Juliette was in her late twenties, was shapely and had long, brown hair which she usually had tied up in a French plait. Juliette lived for her work and was seen as a rising star within the organisation.

Eirik Jensen, a tough, softly spoken Norwegian, looked up and said, 'What is it, Juliette?'

'We've had a request for assistance from the Federal Criminal Investigation Office headquarters in Wiesbaden.'

'What do the Bundeskriminalamt need?' Eirik said, using their proper German name.

'You will be aware that they monitor the neo-Nazis as a matter of course and have agents embedded within them. They have begun to pick up increasing activity within the various organisations.'

'Will we never be rid of these fascists?' Jensen said in a tired, fading tone.

Eirik's parents had lived under Nazi occupation during the Second World War, and he had a particular dislike of fascists and their methods.

'Go on!' Eirik continued.

'The agents are predominantly low level, and so it is not fully clear what is happening, but there is a general excitement among the higher echelons of these groups, which is filtering down to the rank and file. Almost as if something big is going to happen. The German authorities want us to 'make contact' with other European law enforcement agencies, to try to determine what is being planned,' Juliette explained.

'Well, these neo-Nazis are not the sort of people to ignore. They are highly committed and well organised, and their tentacles stretch a long way,' Eirik continued, 'you'd better make it a priority.'

'Yes sir!' Juliette said, promptly turning and leaving Eirik's office, the door lock lightly clicking shut behind her.

CHAPTER SIXTEEN

Harz Mountains, Germany

IN THE ROOM, DEEP IN the woods of the
Harz Mountains, the fire crackled, the dogs
slept, and the neo-Nazis waited silently, each
lost in his own thoughts. The forest was still,
as the rainwater had ceased to drip from the
branches.

Suddenly the silence was shattered by the
sound of running feet in the hall of the lodge.
All of the men turned towards the door as Karl
returned to the room and speaking directly to
Herr Müller he said, 'Sir, Kaspar and Stefan
have tracked them to a property in a hamlet
called Cleobury Mortimer. They cannot get a
good view of the house as it is partially obscured.
The man and woman spent about forty minutes
at the building. There appeared to be one male
occupant in the building when they arrived,
and he has remained there with the driver's

dog while the couple has left in, what looks like the homeowner's car. Fortunately, Kaspar had managed to attach a tracking device to the Audi as a precaution before they left. He had entered the neighbour's garden and by pushing his arm through the dense yew hedge, had placed the tracker on the car's underbody. Klaus and Heinz are now following them at a safe distance, and Kaspar and Stefan have remained and are continuing to watch the building.'

Herr Müller looked pensive. He remained silent for what seemed to Karl, to be an eternity.

Then Müller looked around the room at the others and questioned rhetorically, 'What is going on here?'

The room remained silent apart from the shuffling of a pointer which adjusted its position. The dog's fur had become too hot by the fire. Everyone looked directly at Müller. Eventually, Rolf, moving away from the window, said to him, but for the attention of all, 'We could leave the tail on the couple and then ask the men to pay the occupier a ...*house call*. It might elicit some useful information that could direct our future course.'

The men in the room had not looked at Rolf when he spoke, instead preferring to watch for Müller's reaction. They still said nothing.

Müller thought on and then said to no one in particular, 'Yes, let us roll the dice!'

Turning to Karl, he said in a staccato manner, 'Tell Klaus and Heinz to continue as they are. Get Kaspar and Stefan to interrogate the man who was left in the house. Remind them of the need for sensitivity. They must not alert the local residents. I 'expect' them to get 'all' of the information the man possesses. Then terminate him, unless they feel that he is of further use to us. The dog is NOT to be harmed.'

Karl snapped, 'Sir!' as an affirmative answer and did an about-face and left the room abruptly.

Frau Vogt, who remained in the shadows like an interloper, inwardly sneered at Müller's concern for an animal. She had no interest in any living thing. But then, no one really cared what Frau Vogt thought.

'We are playing a cautious game,' Müller said in a slow, savouring way, '...but it will soon conclude!'

He smiled to the others in the room, offered up his glass in a toast, barking, 'Sieg Heil!'

Suddenly, standing loosely to attention, they repeated his salutation in unison and promptly emptied their glasses. Only Frau Vogt had no glass to empty. The sound echoed out into the silent forest, harking back to an earlier, darker time half a century before. Müller, however, savoured the moment and took a long, congratulatory sip of the Jägermeister enjoying its taste more than ever. Now, the only sound in the room - the rattling of the ice-cubes in his glass.

CHAPTER SEVENTEEN

The Oval Office, Washington D.C., USA

THE MEETING WAS NATURALLY com-
ing to a close, between the newly elected
President and John Murphy, the Director
of the CIA when Murphy said, 'Mr President,
there is just one last thing. I suspect it is of little
importance and will come to nothing in the end.'

'Yes, what is it, John?' President Carl Brown
said casually, as he began to get up from his seat
and to turn towards the window to take in the
view of the gardens.

'We have picked up a lot of traffic involving
the European intelligence community and Neo-
Nazis in Germany relating to the recent killing
of an old man and his bodyguards in England.
The information so far leads us to believe that
he was a former member of the SS.'

Murphy thought that the details would have
had little impact on the President, so he was

surprised to see a sudden tensing of his half-turned face and a distinct, though minor, staggering of his continuing movement.

President Brown was clearly very interested, though he tried not to give that impression. He kept his face turned away from Brown, but said as nonchalantly as he could muster, 'Do you know anything more?'

As he said this, the fingers of his left hand dropped to his desk, almost to steady himself.

Murphy detected a slight change in the tone of the Presidents voice, almost as if the President was nervous.

Murphy replied, 'No, Mr President'.

There was a momentary silence, and President Brown said, again without turning to face Murphy, 'That will be all.'

'Yes, Mr President,' With that, he turned and went to leave, and as he did so, the President said, 'Keep me updated with that last matter.'

'Yes, Mr President,' he said as he turned the door handle and then left the room.

CHAPTER EIGHTEEN

The Director's Office, George Bush Centre for Intelligence, Langley, Virginia, U.S.A.

JOHN MURPHY SAT AT HIS desk in Langley, pondering his recent discussion with the President. 'Why was this relatively uninteresting development in Europe clearly a matter of intense interest to this new President, he thought? More importantly, why would the President want to try to cloak that interest from him?'

A light knock on the door preceded Murphy's secretary entering the room, as she ushered in Tom Miller. 'Thank you, Margaret,' Murphy said as she left the room.

'Good Morning sir,' Miller said as he sat down.

'Thank you for coming, Tom,' said Murphy at the sound of the door shutting, continuing,

'I wanted to talk to you face to face about a discreet matter. I would like you to attend to it for me.'

'Certainly sir,' Miller responded, smoothing his tie as he did so and intrigued by the use of the word, 'discreet.'

Though mid-level in the organisation, Miller had come to Murphy's attention some years before having displayed highly intuitive work on a complicated terrorist case he had been assigned. Murphy had singled him out on several occasions since, utilising Miller's particular skills to significant effect. Murphy had him marked for future advancement.

Murphy continued, 'There has been a development in Europe. It appeared at first blush to be of little significance. However, it may have more relevance than I had previously thought. It involves the murder of an old man in England. He was killed along with his guards.'

Murphy continued, 'The man was an SS Major during WW2, by all accounts and it is believed that neo-Nazis may have been involved in his death. As to why we do not know, though there is clearly a bad smell about it.'

Miller looked bemused. He couldn't imagine why neo-Nazis would want to kill, what on the face of it was, one of their own. Murphy slid a thin file across his desk towards Miller, who picked it up. Murphy said in a hushed tone, 'I do not want any official record of your work made, no one in the organisation must know of your efforts and you will only report to me, face to face.'

'Sir ...yes, certainly, sir.' Miller replied. 'May I ask why?'

'I cannot tell you at the moment, though your work may well assist me in answering that question.'

'I will have funds transferred to a private account that you alone will have access to, and the details are in the file. You must only use independent contractors if you require them. This is a matter of the utmost secrecy.'

'Yes, sir, you can rely on me.'

'Tom, I know I can,' Murphy said with a smile as he stood up saying, 'Good day.'

Miller jumped up and grasping the file to his chest, saying as he left the room, 'Thank you, sir.'

Miller returned to his room and immediately read the thin file. He left for home shortly afterwards to make his preparations. He was, in a sense, greatly honoured that the Director would give him such an assignment, though he worked on it with some small sense of trepidation.

Shortly after this meeting, a whispering campaign began in the corridors of power and the press, explicitly targeting Murphy. Trumped-up allegations relating to his early career and more precisely his conduct towards females under his command gathered steam rapidly.

The skids were clearly under him, and President Brown put him under sustained pressure, before promptly asking for his resignation, with the thinly veiled threat, that he would be sacked and 'thoroughly' investigated if he did not.

Though Murphy knew that he was blameless, he also knew that he was the target in a clearly orchestrated conspiracy to unseat him and to what end, was as yet unclear. Though no evidence was there to be found, he knew that it would craftily be invented. Given the circumstances, Murphy felt that it was better to resign, which he did do, leaving him clear to devote his full attention to unmasking the culprits and their motives. Murphy had a sense that the catalyst for his demise, could well have been traced back to the death of the SS officer and his conversation with the President, though he knew not why.

Murphy was quickly replaced by, as it was said in the press, a more 'appropriate' candidate, Paul Shultz who was put forward by the President.

His nomination had come as a result of 'guidance' from Herr Schwartz.

CHAPTER NINETEEN

Cleobury Mortimer, Shropshire, England

KASPAR AND STEFAN HAD parked their car on the main street a hundred yards further on. Ordinarily, they would have tucked it away in a side street, out of sight of prying eyes. However, the side streets were already full of tightly packed vehicles, and they did not wish to find their car blocked in on returning to it or to have issues with locals having parked in front of their property. An Englishman's home was his castle, or so it was said. Kaspar knew that with car-ownership, an Englishman's estate seemed to have extended to the parking spaces in front of the castle, even though they were on the public road. Frequently too polite to say anything, parking in front of someone else's house was often a source of irritation and always a source of interest.

The streetlights were sparse and the passing

traffic, light. They had waited in the shadows of one of the pollarded lime trees which lined the road. Nearby, yellow honeysuckle gave off an overpowering and rather pleasant scent. The canopy offered considerable cover to the silent watchers, as it had not been pruned recently by the local council, who were trying to save money in the wake of government cuts.

Kaspar felt his mobile phone vibrate in his pocket. He looked at the screen and read the text from Karl, which gave him his orders. The message had not come direct. The men in the Harz communicated in code with an agent in Berlin, who then sent any messages independently, from a disposable burner phone, on to the intended recipient. He knew the meaning, all too well, of 'interrogate' and unlike some others, he took great pleasure in his craft.

Turning to Stefan, he said, 'Make your way around to the rear, and once you are in position, I will knock on the door. Give me a few seconds to talk to the man and then make your way through the back. Remember, we need to take him alive!'

Kaspar pulled his handgun from his right pocket and a silencer from his left, and while still monitoring the property, he effortlessly screwed the suppressor into position. Mirroring his actions, Stefan then, without answer, slowly made off along the road. After fifty yards, he ambled across to the other side of the street and slipped down a side road. Keeping to the shadows, it did not take Stefan long to find an alley that ran along the back of the properties, while continually checking the street for prying eyes. All being clear, he slipped silently into the darkness.

Stefan crept halfway down the access-way, past green and black, plastic wheelie rubbish bins until he saw the house he was looking for. It was set back behind a low redbrick wall topped with blue, engineering brick, half-round copings. A sparse hedge stood proud of the wall's top, and behind could be seen a roughly lawned garden. Stefan nimbly vaulted the boundary, the momentum taking him through the spindly privet hedge, dropping quickly to its base in a crouch. He rubbed the knuckles of his left hand which were showing traces of blood, having scraped his hand on the bricks. The back garden was mostly in shadow, and Stefan sent a text to Kaspar saying, 'Ready'. He wasn't ready, but by the time he had crossed the garden and Kaspar read the message and had walked to the door, he would be in place.

Kaspar felt the text vibrate in his hand and reading it, he glanced around. Seeing nothing untoward, the German crossed the road and made his way to the house. As he walked, Kaspar felt under his jacket checking for the Taser that sat on his hip, clipped to his belt. It was secure and ready, and he pulled the jacket flap back over it. Kaspar entered the short drive between the lines of yew hedge and made no attempt to hide the sound of his steps on the gravel. With the first footfall, he heard the Lab begin to bark inside the house only to be stilled by the sound of a man's voice from within. Kaspar banged the door knocker and saw the frosted outline, through the half-glazed, wooden door, of the man and the dog coming towards him along the passageway.

Stefan had stealthily negotiated the garden and was crouched on a concrete slab by the back door. He had a clear view through the darkened kitchen and along the hallway, which had just been lit by Peter as he had gone to answer the caller. In the garden, at the rear, Stefan had heard Kaspar's footsteps clearly and then the doorknocker sounding. A moment later, the creak of the door opening sounded, and Kaspar then began to speak. Pulling a miniature crow-bar from his inside breast pocket, Stefan left a few seconds and then, rising off his haunches, began to pry the door open levering the door jamb by the lock. The dog was the first to notice and barking, did a volte-face. He came bounding down the hall through the kitchen and began howling and clawing at the door.

Peter had suddenly turned around at the sound of the splintering wood, but just as he did so, he caught, from the corner of his eye, the sight of Kaspar drawing the Taser from his belt and forcing it upwards towards Peter's chest. Peter dropped to a crouch, spun back around and parried the thrust harmlessly above his shoulder. At the same moment, he had slipped his other hand behind the opened door and had grasped an un-sheathed hunting knife from the hallstand. With incredible agility, Peter jumped up, grabbed the door and slammed it solidly back towards the jamb. Kaspar's arm and face took the full brunt of the blow, though he did not drop the Tazer. Peter then swung the door open again and taking the dazed Kaspar unawares slammed the knife deep into the toppling intruder's shoulder. Kaspar winced at the pain, just as Peter himself fell back in agony.

Though Stefan had not been able to break through the door, he had seen the events unfold and had taken his silenced gun from his pocket and had fired two shots in quick succession through one of the door's glazed panels. The first bullet had ripped into the wall by the door disappearing in a puff of plaster dust. The second ran true and had hit Peter in the back of the knee, shattering the joint. As he slid back towards the wall gripping his knee with one hand and the door with the other, Kaspar summoned his strength and fired the Taser into Peter's chest discharging a powerful electric shock. Peter went down into the floor, writhing in agony and then slipped into unconsciousness.

Kaspar, kicked the door shut and staggered to the backdoor. He flipped the bolts to the side, and the door swung open, the lock already having been broken by Stefan's efforts. 'Are you alright?' Stefan asked.

'Not good, but it seems like the knife didn't hit anything life-threatening!'

Stefan walked past him and grabbed Peter, dragging him into the kitchen and hoisted him up and on to one of the wooden kitchen table chairs which had arms. Pulling a handful of cable ties from his pocket, he strapped Peter's arms and legs to the chair. He then took another and tightened it just above the injured knee to prevent or reduce further blood loss. The Lab was cowering under the table and had begun to whimper softly. Stefan leant over and stroked the dog's head vigorously, 'Guter Typ!' - *Good lad!* But Kaiser just shied away.

'I'll go back to the car and get the medical kit – I'll just be a few minutes.' Stefan said.

Kaspar, who was now sitting down and looking decidedly, ashen faced, said softly, 'Fine.'

Stefan returned five minutes later, having had to take longer because of a passer-by, whom he had had to avoid. Kaspar heard him coming down the drive and then through the door, which he had left on the latch. Stefan entered the kitchen, noticing that Kaspar seemed to have perked up a bit. He dropped the black nylon bag he carried on the table and opened it up, without saying anything. Kaspar had taken his jacket off and was deftly pulling his shirt away. The blade had entered high in the shoulder through the Deltoid muscle and though going in deep, it had not penetrated through the back.

Stefan did not clean the open wound but expertly began to dress it, as he had been taught in the military. Grabbing a field dressing from the bag, he opened one end of the plastic wrapper, removing the inner packet. He took the bandages from the paper wrapper and placed the white pad directly over the wound. Kaspar held the dressing in place with one hand, without being asked, while Stefan secured it by wrapping the tails over the shoulder and under the arm and then tying them off with a non-slip knot. He then taped the dressing firmly in place, and once done, Kaspar began to apply manual pressure to the wound for the next ten 10 minutes to help control the bleeding.

Stefan helped Kaspar to put his shirt back on and hearing Peter moan softly, turned to see that he was beginning to come around. He opened the bag again and grabbed a small packet of sleeping tablets. Stefan broke one out of its foil compartment and went over to the fridge. Looking through the contents, he snatched a pack of two pre-cooked chicken breasts. Grabbing a knife from the counter Stefan quickly sliced half of one of the breasts into cubes, slipping the tablet into a cut he had made in one of them. Stefan snatched the pieces up into one hand, bent down and gently threw them under the table near to the dog saying, 'Da gehst du mein Kleines,' - *'There you go my little one.'* The dog did not move for a moment, but true to his breed, Kaiser couldn't pass up a tasty snack. He cautiously leant his head forward and then swiftly hoovered up all the pieces, spending the next few minutes, licking the floor vigorously.

Stefan smiled and stood up looking over at Kaspar who had a look of pure venom on his face and who said, 'Right, let's get to business!'

Stefan smiled and walked in front of Peter,

who winced from the pain of his knee and the overtightened, plastic tourniquet.

'Well, my friend ...we are here to get some information from you. If you freely give us all that we require, then we will release you. But if you do not, then things will go very badly for you. Do you understand?'

Peter, who looked stressed though resigned, said nothing as he stared into the middle distance.

'Firstly, I wish to know who you are and what your relationship is to the two people who just left this house?'

Peter said nothing.

'So ...I see you need a lesson in my methods. So be it!' Stefan said.

He walked over to the gas cooker and turned it on, the auto-ignition lighting the flame. Stefan looked through the drawers and cupboards, finding a solid steel carving knife and an oven glove. He cut a length of fabric from the kitchen curtain and then used it as a gag on Peter who squirmed in vain to prevent it. Stefan then got to work, heating the blade.

The dog, unseen, had begun to snore gently under the table.

Once the steel was hot enough for Stefan's purposes, he held the blade flat and firmly against the top of Peter's hand. Clenching his fist, Peter writhed wildly and cried out in agony, though the muffled sound did not carry. Stefan held the back of the chair with his other hand to prevent it from rocking over with the violent movements of Peter. Kaspar had moved his chair in front of Peter so that he could fully enjoy the show and to make Peter's torture, more unpleasant and degrading for him.

Stefan waited until he felt Peter's pain was subsiding and rather than ask the question again, he began to heat the blade once more. Peter looked on in horror. Kaspar looked on with increasing pleasure.

From the darkened garden, the brightly illuminated ground floor windows of the house looked like movie screens. Sitting against the wall of the alley, but in the garden, under a large, bushy Hydrangea with enormous flower heads sat Yosef, one of the Israeli agents. Through the cluster of stems, leaves and flowers, he observed the unfolding scene with interest and disgust. Yosef could see the blade being repeatedly heated and used on hands, arms and face and then the gag removed followed by the questions, always the questions! Then the process re-commenced. Yosef had ordered his colleague, Ori, to tail the other two Germans. They, in turn, were following the couple, and Ori was expected to regularly report their progress back to the London office based in the Israeli Embassy.

Peter knew that whatever happened, he would die that night. All he could hope was that he died well and that it took a long time before Peter gave up what he knew. That would give time for Rebecca and Adam to escape. He realised that everyone broke in the end, however brave they were – unless they died first.

Yosef contacted London and informed them of the ongoing events, requesting their orders. They responded within 10 minutes, stating, 'Imperative – observe and report only. Do not intervene unless directly ordered to.'

The horrific scene played out before Yosef's eyes. He repeatedly requested to be allowed to stop the torture. He was repeatedly refused. He was straining at the bit to kill the neo-Nazis.

Then suddenly the man in the chair, whose body had been writhing in the most unimaginable pain, was still – his head lolling to one side.

Peter had died, and despite not wishing to, he had given up some information the torturer had required, though not all of it.

Both neo-Nazis were standing and talking between themselves, unconcerned with Peter's death, just perturbed that they could not have delayed it further. Then one of them, Kaspar, walked into the other room and went to a computer that lay on top of a small wooden table. Yosef could see that he was looking for something but could not see what. After a few minutes, he returned to the kitchen and spoke briefly to the other German, who had been packing and closing his bag. Then, rapidly, they both left through the front door, closing it behind them.

Yosef heard the men's muffled footsteps fade as they passed down the gravel path. He went to the back door which had been pushed shut, it swung open with the lightest touch - the only sound from within, the snoring of the dog. Yosef entered and quickly walked through the kitchen, past the corpse, into the room with the computer. In his haste, the German had left the screen open.

Yosef contacted London and told them that the couple were almost certainly heading for St Pancras. He then left the building by the back door, looking down at the dead man and saying in Hebrew, 'God bless you, my friend!'

The unclosed door swung gently in the breeze that was gradually beginning to build, and the dog slept on.

Vaulting the wall, Yosef ran softly down the alley and then along the road to his car. He had placed a magnetic tracking device on the Germans' car, and he picked it up before he had left the street. They were some distance ahead of him, and that was the way he liked to keep it.

Chapter Twenty

MILLER FELT A GREAT SENSE OF disgust, like his CIA colleagues, as they watched Murphy denigrated in the media and effectively removed from his post.

Murphy was always held in the highest regard, in the service and nobody who worked with him believed the allegations. There was some surprise, however, that he had not stood his ground and defended himself more vigorously. Their shock was compounded by Murphy's replacement, who was thought by most to be, a thoroughly unsuitable candidate for the Directorship of the CIA.

Miller had felt torn between his dedication to the CIA and his loyalty to Murphy. On balance, he believed that the work which Murphy had entrusted to him, shortly before his departure, was clearly of the most considerable importance. The fact that it was being withheld from the wider CIA meant, in Miller's view, that it could possibly implicate some of his colleagues or others in positions of power. Independently of Murphy, Miller also considered that there could well be a correlation between Murphy's sudden fall from grace and this final, clandestine assignment.

Therefore, Miller had continued to work closely and covertly with John Murphy, to unravel the Gordian knot that enveloped the former SS man's departure from this world.

Miller had just left Murphy's home, in Great Falls, after briefing him on the latest developments. There was little to report as of yet, but, from what Miller had said, whatever was going on was clearly of vital significance to a lot of people, and they were thoroughly ruthless.

One matter of note which Miller mentioned was that Paul Shultz, Murphy's replacement, had been asking questions about any new investigations that may have commenced. He was particularly interested in any relating to matters in Europe and in particular England and Germany. There seemed to be an emphasis on anything that had a direct link to Murphy. All the departments had been questioned. Miller said that he had been interviewed twice about this, as they knew that he had been in a meeting with Murphy just before he had resigned. Miller, like Murphy, felt that it was peculiar. There was, on the face of it, no ongoing investigation into the neo-Nazi matter. However, Shultz seemed unwilling to have one commence.

Murphy watched thoughtfully, as Miller disappeared out of the driveway heading back towards Langley. A hand against the ornate wooden frame of the entrance he thought, how right his judgement had been concerning that young man Miller. Closing the door, Murphy walked unhurriedly back through the house and out into the garden at the rear. On the light breeze, he could detect the faint smell of damp pine needles. He had both of his hands buried in his pockets, and his mind was deep in thought, as he looked down at the proud Potomac passing by.

'Why was an old Nazi so important that he had to be killed? Why would neo-Nazis kill him – if they even did? Surely, they would have had a natural affinity to the dead SS man? What is the link to the President? Where does Shultz fit in?' His thoughts continued to trouble him, as the light began to slowly fade, and a slight chill descended.

CHAPTER TWENTY-ONE

Harz Mountains, Germany

KARL HAD RETURNED TO THE room and standing before Müller he said, 'Herr Müller, the occupant of the house died while he was being *questioned*.'

Karl did not have to explain the horrors that Peter had suffered before he had died, as all present knew the thorough techniques their men, with relish, would have used.

Karl continued, 'Kaspar said that you *were* correct - that *Schwein,* 'von' Freitann, wasn't working alone, he was working for that scum, the Kreisau Circle, throughout!'

Otto had not used his title, 'von', while a member of the SS, but Karl had pointedly said it with an expression of overt venom.

'I knew it!' Müller broke in, almost screaming and with a twisted smile on his face, 'what else did he say?'

The others in the room watched Müller's hands digging into the arms of the chair and could not fail to see the veins of his neck and face rising, through the parchment skin, threatening to burst.

'The girl 'is' the granddaughter,' Karl continued, 'and the man with her is one of the guards, the most senior. His name is Adam. There was a sealed notebook with a map - von Freitann left it with Adam for passing to the girl in case of her grandfather's death. The dead man did not know the exact contents of the book, but he said that it told of the location of a ...of 'the' briefcase that von Freitann had buried somewhere in former East Germany.'

'Is that all that the man said, Karl?'

'No, sir,' barked Karl, '...he didn't understand the relevance of it, but he heard the girl reading a letter which mentioned a castle to the west of Prague which seemed to be of significance. He could not remember the name, but Kaspar thinks it must be Zbiroh. The man said that the SS had commandeered it during the war.'

'Yes, it 'must' be Zbiroh!' Müller snapped, unable to control his excitement, 'where have they gone now?'

'Kaspar didn't find out before the man died, but he checked the computer in the house. Shortly before the couple departed someone had been looking at the Eurostar website, it was listed in the internet browser history file. I have also heard from Heinz. He says that the couple in the Audi is heading southeast in the direction of London. That's where the Eurostar terminus is located.'

'Good Karl ...Well,' Müller mused, '...we can take from that the clear possibility that they are going to attempt to cross the Channel and head for Germany to retrieve the briefcase. They were smart enough to change cars, but not smart enough for us. Isn't that so Rolf!'

'Yes, Herr Müller,' Rolf replied, smiling.

'Karl, tell Kaspar and Stefan to head to London to meet up with Klaus and Heinz.'

'Herr Müller, our men may be a considerable way behind them. They may need more manpower, if the couple takes an earlier train, they ...'

Müller broke in, 'Yes, quite right, Karl!'

Karl's expression did not change, but internally he felt a great sense of pride – this was the second time Müller had complimented him. He had been in the organisation for many years but only worked at the Harz headquarters, for the last two months.

Müller questioned, 'What resources have we got in or near London who we can trust?'

'There's Herr Carter's group in the East End of London,' said Franz, who had not spoken previously. 'They are mainly hard-line right-wingers and football thugs, but they're well organised and dependable. Carter keeps a tight grip on them. I've used them before on small jobs.'

'Do they have access to guns?' Müller asked, looking directly at Franz, as a spark exploded out of the open fire before suddenly burning itself out.

'Yes. And most of those scum are ex-military.'

'Good. I want you to get on to the English immediately. Clearly, they are to know nothing about the true nature of the operation, except that we need to 'detain' two individuals who will be trying to board a train at St. Pancras. They can be told of the existence of the notebook, but they are not to read its contents if it comes into their possession. Emphasise the 'consequences' if they were to be so foolish.'

He spoke in a subtle and threatening manner continuing, 'Tell them that they will be paid well and will meet up with, and be under the direction of, our men. Remind them that, though they will need weapons, this is not to end up in a Hollywood shootout. We need these individuals alive, and the matter dealt with subtly.'

'Yes sir!' Franz said, and he then left the room, quickly followed by Karl. Their leather walking boots pounding along the wooden floor echoing like a parade ground rather than a home.

Then all was quiet once more in the room and in the shadowy forest.

CHAPTER TWENTY-TWO

The Blind Beggar Pub, Whitechapel, East End of
London, England

THE PHONE SOUNDED BEHIND the
counter of the atmospheric, Victorian
public house. It was early in the morning,
and the shrill ring went unanswered for more
than five minutes. Franz, who was becoming
very impatient, was about to drop the handset
when a rough, deep, sleepy voice croaked, with a
heavy dose of aggression, 'What the f ...!'

Butting in, the German said abruptly, 'Herr
Carter, its Krüger.'

'Uh ...oh, sorry, Mr Krüger ...we had a lock-
in last night, and the customers have only been
gone, uh' Carter, who spoke in a gruff, Cockney
accent, looked at the large, wooden, Edwardian
clock on the wall, '...um, an hour.'

Uninterested, Krüger barked, 'We have a job
for you, it's urgent, and it's vital to us, you will be

paid well,' Krüger continued, 'you'll need three more men with handguns, and I need your team at St Pancras station within the hour.'

'Blimey! ...well ...ok ...sure,'

Carter was about to ask what it was all about, but he held back – he knew these Germans were not the talkative type.

'Make sure they are your best men and bring some rope or handcuffs, cloth for gags and a fully fuelled van!'

'You will meet at least two of our men, Klaus and Heinz, either when you get there or very soon after. You've dealt with Heinz before - did you keep his phone number?'

'Yes, I have it.'

'Gut!'

'Right, consider it done!' Carter replied, but before he had finished the line had gone dead, Krüger having promptly put the phone down.

Carter, who was only just beginning to fully wake up, had pulled the phone away from his ear, leaving it hanging in mid-air. Staring into space, he was still trying to make sense of the call. After a few moments, he looked at the clock again – time was ticking. He did not have long to organise things – he replaced the handset thinking to himself, 'Bloody Krauts!'

Then he thought of the money – the one thing he did know, was that they always paid, and they paid very well.

Standing there, in part-soiled, tiger print Y-fronts and dirty white socks with holes in – he looked every bit the picture of the modern man, in crisis. He thought, very briefly, farted and scratched his belly, for no particular reason and then picked up the phone again before ringing a local London number. The call was picked up after a couple of rings, and a sleepy voice said, 'Yeah! Who is ...' Carter said, 'Paul, it's me – we've got a rush job on for the Krauts. It's on right now. I need you to get Dave and Mark, and I'll pick you up outside your flat in five minutes – I'll be in the work van, and I'll have shooters for all of us.'

'Are you taking the p ...'

Paul tried to say before Carter cut him dead with, 'No I'm not! Now get off your arse! Pronto! Can you get hold of the others in time?'

'...well, sure ok. Mark's staying with me as we were going to go to Newhaven on the south coast, feathering for Mackerel. I'll get on to Dave now, he's round at his Mum's – she's in a block of flats, over the back. Don't worry, we'll be ready! What's the full S.P., Pete ...?'

'Dunno, but they seem to be in a bit of a flap about something. It must be important ...We'll soon find out, I suppose. See ya in a minute!' Carter said.

'Laters', Paul said as they both slammed the phones down.

Carter ran back up the stairs to his flat above the pub, leaving an awful stench of body odour, booze and stale tobacco in his wake. He pulled on some paint-spattered, faded blue jeans, a lime green, Fred Perry t-shirt, highly polished red DM boots and a green MA-1 flight jacket, once

144

de rigueur among the skinheads of the1970's and 1980s and still his standard dress.

He had close-cropped hair, a beer belly, an earring and was covered in tattoos of spider's webs, hearts, girl's names and a large one showing his allegiance to West Ham football club. The tats were old and faded and covered his muscled arms and hands, and they extended, in part, up to his neck to the base of the hairline. Hidden by the t-shirt at the bottom of his spine was a large, tattooed, black swastika. Carter's face had a weathered look to it and was, like his arms heavily tanned. It was also unshaven.

Carter pulled a tatty leather suitcase from under his bed and threw it on top of the quilt which lay, untidily, across his bed. Opening it he pulled out three old revolvers and an automatic, checking each was loaded. He went to shut the case, but then lifted the lid again and pulled out a sawn-off shotgun and eight cartridges which he stuffed in his pocket.

The naked girl who lay on the far side of the bed, part-covered by the quilt said sleepily, in a heavy Northern accent, 'Where you goin' you git?'

He ignored her.

She was half his age and pretty, in her own way. She had tattoos on her arms and one on her neck, which was a spider's web, without the spider. It extended up and into her hairline. The hair itself had been close-cropped and bleached white, though ugly black roots showed through. The thumb and forefinger of her right hand played carelessly with her nose-ring while her ears were a mottle of earrings and studs of various kinds. Her slutty, bright red lipstick, which was severely smudged, set her off a treat.

She laughed and said, 'Wot's wrong? Are the ol' Bill comin' roun' for yer?'

It was a pertinent question, as the police often turned up unannounced to speak to Carter about various 'irregularities'.

He turned to her and said aggressively, 'Shut it, you slag before I knock seven bells outta yer!' as he did so, his fist unconsciously clenched.

Imperceptibly a shadow seemed to pass over her face. She knew, from bitter experience, that Carter was as good as his word.

Carter threw the four handguns and the sawn-off into a black Adidas holdall and readily threw the case back under the bed, before making his way out of the bedroom.

Emboldened by his departure, she half rose and threw a pillow after him. It hit the wall with a dull thud. As the door closed, she screamed hysterically, 'You pig! Don't speak to me like that!'

But he was gone. Ordinarily, he would have beaten the young woman senseless for giving him backchat, but he was too busy at that time. As he went, he smiled to himself and thought, 'I'll save that for later when I can really do a number on that cow!' he would make sure that she would have good reason to permanently regret her lack of respect!

Passing a Formica topped, dining table, in

the filthy kitchen Carter grabbed a small wallet, mobile phone and a bunch of keys and chucked them into the sports bag. He threw the bag over his shoulder, descended the stairs loudly and burst, with an almighty crash, out through the front door of the bar which slammed shut behind him. He had to squint while his eyes adjusted to the bright light as he looked about him just in case someone was waiting to 'do him over' or to arrest him. Carter ran through the passing, early morning traffic on Whitechapel Road, sticking two fingers up at a passing motorist who had the temerity to blow his horn at him before he trotted into Sidney Street. From there he disappeared into Raven Row. As Carter trotted down the street, the thug let the holdall fall in front of him and pulled the keys from the bag. Outside a disused industrial site, illegally and badly parked on double yellow lines sat the red, ex-Royal Mail Ford Transit van that he was heading towards.

The van was a wreck, the paintwork was severely faded, marks showed where the Royal Mail logos had once been, and it was impossible to find a panel which had not sustained dents and scratches. He unlocked the van, threw the bag into the passenger seat and jumped, surprisingly nimbly behind the wheel. The vehicle had the smell of cement dust and oil which, though powerful, was unable to fully mask the odours emanating from the driver.

Carter started the engine, it appeared, before he had been fully seated. The starter motor made a harsh metallic scraping sound, as the van skidded off down the side street, belching thick, black, toxic smoke from the exhaust. The van's diesel engine sounded utterly unhealthy, but the vehicle drove surprisingly well. He handled the van aggressively and competently through a network of small streets and larger roads, coming to a sharp halt outside a set of run-down, Council owned maisonettes. On the wall outside sat two men, both looking, every bit, the epitome of the classic, London thug. They jumped up as the vehicle stopped just as a third man, looking much the same, came running at full pelt, down the street coming to a sudden stop by the van.

Paul opened the side door, and Mark jumped into the back and sat on the floor. Dave followed suit, and as he climbed into the van, he turned to Carter, who had his window down and said in an excessively loud voice, 'Alright mate!' Carter ignored him but said something, particularly nasty, under his rancid breath.

Slamming the side door shut, Paul ran around to the passenger side and hopped in pushing the bag of weapons to the floor and closing the door behind him as the van sped away. They were all London boys and knew the backways well. Carter had no problem finding the fastest route through the maze of twisting streets and passageways, and fortunately, the traffic was not yet at its worst.

As they drove, Paul doled out the guns, and he and Mark tucked them into their jackets. Dave, in a rush to meet up with the others, had left the house without a coat. Looking around, he put on a black, Donkey jacket that lay on the floor of the van beside him, placing his revolver into the side pocket. He left the shotgun in the bag with the automatic for Carter. Dave said in the direction of Paul, 'So what's going on then?'

Carter answered snappily, 'It's a job for the Jerries. I don't know what's going on, but they wanted us tooled up and with our own transport!'

Carter thought Dave too mouthy and frequently quite irritating, finding it difficult to hide his contempt. But in other respects, Dave was an excellent foot-soldier. Continuing more generally, Carter said, 'I reckon it may be a snatch. We're meeting up with two of their lads at St Pancras, after that who knows?'

Paul said, 'Do you know who we're meeting?'

'Yeah, someone called Klaus and that bloody arrogant bastard Heinz!'

'Bloody hell! That tosser gives me the bleedin' creeps!' barked Mark.

Carter said cynically, 'He gives us all the bloody creeps!'

After that, they were all silent as Carter deftly weaved his way towards the train station. Thirty minutes later they drove by Kings Cross Station and then past St Pancras which was adjacent to it. He slipped down a side street opposite the station and parked, again illegally, on Bidborough Street. Carter pulled out his phone and made a call which was answered on the first ring, 'Carter, where are you now?' Heinz barked before Carter could say anything.

'We're opposite the station parked up ...maybe a couple of minutes' walk away.'

'Gut! Wait there for further orders! Our ETA is approximately 1:00 p.m. I will contact you when we are closer – remain ready for my contact'.

Carter replied icily, 'Right!' but Heinz had already ended the call before hearing his answer. It was an order, and Heinz did not require a response, just obedience.

Carter, whose face was red with anger, turned to Paul and said slowly, 'I would take great pleasure in throttling that bastard!'

Mockingly, Paul said, 'Join the queue!'

Ten minutes later, Heinz telephoned. Carter answered it at the sound of the first ring and before he could say anything Heinz said, 'Herr Carter!'

'Yes!'

'Leave one of your men in the driving seat of the van. Tell him to keep the engine running and the doors unlocked. You and the others go to the steps at the front of Saint Pancras which lead over to Kings Cross and wait at the base of them. We will bring two people down the stairs, and you will assist us in getting them into the van without any unnecessary disturbance. You understand! If there are any changes to your orders, then I will call you.'

'Yes,' Carter said, through gritted teeth, his face flushed red with anger.

Heinz continued menacingly, 'Tell those thugs of yours that this is a sensitive matter and there must be 'no' unpleasantness.'

Carter, speechless with fury, heard the click on the line and pulling the mobile from his ear yelled, to no one in particular, 'Bloody bastard!'

Still seething he looked around at the others saying, 'OK let's get this over with. Dave, you wait here. We might need to make a swift get-away, so keep the engine ticking over and don't lock the doors.'

Dave began to grumble, and Carter snapped, 'Shut it!' For once, Dave did remain silent.

Carter grabbed the sawn-off, and the automatic and along with the other thugs jumped out of the van and headed over to St Pancras. He stuffed the automatic into his jeans waistband at the back and tucked the shotgun inside his jacket and held it under his arm. He loved the feel of the weapons, and he relished the sensation of power and single-mindedness he had when he carried them. The three of them waited at the base of the stairs as 'ordered', looking 'relatively' unobtrusive, like any other bunch of yobs just hanging around, being swallowed up among the London crowds.

Chapter Twenty-three

Embassy of Israel, Alpenstrasse 32, Bern, Switzerland

EZRA GOLDMANN, THE MOSSAD Controller in the Swiss Office in Bern, was looking out of the window at nothing in particular. He was saturnine by nature, but on this specific day, he was particularly humourless. Ezra knew that Mandler was disappointed with him, Ezra also knew that Mandler had good reason. The day had begun with a burst of warming sunrise, though he had hardly appreciated it as he had been up all night and was running on empty.

The door opened and a young woman, Miriam, walked in saying, 'We've heard from London. The agents say that two of the neo-Nazis have just tortured a man to death in his home in a small town in Shropshire. The couple who fled the Hall had met up with him just before leaving for London. They had been followed by the other two Germans. Our agents believe that they are heading for the Eurostar.'

Ezra had briefly turned to look at her when she entered, but as she began to speak, he had slowly returned his gaze back to the skyline outside. He enjoyed the smell of her perfume as it reminded him of his wife, who had died two years earlier.

She had not knocked and had a familiar way with Ezra, having worked as his assistant for the last four years. She looked at his sombre face and felt a sudden sense of sorrow for him. He was a fair and kindly boss, and he looked like he had a considerable weight on his shoulders. There had been talk in the office, that he had made a grave error of judgement in this matter.

She waited in silence with the door ajar behind her. Eventually, Ezra said, 'Tell London to get six more agents to St. Pancras. Make sure they are all armed. Which agent is in charge?'

'Ackerman, Yosef Ackerman, sir,' she replied.

'Ackerman ...yes, yes ...I know him, he's a good man,' he carried on, 'tell them that they are to observe what is going on and to report back any activity immediately to this office and not first to London. Impress on them the importance of this situation. Under no circumstances are they to lose contact with the Germans or to play any other part in the unfolding scenario.'

'Yes, sir,' she said as she disappeared out through the door. So gentle was she with the door handle that he hardly heard it being pulled shut. Ezra did not move, save for his eyes darting back momentarily, as the door latch engaged.

CHAPTER TWENTY-FOUR

THEY HAD SAT IN SILENCE AS Adam drove deftly through the country lanes and then on to more major roads, passing towns with names such as Kidderminster, Redditch and Stratford-upon-Avon. Always their progress fluctuating between southerly and easterly, they sped on, before eventually merging onto the M40 motorway, southbound.

The Audi effortlessly ate up the motorway tarmac, the car's shell masking the sounds of the high speed and giving them the sense of a more leisurely journey.

Rebecca had listlessly watched the ever-changing scenery of the drive thus far, but the monotony of the motorway made her turn her mind back to recent events.

She leant forward and pulled the notebook

155

from her handbag, which sat in the footwell in front of her.

Opening it up she looked at the entry on the first page, which had been written in pencil, on what was by then dog-eared, yellowed paper which was rough to the touch. It was dated July 1945. Her eyes teared up as she thought of the man, her grandfather, who had written it, all those years before. As she did so, she gently bit her lip.

Rebecca started to read to herself, and after the first paragraph, she began to feel a mild sense of shame. The man beside her, Adam, had risked his life to save her. Also, he had, for many years, protected her grandfather and had been the faithful keeper of the book. Dwelling on it, she felt that he had as much right to know of its full contents as she did, maybe more.

'I'll read this as we are driving,' she said, turning to look at him.

'If you wish,' he said, keeping his eyes fixed on the road for the most part. Rebecca had noticed throughout the drive that he had spent nearly as much of his time looking behind them, via the rear-view mirrors, as he did ahead.

She began, 'It's dated 24th July 1945.'

'A while after the war had ended,' Adam mused, '...I expect it would have been too dangerous for him to keep a written record, while hostilities continued.'

Rebecca then began to read aloud, *'In late January 1945, I was withdrawn from the front line and sent for treatment and then to* recuperate in a Castle, south-west of Prague. I had been severely injured by a Russian grenade while trying to drag one of our wounded men, an SS-Unterscharführer, back to our lines. I later heard that he had died of his wounds. The fighting through the Carpathians had been brutal. While in the castle, I was told that I had been recommended for a commendation for trying to help the, by then, dead man. It meant nothing to me. In February 1945, I was next transferred to Berlin, to a specialist hospital, to further aid my recovery. I was sad to leave that magnificent Castle, which appeared so far away from the realities of the war.

Two months after arriving and with my health improving increasingly, I was summoned to the Reich Chancellery in mid-April. I was to meet the Reichsführer-SS, Heinrich Himmler. I felt immensely troubled. He was a man I utterly despised, but I also knew the horrific depths of evil which he had sunk to. I had no idea why I had been summoned to meet him. I was concerned that his henchmen may have tortured a confession out of some poor unfortunate, thereby implicating me in some manner.

I was taken from the hospital, where I was being cared for, by two vicious looking SS-Obersturmführer. They were officious and curt in manner. One sat on either side of me in the back of the black Mercedes-Benz staff car which displayed SS pennants on each front wing. It was driven by an SS-Oberschütze. No one talked throughout the journey. The nurses had made a fuss of me and had polished my boots, making ready my uniform and medals. They looked admiringly at their work, as I positively and superficially gleamed. The others in the car were all immaculate. We must have looked incongruous to the bedraggled population as we drove through the burning ruins of Berlin, that once mighty city which now lay in tatters, with the worst yet to come.

I remembered my earlier life and happier times with friends and family, having come to a kind of inner peace with myself. Risking death many times before, in the heat of battle I now faced, potentially, a bitter end with the master of death himself, Himmler.

As the car came to a halt at the steps of the Reich Chancellery on Voss Street, the officer nearest the pavement opened the door and stepped out. He stood to attention, holding the car door for me. I climbed out and was followed by the other soldier. With a wave of his arm, the first Obersturmführer urged me to mount the steps, and then each of them fell in, one on either side of me.

Two SS sentries stood in front of the middle two of the four, square columns which supported an enormous eagle on the façade. Passing beneath the giant stone relief, I wondered how many men had died to provide for such opulence.

As we entered the main foyer, through large, impressive doors, I was marched down a long corridor watched by an SS officer who sat at a *large oak table, off to one side. He was leisurely taking notes. It was a very grand building and was teeming with military personnel and administrative staff, frantically rushing around. They were entering, what everyone knew to be, but no one dared to say, the final death throes of the Third Reich.*

I was eventually brought to a halt at a nondescript set of double doors, with a sentry to one side. He remained, stood to attention and did not move or say a word. The taller of my escorts knocked loudly on one of the wooden panels, and a few moments later one of the doors was swung open by a middle-aged woman in a dark blue outfit, set off with a cream blouse. She looked rather stern. Seeing us, she stepped aside, and I was next led into a large Chamber. It was hung with opulent oriental rugs and lit by two enormous, crystal chandeliers. The walls were painted in a deep lemon-yellow colour, picked out with cream detailing. The room had a large, patterned carpet, but little else inside, save for a few covered chairs around the edge. At the far end, a group of SS officers stood talking, and as we approached, they pulled apart to reveal Himmler himself, staring at me with a deadpan face. As I was brought to a halt in front of him, we all gave the Nazi salute.

He said, 'Ah, Sturmbannführer Freitann, I believe.'

'Jawohl, Herr Reichsführer,' we said in unison.

He did not return our salute but asked the

officers he had been speaking to, to leave. They all saluted and went immediately. A request from Himmler was always to be viewed as an order - to be followed immediately. He gave the departing men a salute that looked more like a weak wave.

Once the door had been shut, he turned back to us, saying in a mildly, sinister voice, 'I have been looking forward to this day for some time, Freitann.'

With that, he unbuttoned his tunic and slipped his hand inside, pulling out what I first thought was to be a Walther PPK pistol. In fact, it was a small black case.

Himmler smiled as he, no doubt, relished the strained look on my face.

He said nothing for a moment and then said, 'It is always a pleasure to decorate a brave soldier of the Third Reich.'

He opened the box to show the Swords clasp for the Knights cross and he then came towards me, with an outstretched hand. As we shook hands and he passed me the award, he said, 'Congratulations Freitann. I hope you are fully recovered from your wounds now?' His grip was neither weak nor firm, but his hand was stone cold, lifeless.

'Yes, tha ...thank you Herr Reichsführer.' I replied as the weight perceptibly began to melt away from my relieved shoulders.

He looked at my two escorts and waved them away. Waiting for them and the woman, who had stood silently at the back of the room, to take their leave.

'Von Freitann, isn't it?' The way he spoke engendered such menace. But to look at his face, he seemed to have a pleasant, smiling visage.

'No, Herr Reichsführer,' I barked, '...excuse me Herr Reichsführer. I do not wish to appear abrupt ...but I have removed the Von from my name and have not used it for many years.'

'Now, why would that be?' he questioned, his eyes looking highly inquisitive.

'I do not feel that, in the modern age, it is appropriate to hark back to the days of the nobility. I wish to excel in the meritocracy of the Third Reich and not to live, falsely, off the past. I ...I hope you understand, Herr Reichsführer?'

He did not respond, but just looked piercingly into my eyes, and then he smiled cryptically.

He next said, 'I believe you stayed at Castle Zbiroh for part of your treatment.'

'Yes, Herr Reichsführer. It was enjoyable.'

Uninterested, Himmler continued, 'How long were you there?'

I suspected he already knew the answer to the question.

'Just under two months, Herr Reichsführer.'

'And did you travel much in the region?'

I was very concerned about his line of questioning, which made little sense to me, but which clearly meant a great deal to him.

'Yes, I regularly walked the grounds and went into the local villages and towns for trips with some of the other soldiers ...Herr Reichsführer.'

'It is not far from the Front now, is it?'

'Our glorious armies will ...'

'Yes, yes, yes ...answer the question!' he snapped; a sense of frustration visible in his countenance.

'No, not far, Herr Reichsführer.'

Himmler's evil eyes stared, once more, piercingly into mine for a moment. Then he said, with a deadpan face and quite abruptly, 'Goodbye ... Sturmbannführer Freitann.'

Surprised, I snapped my heels and saluted, expertly turning and marching to the door. I felt those evil eyes burning through my shoulder blades as I went. As I came close to the door, it opened. The secretary had heard me coming. I was marched back through the vast Reich Chancellery, out through the doors and down the steps to Voss Street. As we descended the steps, I saw our driver gliding into the pavement with the Mercedes, stopping just in front of us. Still, no one spoke. I was driven back to the hospital and dropped at the front door. The officer who got out of the car to let me out saluted and said, 'Congratulations, Herr Sturmbannführer.' I saw that his words had been accompanied by a slight sneering grin, which had been thinly disguised.

I watched the car drive away and stood there just staring at it. As it disappeared into the light traffic, most of it military, I wondered if I had entered some nightmare world and what reason the puppet master had had for questioning me.

Once the car was out of sight, I turned and walked into the grounds of the hospital. The place was brimming with nurses, pushing wounded soldiers in wheelchairs or walking with them. It was a terrible sight to view all of those young men, once the flower of Germany. It was sad to think, but they were probably the lucky ones.

I walked back to my ward and was fussed over by the nurses who wanted to know if I had met Hitler. As I told them of my day and that I had received the award from Himmler, they became less effusive. Even among hard-line Nazis, the mention of that name gave them a chill. I wondered if they had known, how many of them would have considered if I would ever return.

Later that day, the Matron came to me, saying that they had to pack my belongings and that I was to be discharged early the next morning. She said that a car would pick me up from the front steps at 7.00 a.m. sharp. The kindly Matron seemed slightly rattled, and just as she was about to leave me, she turned back and gave me a kiss on my cheek and a tight hug. Typically, I would have felt warmth, from someone such as her, quite endearing – on this occasion, it had the sense of someone walking across my grave - a portent of doom. I felt as if she was scared for me, though I did not know why.

I was accustomed to sudden, unexpected orders or changes to them while in the army, but coming so close to my meeting with Himmler, I felt very uneasy.

Rebecca was drained by it all and seeing Adam turn to look in his mirror once more, she stopped reading and snapped, 'What are you looking for!'

'It's nothing, don't worry,' he said, 'I'm just cautious by nature ...and by nurture.'

'Is someone following us?' she said, with a faint sensation of hysteria in her voice and in her facial expression.

'No ...not that I can see anyway. I just wondered how these people knew about my place, the farm. I didn't see anyone follow us from the Hall. I'm sure it's nothing to worry about. I expect they were monitoring the Major and all the guards for quite some time, building up profiles of us, as they went along. I just like to be sure, that's all.'

Rebecca sensed a sickly, leaden feeling in the pit of her stomach as she stared through the window into the darkness of the passing countryside, as her mind drifted off into nothingness. Her body and mind were utterly exhausted, and it wasn't long before she slipped into a deep, cathartic sleep.

Adam drove on, unable to shake an acutely primaeval sensation deep in his psyche. Though he could see no pursuers, he sensed that they were there, lurking in the shadows. Waiting. Watching.

CHAPTER TWENTY-FIVE

Police Station, Cleobury Mortimer, Shropshire, England

FOLLOWING SEVERAL COMPLAINTS, from neighbours of a dog barking incessantly in the garden of a house in the town, two police officers had been dispatched in a car to investigate. One of the officers who had attended, what had appeared to be a very minor matter, had just radioed the station and had spoken to the Duty Sergeant.

The officer had detailed what he had found. The constable had also spoken to some of the neighbours and had recounted their statements to the Sergeant.

Sergeant Davies was ex-Royal Navy and had been in the police force for over twenty years. He 'had' felt that he had seen it all ...until now.

Davies told the Constable to touch nothing and to wait for further orders. Putting the phone down, Davies called out to a female constable in the back office, 'Baker, get four more officers down to that house with the dog and tell them to cordon it off.'

Bemused, she responded, 'Ok, Sarge.'

Picking up the phone again, he stopped and called back over his shoulder to Baker, 'Oh … and get a kennel to pick up the dog to look after it until we can find someone to take it off our hands.'

Looking momentarily at the keypad, he tried to process what he had just been told, but it was almost unimaginable. From memory, he tapped in the number of the West Mercia headquarters in Worcester.

He spoke, initially, to a Sergeant in the main office, but was promptly put through to Chief Inspector Elkin, who he had never dealt with before.

'Sir, I'm calling to let you know about a serious incident we have just attended at one of the houses in the town,' Sergeant Davies said. He reported, in a matter-of-fact manner, what he had been told by his Constable.

The Chief listened intently and did not interrupt. When Davies had finished, there was a short silence, and then the C.I. asked about the background of the deceased. The Sergeant told what he knew of him, 'The man's been …or had been living in the village for approximately five years. He was a friendly chap, I saw him occasionally in the local pub, and I had spoken to him a few times, but only briefly. The deceased tended to keep himself to himself. I'm not really sure what he did for a living, maybe working on one of the local country estates – he was always smartly turned out. I understood he was ex-military ...one of the Guards regiments I think.'

'Was he anything to do with Hereford?'

'Not that I know of, but those SAS guys tend to keep their business pretty hush, hush ...maybe, I suppose he could have been. He looked like he could handle himself in a tight jam.'

'It makes you wonder, Sergeant, what sort of individuals could have been capable of doing this to a man like him?' the Chief said.

The Sergeant said nothing but began to feel an increased level of concern for his officers at the scene.

'Look, Sergeant, this isn't the first curious incident to cross my desk recently. I have just had a triple murder with mutilation involved, up at a place called Rook Hall in Shropshire. It was a professional job with multiple killers, and some of the deceased also appear to be ex-military, Foreign Legion if the tattoos are to be believed. First indications seem to point to automatic weapons having been used. I'm putting all of the local armed units on alert, and I am dispatching teams to Rook Hall and now to your location. Forensics are already at the other crime scene, and I'm also going to send a forensics team to you as well.'

'Right sir, I'll let my men know.'

'Keep me fully and promptly informed, Sergeant.'

'Yes sir', he said just as the Chief rang off.

Davies immediately called through to the Constable he had spoken to earlier, 'Royce, I've spoken to headquarters – it looks like something nasty is going on. The perpetrators are a vicious bunch, and this doesn't look like it's the first incident. They may be using machine guns or other weapons. There will be an armed response team and forensics boys, on-site shortly. Tell the others to be careful and to touch nothing. Remember, no heroics!'

'Yes, Sergeant.'

'Look after yourself, Pete!' the Sergeant said as he finished.

Peter Royce had never heard Sergeant Davies call him by his first name before, which left him feeling spooked.

Constable Baker had overheard the conversation and said nervously, 'What's going on Sarge?'

Momentarily confused, as he was dragged out of his thoughts by the interruption, Davies said, 'Uh ...I ...I dunno, it looks like we have some extremely savage individuals on our patch, and they are seriously tooled up.'

Baker, who had always had a soft spot for Constable Royce, ever since they had had a bit of a fling a couple of years before, looked horrified.

Davies continued, 'Get an urgent call out to all of our boys and tell them that there appears to be a team of highly skilled professional killers in the area, who are carrying machine guns. Let the lads know that they have killed several people already and that our men are not to intervene under any circumstances. If they see anything, then they should monitor the situation and report back immediately and await an armed response team.'

'Yes, sir!' Baker said softly as her heart pounded uncontrollably.

'And you had better warn all of the local forces as well!' Davies barked over his shoulder as Baker rushed off to make the calls.

While Sergeant Davies was making his arrangements, Chief Inspector Elkin was patching a call through to New Scotland Yard in London.

CHAPTER TWENTY-SIX

New Scotland Yard, Police headquarters, London, England

'SIR, I'VE GOT CHIEF INSPECTOR Elkin on from West Mercia,' the Scotland Yard operator said, 'he says it's urgent.'

'Sure, put him through!'

As the line clicked and the call was transferred through, Chief Superintendent O'Connor said, 'Hello Jack, what's this about then?'

'We've got a serious problem over here, Chief Super.'

Intrigued, O'Connor said, 'Go on.'

Elkin proceeded to faithfully recount the events in Shropshire. When he had finished, the Chief Superintendent said thoughtfully, 'Right. That certainly is profoundly serious.'

He continued, more to himself than questioning Elkin, 'Why would they kill a man and then dress him in an old, military uniform and after that rip off a lot of the insignia and burn it?'

'Have you any idea where these people are now?'

'No sir, not yet.'

'Was that all, Jack?'

'Well, it's probably nothing sir, but one of the neighbours, close to the house in Cleobury Mortimer, thought he heard people speaking in the street in front of his house. We believe it would have been around the time of the killing. He said they spoke in hushed tones, but his window was open, and he was certain the language was German.'

Elkin continued, 'The witness is pretty reliable. He served three years with the British Army of the Rhine in the Kings Royal Hussars I believe.'

'German?' the Chief Superintendent said ponderously, 'maybe it's nothing, Jack and maybe it's everything!'

'Oh, ...there's one other thing. It appears that the old man who was killed at Rook Hall was foreign, possibly Swiss or German.'

The line was silent for a moment, and then O'Connor said, 'Right Jack, leave it with me. Keep me fully informed of any developments, as they occur.'

'Yes, sir,' Elkin said as the Chief Superintendent rang off.

O'Connor sat for a moment deep in thought, tapping a pen lightly on the desk. He then rang through to his assistant in the next room, 'John, please get me Sebastián Caro at Interpol and ask Mason and Blackford to come to my office, pronto.'

'Right you are, sir,' said the assistant.

Five minutes later, the assistant put Caro's call through to O'Connor, 'Sebastián, how are you?'

'Fine thanks Patrick, how are you?'

'I've been better Sebastián ...we've got a tricky problem developing over here in Shropshire, and there may be a German connection.'

O'Connor saw Mason and Blackford arriving through the glass of his office wall and waved them to come in.

As they sat down in front of his desk, O'Connor recounted to Sebastián what he had been told by Chief Inspector Elkin and then said, 'So now you can see why I have called you.'

'Yes ...and I may be able to offer some assistance. My colleagues have been working on something which may be related to this, concerning fascist groups in Europe. I will ask one of them to call you back.'

O'Connor put the phone down and said to the two officers before him, 'Well lads, you heard that.'

'Yes, sir!' they said in unison.

'It's a nasty business, I can tell you.' He continued, 'I want the two of you to drop whatever you are working on and concentrate on these incidents. Your main contact will be Chief Inspector Elkin from West Mercia Police. I want this given top priority. That was my contact at Interpol I was speaking to. They may have something ...I will let you know.'

'Yes, sir,' they both said once more.

As Mason and Blackford were about to leave, the phone rang. O'Connor answered it, and his assistant said, 'I have Interpol again.'

'Put them straight through,' he said as he waved Mason and Blackford to sit down again.

'Good Evening Patrick, its Eirik. I have you on speaker and with me is Juliette Dupont one of my colleagues.'

'Good Evening Eirik, thank you for calling back so promptly, I will put you on speaker also, as I have two of my officers with me, who will be heading up the case. They are Frank Mason and Mark Blackford.'

'Certainly, Patrick.'

The sound on the line imperceptibly altered, as it went to speaker - Eirik continued, 'Good evening gentlemen.'

'Good evening, sir,' they both said.

'Well, Sebastián has briefed us on your difficulties in England. There may be a connection with a matter we have been dealing with in conjunction with the German Bundeskriminalamt. There has been a noticeable increase in activity among various neo-Nazi groups in Europe and abroad. We believe that the senior members of those organisations are working on something important to them and possibly game-changing.'

'Do you have any ideas about what it is yet?' O'Connor said.

'No, not yet. It must be crucial, though, as the

rank-and-file members are not being told the details at present. We have some embedded agents at a lower level in deep cover, and they are unable to find out anything,' Jensen continued.

'What is the link to the events in Shropshire, sir?' Blackford asked.

'One of the neo-Nazi organisations has sent some of its members to the UK recently. There's nothing unusual in that, as all of the various fascist groups around the world tend to maintain close ties. However, we have studied the individuals more closely. We found that a greater number have gone this time, compared with previous trips. All the individuals have prior military service, with two of them suspected of multiple murders in Germany and Austria. However, most striking was the fact that they all travelled separately for some reason.'

'Can you forward their details to us as a matter of urgency?' O'Connor said.

'I am preparing the relevant background information on these people and everything we have on their known contacts in the UK,' Dupont responded, 'I'll send it over to you within the next thirty minutes.'

'Thank you, Juliette,' O'Connor said, continuing, 'Well then, I think we can leave it there for now, and we will be in contact with you as soon as we have anything further to report.'

'Thank you. Goodnight to you all,' said Eirik.

'Goodnight,' responded O'Connor and the two officers as O'Connor killed the call.

'Well, there you have it, lads. This may yet

turn out to be something of great importance. Keep me updated at all times.'

'Yes, sir!' the officers said as they left the room.

CHAPTER TWENTY-SEVEN

M40 Motorway, South of Oxford, Oxfordshire, Central England

REBECCA HAD SLEPT THROUGH several junctions on the motorway. Suddenly she burst out of her slumber in a cold sweat, finding herself gripping the passenger door's fascia tightly with one hand and Adam's muscular forearm with the other. Rebecca was confused and still groggy and had woken from a nightmare. Collecting her thoughts, she let go both hands feeling a mild sense of embarrassment. Rebecca looked at his arm, which had not flinched, and could see the marks of her nails deeply embedded in the skin, 'Sorry ...I ...I just had a bad dream,' she spluttered.

He did not answer. He just turned briefly to look at Rebecca and gave her a warm half-smile, before returning his gaze to the motorway ahead and once more, behind.

Rebecca adjusted her seating position, having sunk lower into the seat during her sleep. She rubbed her eyes and felt, in some ways, better for the rest.

Rebecca looked out of the windows and could see the sky was gradually beginning to lighten.

Her mind kept going back to her hold on his arm. His strength, the warmth of his body, the self-control. Inwardly she tried to shake herself out of her thoughts as her emotions ran wild.

After a few moments and with no notice, she began to read aloud from the notebook again, from where she had left off. Adam noticed that her voice had developed an unexplained quiver as she continued.

The next morning the same car and driver had arrived but without the escort. I was driven, in silence, to Fliegerhorst Berlin Gatow, the airfield in the western outskirts of Berlin, in the Spandau district. As we approached the front gate, the Luftwaffe guard, who appeared to be no more than 13 or 14 years old, lifted the barrier to allow the car to enter. The lad's oversized helmet looked quite ridiculous, as his head was almost disappearing inside it and his shabby uniform looked two sizes too big for him. He appeared to be petrified. Everyone was terrified at that time. Usually, the driver would have been stopped, and his and my identity would have been thoroughly checked. But, in the closing days of the war, speed was essential, and the guards at the airfield had become used to some very strange comings and goings.

We drove through the gate and across open ground covered in rough grass. It had been neatly cut at some point but was now appearing very shabby. Few Luftwaffe personnel were to be seen, and the aircraft were also sparse on the ground. I was driven at considerable speed past some barracks, then by, what looked like, the lifeless officer's club and finally into a large hangar. The only plane inside was a Fieseler Fi 156 Storch. They were generally used for medical evacuation and as spotter planes, among other things. The Storch had exceptional flying abilities, though they flew relatively slowly.

As we entered the hanger, an old man dressed in a grey boiler suit began to rotate the propeller six or seven times. I had seen it done many times before and knew that it was to get rid of oil which had settled in the bottom of the downward-pointing cylinder of the inverted V8 engine. Completing his task, the weary, old man slipped under the wings and released the chocks, and the pilot started the engine. The plane's propeller began to rotate and the cylinders, grumbling, began to fire up, followed by clouds of thick black smoke and an acrid smell.

The driver had stopped by the side of the plane, and then he jumped out of the vehicle. He stood to attention as he opened the car door, and as I got out, I saw the pilot lean over and open the side door of the plane from inside. It was clear that I was expected to board and so I walked under the wing and climbing in, I dropped back into the seat behind the pilot. The noise was deafening as it echoed around the hangar. The pilot passed me a cloth flying helmet which had a throat mike and earphones inbuilt. As I placed this on my head and strapped myself in, the car's driver passed me my small luggage bag which I put on the floor between my feet. He then pushed the plane's door shut, and as he left, he gave me a quizzical look. I did not see him get back into the car as the next moment the plane was turning gently and taxiing out of the hangar, swinging quickly on to the taxiway.

I heard the pilot chattering wildly to the control tower, before stopping the plane abruptly. The pilot began to power up the engine, and moments later he had released the brakes, and we were racing along the taxiway. After what seemed like only sixty or seventy yards and just short of a bunker, the plane lifted off the concrete, parallel to the runway. It rose into the air effortlessly, and as we gained height, I could see the ruins of Berlin off to one side, with, everywhere, plumes of smoke rising, explosions bursting and, in the distance, the impending onslaught of the Russian Menace. As I watched the horrors of the scene below, a great wave of sadness passed over me.

The little Storch had exceptional take-off and landing abilities and the pilot, in his eagerness to leave, had not wanted to wait until he had reached the main runway before he made his escape.

The flyer banked sharply, and we readily put Berlin behind us. Though I was not to know it at that time, I was never to see the city again.

The pilot gained some height and reaching one thousand six hundred feet, he levelled off just below the cloud layer.

I next saw him raise his hand to press against his throat mike and he spoke to me in exuberant terms, 'Good morning sir, my name is, Wilhelm. I cannot tell you how glad you have made me. This assignment has been sent from heaven. I had given up hope of ever getting out of Berlin before the Russians ...' In his excitement, he had forgotten that I was a Major in the SS and his sentence trailed off, as he choked on the final words.

'Hello, Wilhelm, my name is Otto. Don't worry, you are among friends. We will all be glad when this wretched war is over!'

We were silent for a few moments, and then I asked, 'Where are we heading?'

He was thoughtful for a moment, and then he blurted out, 'They said it was classified ...but maybe you should be told,' I wondered what he meant by that, as it did not make it sound overly enticing.

He continued, 'I am to land in a field close to the Castle of Wewelsburg. After that, I do not know.'

The name Wewelsburg clearly meant something to the pilot, judging by his tone, and it certainly had resonance for me. It was the spiritual home of the SS.

I felt that Wilhelm would have been quite content, if I had asked him to continue on his westward journey past the castle and over the approaching frontline of the Allies, into internment in a prisoner of war camp.

I sat, trying to make sense of the past hours. If I was to be tortured and killed, then Himmler had had plenty of chance to do so already. Maybe he was just toying with me for his own mad amusement. It seemed unlikely though, as that monster had a lot on his mind in the closing months of the war, saving his own skin for one. However, I reasoned that it was more probable that he wanted me for some mission. Possibly, something to do with the Castle Zbiroh or at least that region of the Protectorate of Bohemia and Moravia that he had questioned me about.

I decided that there might be something that could be of importance in this journey, to a future Germany and to help in bringing people like Himmler to justice.

The cold became more intense inside the aeroplane, the further we rose, and it smelt quite damp. I was glad of my overcoat, and pulling up the large collar, wrapped it closer to me.

I asked Wilhelm, 'How long until we land?'

He replied in a dejected voice, 'About one hour and thirty minutes depending on any headwind or tailwind.'

Ten minutes later, as I dozed, the plane

suddenly lurched sideways violently, waking me from my slumber. I felt a thundering as the tailplane was strafed by cannon fire from, as I saw, a British Hurricane fighter that had just disappeared past us, at over three times our speed. The visibility in the Storch was better than in any plane I had ever travelled in, and it felt like I was sitting in a goldfish bowl. Pleasant for sightseers, but very unpleasant when you are the main target in a shooting match, with death as the prize.

Wilhelm, who had clearly not seen the plane before it attacked seemed to quickly regain the stability of the aircraft, and as I heard the Storch's engines begin to labour even harder, the little plane began to climb once more. I looked over my shoulder to see the Hurricane banking, far off to our left and preparing to come in for the final killer run. The little Storch was climbing reasonably swiftly, but the base of the cloud seemed a lifetime away. I kept watching the cloud base and the Hurricane, which was now coming out of the turn and heading straight for us. I was transfixed by it, as I saw the cannons opening up, spraying us, I could feel the shells hitting home into our fuselage, but then at that moment, we seemed to dramatically ascend into a murky world which became, suddenly, quite opaque. It was a strange sensation as we entered the relative comfort of the cloud, almost like ascending to Heaven but still hearing the danger of the whizzing shells. Once entirely in the cloud, Wilhelm violently altered course. The *sound of the fighter planes attack faded and stopped, and we both breathed a sigh of relief.*

Shortly afterwards Wilhelm appeared to alter course again. I had become totally disorientated, but he seemed to know where he was going. I presumed that the pilot had returned to the original route. Much to my unease, however, he did not descend from the cloud. Though I understood his reasoning, I did not like to fly generally and certainly not without any visuals. Eventually, he said, 'We are nearing the target.'

Clearly, he had operated as a bomber or fighter pilot previously, judging by his turn of phrase.

He began to descend and suddenly the cloud dissipated, and we were in daylight again looking out at a calm rural scene, so vastly different from the Berlin I had left.

The pilot took a careful look around, as did I, but we were very much alone.

Seeing the castle, Wilhelm said with an air of dejection, 'There it is. We'll be landing soon.'

I could not see the castle ahead amid the landscape but took his word for it. We were losing height constantly and then, I saw it, off to one side and in the distance. It stood perched on a heavily wooded hilltop. It was an impressive fortress with enormous walls which connected three round-towers, giving it a triangular layout. Wilhelm flew over the village of Wewelsburg and off to the side of the castle. We had a majestic view as we were now cruising at 300 feet above the battlements.

Wilhelm circled the hilltop and radioed to the Castle for instructions. He was ordered to land south of the village in a small grassy field, near to the main road. He circled and made his final preparations, stabilising the plane and dropping his airspeed and flaps as he continued the descent. Coming near to the ground Wilhelm reduced power and pitched the nose up, giving some more flap, while at the same time allowing the plane to flare. When we were a few feet above the ground and moving relatively slowly, the plane just began to gently sink into the grass. It was a perfect, soft landing, though the ground, which had looked very flat from the air, was clearly quite irregular and the plane bounced and rocked to its final stop.

As I was climbing down from the Storch, a Kübelwagen pulled alongside us, with an SS driver and an officer in the front seats. The officer jumped out and giving the Nazi salute, which I returned, he said, 'Sturmbannführer Freitann, you are to come with me to the castle.'

He then turned to the pilot and said, 'You are to wait here, Hauptmann. We will have further use for you.'

Wilhelm turned to me and said somewhat cryptically with a half-smile on his face, 'Good luck in the future, sir. It was a pleasure meeting you.'

I had a distinct impression that he felt that my future might be a short one.

As I climbed into the Kübelwagen, a truck was pulling off the road and heading towards us. Including the driver and an Unteroffizier beside him, there were four other soldiers in the back - all SS. They came to a stop just as our car began to drive towards the gate. At that point, the Storch with its propeller still turning, suddenly roared into life and began to pull away from us heading, back down the field, clearly, as fast as Wilhelm could force it.

The officer screamed at his driver, 'Stop!'

The Kübelwagen swiftly skidded to a halt in the slightly damp grass, as the officer jumped out shouting, 'Traitor! Kill him! Kill him!'

I turned to see the plane about thirty yards away as the officer, and all the other troops began, while dismounting from their vehicles, to open fire on the disappearing aeroplane as it made its dramatic break. I desperately willed Wilhelm to make good his escape, but I felt, given my present company, that I should show some camaraderie with my 'fellow' SS. So, I pulled my Luger from its leather holster and began to fire at the trees, aiming slightly to the left of the aeroplane.

I stared at the Storch as it picked up speed and began to lift up and away from the grass, 5 feet, then ten feet, then fifteen and then ...just as I felt he was going to make it the left-wing suddenly caught fire. Seconds later the Storch exploded, crashing to the ground in a burning heap, moments afterwards. There was absolutely no hope for poor Wilhelm, who must *have taken his fateful chance to make his escape to the Allied lines. I expect that he had felt that his next journey would have been back to Berlin if he ever managed to make it. I had seen much death in the war, but I felt utter despair to see the plane's wreckage burning close to the tree line. Surrounded now, as it was, by the SS killers who were jumping for joy in front of Wilhelm's funeral pyre as the thick black smoke wafted above them, it was a truly appalling sight. Almost pagan. What an abominable waste of a brave, decent young man.*

The officer turned to me, smiling in triumph and saying, 'That traitor will never see home again!'

I was unable to make a reply or even to give any false sense of recognition of this creature's apparent triumph.

Rebecca stopped reading for a moment and glanced out at the passing countryside. Her eyes were filled with tears. She could not explain why, but she was overcome with a tremendous sense of sadness for the long-dead Wilhelm. She wondered if he had any known grave or even if his family ever knew what had become of him. He had only wanted to live, and yet he did not.

Rebecca also felt a growing sense of understanding and compassion for her grandfather. No wonder he had wished to keep her from the horrors which he had witnessed.

She silently wept almost in remembrance of

that kindly old man who had been such a constant in her life.

Adam turned to her and asked, 'Are you alright?'

She ignored his question, and after a short silence, she continued to read.

We all climbed back into the Kübelwagen, and the driver sped away, leaving the legion of ghouls to their enjoyment. We continued on through the village, the acrid smell of burning oil and rubber still in my nostrils and eventually climbed up through the trees to the castle.

Wewelsburg Castle lay to the northeast of North Rhine-Westphalia, and it was the spiritual centre of the SS cult. Even the mention of it left me with a sense of foreboding. On our arrival, we were stopped by four SS guards who looked like particularly trigger-happy creatures. Once my identity documents were thoroughly checked, I was asked to wait for a moment by the sentry post, as the Kübelwagen and its occupants reversed back and then turned, making off towards the village.

Momentarily, an SS General, SS-Obergruppenführer, in full dress uniform, attended and told me to follow him. I had never seen him before and was surprised by the appearance of such a senior officer. I was utterly apprehensive, unable to think of anything else, but my real mission as a sleeper in the SS for the Kreisau Circle.

They must know, I feared.

I followed the SS-Obergruppenführer through the courtyard of the castle to the entrance to the West Tower. On entering the tower, I was led down to the basement where I met, not Heinrich Himmler, but SS-Oberführer Gartmann. I had seen him at a function many years before, but only briefly. He was a man who was little known outside the upper circles of the SS. But he was more feared than Himmler in many ways, for his ruthless, savage cruelty. It was widely known that he had power well beyond his rank. 'Der Schatten', 'the Shadow' as he was known, was a man to be genuinely feared. I gave the Nazi salute and came to sharp attention, clicking my heels and crying, 'Heil Hitler'.

Gartmann gave the General a sharp glance, and he too suddenly clicked his heels, saluting at the same time and then retired closing the door behind him. Der Schatten ignored me initially and then walked behind me, while I remained at attention, hearing moments later, the sound of a key turning, which I took to be the door being locked. The room was empty apart from a small, oak table and an ugly, matching chair. He returned and stood before me, saying, 'So we meet, at last, Sturmbannführer Freitann.'

He did not smile but just stared, unblinking, deep into my eyes with an utterly lifeless face. I did not know what to say in response, but blurted out, 'Yes, Herr SS-Oberführer ...it is an honour to ...'

Gartmann, disinterested, cut me short

saying, 'Sturmbannführer, I have chosen you 'personally' for a mission of the utmost secrecy and importance to the Reich and to our Fuhrer.'

He fixed me with a blank stare, shrouded in evil, which sent a cold shiver down my spine. After what seemed like an age, he turned, before moving towards a steel safe built into the tower's wall. The blackened, steel door of the safe was embossed with two large SS runes fashioned from what looked like platinum. The private safe had been built into the basement of the west tower during the mid-thirties, and only Himmler, Gartmann, the SS-Obergruppenführer and the castle Commandant knew of its existence. The open door shielded the interior, but I saw him remove a metal box which had a handle on each end. It was black, and when Gartmann placed it on the table, I saw that it had been welded shut along every seam. It had the SS symbol emblazoned on its face, again in the same platinum.

Locking the door once more, Der Schatten ordered me to pick the box up and to follow him. The case was moderately heavy, and I did as I was ordered. On leaving the room, the SS-Obergruppenführer and six SS guards, who had been waiting outside, followed us, as I was taken to Die Gruft, the vault. I had heard tell of this place before, it was the inner sanctum of the SS cult, but I had never met anyone who had entered it, or who had admitted to entering it – it was known as the 'Himmler crypt' by many within the SS.

On entering, I found a dark, vaulted room with twelve pedestals around its exterior. On three of the plinths stood SS-Obergruppenführers in full dress uniform, like the previous General. They were draped with black cloaks and hoods with an inner, red silk lining and the SS emblem on the right breast, emblazoned in silver thread.

SS-Oberführer Gartmann and the General who had followed us walked ahead of me and took their places on empty pedestals. They now wore robes, and each of the plinths was lit by a sombre light.

It was in this dark, formidable and unspeakable place that I had to swear a blood oath of loyalty and secrecy to the Fuhrer, the Reich and the SS. I was to carry out their task with no regard for my own personal safety and with unerring diligence.

I did not feel bound by their abominable oath, made in their most hallowed ground as they were, in my eyes, the embodiment of pure evil. However, breaking the vow has prayed on my mind ever since.

Following the ceremony, nobody moved or spoke, though all eyes watched me like falconer's hawks. Behind me, the door softly opened and I was then ushered out by an SS-Obersturmführer, impeccable in his full-dress uniform, but not before I gave the most perfect Hitlergruß, Nazi salute, which I had ever managed.

Thankfully, I was never to see Gartmann or the vault again. As I followed the

SS-Obersturmführer into the courtyard, I felt beads of icy sweat running down my back. I could hardly walk in a straight line as my body felt as if it were inwardly convulsing, while my mind was in wild elation at having escaped un-tortured and without being brutally murdered.

On reaching the daylight, the SS-Obersturmführer turned suddenly to face me, and from his tunic pocket, he pulled two sealed documents. He slipped them into my side coat pocket, as I still carried the box Der Schatten had given to me. As he did so, he said, 'Herr Sturmbannführer Freitann, one of these envelopes contains your orders and the second a letter of authorisation from Reichsführer Himmler which 'will' ensure that you get full co-operation from all members of the German Forces, whatever their rank. You will open them immediately, having left the castle with the column. Memorise the orders and then destroy them. Do not mention the contents to anyone else apart from the commanding officer at your final destination. He does not, at present, know of these plans.'

I suspected that the authorisation, supposedly from Reichsführer Himmler, was possibly a forgery of Gartmann's making.

I was then led to and ushered into a waiting Mercedes-Benz W150 cabriolet staff car with SS pennants on the fenders. An SS driver and an SS-Hauptsturmführer sat, unspeaking, in the front seats, while I sat alone in the back. The

SS-Obersturmführer called the officer out of the car and out of earshot of me, he handed him a book and then a further sealed envelope. He spoke very intently and furtively to the officer, who then saluted and spun around, marching back to the car. The SS-Hauptsturmführer had an intensely determined, aloof and proud look on his face. Whatever he had been given was of great importance, and I felt, related to my fate.

We set off, and three Opel Blitz trucks followed behind. The first open-top truck had twelve clearly battle-hardened, Waffen-SS soldiers in immaculate uniforms sitting in the back. A driver and an officer rode in the front. The other two trucks only had a driver in each, and their covers were also rolled back. The vehicles were immaculate and were all painted in a matt, dark grey. We left immediately, and shortly afterwards, I read the orders and as instructed, pulled a lighter from my pocket and destroyed them. I was to take the convoy to Zbiroh as a matter of urgency and then to deliver the box to the castle's Commandant. Nothing was said as to what I was meant to do after that point. I spent the following hours trying to assimilate what I had just learnt and its possible consequences.

We travelled south-east, under my direction, towards the border with the Protectorate of Bohemia and Moravia. Later, that first day, we stopped briefly on the side of the road to eat dinner, before moving on again. During the rest stop, I overheard some of the soldiers chattering.

They mentioned that Himmler had ordered the SS to destroy the Wewelsburg Castle, on what was to be, just two days before the U.S. Third Infantry Division took possession.

The convoy had to detour occasionally because of advancing American troops. On the second day, as we drove along an empty stretch of road through open country, with the light beginning to fade imperceptibly, we heard the sound of an aeroplane rapidly approaching us. All heads turned, and the officer with me shouted violently at our driver to speed-up, which he did, dramatically. I was pressed back into the seat as I looked behind and saw the slower trucks increasingly, dropping further behind us. The troops in the first vehicle had just begun firing their weapons at the fighter, as all three trucks began to be strafed by an American P-51 Mustang. The Major and I had both drawn our Lugers, and we started to return fire, my shots going, purposefully, very wide, at the passing plane. The first two vehicles were ripped to shreds by the blast of bullets with the second truck exploding in a ball of flame as it was then hit by one of two small bombs which the fighter had dropped as it passed over. The second bomb had missed the first truck exploding in the ploughed field close-by, spraying the air with mud and shrapnel. The first truck suddenly veered off the road and slipping into the ditch that ran parallel to it, rolled onto its side with the few surviving troops spilling out onto the muddy field. Many now hung dead or dying *from the effects of the strafing, the blast and the tearing shrapnel. All appeared injured, except the driver of the last truck who had stopped and had come running, clasping an MP 40, to assist his comrades.*

Our car had stopped momentarily as we viewed the scene. We were almost one-hundred yards ahead of the trucks; while the Allied fighter was making a wide bank to prepare for a second pass. I turned to the Major who was rapidly reloading his Luger and then, lifting my pistol, I shot him once through the temple. He fell back over his car door and slipped out onto the road in a lifeless heap. The driver had half stood up, staring in disbelief at the now motionless officer as I then also shot him twice in the chest. He slumped back into the seat, dying, as I vaulted out of the Mercedes-Benz. I ran to his door and opening it began dragging his body out. The driver of the third truck had had a good view of the unfolding events, as he ran forward to help his friends, still facing towards our vehicle.

As I had just finished pulling the driver clear, I looked back and saw the running man begin to loose off shots at me from his submachine gun. Running to the other body, I lunged at the officer's tunic and retrieved the envelope he had been given at the castle. I jumped into the car, which was still running and ducking my head, put the car in gear and slammed the accelerator to the floor. I heard the running SS driver shouting, 'Halt!' and felt the occasional bullet hitting the car's metal exterior and saw others spitting up dirt on the road and amid the ploughed field. The Schmeisser, as it was often erroneously referred to, was not a long-range weapon fortunately and in the hands of a stressed and running man, even one from the elite SS, it was not enough to stop me.

I heard the weapon spatter bullets at me for a few bursts more, as I raced away, but with the sound of the approaching plane coming once again, the gun stopped. I looked back and saw the Mustang descending once more, at a steep angle this time. It was making directly for the trucks, and as its weaponry began to let fly, the surviving soldiers desperately tried to return fire. It was carnage, I turned back to the road and raced ahead as fast as I could go.

Seeing the road disappear into a large wood a few hundred yards ahead of me, I desperately prayed that I would make it. I heard the plane's guns suddenly stop and looking back I saw that it had passed over the trucks and was now in a steep bank and turning towards me. I could not outrun it on an open road, and it would be on me in seconds. I waited and waited, and at the sound of the first shots, I stood on the brake and brought the car to a swerving stop just atop of the upper edge of one of the drainage ditches at the roadside. As I did so, I saw sparks fly as the tracers ripped through the road ahead of me and then I saw them carry on into the ploughed field churning it up.

The sudden halt flung the book, the officer

had received and which had lain on the seat beside him, into the car's footwell. It was the infamous, *Mein Kampf* by Adolf Hitler. I knew that I had little time before the pilot came back in for the kill, and he would not be fooled next time. I pressed the accelerator to the floor, as I pushed through the gears, dragging the car back to the road and back towards the wood. It seemed to take a lifetime, and my eyes were repeatedly drawn to the plane as it turned, my ears listening to every change in the noise of its engine. The American was banking above the trees in an attempt to come directly at me. Making the turn he powered down towards the vehicle, but as I got to within spitting distance of the wood, the lofty tree canopy gave me some protection from the rounds as they ripped through. The back seat was torn, shredded by bullets. But apart from that and being hit by shattered, falling branches, thankfully I was untouched. Seconds later, I was deep into the dense wood and racing away. The pilots firing stopped, only to recommence momentarily as he passed over the other vehicles once more. I heard some small arms, return fire from the surviving SS men, but less than before. I listened to the engine of the American's plane, hoping that he would not return. Thankfully, the noise gradually became less laboured and fainter as it continued on towards its home airfield.

I drove as fast as I could for several hours, praying that the men in the convoy had all been killed. Or if some had survived, that they had no radio or none that had survived the Mustang's attack, with which to contact Wewelsburg. I felt sure that they would be unable to follow me as the two destroyed vehicles ahead of the third truck would block its path, and it would be impossible to cross the ditches on the side of the road or the ploughed fields. It was also possible that the last truck may have been destroyed in the final sweep by the American pilot. He had, after all, proved himself a very efficient aviator and killing machine.

Instead of continuing south-east, I headed due east. Many routes were empty, but then the main roads were often filled with a mixture of petrified civilians fleeing the frontline and dejected troops heading for it. There were few roadblocks, and once I showed the letter from Himmler to the few I did come across, the terrified guards hurried me through.

It was too dangerous to retain the box for much longer. Having it in my possession might well be enough to have me shot, by either side, dependant on its contents. I also had no intention of the Nazi's gaining control of it ever again.

Eventually, I came to a heavily forested region, with few villages, East of Arnstadt in Thuringia and having seen nobody for some time, I pulled off the road turning onto an old, dirt track. The going was bumpy but relatively good as the soil was not very waterlogged. The trail seemed as if it had not been used for a long time. It was in this lonely place near a rocky outcrop that I buried the box and the book wrapped in my greatcoat and a waterproof tarpaulin from the boot of the car, using an entrenching tool that was strapped to the staff car's side.

Resting, from my efforts, I then opened the letter that the officer had been given at the castle. It was marked 'Top Secret', burn once read. It had clearly been opened by the officer, but for some unknown reason, he had not destroyed it. I have never understood why, but he may have kept it to protect himself from charges of murdering a fellow SS officer. For the letter, which was purportedly from Himmler himself, explained that I was to be used to direct the other soldiers to a castle, which was unspecified. It explained that the box contained a briefcase with documents inside. These told of a large cache of gold and other valuables, which were to be retrieved and it went on to say that details would be disclosed of its final destination by the senior officer at the castle once he had read the orders in the sealed box. At that point, I was to be shot. I felt a deep sense of dread coupled with elation, as I read those words, realising how incredibly fortunate I had been.

The total secrecy with which the SS had shrouded the Castle Zbiroh and its deliberate omission from maps had, as it turned out, worked against them in the last chaotic days of the war and had been my saving.

I sat on a rotting log for half an hour, collecting my thoughts. I then made my escape after *drawing the map and taking careful notes of the location.*

Unknown to the Major, along with the details of the exact location of the cache of hidden gold there lay a sealed file detailing not only its final destination but also the orders as to its future use. The name scrawled across the front of the papers in black ink, supposedly by Himmler himself, was, Das Spinnennetz, the Spider's Web.

I headed south-west after this, towards the Swiss border and the allied lines. I knew that if I fell into the hands of the SS, then my future would be very unpleasant and very short. I was captured at a roadblock set up by a panzer division. I had mistakenly left the letter from Himmler in the pocket of the, by then, buried greatcoat and the troops took me to be a deserter. After some animated discussion as to whether I should be summarily executed or not, I was loaded onto a cattle wagon on a train bound for Berlin. The Panzergrenadiers had clearly erred on the side of caution just in case my story about being under the direct orders of Himmler, was actually true.

There were German troops in the flatbed wagons at both ends of the train being transferred to Berlin. The carriage that I was loaded into was packed with British and American P.O.W.'s, who viewed me with complete suspicion until they realised that I was even more intent on escape than they were. The train slowed down every now and then, so we enlarged a pre-existing hole in the floor of the truck with a pocketknife which I had, concealed in my trousers. Fortunately, the troops, who had thrown me on to the train, had only taken my sidearm and had not thoroughly searched me. It was pitch black, and there was no food or water. We managed to make the hole in the base of the truck large enough to get through, by eventually working some planks out. When the train slowed, I slipped out, dropping on to the tracks along with several of the other men. We each rolled out between the wheels and ran for cover down a grass bank into the dark woods that flanked the line. I heard shouting behind me and then machine-gun fire and rifle shots. Close by I could hear yelling from a man who had been hit, but the train carried on without stopping. Wherever they were going, they were in a hurry.

I lay in the scrub until the train was out of sight, hearing the others grouping together and then gradually making their way off. I felt I had a much better chance on my own, being German in what was still German-held territory. I waited for them to leave and then started to make my way back down the tracks towards the south. I was also fearful of being caught by the allies, thence to be put into a P.O.W camp, as these would be full of SS and Nazi sympathisers.

I made my way to Austria, and while hiding in a vineyard, near the Swiss border, I was discovered by a local man. He let me sleep in a barn, and I ate with his family. The poor man had lost two boys on the Eastern Front, and he had, though not a Nazi, no love for the Allies either. I stayed for a week, assisting around the farm after which they then arranged for me to be helped to cross over to Switzerland. Smugglers, who were formerly alpine guides, before the war, helped me to cross the mountains and the border. The journey was gruelling, and I developed pneumonia on the trek.

When I got to Switzerland, which was neutral, I contacted British officials at the Embassy and told them some of my past, helping to fight the Nazi's. They put me in a private hospital to recover and then I began to assist them, processing the mountains of documents which had been found in the Nazi archives. Many of the ones that I dealt with related to stolen artwork, gold and diamonds. They had been hidden in locations such as salt mines in Germany and across former occupied Europe. Others had been spirited away through Spain and Portugal to South America and Africa or into the vaults of the very private, Swiss banks. I left eight months later and was sent to England. While in London, I continued my work there, with the British Government, who also gave me a false identity to protect me from potential reprisals against me by former Nazis.

I did not tell the British of the existence of the box as I did not know fully what its contents were, but I did believe that they were of *immense importance. I also felt that whatever secrets were held within, might be more appropriately passed into the hands of a future, democratic Germany, dependant on what those secrets were.*

I could not retrieve the buried items after the war because they were in the Russian zone and then, later, they constructed the Iron Curtain, which put a final halt to any thoughts, which I had, of recovering it.

With the fall of the wall, it was eventually possible to go to the wood to retrieve the metal case and the book if they had survived. However, I was old and frail by then, and I felt that maybe I should let sleeping dogs lie.

I was also concerned that the former Nazi's had not truly gone away and that a prize, seemingly this great, would be worth the wait.

During my work for the British, I gradually came to believe that I had put together the jigsaw. Some documents which they gave to me to study were transaction records of the Reichsbank, which were discovered in a salt mine near the Thüringian town of Merkers, in April 1945. Within these records were held detailed lists of multiple shipments of gold during the war and in particular, one substantial transfer which interested me, as Himmler had ordered it personally. I felt that I had been chosen specifically because of my first-hand knowledge of Castle Zbiroh and the surrounding area.

I had read that the gold had formed, the

large part of the National Bank of Belgium's reserves. At the start of the war, shortly before the German invasion, the Bank had transferred it to the Banque de France, in their Bordeaux and Libourne branches, as a precaution. After France and the Low Countries were attacked, the Belgians tried to get the French bank to transfer their 198 tonnes of fine gold to the U.S.A. Therefore, the Banque de France had asked the French admiralty to transport the Belgian gold to America. The ship carrying the gold never went to the United States and instead, made its way south eventually docking at Dakar, the capital of the French colony of Senegal, in West Africa. From there it was transported inland to the military base of Thiès and then 500km deeper into the Sahara to Kayès.

In late 1942, Pierre Laval, who was the Minister of Foreign Affairs in Marshal Petain's collaborationist Vichy government, then had it sent on to Berlin, via Algiers and Marseille and into the hands of Goering and Himmler. It was, once more, melted down into gold bars and stamped with the Nazi Eagle at the Prussian Staatsmünze, the State Mint.

The Nazi's tried to hide its true origins by hallmarking it with the years 1936 and 1937. These ingots were supplied with false documentation, and a substantial quantity of them were then transferred to the National Bank of Switzerland by the Nazis.

However, records showed that a considerable proportion of the gold, along with other looted bullion, had been transferred to a castle in what was by then former Czechoslovakia under the orders of Himmler, but the exact destination was not specified.

I learnt later that Himmler had entertained dreams of creating a vast, personal country estate in the region when the war was over. Castle Zbiroh was to have been his family home, to be adorned with the stolen artwork of Europe.

CHAPTER TWENTY-EIGHT

St Pancras International, London, England

THE M40 EVENTUALLY TURNED Into the A40 as it came close to the outskirts of London and the traffic congestion rapidly increased, though it was still moving fairly swiftly. Adam turned up onto a slip road, and at the overhead roundabout, he took the first exit left onto the A4180 towards Ruislip.

As he did so, he passed the RAF Northolt, Polish War Memorial, surmounted by a bronze eagle, commemorating the contribution of Polish airmen during the Second World War.

He continued straight on for just over a mile passing a builder's merchant, petrol station and then to the left the end of one of the RAF runways. Adam was looking at the side streets for a relatively inconspicuous place to park. Then coming level with the main gate of RAF Northolt again on the left Adam slipped into the filter lane to the right stopping behind a battered, white, builder's van that was waiting at the traffic lights. Shortly after coming to a halt, Adam noticed the green traffic light arrow illuminate, allowing him to proceed and he followed the van into Bridgwater Road. Adam spotted what he was after on the right, after passing some newly built flats and just beyond an overhead bridge. A long stretch of road that had no yellow lines along it to prevent parking.

There were a lot of free spaces, and he manoeuvred in between an old, rusty, white BMW and a much newer, blue SUV. Parking up Adam pulled his bag from the boot, as Rebecca climbed out and shut her door. Then he locked his pistol and the two spare clips of ammo he carried, inside the boot of the car hidden under a rug. While Rebecca stood on the pavement waiting, Adam surreptitiously moved through and around the car, wiping away fingerprints with a piece of cloth from his pocket. Locking the car, they walked a hundred yards along the tree-lined street of bay-fronted houses. The few trees had, recently, been trimmed and the pavement was still scattered with torn leaves and broken twigs which had escaped the Council tree surgeons.

They smelt the powerfully exotic aromas of herbs and spices being cooked into what was probably soon to be a delicious curry for a nearby homeowner. It reminded them both that they were starving, a reminder that they could have done without. Rebecca forced herself to forget her thoughts of what it would taste like.

Rebecca and Adam gently brushed against each other occasionally as they manoeuvred along the street dodging tree trunks and badly parked vehicles. Longing for those brief moments of intimacy each time, Rebecca's worries briefly waned.

On reaching the main road, they turned towards Ruislip Gardens and kept walking until they reached a relatively open stretch of the highway, where they then waited. It was much busier and louder with a lot of traffic and the sound of a police cars siren wailing in the distance. Adam watched in both directions for a black cab to pass by, displaying the amber taxi light on top, thereby showing that it was available for hire. It didn't take long before one came into view, and Adam hailed it down.

As they did so, Klaus and Heinz passed them on the opposite side of the road. They carried on for one further street and turning into it, they promptly made a U-turn and headed back, after their quarry trying not to look at them directly.

The taxi driver had been making his way into central London, and he waived in acknowledgement to Adam as he was passing by. Flicking his indicator on, the man turned back into Bridgwater Road where they had emerged from. They walked around the corner and found the cabbie pulled up, awkwardly, on the pavement a little way down.

The driver ran his window down, and Adam said, 'St Pancras International please'.

'Right you are Squire!' the Cockney driver said, as Adam opened the rear door for Rebecca.

Hearing the foreign accent, he presumed, 'You after the Eurostar?'

'Yes, please,' Adam said.

Rebecca climbed in and sat on the back seat. Adam followed her, shutting the door behind him as he slid in beside Rebecca.

The driver had flipped the meter on, and within thirty yards, the cabbie turned into the entrance to Carmichael Close and in one manoeuvre made a complete turn in the street, heading back towards the main road. At the junction, he turned left as the lights were green and headed off on his way.

Unseen and four cars behind, Klaus and Heinz followed in pursuit.

London never seemed to be lacking congestion, and it was, as usual, relatively slow going. The cabbie was very talkative and did not seem to need much response to keep up the flow of gripes, information and gossip he provided on vastly diverse topics. Adam was uninterested, but Rebecca seemed to enjoy his patter and every now and then she would respond to him in, what appeared to her, an appropriate manner. Adam wondered if, by keeping her mind occupied, it helped her to cope and to keep her thoughts, from the horrors which she had recently been exposed to.

The going was slow all the way, and Rebecca noticed that Adam continually turned back to view the cars which followed. He pretended that he was looking at her or at the sights of London to make it less obvious, but close up, she could see his eyes darting back behind them. Adam had done much the same all the way from Shropshire while driving, methodically looking in his side and rear mirrors. He was so diligent that he seemed almost as if he was taking a driving examination. She wondered if he was just naturally suspicious or if it was this current situation alone which demanded it.

Rebecca found it in some ways unnerving, but also strangely comforting – giving her the feeling that she was safer with him by her side. They ploughed on into London passing through Lisson Grove, Regents Park and then past Euston Station before eventually coming to St Pancras. It had been transformed with a vast regeneration and construction effort, as had Kings Cross Station which lay just to the east.

Klaus and Heinz, unwilling to get too close, had lost them in the traffic as they melded into the swarm of other taxis and general congestion. The Germans were not overly concerned, however, as they had a good idea where Rebecca and Adam were headed, and so they maintained their course.

Rebecca looked ahead through the windscreen of the taxi at the magnificent Gothic edifice of St Pancras. It always enthralled her in the past, though it had previously lain there in a state of partial decay. Now its elegance, charm and beauty was restored, and the grand terminus hotel had been brought back to life.

The taxi driver pulled into the filter lane and turning his blinker on, waited for a green turn light. The cabbie followed the car ahead and turned down the access road between King's Cross and St Pancras. He had only driven a hundred yards or so when he pulled over onto some double yellow lines beside large modern, metal bollards. They surrounded the grand, open, arched, oak doors which served as the side entrance leading to the Eurostar foyer. 'That'll be Thirty-one quid!' squawked the driver, happily.

Adam handed him forty pounds and said, 'Keep the change.'

A loud click signalled the doors being unlocked and the cabbie said, 'Cheers mate! Do you need a receipt?'

'No, thanks,' Adam said.

As Adam opened the door, he grabbed his bag and climbed out onto the pavement. He turned and holding the door open, waited while Rebecca exited the cab. The driver who clearly abhorred a silence and finally seeming curious about them said, 'Going anywhere nice?'

For the first time, he really appeared interested in them, rather than in his own monologue. No doubt, he was looking for new material to pass on to his next passenger.

Rebecca replied, 'The future.'

Adam shut the door and called, 'Thanks!' over his shoulder as he scanned the road behind them once more. He did not notice the two men, among the throng, who had just entered the street on foot, having quickly parked their car badly in a side street.

Swiftly, he walked through the door into the foyer, leaving the cabbie speechless. The man smiled and then drove off, forty pounds better off. Adam and Rebecca passed through the magnificent Victorian brick arches into the modernity of the Eurostar terminal passing the glass-enclosed office for the premier class passengers. They walked towards the row of ticket machines on the left, which sat like sleeping robots against the wall. It was busy with people from all over the world, mostly heading to the continent or into London. Somewhat incongruous, two unarmed French Gendarmes passed by in the opposite direction. As Adam went to one of the machines, dropping his bag, he saw the officers disappear into an almost unnoticeable passage beside the Premier class.

Adam pulled some sheets of paper from the side pocket of his jacket. Quickly, scanning them, he entered his details into the machine, and it promptly disgorged the train tickets. Adam placed them into his inside jacket pocket and asked, 'Would you like to grab a Coffee? We have some time to kill.'

'Sure, why not!' Rebecca lazily responded.

He picked up his bag and swung it over his shoulder, turning towards the main concourse and its magnificent, cast iron and glass roof. This formed the backbone of the station and was why it was often called the cathedral of the railways.

He moved forward, opening his palm to show

the way for Rebecca to walk with him. Again, she noticed that though he appeared to look at her, he really looked just past her, into the background. Rebecca felt a cold shudder run through her body, giving her a deep sense of foreboding. She did not know fully, what had caused the sensation of doom that she suddenly felt, but deep in her subconscious, she had noticed a change in Adam. In his face. It had tensed, ever so slightly, he appeared more alert – like a cat on the prowl, almost ugly. Adam moved forward, and Rebecca followed him, the sense of gloom gradually dissipating as her mind wandered. Rebecca had seen St Pancras many times before, but it never failed to uplift her, its elegance was almost otherworldly.

Nearby a commuter, with time to spare, had stopped and was sitting at a tired, nondescript, upright piano pushed up against the back of a glass elevator. Someone had given it a rough paint with a cornflower blue emulsion using a cheap bristle brush. Oddly, it lent a gloriously dignified style to the tatty antique. It was like an elderly woman who had put on a touch too much makeup, which had the effect of making her quite sweet and rather adorable. The young man, probably a student, who sat at the keyboard was wearing faded, scarlet, Concourse basketball pumps, one with a shoelace and one without. His jeans were barely blue and had seen much better days and his Lonsdale sweatshirt clearly doubled as a towel, for it was rather shabby. He was a scruffy looking individual who had an intelligent, kindly and charmingly, vacant face.

However, the way he stroked the keys was delightfully enchanting. The gentle classical tune had an intoxicating effect which encouraged many of the passers-by to stop to listen or to glance over and smile as they slowed before continuing on their way. The closer she came to him, the more it affected her. When they had first entered St Pancras she had, ever so faintly, heard a happy chord, which had added a warm, enticing sensation to the building. Suddenly, the impromptu pianist seamlessly slipped into a slightly, more contemporary piece by Trenet - La Mer. His performance of it was shocking and outrageous and utterly captivating. He seemed oblivious to the small group who had gathered to listen and to pass a few moments in ecstasy. The majority of people passing by turned right and walked along the main concourse underneath the champagne bar, all affected in some subtle way by the melodies.

As Rebecca and Adam passed a shop selling exotic toiletries, L'Occitane, he stopped abruptly and turned his head, looking about, as if he had lost his way. Rebecca was captivated by the beautiful aromas which wafted past her out of the shop. Adam looked bemused and then said, 'I know where we can go.'

He suddenly grabbed Rebecca's wrist to her immense surprise and began to stride on once again, towards the escalator that ran through the centre of the cavernous building. Adam seemed quite jolly, and Rebecca was rapidly coming to the conclusion that he was, a rather peculiar person, to the extent that she wondered if he was, in fact, entirely unhinged. He seemed oddly pensive much of the time, peppered with sudden, though minor, mood changes and subtle touches of tenderness or kindness. Adam, impatient, did not stand on the moving treads, preferring to increase his speed by walking up the escalator at quite a pace. At all times, he maintained a gentle toddler-like grip on her wrist, tugging encouragement as they went.

At the touch of his authoritative grip on her wrist, she had initially been taken aback by this sudden, almost intimate gesture. However, Rebecca increasingly felt a sense of embarrassment, and she gently tried to release herself from his grip. However, Adam would not release his hold. She found that she could not stop thinking about her body touching his, her skin against his. Rebecca felt childish and tried to get a mental grip on her senses. She had a slight flush in her cheeks as she also sensed something baser in her being.

As Rebecca tried to look at the broader picture, she began to succumb to an intensifying and primal fear in the pit of her stomach. It was not a fear, however, that she disliked, not in the usual sense. The concern which Rebecca had begun to be affected by was that Adam would release his hand, that he would release her. She tried to rationalise the sensation. Rebecca did not know him, not really. She was also, oddly unnerved by him, scared even. She perceived that there was little connection with him, for all his courtesy and concern he was at all times distant, almost as if he was preoccupied. Throughout the time, they had spent together Adam had, for the most part, shown her no real interest. Rebecca could tell when a man liked her. It happened so often. Adam seemed to fluctuate between glances displaying, what could almost be, fondness and then occasionally, utter indifference. Rebecca was beautiful, to the point of striking and the attention it engendered, from men in general, was at times a mild annoyance for her. Adam 'appeared' to be almost totally oblivious to her charms, her beauty, her femininity. She could not understand it, and in a mildly irritating way, she found it quite captivating.

Bounding off the top of the escalator, Adam seemed to be pulling on her arm much more firmly and persistently than previously, to the point that it began to hurt. Rebecca gave a soft squeal of pain, and though it was, in part, exaggerated she had hoped for some sort of acknowledgement - there was nothing. They walked across the gangway to the sidewall, doubling back towards the champagne bar and continuing on their way. As they did, so they had, unknowingly, passed by two police officers who were stood inside a doorway, hidden away from the main thoroughfare. They were not the ordinary London 'bobbies' of tourist literature fame. Both men wore blue, peaked caps, chest armour and they each carried submachine guns with handguns strapped to their right legs. They looked quizzically at Adam and Rebecca as they passed by and then turned their gaze to look elsewhere.

Adam carried on his path, back past the Eurostar which lay below and onwards towards the trendy Booking Office Bar at the rear of the station. He repeatedly looked towards Rebecca to give her a comforting smile and then, methodically each time, as was his way, he would glance back past her. Adam stopped momentarily to look at the bronze statue of John Betjeman that stood on the concourse. As he appeared to stare at it, Rebecca saw him looking straight past the larger-than-life cast, scanning the station beyond. Adam then turned abruptly, once more pulling Rebecca with him while continuing up towards the front of the station. Passing a skeletal, glass lift he suddenly turned sharply left, nearly wrenching Rebecca's arm from its socket.

She squealed, 'Adam, you're hurting me!'

He turned back and did not look at her. Instead, he looked straight past her, through the lift panes at something or someone beyond.

'I'm sorry, but we must hurry!' he said.

Before she could respond, Adam had broken into a trot pulling her along with him. There were few people around, but some of the customers in the outside terrace of Carluccio's restaurant turned to observe them in wonder. As she glanced at the customers, she saw some of them look at her and at Adam and then back beyond them, at something else that sparked their curiosity. As Rebecca followed their gaze, she became acutely aware of another set of running footsteps some distance behind her.

Continuing to be dragged, she looked back to see two athletic men, with the look of mobsters, following them with an intensity of expression which was terrifying. Rebecca let out an involuntary scream. Adam pulled her on as they passed an enormous bronze statue of a man and woman in a tender embrace. Just beyond the artwork, could be seen three-arched brick passages which were completely open to the exterior. They had served as one of the old entrances into the station, and they led on to a large, cobbled ramp for cars when drivers were dropping off passengers. Adam raced down one of the passages pulling Rebecca as fast as she could run.

As they were about to exit the station onto the cobblestone ramp, Adam ran headlong into a man running in the opposite direction who was just coming around the corner. It was Carter, who had heard a woman's scream and had come up, alone, to investigate. As Adam fell, he let go of Rebecca's hand, leaving her barely standing. The two men lay sprawling on the floor, allowing Carter's jacket to fall open displaying the handgun protruding from his pocket and still in its place. In an instant, Adam had grabbed the automatic with one hand while holding Carter by the throat, with the other. Violently, he smashed the gun's butt solidly into his prostrate victim's face, leaving him momentarily unconscious. Adam turned swiftly, still in a crouching position and looked up at one of the men, Klaus, who had been following them and who now stood behind Rebecca, holding her with one hand and pressing a gun into her waist with his other. Adam levelled the automatic he now held directly at Klaus, aiming purposefully at his face. Rebecca looked thoroughly petrified, stifling a scream.

The second man then appeared from behind a red marble pillar. He pointed his gun directly at Adam. Looking down at the unconscious man on the floor, he laughingly said, 'I see you have met Herr Carter. He never could follow orders. He had better be alive for your sake! Where is it?' he continued.

Before Adam or Rebecca could answer, they were distracted by a commotion within the station. Some shouts and screams could be heard from people who were clearly in a state of agitated panic. Heinz left his partner holding Rebecca and ran back along the passage to see what was happening. As he did so, he either forgot or didn't care that he had his gun in his hand. Emerging from the tunnel, he instantly became visible to the two police officers who had become suspicious and who had followed the two pairs of people. One of the officers dropped to a kneeling position with his semi-automatic carbine at his shoulder aimed at Heinz. The other officer stood bolt upright, with his Glock 17 pointed directly at the gunman barking orders at him. Heinz, who was overly aggressive by nature and a habitual chancer went to raise his gun towards the officers to shoot. Instantaneously, the officer's shouts stopped only to be replaced with an explosive burst of automatic fire. Adam saw the German thrown back, with immense force, falling to the floor behind a pillar, leaving a cloud of blood spraying through the air.

Still holding Rebecca, Klaus had suddenly turned to look at the ruckus. As he did, he had cautiously shielded much of his head with Rebecca's, but in doing that he had exposed more of his arm and shoulder which held her. Adam took the opportunity and loosed off a bullet. The squeal of pain followed instantly after the round broke through Klaus' collarbone. His hand fell away, releasing Rebecca and she ran hysterically towards Adam preventing him from firing a second clear shot. She slammed into Adam and now with a better view, he fired at Klaus who, writhing in agony was just raising his gun hand towards them. Adam had aimed at his heart, but the shot had gone wide as Rebecca had been struggling to get away. The bullet clipped his upper wrist – enough to stun him and prevent return fire. Adam pulled Rebecca out of the passage and across the cobblestones of the ramp past the prostrate Carter. The thug was still groggy, though he was beginning to stir. The pair ran towards an old stone staircase which descended to the hubbub of the busy streets below.

They heard behind them, once more, barked orders from the firearms officer who had, it appeared, now turned his attention to Klaus and possibly Carter. Just as Rebecca and Adam were about to disappear down the steps, they heard more shouting and another violent burst of automatic fire. As they ran down the steps, they saw the two waiting thugs who both had concerned looks on their faces and their revolvers had been part-drawn. They looked, in dress, not dissimilar to Carter, who Adam had just been unceremoniously introduced to. He hid his gun behind Rebecca who was in front of him and who was crying, and he said to the two men, Paul and Mark, 'Your friend up top said to tell you both to get up there pronto! It looks like some sort of fight!'

The two villains looked nervous but, even so, they ran up the stairs, weapons at the ready and straight into a firestorm.

Carter had left his phone in the van, and it was Dave who answered when the anxious Herr Krüger called to find out what was happening.

'Carter!' he bellowed.

'No, it's Dave. I work with Carter.'

'Where is he ...what's going on? I can't get my men on the phone.'

'I dunno. Carter told me to wait in the van!' Dave said.

'You will get out and find out what is happening and then call me back immediately!'

Dave had no time to answer, as Herr Krüger had slammed the phone down. He got out of the van and began to walk along the street, but before he had gone very far, he knew that something had gone horribly wrong. He could hear sirens screaming in the distance and a general commotion. At the end of the street, people were hurrying away on foot from the St Pancras area. As he got to the corner, he saw armed police ahead of him standing on the ramp of St Pancras and unarmed police beginning to cordon off the train station.

In the swarm of people, he noticed what looked like a husband and wife coming towards him, they were elderly, and the man looked pensive as he supported and comforted the woman who was crying uncontrollably.

Dave said to them as politely as he could, though he came across as grossly abrupt, 'What's happened ...I was going to catch a train.'

The man who appeared 'rather well to do' and would, in normal circumstances, have avoided any interaction with an individual like Dave said, 'It's been awful the police have shot some men. It looked like the perpetrators were trying to abduct a young couple.'

Dave was shocked by the news, though he suddenly felt like retching on hearing the man's use of the poncey word, 'perpetrators'. Dave thought that the old fool would ordinarily make himself a perfect target for a particularly vicious mugging.

Dave said sharply, 'Are they all dead?'

The older man did not answer him but went on to say, 'We were just trying to have a meal at the station when ...'

'Are they all dead?' Dave asked again, but this time more bluntly.

The elderly gentleman began to regard Dave more suspiciously.

He said to Dave, 'No ...no some of them looked dead, though others seem to be wounded - but I did hear a policeman say that the man and woman they were chasing, managed to escape.'

Dave had lost interest in the older couple, and hastily walked off in the direction of the van. The old man looked at him as he took his leave, making a mental note of Dave's description and of the vehicle he climbed into. He intended to speak to the first policeman he could find about that curious individual.

Dave was scared. He had just got out of Wandsworth Prison after a two-year sentence for a serious assault. He was not going to wait around to get his collar felt again and anyway, it did not sound like his mates would be turning up anytime soon.

As Dave climbed into the van, Herr Krüger, unable to maintain his calm called again, 'What is happening?'

Dave said, 'It sounds like it has all gone belly up! I can't get close to the station, but there are sirens and armed police everywhere.'

'I believe some of our men have been killed or captured and that the people you were after got away. Was it a man and a woman?'

Herr Krüger did not answer, lost deep in thought.

Dave said, 'How am I going to get paid? I need to get out of here!'

Krüger, temporarily shaken by Dave's inane

request, stared at the telephone with a look of pure evil, just before cancelling the call. Fleetingly, he wished that Dave had been within his reach so that he could give him a truly 'appropriate' response.

Dave screamed down at the phone, at the dead line, 'You bloody bastards!'

He then put the window down and threw the phone out, putting the radio on as he did so to see if there were any news flashes. He belched loudly and felt better for it. As he drove off, he decided that it was about time for him to take a very long vacation to southern Ireland. He would pay a visit to some friends he had made, in the travelling community. He had met them when he had been involved in illegal bare-knuckle fighting.

Krüger turned to Herr Müller, 'It looks like our plans have gone awry. Armed British police seem to have intervened. Several of the men, ours and the London gang are believed to be dead and/or captured.'

Herr Müller, uninterested by the rising death toll, said anxiously, 'What about the two we are after?'

Krüger, swallowing hard before he answered, said, 'It appears ...that they got away.'

Müller was beside himself with rage, screaming at the top of his voice. All the others in the room remained impassive and silent.

When Müller had stopped, and after a short, respectful, silence, Krüger said softly, 'Maybe all is not lost, Herr Müller.'

Müller looked up at him swiftly, like a drowning man grasping at straws, 'What do you mean?' he barked.

'Klaus told us that the couple's car was parked close to RAF Northolt. These two may go back to get it, as they know we are after them and they have few options left. They don't seem to be keen on going to the police, for whatever reason. We could contact Kaspar and Stefan, who are nearing London. If we tell them the general area, we could get them to try to pick up the signal, once again, from our tracking device on their car.'

Herr Müller looked contemplative. After a few moments, he said, 'Yes, it may work. Get on to them immediately. But make it clear that they are only to 'follow' these people for the moment and to report back regularly. I don't want them spooked any further.'

Krüger called and spoke to Stefan telling him what to do. Putting down the phone he said to Müller, 'Stefan said that they can be there in approximately thirty minutes.'

Herr Müller did not respond. He just stared at the ice floating around in his glass, and the room fell, effortlessly, back into silence.

Adam and Rebecca had run through the melee which by then surrounded the two stations of St Pancras and Kings Cross and had hopped on to a passing red London bus to escape the area. As Adam glanced back, he saw one of the armed police officers appear on the pavement at the base of the steps, frantically looking around him. The passers-by, already shocked and scared by the sound of repeated gunfire and now the sight of him added to the officer's confusion by scattering and screaming. Then Adams view was obscured by another bus which also had the effect of obscuring them from the officer. They were on the number 10, and after several stops, they jumped off near the British Museum. Rebecca and Adam walked a few streets away before Adam hailed a taxi back to Ruislip. The taxi driver tried to chat to them, but he soon realised that they were uninterested in talking to him or to each other and so, rolling his eyes in disgust, he turned the radio on. The cabbie began to listen to music on Capital FM while Rebecca and Adam sat looking out of their windows, both deep in thought. Eventually, Rebecca's head lolled back into the seat, and she drifted off into a deep sleep, utterly drained from the mental exhaustion of the most recent, violent events.

Ten minutes later, the news started to play. During the broadcast, mention was made of two sets of gruesome murders around Shropshire, several deaths in a place called Rook Hall and one in Cleobury Mortimer where the individual was tortured before being killed. Police had released a statement that they were looking for two individuals, giving Adam and Rebecca's names and descriptions. The broadcaster explained that the suspects may be accomplices or that it was equally possible that the woman had been abducted by the man. The police said that they were acting on a tip-off. What they did not say was that the caller had had a German accent. The

senior investigating officer also said that anyone who saw the suspects should not approach
them, as they may be armed and dangerous.
Instead, the detective had asked that members
of the public should call the police immediately,
on 999, if they spotted the individuals.

Adam continued to gaze out of the window,
but his expression had imperceptibly changed.
His stare was harder and tinged with a subtle
sense of regret. He wished that he had never involved his friend. Sadly, it was becoming clear as
to how the 'reception committee' had known of
their whereabouts.

Once they arrived in Ruislip, Adam asked
the taxi driver to stop. It was a couple of hundred yards from where their car was parked. As
the driver abruptly pulled over onto the kerb,
Rebecca woke with a jolt. She was still groggy
and getting her bearings when Adam opened
the door and jumped out of the cab, extending
his hand to her. She took it and crouched as she
exited the door. Adam paid the driver through
the open front window saying keep the change
before slamming the rear door shut. They slowly
began to walk away in the direction of the car. A
few moments later, they heard the taxi pull off in
the opposite direction, eventually disappearing
up a side-road.

The pair continued, in silence, along the
street to the car and Adam, unlocked it, saying,
'Jump in.'

He threw the bag and the skinhead's gun into
the boot and then got in beside Rebecca.

As he was about to start the car, she grabbed his forearm and said in a tearful voice, 'Adam, what is happening, what are we going to do?'

He looked pensive saying, 'I'm not fully sure what is going on, but I have an idea. Whoever is after us clearly wants the box and the gold. We will certainly not be safe until we can find it ourselves and keep it from them 'permanently'. We need to head to Germany via an alternate route and see if we can find what they are after.'

'But how will we get there if these people are following us?'

'Don't worry, we are not going to go through any of the main ports or airports. If it is, who I think it is following us, then they are very resourceful, and they will be watching them. These people have waited a long time, and they have a very great deal to lose. I am certain that they will now throw everything they have at this.'

'Shouldn't we call the police,' she said.

'No, certainly not! I heard a report on the radio that the police are looking for us. They believe that we committed the murders,' he felt it best not to specifically mention the horrors at Cleobury Mortimer.

'But surely they would believe us!' she cried.

'Maybe, maybe not ...but it isn't worth taking the risk. Anyway, these people who are after us are pros, and they have many friends. Once we gave ourselves up, we would be sitting targets.'

'Don't worry, I know someone who should be able to help us.'

Adam turned the key and began to drive,

passing a map to Rebecca while laughingly saying, 'Ever used one of these before?'

She smiled coquettishly, saying, 'I was a Girl Guide, you know!'

'Good then get me heading towards the north Norfolk coast. And make it snappy!'

She smiled through her anguished face and tapped his arm in a mocking slap before turning back to the map. After a few moments, she said, 'OK, turn left at the end of the road and then head straight for a mile or two. I'll let you know what to do after that when I'm good and ready!'

He glanced over at Rebecca, who looked at him with a darkly, mischievous smile, which made him laugh out loud.

Unseen a few streets and several hundred yards away, Kaspar and Stefan were peeling off a slip road heading towards RAF Northolt. They were happy that they had just picked up the signal from the tracking device and even more pleased that it was moving and that they had almost certainly found their quarry once more.

Several miles away, lying half-naked, in a bed with filthy sheets, in a filthy room above a filthy pub in the Whitechapel Road, the young girl with the tattoos, bleached hair and ugly black roots slept on. She was unaware of the fate of Carter, oblivious as to her lucky escape if he had ever returned.

She had had a sad life thus far and had never been given any breaks. She didn't know it then, but her luck had changed, and it would continue to change – for the better.

CHAPTER TWENTY-NINE

Embassy of Israel, Alpenstrasse 32, Bern, Switzerland

MIRIAM RANG THROUGH TO Ezra's office, 'Sir, I've got Yosef Ackerman on from England.'

Without saying anything further, she put the call through, 'Mr Goldmann, its Yosef. There was an incident at St Pancras. The fascists tried to confront the couple, they seemed to have help from some London skinheads. By chance, they were surprised by an armed police patrol, and there has been at least one fatality, possibly more.'

'The couple?' Goldmann asked nervously, feeling sweat suddenly beading on his temples.

'No, sir. They escaped during the disturbance - it appears unharmed. We trailed them back to their car near Northolt and are now in pursuit of them. They are heading towards East Anglia.'

'Are they aware of your presence?'

'No, sir,' continued Ackerman, 'but we are not the only ones tracking them. The two Germans who killed the man in Cleobury Mortimer are also tracking them. They seem, currently, to be content to shadow the couple.'

Goldmann thought to himself while staring from the window at nothing in particular, before continuing, 'Do you have any understanding as to why?'

Ackerman continued, 'I'm not sure, maybe they are waiting for reinforcements, or maybe they don't want to end up in another bloodbath. The British will be beginning to put 'two and two' together, and things may start to get a bit more difficult for these Germans now.'

'Are you any closer to understanding what is going on?'

'No, sir, but whatever it is, it is clearly crucial to the neo-Nazis for some reason.'

Goldmann distracted momentarily by the sound of a low flying aeroplane, said in a slow, methodical tone, 'Yosef, this is of the utmost importance to us. No effort must be spared in finding out what this is about. Do not let these people know that we are on to them, but if a clear opportunity presents itself to increase our knowledge, then you have my full authority to do whatever it takes.'

'Yes, sir, I understand.'

Goldmann put the phone down and looked out across the city of Bern, placing one hand against the glass as if to steady himself. He liked the place, but it was no substitute for his home in Haifa, in the north of Israel. Goldmann often thought, on colder nights in Bern, and there were many, of his home close to the Mediterranean coast. It had a glorious sea view. He could, at these times, almost smell the almond blossom and taste the figs and pomegranates that grew, so readily, in his garden. But there was nothing so wistful, as the memory of the warm, salt-laden breeze that would come off the sea, while Ezra relaxed in his garden under the lemon trees. It was at points like this that Goldmann wished he were back there sipping a chilled glass of his favourite Sauvignon Blanc from the Recanati winery in the Hefer Valley.

He thought for a moment, of the strange goings-on in England, but could make little sense of them.

After a short while, Miriam came into his office saying, 'Is everything in order, sir?'

'Yes, for the moment,' he replied, continuing, 'please place a call through to the collections department in Tel Aviv for me?'

She disappeared without saying a word, and moments later the phone rang, 'Tel Aviv, sir!' Miriam said and passed the call through.

Goldmann said to the operator, 'Its Goldmann in Bern, I need to speak to Ariel Mandler!'

'Yes, sir,' the operator said and passed the call straight through.

'Good news, I hope, Ezra?' Mandler said, in what felt, to Goldmann, like a mildly hostile tone.

'Yes, sir ...I believe so - well, interesting anyway.'

'Go on!'

'The neo-Nazis had tortured and killed one associate of the couple and have just been involved in a serious incident at St Pancras train station when they were trying to apprehend the two of them. A British armed police team surprised the neo-Nazis, and there have been fatalities. The Germans were also using hired, local thugs. The couple escaped, it appears unharmed, and they are being tracked by the Germans as they head towards East Anglia by car. Our men are keeping close surveillance on them. It is still unclear what, exactly is going on, but whatever it is, it is clearly greatly important to them.'

Mandler said nothing for a moment, and Ezra began to feel slightly uneasy. Then Mandler said, 'We are making some progress 'here', Ezra. We believe that the old man who was killed at Rook Hall was given a false identity by the British shortly after the war. We do not yet know why. However, we are sure that he was not a Swiss national, as all the current documentation we have on him appears to show. We believe he was actually German - an SS officer. Which one and why he was so important, we are yet to determine.'

Mandler, stopping momentarily, pressed his left hand down, flat onto the table, and then said, 'I feel that the key to this conundrum will be found when we discover the old man's true identity and begin to piece together his past. If this were revenge for some long-ago misdeed, then I would have thought that they would have contented themselves with killing him and 'maybe' anyone else they found at the location. The old man seems to have tried to defend himself with a gun when they came for him, and we believe that he was shot by mistake before he could give up what they required. Therefore, if it was not revenge, then he must have had something that is of great importance to the neo-Nazis. That may explain why they are tracking the couple now, rather than just terminating them. The Germans may believe that either the granddaughter or the bodyguard have what they seek.'

'Might I ask, if you have any idea what they could be after, sir?'

'No, we don't know ...yet,' Mandler said ponderously.

Then, after a short silence, he continued rapidly, 'Right Ezra, keep your men on this. Top priority! If we get anything here, then I will inform you, but for now, just watch and wait. This may be much bigger than we can currently imagine.'

The line suddenly went dead, and Ezra, his forehead moist with perspiration, put his phone down, contemplating what had been said to him.

CHAPTER THIRTY

Collections Department, Mossad headquarters, Tel
Aviv, Israel

MANDLER RANG THE BUZZER on his
desk.

A moment later, Daniel opened the
door and walked into the office, bringing with
him a gusting wave of the cheap aftershave,
which he had lathered himself in. Mandler knew
that Daniel fancied himself as a ladies' man,
and it was probably for the benefit of the young
women in the accounts office. Mandler smiled
cruelly to himself, thinking that one whiff of it
would probably be more likely to make their
eyelashes fall out than to make them attracted
to him in any way.

'Well, Daniel! Do you have any further information about the identity of this 'Swiss' national?' Daniel noted the sneering intonation which

234

Mandler used when he said the word 'Swiss', which he clearly believed was a fallacy.

'We have been working on the lists which you requested of SS men who were alive and then disappeared after the war.'

He continued, 'It is a laborious task as many of them purposefully hid from the authorities or were the subject of reprisals after the war and probably lie in unmarked pits, scattered across the countryside of Europe. Therefore, we have focused on those who ended the war with Sturmbannführer rank, who possibly had mention of Switzerland in their records. This has been relatively fruitful and much more manageable.'

'Well, do you have any names yet?' Mandler questioned, mildly irritated by the delay.

Daniel, enjoying his moment of importance, said, 'Yes, we came up with twenty-three names. Of those six were eventually captured and executed for war crimes, five others died while serving their prison sentences. Three were given over to the Russians and were never heard of again, but I feel confident that they will not have survived captivity, very long. Hugo Winkleman was caught in late 1946 but was shot dead by American MP's while trying to escape. Carl Dietrich died of cancer in 1952 in Rome. Then Hermann Raeder died in early 1963 in an unexplained house fire in his cabin in the mountains of the French Pyrenees. He had lived alone there, for some time before his death. Former members of the French Resistance were suspected of causing the arson, but no charges were ever brought by the local police, unsurprisingly. And one, Alfred Holle, has been tracked down to Hannover, where he still lives with his wife in the suburbs.'

'And the other five?' Mandler barked, impressed as always with Daniel's work, but tired of listening to him.

Daniel looked slightly put out, but said, 'We have their names, but that is all at present. We are urgently searching the files to find out exactly who they were and what they did during the war. As you know, the Germans kept meticulous archives throughout the war, on everything. It means we should get quite a bit of background, but it will take some time to go through the wealth of information.'

'Their names?' Mandler said, fatigued to have to wrench everything from Daniel.

'Werner Graf, Adolf Shultz, Walter Gille, Otto von Freitann and Theodor Model.'

As Daniel reeled off the names, Mandler had picked up a pen and lazily scribbled each of the names on a notepad, for future reference.

'A member of the aristocracy among them, hey? Unusual!'

'Yes, von Freitann. He should be easier to track because of his elevated background,' Daniel took a slight pause and then continued, 'the British Embassy man is called Thomas Hopkins, and he 'is' MI6. However, we don't believe that he is acting in an official capacity regarding the neo-Nazis.'

'Why not?' Mandler looked up, trying to hide his surprise.

'Our moles in MI6 were unable to discover any information concerning this, though maybe because it is being dealt with on a strictly need to know, Ultra Top-Secret basis. However, more importantly, Hopkins went through a very messy divorce several years ago, and he has three girls at private school, and he incurred quite serious debts to prove it. Recently those debts were settled in full with the monies coming from a Swiss bank account. We are continuing to keep him under surveillance.'

'Well, well, Mr Hopkins! Someone has been a very naughty boy!' Mandler continued, 'Well done, Daniel!'

Daniel was slightly taken aback by the compliment, as he knew that Mandler did not particularly like him, and he very rarely complimented his work.

'Thank you, sir,' he spluttered.

'I wonder, what the neo-Nazis would have been paying him for!' Mandler asked rhetorically.

He was silent for a moment and then said, 'How are the technicians getting on with cracking the communications in the Harz?'

Daniel nervously brushed the pocket of his trousers saying, 'It's proving difficult sir, the Germans have ramped up their electronic security, possibly because of their current activities. The team are working flat out, they will crack it, I'm sure, but I can't say when.'

Mandler retorted, 'Right, you must keep the pressure on.'

'Yes, sir,' Daniel said as he turned and left the room.

Mandler sat back in his chair and looked at the items on his desk. The paper, a pen, a stapler, a rubber band and some treasury tags. He played around with them, moving each item into its particular place and into proper order. While he did so, he pondered the various events and tried to make sense of them.

He ran his eyes down the list of names he had just scribbled down. His eyes kept coming back to von Freitann. It was unusual to find the aristocracy in the SS. 'Could this man, or his background be the key he wondered?'

Unable to come to any firm conclusions, Mandler left his office and headed to the canteen to get a coffee. The noises of activity from his busy team, as he passed them by, was encouraging.

CHAPTER THIRTY-ONE

A134, Road, south of Bury St Edmunds, Suffolk, England

REBECCA TOOK ADAM THROUGH the streets of north London and out towards Chelmsford. The route she chose kept them away from the motorway and stuck to the more minor roads. There was no particular reason for her choice, but that, oddly, it made her feel a little more inconspicuous, maybe safer. Once outside the M25 motorway which orbited London, they encountered less traffic and increasingly, open countryside which relaxed her. For much of the journey, they remained in silence. When she had tried to put the radio on, Adam had stopped her explaining that it disturbed his concentration. Rebecca thought about this for a moment. She then decided to add 'high-maintenance' to the negatives side of the mental tally which she was keeping of his qualities or lack of them.

As they neared the historic market town of Bury St Edmunds, Rebecca said, 'Can we stop? I'm exhausted, and I'm starving too!'

Adam said, 'Yes, of course. Let's go into the next town and see what we can find.'

They drove into Bury St Edmunds and followed signs to the centre, parking up in a pretty cobbled square surrounded by historic buildings and close to the ancient cathedral.

Two hundred yards behind them, the blue Mercedes-Benz GLC Coupé pulled into a side road, having seen that their quarry had stopped moving. Kaspar and Stefan looked at the satellite navigation system to view the area ahead.

Kaspar said, 'Get out and see what's going on. If they start moving again, then I will come and collect you.'

Stefan said nothing as he left the vehicle and walked nonchalantly up to the square.

Adam had stopped close to an imposing ivy-covered, Georgian style building, which had a dominating effect on the square. It turned out to be the Angel Hotel, a family-run concern which had, in its time, played host to guests as diverse as Charles Dickens and Angelina Jolie. Rebecca was struck by how quiet the sleepy little place was compared to the hustle and bustle of London.

As they climbed the hotel's entrance steps, Stefan watched from the corner of the street for a moment and then carried on across the square.

He entered the hotel and walked past the reception desk and into the bar, on the face of it paying no attention to Adam or Rebecca who were booking their rooms. Stefan stood next to another customer who was already leaning against the bar. He ordered a drink and immediately struck up a conversation with the man about the town, offering him a drink also.

To anyone watching and to Adam in particular, whose eyes had followed him, he appeared just like any other local, meeting a friend for a drink.

When Stefan heard Adam and Rebecca finishing and going to their room, he waited a few minutes and then left abruptly. As he descended the steps to the hotel, he felt distracting pangs of hunger as he caught faint smells coming from the restaurant.

The drinker who Stefan had been speaking to looked stunned and watched him leave, turning to the barman saying, 'Don't you find foreigners bloody overfamiliar and just plain odd!'

The barman, who was Italian, just smiled saying, 'Maybe he fancied you!'

The customer nearly choked on his drink and gave a heartfelt grimace.

Stefan made his way back to the car, calling Kaspar on the way to update him, 'Kaspar, they have booked into a hotel called The Angel. I followed them in. They said it was just for the one night.'

Kaspar tightly clenched his fist and barked,

'You fool you shouldn't have gone in there after them. They may have spotted you.'

Stefan was irritated, 'No, they suspected nothing I went into the bar for a drink. There were many others there.'

'Right, stay in the square and remain at a distance. Keep a close watch on the car in case they are trying to throw us off, to make an escape. I'll relieve you in an hour. I will tell Germany what's happening.'

'Right!' said Stefan, ending the call.

Adam and Rebecca took two adjoining rooms overlooking the square, and after refreshing themselves, they went down to the restaurant and ordered a meal.

While they waited for the food, each had a pre-dinner Gin and Tonic. Adam said, 'I've contacted my friend in Brancaster, on the coast. We'll meet him tomorrow, and he'll take us over to the continent.'

'In what?' Rebecca asked with a look of mild surprise.

'Ha,' he smiled, 'in his fishing boat.'

'You really know how to treat a lady, don't you!' she grinned, forgetting the horrors of the day temporarily.

He smiled and stared straight back at her, with an inquiring, kindly look.

They had both ordered the grilled mackerel with beetroot risotto to start and then she had the sea bream as a main course and Adam had the venison in red wine, from the nearby Elveden estate. Rebecca had a glass of Chardonnay while

Adam tried a pint of the local ale. They chatted about her schooling, her hopes and aspirations and also about Adam's time in the military. However, they did not speak of Rook Hall or her grandfather or St Pancras. After dinner, they took a leisurely stroll around the town centre and then went back to the hotel. Rebecca was glad to be back at the Angel as the sky had been clear, but it had turned quite cold. They sat beside the open fire in the lounge, enjoying the heat from the burning wood and a fresh bottle of Chablis. They were silent, for the most part, enjoying the atmosphere and increasingly, each other.

Kaspar and Stefan had taken a chance and had not followed them on their walk. It was a small town, and there were few people about, on that evening. They had probably already seen Stefan, and it would be too dangerous for one person alone to follow them given the circumstances.

Even so, Kaspar, whose watch it was, gave a sigh of relief when he saw that they had re-entered the square.

It had been a cold and problematic night for Kaspar and Stefan. They had extended their respective watch periods to, two hours on and two hours off. It allowed time for each one of them to have a decent sleep in the car at any one time.

They were glad of the morning, when it came, to break the monotony of it all.

Adam woke early, but Rebecca slept in until gone 10.30. When she awoke, she showered and dressed and knocked on Adam's door. They ordered a late breakfast in his room. Rebecca had smoked salmon, scrambled eggs peppered with spring onion and toast washed down with a pot of English tea. Adam had two Craster kippers with a side of samphire, toast and a mug of piping hot, black coffee. The food was delicious, made all the better by their continued exhaustion.

Rebecca had worn the same clothes for two days, and she felt awful. She said, 'Can we 'please' go to a store to buy some clothes?'

'Yes, certainly. We could go into town before we head off,' Adam said.

Her mood visibly lifted and she said, 'Well, come on, let's go. I love shopping.'

'Oh, no! What have I let myself in for!' he grimaced laughingly.

With that, she raced to the door, holding it open for him, to usher him along.

They meandered through the maze of shops, buying a set of casual clothing, a pair of shoes and some beauty products. They also bought some toiletries and a small luggage bag to carry it all in.

Kaspar who was on watch again, when they left, let them go unfollowed once more, his confidence having been buoyed by their return on the evening before. He was also concerned that in the narrow streets a tail would be readily spotted.

Again, they returned, nearly two hours later just as Kaspar, who was on watch once more, was beginning to fear that they had absconded.

Kaspar held a digital camera with a telephoto lens which he had taken from the boot of his car. Taking the opportunity, he took some photographs of their faces for onward transmission to Germany.

Adam put the luggage in the car before they returned to the hotel with two smaller plastic bags. Kaspar thought to himself, 'So you look like you might be going on a trip somewhere!'

He phoned Stefan who had gone to refuel and said, 'Be ready. I think they may be heading off soon.'

'Right!' said Stefan.

Forty minutes later, both having changed their clothes, Adam and Rebecca emerged from the hotel, and headed for the car, while Kaspar made a quick call to Stefan.

Just as Stefan was pulling the car into the square, Adam's Audi was leaving it at the far end.

'Right let's see what they are up to!' Kaspar said to himself as he jumped into the car.

As Stefan drove away in pursuit, Kaspar put a call through to Germany, to update them.

CHAPTER THIRTY-TWO

Brancaster Staithe, North Norfolk Coast, England

ADAM CONTINUED TO FOLLOW Rebecca's directions, as she read from the map. They carried on northwards heading along the A134 through the pines of Thetford Forest and then on past the small market town of Swaffham. Adam continued to watch the rearview mirror looking for anyone tailing them, but he saw nothing to concern him. The neo-Nazis had shrewdly held back as far as possible, while still remaining within the range of the tracker, to prevent Adam from spotting them.

Just before reaching Castle Acre, they watched two fighters from a nearby military base as they flew low across the road ahead and then out towards the coast. The roar of their engines brought back memories of Adam's own past in the army. Adam turned off the main road and headed across country on minor back roads, before coming to Great Missingham and then onwards to the small village of Docking. After reaching it, they began to taste the salt in the air wafting off the sea a few miles ahead. It was only a short drive further to the tiny coastal, fishing village of Brancaster Staithe where they turned off the road into Harbour Way, pulling up in a makeshift car park by the water.

They climbed out, and both took a lungful of fresh sea air.

'Isn't it quaint?' Rebecca said as she turned to Adam, her hair lightly dancing in the breeze.

He looked directly at her and after a slight pause, said, 'Yes, very pretty.'

Rebecca's cheeks flushed, and she turned back to look out across the salt marsh, crisscrossed as it was with inlets, and then out towards the sea. Adam, however, continued to look at the profile of Rebecca's face, totally entranced by her.

She turned suddenly to speak to him saying, 'Adam, shall we ...' but stopped mid-way through the sentence as she saw that he had continued looking at her, but struck silent, more so, by the look on his face. She blushed and stuttered, 'Sh ...shall we get something to eat over there?'

Rebecca felt unnerved as she pointed past Adam, encouraging him to look over at a small wooden cabin standing on its own. It had a painted sign emblazoned across the top, 'The Crab Hut'.

He did not turn away at first, but then looked over and said, 'Sure, I'm hungry, and I love seafood.'

Slowly, they both began to make their way over to the hut, each lost in their own thoughts. Climbing the wooden steps to the serving hatch, Adam read off the day's offerings, scrawled in chalk on a small blackboard.

'Crab sandwich, dressed crab, lobster baguette, mussels, cockles, whelks ...'

Rebecca cut him off exclaiming, 'Whelks ... what on earth are they?'

Adam, feigning shock, said, 'You've never had whelks! You haven't lived, Rebecca! You must try them!'

'We'll have a pot of whelks for the young lady, and I will have a pot of cockles,' he said.

Adam had winked at the elderly gent serving him as he asked for the whelks and the man had knowingly smiled back.

'And for your main course?' Adam said, looking down at Rebecca.

'I shall have the lobster accompanied by a glass of your finest bubbly,' she replied, smiling.

'Lobster we can do, but they are fresh out of Champagne! How about a goblet of the local apple juice instead?' he grinned.

'Perfect!' said Rebecca, laughing softly.

He turned to the owner and said, 'Can we also have one lobster baguette, one Crab sandwich and two apple juices please.'

'Coming right up sir!' the kindly old man said, as he passed Adam one punnet of whelks and one of cockles. He then handed him a pepper pot and a small glass bottle of malt vinegar.

Adam paid and said, 'Thanks, we'll come back for the rest.'

They walked over to the shore and Rebecca leant against a wooden post. They both breathed in simultaneously as a refreshing gust of salt-laden wind passed over them. Adam gave her the whelks, and then he sprinkled pepper and vinegar on both of their punnets. He handed her a small wooden fork he had picked up at the cabin and said, 'Enjoy!'

Adam tucked into the cockles with relish and finishing them, turned to Rebecca, who was still vigorously chewing her first whelk. She had a look that was a mixture of horror and disgust across her face.

'Are you enjoying it?' he said, smiling.

She could not talk but gave a downcast look with her eyes. She then offered Adam some, but he said, 'No thanks, I can't stand them!'

Her face instantaneously changed to a look of shock and then she began to laugh uncontrollably, nearly choking on the whelk, as she tried to slap Adam's arm.

He laughed out loud, and as she swallowed hard, to devour the whelk, she laughingly coughed out, 'You scoundrel! How could you!'

She grabbed at him and fell forward against his firm chest as his arms suddenly came up to brace her shoulders, touching her soft skin. Their faces desperately close, stopped their mirth momentarily, as they looked into each other's eyes. He could feel the warmth of her skin and smell the intoxicating scent of her perfume. He felt uncontrollably drawn to her and her to him.

They stood in silence for a moment, the only sound - the wind across the marsh and the ever-present gulls.

Adam began to feel awkward. He had a job to do, and an emotional attachment at this time would undoubtedly be troublesome. Also, her grandfather had employed him, and he was expected to protect Rebecca.

Adam pulled away, suddenly cold, saying, 'Let me just get the rest of the meal!'

Rebecca was shocked and felt deeply saddened, she could not understand his reaction. Feeling hurt and slightly foolish, she turned to look out to sea once more, trying to make sense of her emotions.

She heard a loud, deep call, 'Adam!'

Rebecca spun around quickly to see a rough-looking, seafaring man in overalls and a dirty pair of large black Wellington boots, walking over towards Adam. He carried with him an enormous smile across his face.

Adam was walking down the wooden steps of the hut with the food and drinks, and he called out, 'Tom, great to see you again!'

They gave each other a hearty embrace, and Adam said, 'Come and meet my friend Rebecca!' He turned to face her, and they walked down the slipway towards the water, Tom calling over his shoulder to the man in the hut, 'Hey, get another crab sandwich on the go for me, Timmy! I'm famished!'

Tom was a great hulk of a man. His age was difficult to estimate, but maybe mid-thirties to mid-forties. He had a heavily weathered face with a deep, nut-brown tan and one of the gruffest voices Rebecca had ever heard. But for all of that, he was a jolly, friendly soul who oozed kindness and a faint smell of oily fish.

Rebecca shaken from her dark mood by Tom's ebullient nature said, 'Hello Tom, I'm delighted to meet you.'

'Likewise, I'm sure,' said Tom.

'Well, this is a thing Adam - Germany, is it? There'll be no questions asked! ...I'm happy to help. Do you both want to follow me?'

'Sure,' they said in unison.

'Ah, just a tick ...' Tom said as he slowly trotted back up the slipway, looking faintly ridiculous in his wellies.

He ran up the stairs of the hut and grabbed the crab sandwich from Timmy, shouting, 'I'll sort you out later Timmy, I've got no cash on me at the moment.'

A muffled response came from Timmy and then Tom re-joined them.

The three of them walked along the shoreline for a while until they came to an old wooden jetty with a couple of small fishing boats moored up alongside. The boats looked like they hadn't seen paint or hadn't even had a good scrub in years, but apart from that, though rusty, looked seaworthy.

'Come on board, we'll cast off come the next

tide,' Tom said as he, surprisingly nimbly, jumped onto the deck of 'The Jolly Seagull'.

'I just need to get our bags, Tom,' Adam said, and he jogged back to the car as Tom held out a helping hand to Rebecca. She took it to steady herself as she climbed aboard, noticing that his skin had the feel of well-worn leather. 'Thanks, what do you catch?' she enquired.

'We set pots for crabs and lobster mostly, but I often take anglers to a few wrecks further out into the North Sea. There we can find anything really ...bass, tope, cod, mackerel ...you name it, we got it!' Tom chuckled.

'You fish?' he continued.

'No, not really ...I tried fly-fishing once with my grandfather, but I found it a bit boring. Sorry!'

'Well, maybe the two of you could come sea fishing with me one day ...when you have more time, that is! Boring it ain't, I can promise you!' he said smiling.

She wondered if he thought they were 'an item', but maybe he was just gracious. 'Who knows!' she said with, he thought, a faint hint of sadness.

He showed her into the small cabin, pointing to a lightly padded bench as he said, 'It's not the Waldorf, but it's all mine! Make yourself comfy while I get ready.'

She sat down and watched Tom busy himself with the controls, before he disappeared down through a hatch into the bowels of the boat, like a rabbit down a hole. His head reappeared from below five minutes later, just as Adam was clambering aboard with the bags. He had put the gun he had picked up in St Pancras into his jacket pocket and his own weapon, with the spare clips, into his bag.

'Adam pass them down to me, and I'll stow them away.'

'Sure!' Adam said, as he dropped one and then the other bag down into Tom's outstretched arms before they disappeared into the hold.

Adam sat down opposite Rebecca, who pointedly avoided his gaze. He felt a slight sense of unease as if he had done something wrong. Then Tom reappeared and started the engine, saying, 'Adam can you let go the lines and we'll be off.'

'Sure thing!' Adam called as he went out onto the deck and then hopped over the side on to the harbour planks. He let go the bow and spring lines, throwing the gathered rope into a pile. Adam then gave the boat a gentle push with his foot nudging the bow into the small channel. He then untied the stern line, and while still holding the ship on the cleat he jumped back aboard the Jolly Seagull, releasing the line as he went and pulling it through before throwing it on the deck. The boat gently drifted away from the harbourside before a rev of the engine proceeded to take it forward at a slow pace along the channel. Adam leant over the side and pulled up the three old tyres which were being used as fenders as the boat chugged on its way.

He then walked back into the cabin, gently swaying with the motion of the boat as he went, before sitting down again, in silence. Rebecca was looking out of the grimy window and keeping to herself. Tom was busy navigating through the narrow, twisting channels of Mow Creek and then on to Norton Creek through the desolate salt marsh. The waterways eventually led out to The Wash, a large bay surrounded on three sides by the counties of Lincolnshire and Norfolk. This then led on to the open sea.

As the boat entered The Wash, Tom gave it more power and brought her up to a cruising speed of 18 knots reasonably quickly. He typically hugged the shoreline until they were out into the North Sea. The colony of gulls that followed the boat gradually began to peel away and headed back towards the coast, screeching excitedly as they went. Tom returned to his jolly manner and started chatting busily with Adam. Rebecca had taken the opportunity to look at her phone and to send a text, subsequently receiving a response, before slipping the phone back into her coat. She had believed her actions had been unseen. Unknown to Rebecca and perplexed, Adam had watched her in a reflection in the window.

She looked up and out across the water, feeling the bracing salt-laden breeze which, she found revitalizing and cleansing. She felt tired, not just physically, but utterly exhausted mentally.

Their progress had been watched through powerful military-grade binoculars, by Kaspar. Stefan had parked up, while Kaspar had walked along a part of the nearby Norfolk Coast Path to get a better vantage point. Anywhere else he may have been noticeable, but there he was inconspicuous. He was just another crazy bird watcher among many others with similar binoculars and enormous cameras fitted with telephoto lenses.

As they began to make their way out of sight, with an easterly heading, Kaspar called Germany and gave them a further update.

Krüger said, 'So, it looks like they are heading to the continent by boat. Right, keep a watch on them for as long as you can and keep reporting back. What's the name of the boat, and what does it look like?'

Kaspar said, 'It is called 'The Jolly Seagull' and it has a black hull, up to just above the waterline and then the main body of the boat is bright red, the cockpit is a dull white. It looks like it needs a new coat of paint and it is approximately forty feet long. Apart from that, it seems like any other fishing boat.'

'I'll get some of our men on alert in Germany, Holland and Belgium,' Krüger retorted, as he finished writing his notes and rang off.

CHAPTER THIRTY-THREE

The Salthouse Dun Cow Public House, Salthouse,
North Norfolk Coast, England

KASPAR WALKED BACK TO THE car and
climbed inside.

'What's happening Kaspar?' asked Stefan.

Kaspar thought for a moment and said, 'I'm
not completely sure, but it looks like they are
trying to get to the continent in a fishing boat.
We need to watch them for as long as possible
and report in.'

'Kaspar said come on let's go. We'll drive
along the coast for a while and find another spot
to watch their progress.'

The Germans headed on through the villages of Burnham Deepdale, Burnham Norton,
Burnham Overy Staithe and Wells-next-the-Sea
stopping regularly where the landscape afforded
a good view. They tracked the steady progress of

the small fishing boat as it continued to hug the coast on its relentless voyage east.

After Wells they drove further along the coast road towards Stiffkey, Morston, Blakeney and Cley next the Sea, the Jolly Seagull mostly within sight.

At Salthouse, the Germans turned off the main coastal road and drove out along the beach road to get a closer view. They could see that the boat, though it was keeping its course, was further from the coast as it was at this point that the Norfolk coastline began its gradual curve towards the south giving the county its distinctive shape. 'The Jolly Seagull' was heading out to the east, deeper into the North Sea. Kaspar took a compass from his pocket and checked it to gauge the boats bearing. He then telephoned Germany and spoke to Krüger, 'They're now heading out to sea, towards the east. Their bearing seems to indicate that they are making for the coast of the Netherlands or possibly Germany.'

'They are after the gold!' Krüger barked.

Herr Müller looked up at him, 'What's happening Krüger?'

'It looks like the boat is heading to the coast of the Netherlands or Germany.'

'Is that so?' Müller said, pondering this new development. He continued, 'So the flies willingly come to the web! We will be waiting for them!' He continued, 'When do you think that they will get to the European coast?'

'I'm not sure ...clearly, it depends on where they are making for, but possibly early morning

...maybe by three or four, by then they would be off the Netherland's West Frisian Islands. If they are heading to Germany, then they may do as they did in Norfolk and hug the coastlines of the islands.'

Once the boat was out of sight, Kaspar and Stefan went back to the car and headed back to the coast road again and then on to a nearby pub, The Salthouse Dun Cow, which they had passed on the way. The Germans sat down for a rest and for a meal of haddock and chips which they polished off with a pint of the local ale, Moon Gazer. They enjoyed the strong flavour of the hops in the beer, but most of all they enjoyed the rest – they were both close to collapse.

CHAPTER THIRTY-FOUR

THE JOLLY SEAGULL MADE ITS way, relentlessly, further out into the North Sea,
which was untypically calm. This did not,
however, improve Rebecca's spirits, as she was
not the best of travellers. The cramped conditions of the cockpit coupled with the unpalat-
able smell of fish and oil fumes from the boat
made for an unsavoury mix. Much of the time,
she felt a mild sense of nausea.

Adam and Tom, conversely, seemed unfazed
and chatted through the evening about the past
and everything but, the current events. They
were clearly great friends, and she listened and
jealously watched Adam's happy ease with Tom.
It gave her a greater appreciation for Adam and
a growing fondness.

As the evening passed through to the early
morning, Rebecca effortlessly began to slip into

an uncomfortable sleep, wrapped in an old blanket and lying against the corner of the bench. The occasional wafts of salt, laden air, coming from the open doorway gave her some respite from the unbearable stench and the taste of iodine in her mouth.

The journey was rather uneventful, and they saw scant, passing shipping and what they did come across, showed itself fleetingly as distant lights on the horizon.

Rebecca occasionally woke with the irregular motion of the boat and on one occasion prompted by Adam's brushing by her, as he walked out on deck to take in the breeze and to look at the spectacular star-filled sky. Rebecca watched him for some time and then decided to follow Adam out. She slipped in beside him and said, 'What an incredible sight.'

'Yes, it's beautiful. You feel so insignificant when you look up at it.'

At that moment, as if on cue, a shooting star, shot its dying light across the heavens.

'Look at that!' she said, grabbing Adam's arm as she did, 'It's meant to be lucky, isn't it?'

Adam looked down at her, with an oddly expressionless face. He then said softly and with great emotion as he looked into her eyes, 'Yes, ...it is.'

She drew away from him, slightly unnerved, but then helplessly flung herself fully back into his arms as she was thrown by the motion of a rogue wave slamming into the side of the boat. She had let out a sudden scream of fear.

He laughed out loud, as he looked at her shocked face looking up at him. Though Rebecca took great comfort from his arms around her, she felt quite childish and pulled away from him. She then made her way back inside to wrap up once more. She stayed awake for a long time, glancing out on the deck at Adam who remained there, alone with his thoughts, silhouetted against the night sky.

She found it difficult to drift off and even more difficult not to think of Adam, but eventually, exhaustion overcame her, and she passed into an uneasy sleep.

Before returning to the cabin, Adam pulled Carter's handgun from his pocket. He looked at it thoughtfully, ran his thumb almost tenderly across the grip and then threw it out into the darkness, hearing the splash as it began its descent into the depths.

Chapter Thirty-five

Harz Mountains, Northern Germany

KRÜGER CONTACTED HIS MEN who were based in Belgium and northern Germany to put them on standby. He also arranged for one of them, who was based in Brussels, to hire a private plane. The man was to have the pilot intercept the route of the Jolly Seagull and once its general course was confirmed, to head to Norfolk to pick up Kaspar and Stefan.

Once the arrangements were made Krüger called Kaspar, saying, 'In a few hours a twin-engine Beechcraft Baron will be landing at a local airfield called Little Snoring. I want you to head there and meet up with Leopold, who is on board. Track the boat's course and then, land somewhere close to wherever they are making for and await further instructions.'

'Yes, sir!' said Kaspar, 'Can you tell me where this ...Little Snoring is?'

'It's approximately twenty miles south-west of your current location. Keep me informed at all times and *do not* lose them.'

'Certainly, sir!' Kaspar barked.

The line went dead, and he turned to Stefan, who was just finishing his second pint of Moon Gazer, 'Let's get going, Leo is picking us up in a light aircraft in a few hours.'

Stefan responded unenthusiastically, 'Where?'

'Little Snoring airfield,' Kaspar responded, rolling his eyes as he said the name.

Stefan, who was just beginning to relax, laughed, 'Are you joking?'

'I know! Only the British would call a place something so ridiculous. Come on, pay the bill and let's go.'

Back in the forest, Krüger stood before Müller and said, 'The arrangements are now in place. We will track them to their destination on the European mainland, and then we will intercept them. Our operatives can efficiently 'extract' the information we need.'

'No,' Müller snapped, 'I do not want another 'mistake' during questioning, like the one in Cleobury Mortimer. If they die while being captured or without giving us the information when they are being interrogated, then it will be lost to us forever. No! Let them go and get our men to follow them, carefully this time! They can lead us all the way to our birth-right.'

'Certainly, Herr Müller,' Krüger replied.

Müller growled through gritted teeth, 'Only after that will they be shown what it is to incur my displeasure.'

Though Krüger smiled and gently nodded in response, a terrifyingly cold shiver ran down his spine. He prayed that he never incurred Herr Müller's displeasure.

CHAPTER THIRTY-SIX

Norderney, East Frisian Islands, off the North Sea coast of Germany

THEY HAD, UNNOTICED AND sometime before, passed the East Frisian Islands of Borkum and Juist to the west of Norderney and then the Norderneyer Seegat. It was a channel, nearly two miles wide, between the islands and it led to the shallow Wadden Sea and its extensive mudflats, known as the Watten. During this crossing, the boat seemed to be more mobile, in all directions.

The dawn was still two hours away. The Jolly Seagull forced its way through the waves past the principal area of population towards the western end of Norderney. The squalls of the North Sea crossing were now left far behind. The Jolly Seagull sailed on, three miles out from the mainland. A stiff breeze was blowing with just more than a hint of rain in the air. The waves were not strong enough to break the bow regularly, but occasionally the cockpit was sprayed with a liberal dousing of saltwater and a tremendous crashing sound. Tom could see the dark outline of the lighthouse on Norderney with its vibrant intermittent beam. It was a beautiful red brick structure that had safely guided Tom and many other sailors for more than a hundred and thirty years. Some of the buildings on the mainland were beginning to show the first signs of life with windows suddenly lighting up here and there. The small boat continued on its tireless path as Adam, Rebecca and the captain huddled in the close confines of the cockpit. Adam had just returned from the tiny cabin below, having filled up three large metal mugs, full of piping hot Bovril. The three of them were well wrapped up, but the cockpit still felt damp and cold, and the warm drink was a welcome treat. No one had spoken for some time, the captain busy with the boat, Adam and Rebecca lost in their thoughts.

Suddenly Tom piped up, 'That's Norderney. We will be heading to the east of the island where it's less populated, as it's a National Park. There shouldn't be anyone around at this time. My friend Jürgen will come out to meet us, and he will transfer you to the coast. Jürgen will leave you there, and he has arranged for one of his friends to take you to the ferry over to the mainland.'

There was a small airfield on Norderney, but Adam had not wished to use it to fly the next stage of their journey. Indeed, it would have been more convenient and faster, but there might be some awkward questions to answer and a flight plan to lodge.

The boat kept chugging along on its path and Adam noticed that the captain was deliberately bringing the Jolly Seagull closer to land, but despite this, they were still over two miles offshore. Tom leant towards the Raymarine VHF transponder, tuned it to the required channel and picking up the fist-mic, he barked, 'Jolly Seagull to Blue Fish, come in.'

After hearing nothing for a period, he said again, 'Jolly Seagull to Blue Fish, come in.'

There was a harsh crackle on the radio, and a Germanic voice with a wind laden encore said, 'Jolly Fish, this is Blue Fish, over.'

Tom replied, 'Blue Fish, what's the weather like where you are? Over.'

'Jolly Seagull, the weather is getting better, over.'

'Jolly Seagull, thanks and out.'

'Blue Fish, as you may have suspected, is Jürgen,' Tom said, 'that pointless conversational alerts him to start heading out to rendezvous with us.'

Adam smiled and said, 'Tom, how very 007 of you!'

They both laughed, but Rebecca just sipped at her Bovril, while trying to hold onto the sidewall with her other hand to steady herself. Her only wish was to reach dry land as soon as she could.

The sky was gradually getting lighter as the dawn began to break and they started to notice the inflatable a long way off, as it bounced violently through the waves. How Jürgen remained in it was a mystery to all. As he continued his approach, Adam retrieved their bags in readiness. Tom didn't alter his course, and within fifteen minutes, Jürgen had skirted the back of the Jolly Seagull and skilfully pulled alongside on the seaward side.

Adam had gone out on the deck and called mockingly, 'Ahoy, Blue Fish!'

As he did so, he picked up the faint hint of pine coming off the land, carried on the breeze.

'Ahoy, to you, Englishman!' he replied jokingly.

'American, if you please!' he called, as he waved to Jürgen.

Both boats continued their forward momentum, but they synchronised down to a slower pace. Tom shouted through the open cockpit door, 'You'd better look lively. I don't want any prying eyes wondering what we are doing. Good luck to you both.'

Adam dropped, first one bag and then the other over the side into the inflatable. When he turned, he saw Rebecca nervously making her way towards him across the slippery deck, a look of trepidation etched across her face. Adam was kneeling by the gunwale, and he held out his hand to help steady her. Rebecca grabbed it with such a lunge, that she fell forward, towards and against him. He said above the noise of the wind and engines, 'Don't worry, I'll help you down, and we will be on the beach in a short while.'

He carefully moved her towards the gunwale and then effortlessly picked her up and lifted her over the side of the boat, leaving her feeling like a rag doll. Hanging in mid-air, she just stared up helplessly at Adam. She felt as if she was his to do with as he pleased. Rebecca was gripping his arms very tightly as she felt the wind and spray intensifying against her body. He called out to her, 'Release your grip!' and with that, he leant further out of the boat and lowered her down towards the bouncing inflatable. At the last moment, as the prow of the inflatable rose on a wave, Adam released his grip and Rebecca bumped, softly, onto the floor of the craft, her hands, which had not released their hold on him, wrenched free of his arms by the force of gravity.

A moment later, he had jumped the gunwale, holding on with one hand. As the inflatable rose up once more, he suddenly dropped down into the small craft, landing with a bump beside Rebecca.

Steadying himself, he waved and called out, 'Thanks Tom!' above the sound of the engines and the wind.

Then as Tom smiled and waved back from the cockpit, the inflatable abruptly pulled away from the Jolly Seagull. In doing so, it completed a near-360 turn. Jürgen sliced through the bubbling wake, which was coming off the fishing boat, as he guided the little craft, turning it and heading inshore.

Jürgen bounced his way across the waves,

the occupants being liberally splashed with sea spray. It was a cold passage and left Rebecca yearning for the comparative warmth of the boat. She, like Adam, held the grab rope towards the front of the small boat while Jürgen sat at the rear controlling the powerful Mercury outboard motor. Unlike Adam, who looked directly at the beach ahead and who seemed unaffected by the cold and wet, she tucked herself down as low in the inflatable as she could.

Coming closer to the beach, Adam saw a man, who had, previously, been hidden in the dunes, show himself by walking down on to the sand. He turned back to look at Jürgen who called out above the noise of engine, waves and wind, 'It's my friend, Paulos!' On hearing this, Rebecca looked up to see Jürgen throw her a smile, as Adam turned his gaze back to the beach. She decided to brave the weather and peered over the splash guard, which seemed to offer no protection to her at all, and saw a little way off, the man Paulos walking towards the water's edge. The noise from the outboard changed as Jürgen began to reduce speed until, with one last surge of wave and power, the base of the boat slid firmly, up onto the beach. Almost before the boat's movement had stopped, Adam had jumped out. Paulos, holding the grab rope at the bow, proffered a hand to Rebecca who, taking it, climbed out unsteadily on to the sand, glad that she was on dry land once more.

Adam turned to Jürgen who handed him a couple of small fishing rods and a canvas bag that had lain in the bottom of the boat. Jürgen said, 'There are few people about this early in the morning and at this time of year. If you have been seen landing, then this is as good a cover as any.'

Adam opened the bag to see two respectably sized Pollack, 'Thanks for all you have done for us Jürgen.'

'No problem, it's added some welcome excitement to my life!'

Paulos and Adam then began to push the craft back into the deeper water. In moments, Jürgen had spun the boat around and with a smile, disappeared back out to sea.

Paulos looked at them both and said, 'Come on, let's go and get you warm and dry.'

Adam and Rebecca followed him up the beach, and they quickly melted into the grass-covered sand dunes. They walked for ten minutes, feeling a little less cold than before as the dunes sheltered them from the wind. A light plane passed over, just to the south. Adam looked at it but felt that it posed no threat as it did not seem to make any alterations in height or direction as it continued on its way. Eventually, they came into a clearing with a group of long wooden buildings. On one of the buildings was written, 'Weisse Düne'.

Paulus said, 'It's a highly-regarded gourmet restaurant, you will have to come back during opening hours one day when you have more time.'

They followed him between the buildings,

where Paulos opened one of the doors and ushered them in. It was a small, minimalist room with a single bed. It had walls painted in faded, pastel creams and blues and it smelt of lavender. It was spotlessly clean and refreshingly warm.

'There's a shower through there,' he pointed and said casually, 'and I have left out some dry clothes and footwear for you both and a couple of rain jackets. I hope they fit.'

Paulus leant down and pulled out two small rucksacks continuing, 'Here you can put your stuff in these. I'll wait outside for you – we had better hurry as I would like to get away from here before anyone begins to wake up and I want you on the first ferry – you will be less obvious on the mainland.'

He opened the door, allowing an unwelcome gust of chilly air in and then he was gone.

Adam had dropped the fish and the rods outside the door but had brought their own bags in. They were damp on the outside, so he emptied their contents out and onto the bed and re-packed them into the rucksacks.

Adam said warmly, 'You go first.'

Rebecca, looking bedraggled and cold, said nothing, but just leant down and grabbed the set of women's clothes that had been left out for her. She walked into the small shower room and quietly closed the door without looking back. Adam stood staring at the door for a moment and then turned to glance out through the window at the ever-lightening sky. A small pool of water had formed around where he stood, as the drips from his clothes pooled together. Adam listened attentively as the droplets fell and hit the floor. He smiled to himself as he became more aware of a nasty smell of fish and oil which came from his clothes. He looked awful – wet, cold and covered in sand and salt, but most of all, exhausted.

He heard the shower turn on, and his thoughts went back to Rebecca. It had been a terrible experience for her, but she was clearly, given what had occurred, an incredibly resilient young girl. He lightly shook his head. Young girl, he thought – she is not a young girl, she's a young woman! He found it difficult to keep her from his mind. He knew that it was important that he kept a clear head for the forthcoming events, but he had begun to feel a deepening fondness for her.

Rebecca spent some time in the shower, gradually unwinding in its warmth. She had gargled with the refreshing water to rinse away the taste of sea and salt. Then Adam turned as the shower door suddenly opened, and she reappeared amid clouds of steam. He saw her looking spotless in a pair of oversized, faded blue jeans, a cream blouse and a vast blue fleece. She wore no make-up, and her beautiful face shone out of a wild mess of un-brushed hair.

'You look wonderful,' he said.

She laughed and said mockingly, '...Oh, really! I bet you say that to all the girls! I've certainly felt better, that's for sure!'

She looked him up and down slowly and looking profoundly serious, mocked, 'You look ...er ...interesting!'

Adam laughed, saying, 'I'll take that as a compliment ...and before you say 'anything' else, I'll jump in myself.'

He smiled at Rebecca and then disappeared into the shower room, grabbing his set of clothes on the way. As he passed by her, she abruptly crossed her arms, hugging herself tightly. A sudden, almost uncontrollable urge swept through her body at that moment – one of absolute desire – the desire to hold him close to her and never to let him go. Her cheeks flushed red at the thought of it and at the idea that he could see her inner thoughts written bold across her whole being.

She mentally shook herself and tried to put him out of her mind. When Adam came out, he was wearing a pair of close-fitting, chocolate corduroy trousers and a beige cotton shirt. He too had a fleece, but his one was slate grey.

He said, 'Not my choice of outfit, but it's nice and warm.'

She secretly thought he looked fabulous, though she said sardonically, 'No, you won't win any fashion contests!'

Adam looked at her, as she smiled back at him seeming happier than he had seen her appear since they had left Rook Hall. Rebecca had brushed her hair, and she looked radiant. She had put on a pair of red converse basketball shoes that looked one size too big and she was wearing one of the two green raincoats which had been left for them.

He sat beside her on the bed and pulled on

the pair of leather boots he had been left and then stood up, putting his raincoat on as he did so. Rebecca had already filled her backpack with her belongings, and she slung it across her back as Adam finished packing his rucksack. Grabbing the bag, Adam went to the door and opened it, and Rebecca walked out ahead of him as he left and shut the door behind them.

Paulos, who had been waiting for them, said nervously, 'Come on, let's go.'

The breeze was brisk and refreshing as it brushed Adam's face, and it carried the evocative smell of the sea.

They walked for another ten minutes before Paulos stopped beside a yellow Volkswagen Beetle, which was clearly suffering the effects of rust. It looked like it had been built in the 1960s or maybe even before. The car was parked, mostly, off the road and on to the sand. Paulos opened the door which was not locked, and they all climbed in. He drove the short distance to the ferry before pulling into the car park. Paulos had not stayed but had said goodbye and wished them good luck when he departed.

They waited at the quayside, in the harbour, for the AG Reederei Norden-Frisia ferry and then, along with a few commuters and tourists, boarded the 8.00 service to Norddeich, near the city of Norden on the mainland. Once they had reached Norden, they hired a car for their onward journey.

Chapter Thirty-seven

JadeWeser Airport, Wilhelmshaven, Lower Saxony,
Northern Germany

THE BEECHCRAFT BARON WAS set up on final approach, its lights glowing through the darkness. The noise of the powerful engines was deafening. Kaspar looked out and smiling, as he saw the glaring runway lights ahead, said, 'Back in the homeland!'

Leopold and Stefan gradually came out of their slumber and looked out into the fading black of the early morning.

They all wore headsets and heard the chatter between the pilot and the tower as they began to gradually descend, before settling into a gentle landing, with a screech of the tyres as they touched down.

The men contacted Krüger in the Harz Mountains, once they had exited the aeroplane. He ordered the three of them to use the car, left at the airport for them and to make their way towards Norderney. Krüger had had the photographs of Rebecca and Adam, which Kaspar had sent, forwarded on to their operatives.

The three men set off and were diverted to Norden part-way through their journey, where they kept watch for the couple. The Germans were updated by other neo-Nazis, who remained on watch in the area - the couple were heading to Norden in a taxi. It was unclear to the watchers what form of transport would, however, actually be used by their quarry.

Leopold monitored the busy train station and Kaspar and Stefan kept a lookout at the two-car hire firms.

Within an hour Stefan had seen them arrive at the Sixt car hire office, which he had been watching and he called Leopold and Kaspar to come to him with their car.

Within twenty minutes they were on the road following Adam and Rebecca at a safe distance, heading towards the south-east.

Kaspar contacted Krüger once more and was told to keep him updated.

Deep in the Harz Mountains, Krüger turned to Müller and said, 'Everything is going to plan, Herr Müller. Kaspar and the others are tailing them. I will warn our men, in the regions they may pass through, to be on alert.'

Müller looked pensive but said nothing in response. A life's work hung in the balance!

Chapter Thirty-eight

Collections Department, Mossad headquarters, Tel Aviv, Israel

THE PHONE RANG ON ARIEL Mandler's desk. He was exhausted, having stayed at the office since news of the neo-Nazi's activities had broken. To the side of him, a camp bed had been installed, and the tousled bedclothes were evidence of his recent occupancy.

He leant across the desk, sighing as he did so and picked up the phone.

'Yes!' he said.

'Sir, I have Mr Goldman on the line from the Embassy in Bern,' the operator said.

'Good, put him through immediately!' Mandler snapped, the fatigue suddenly falling away from him.

There was a click on the line, and Mandler said, 'Well, Ezra! What do you have for me?'

'Hello, sir. I've heard from our agents in

London about the St Pancras matter. The two German neo-Nazis were shot and killed by the police. A member of a right-wing, London skinhead group was also killed, and another was wounded. He is in hospital under armed guard. A third member of the London gang was also taken into custody. The two men are saying nothing, and the police are bemused, as to what has been going on. They have, however, made the link to the murders at Rook Hall and Cleobury Mortimer.'

Ezra paused for breath, continuing, 'Our agents have made certain inquiries having stalked the neo-Nazis. They have found that the couple escaped St Pancras and eventually travelled to Germany, by use of a small fishing boat. They were watched from the shore, as they left England, by the Germans who had followed them. Our men continued to shadow the Germans, who eventually went to a small, nearby airfield. A hefty bribe to one of the men in the control tower served to release their flight plan to our agents. This showed that the two Germans then flew to an airport at Wilhelmshaven, by private plane. We had agents in Germany waiting for them. When they arrived, there was a third man with them, and they then drove to a coastal town called Norden, where they picked up the trail of the man and woman again. The neo-Nazis are tracking them once more, and they are heading in a south-easterly direction, by car. We are monitoring the situation.'

'What about the ...' Ariel began before being

interrupted by a sharp tap on the door, which briefly preceded Daniel entering his room.

'Hold on, Ezra!' Ariel said, knowing that Daniel would not have interrupted him unless it was imperative.

He looked at Daniel, who began, 'Sir, I think we have the identity of the old man who was killed in Rook Hall.'

'What! ...You think you have?' Ariel questioned.

'Yes, we have tracked Adolf Shultz and Walter Gille down. They are both currently living under assumed names in Germany. Werner Graf was also living under an assumed name, and he died of cancer two years ago in Lisbon. That's when his true identity came out. Theodor Model had been living in Italy for many years under his own name. He is currently serving ten years in San Vittore Prison in Milan for his part in a multi-million Euro financial fraud. The Swiss are currently trying to extradite him on other unrelated matters.'

'And then there was one!' Ariel joked, 'the aristocrat!'

'Yes sir, Otto von Freitann. I am certain that it is him. We have a photo of von Freitann in uniform from the war, which was taken for his SS identity papers. It bears a striking resemblance to his photograph which he sent to Her Majesty's Passport Office for his most recent passport application. Also, von Freitann disappeared, without a trace, just before the end of the war in southern Germany. A few months later Oscar

Accola made his first appearance in Switzerland. We also checked the WW2 awards and medals which did not get destroyed in the fireplace at Rook Hall. We found that von Freitann was a recipient of them all.'

'Was there anything else?'

'Yes, he had been picked up, just before his disappearance at a roadblock operated by German soldiers. They thought he was a deserter and they arrested him. He subsequently escaped while being transported, with other prisoners, deeper into Germany. However, the records from the Panzergrenadiers who caught him, show that von Freitann claimed that he was on a top priority mission with a small convoy of SS soldiers, who had been attacked by an American Mustang. The others had been killed and he, alone, had escaped. When he failed to produce his letter of authority, they stopped believing him. The Panzergrenadiers had not shot him on the spot because he had been in the uniform of an SS-Sturmbannführer, and he was driving a Mercedes-Benz staff car with pennants which had clearly been hit by large calibre fire. However, from their report it did, it appeared, cross their minds, that he had stolen these items.'

'And?' Ariel said.

'He had said that he was operating under the personal authority of Heinrich Himmler on a matter of the utmost importance to the Reich. Like the soldiers, I didn't believe it either. However, I checked back through von Freitann's war records, and during the April of 1945, shortly before his capture, he was summoned to the Reich Chancellery from his hospital bed, where he was recuperating from wounds. There is no record as to why. The next day he was discharged early. We can place Himmler at the Reich Chancellery at that time. I also went on to check if there were any reports about an SS convoy being attacked at the location von Freitann had mentioned when he was captured. The USAAF records mention such an attack in that area by a fighter pilot called Jack Lord who had been flying a Mustang. They also state that three trucks were destroyed, and that one staff car got away with a single officer at the wheel.'

'Very well done, Daniel!' Ariel said, 'Ezra you heard ...'

Daniel cut in, 'Sir, there was something else in the USAAF records.'

'Well, go on!'

Daniel continued, 'I found something curious. In the pilot's report, he said that his initial attack focused on the three trucks as the staff car had quickly pulled ahead of the other vehicles while the fighter was on its final approach. Then, while he was banking around to press home a second attack, he saw one of the SS officers in the staff car shoot the other officer, who accompanied him and then he shot the driver. The man was subsequently fired on by one of his own soldiers in the convoy, before making his escape.'

Ariel was very impressed; Daniel had done

outstanding work. He said, 'That is excellent work, Daniel,' he then waved his hand indicating that Daniel, who was beaming, could go.

Ariel continued, 'Well Ezra, you heard that?'

'Yes, it's incredible ...if true.'

Ariel went on, 'Well, there does seem to be evidence to corroborate the story. It looks as if this von Freitann may have double-crossed his compatriots. And if that were the case, then it would explain a great deal. But what had he been entrusted to do that was so important? Something that would eventually lead to his death, so long after the war?'

Neither of them spoke for a moment, then Ariel said, 'How are the electronics team doing?'

'They are working flat out, but the neo-Nazis security is top-notch now, and there is no progress yet,' Ezra replied.

'Right - well keep them at it. I want all our resources on this. It must be of the greatest importance to these fascists and therefore to us. I'll speak to you again,' Ariel said, without waiting for a reply, as he replaced the handset.

Chapter Thirty-nine

Erfurt, Thuringia, Germany

ADAM HAD LEISURELY DRIVEN through the day and arrived in Erfurt, the capital city of the German state of Thuringia, in the mid-afternoon. Both Rebecca and he had discussed going directly to the location to search for the box but had decided that a good night's sleep, after the previous night's sea passage, was more desirable. Adam parked in the old town, and they booked into the Hotel Krämerbrücke. Rebecca had never been to Erfurt before, and she marvelled at the beauty of its medieval buildings, which had escaped severe bombing during the Second World War.

They went to their rooms to freshen up and then went out together for a walk around the historic streets, eventually stopping at the quaint, Gasthaus Feuerkugel for dinner. They asked the waiter for recommendations. Subsequently, they ordered Zwiebelsuppe, a traditional onion soup which smelt amazing and the Thüringer Klöße, grated potato dumplings. Both courses were local Thuringian dishes and were very welcome after the days travel. They accompanied the meal with a chilled bottle of Kruger-Rumpf Riesling and talked long into the evening. Neither mentioned the recent events, which engulfed them, instead preferring to discuss happier times in the past or potentially in the future. Rebecca thought, how easy Adam was to talk to at that time and how much she enjoyed his company. Likewise, he was utterly enthralled by her. Watching him across the flickering candlelight, Rebecca wondered what she would have done without him as a dark shadow passed over her soul.

She watched his face studiously as he discussed animatedly, about his days in the Legion and of his many travels. He had rugged features which were softened by kind eyes and a face which readily fell into a smile. But it really was his eyes which captivated her, they had a sparkling, hypnotic quality which magnetically drew her to him.

'Rebecca? ...Rebecca?' she heard him say through the fog of one glass of white wine, too many.

'Um ...yes, yes sorry,' she said, feeling her face blush, as she mentally shook herself into consciousness and sensed that he had seen something in her that she had wished to conceal.

'I was just wondering if you would like to go, as tomorrow is a big day.'

She most certainly did not want to go, as she felt so contented, but said, 'Yes, of course!'

As they left the restaurant, Adam fleetingly lay his hand on the small of her back guiding her through the door. The unexpected and sensitive gesture sent waves of emotion racing through Rebecca's body.

They took a leisurely walk back to the hotel. Rebecca felt so content with him - so happy. She desperately wanted to hold his hand to complete the moment, though she somehow felt ill at ease at the thought of placing her hand in his.

It was an enchanting walk, listening to the happy, animated chatter from the restaurants and bars and taking in the glorious smells from the kitchens. The sky was alive with magnificent, darkening cloud formations and the sound of birds.

They walked on in comfortable silence, and after entering the hotel, they parted at the door of her room. As she closed the door behind her, hearing Adam's open and close along the corridor, she felt a deep sense of longing and sadness overcome her.

Unseen, during the night, in one of the streets of the old town, Leopold crouched down and attached a tracking device to the Sixt rental car, which Adam and Rebecca had hired.

Rebecca found it difficult to sleep, but once she did, her eyes did not open again until 10.00 a.m. They had not arranged a time to meet, that morning, but she did feel that she had slept in for too long, though she knew that it had done her good. Rebecca rang through to his room, but there was no reply, so she telephoned down to the front desk. She was told that Adam had just arrived back and had gone through to the breakfast room.

Rebecca showered and got dressed, wondering all the time where he had been. Arriving in the restaurant, she walked over to Adam, who beamed, 'Hello, sleepyhead!'

She smiled saying, 'I'm sorry, I normally wake early, but I really did need that rest.'

Adam's plate was covered in slices of various local sausage and cheeses, and he was busying himself, cutting up some dark brown, rye bread. He already had a glass of orange juice, and the waiter had just arrived with a pot of coffee. She saw a small bag on the table and presumed that Adam had been shopping. Seeing her look at it, he said, 'Ah, I just bought a topographic map of the area, as I thought it may help us in our search.'

'You are actually quite handy to have around,' Rebecca said sleepily, 'I could get quite used to you!'

She had let it slip unthinkingly and blushing, felt like biting her tongue.

Rebecca noticed that he had glanced up smiling and then, sliding away as fast as she could, she said, 'I'll just get some breakfast.'

CHAPTER FORTY

.

AFTER BREAKFAST, THEY HAD checked out of the hotel before beginning to drive south, to the east of Arnstadt. On reaching Kirchheim, they turned to the east to start to follow the route of her grandfather's map. They carried on towards Hohenfelden and then, passing through, took the road to Nauendorf and beyond. Just over a mile further on and after the three bends in the route, which were indicated on the old pencil-drawn map, Adam pulled off the tarmac on to the side of a rough track leading deep into a forest.

'Well, this looks like it could be the spot, but much may have changed in over half a century.' He said as he turned the engine off. Adam pulled out the map he had bought and studied it against her grandfather's drawing.

He continued, 'They look pretty similar, but

there may have been extensive logging, and these access roads into the interior could have altered over time, but maybe not.'

'Well, let's get going!' he said, suddenly looking up at Rebecca. He stopped momentarily as he saw her face, deep in thought and with a sad countenance.

'Are you alright?' he asked.

'Yes ...I'm sorry, it's just that I can't help thinking of my grandfather, here, all those years ago. He must have felt terribly alone ...scared even.'

'Forgive me, Rebecca,' Adam said benignly, as he laid his hand on hers, 'I can be a bit insensitive at times. I'm sure that all of this must be exceedingly difficult for you.'

She looked up at Adams warm and kindly face and had a sudden urge to kiss him tenderly, though she held herself back.

'Don't worry Adam, I'll be fine.' She looked over at him and said in the softest of voices, 'I'm so glad you are here with me.'

Adam smiled, the biggest smile she had seen yet, and he said as he winked at her, 'Well then, do you fancy a walk in the woods with me?'

She laughed suddenly, breaking her mood, saying, 'But it's full of big bad wolves!'

They both laughed and got out of the car. Adam grabbed a small shovel and a nylon sack from the rear seat, saying to Rebecca as he did so, 'Some more of my morning purchases!'

They then began to walk down the track, deeper into the trees. Rebecca thought, how beautiful it was, with only the sounds of nature around them. The trees were alive with the chatter of birdlife and leaves rustling, under the press of a faint breeze.

Adam said, 'It doesn't look like anyone has been down here in a while. I've noticed very few tyre tracks, and the ones that are visible are pretty washed out. There are also many leaves and broken branches on the track which have not been pressed into the mud.'

She smiled in response, wondering if he ever switched off and enjoyed life for the moment?

Adam kept looking at his watch and continued at a steady pace. She laughingly asked, 'Are you late for a meeting?'

'No, but your grandfather said that he drove down the track for just over half a mile, before making his way to the right towards a rocky outcrop. I reckon that should be around 15 minutes or so at walking pace along this track.'

'Why didn't we drive?'

'We are just two tourists, going for a walk in the woods and no one will hear us on foot. Besides your grandfather drove a military vehicle, which was made for these roads, our little compact, with its road tyres and weak suspension, probably wouldn't make it a hundred yards. It would also be challenging to explain as to what we were doing driving into the forest.'

Rebecca felt slightly foolish and wished she had never asked and returned her thoughts to the natural beauty and sounds of the forest as they continued walking.

Adam looked at his watch again and suddenly stopped, 'Right, that's fifteen minutes gone.'

He looked at the map and said, 'The contours on the topographical map indicate a slight rise in the landscape off to the right, maybe eighty to one hundred and fifty yards into the trees. This may be the rocky outcrop we are looking for.'

He began to head off the path, and Rebecca followed. The trees were dense but the going underfoot was relatively good. It took them nearly ten minutes before they located the rock formation which rose, out of the forest floor. It was not an exceptionally large formation and only rose to approximately fifteen feet before disappearing back into the earth.

Adam looked at the map and the notes which he carried and compared a pencil drawing of the outcrop to what he could see. He walked around the perimeter until he found a match, 'That's it!' he exclaimed, showing Rebecca the drawing which she compared to the rocks before her.

'It's incredible!' she whispered.

'Right, then that means that we need to dig just under that overhang,' Adam said, as he dropped the maps and the nylon sack and walked over to a patch of dry soil beneath a protruding piece of rock.

He dug down through the soil, which had, mostly, been protected from the elements by the rock and had been further desiccated, by the action of the surrounding tree roots.

The soil itself was relatively easy to dig through, but his progress was slowed as he had to slice through layers of roots. Nearly three feet down, he hit something hard. He stopped momentarily and then began to square off the base of the hole, revealing a dark green sheet, covered bundle. He used the shovel to prize the item out of the hole and once loosened, picked it up, lifting it onto the side.

Adam climbed out of the pit, and they both just stood, part in disbelief and part in anticipation, looking at the bundle. Adam leant down and pulled off the old tarpaulin, and the tattered, somewhat rotted, military greatcoat underneath to reveal, a large book and a dusty, black, metal box. Clearly emblazoned on the front was the SS symbol which still shone brightly.

Adam examined the box and said, 'It's welded shut. I will have to get some tools to break into it.'

He picked up the book. The outside was moderately deteriorated, but on opening it he read out incredulously, 'It's 'Mein Kampf!' Unbelievable! ...This copy has been signed personally by Adolf Hitler!'

Adam threw the greatcoat and tarp into the hole, shovelling the soil back on top. He grabbed a few handfuls of leaves and twigs and scattered them over the disturbed earth to further disguise it. He then threw the shovel far off, into the undergrowth, before they headed back to the car with the box and the book. Catching a faint breeze, Rebecca thought that she could smell a very light scent of Eau de toilette in the air. It was one that she recognized but not one that

Adam used to her knowledge. And anyway, he was downwind of her. She looked about to find its source, by which time it had gone. Passing it off as her imagination she carried on, thinking no more of it.

Partway along the track, Adam suddenly stopped as a startled bird took flight, off to the left and deeper into the forest. Rebecca looked at him and felt petrified as she saw the intensity of concentration on his face. She also observed that he had deftly drawn a pistol from his pocket. They both waited in silence for nearly ten minutes, until Rebecca could take it no more. She laid her hand gently on his arm and said in a hushed voice befitting the tense situation, 'What's wrong, Adam, you are scaring me?'

He said nothing but put his finger to his mouth, signifying that she should remain quiet. He then waited another few minutes before indicating that she should follow him. They crept silently off the track and into the woods, just enough that they could still make out the trail though they were themselves mostly concealed. They slowly passed through the trees, following a parallel route towards the place where the car was parked. Then, a few moments later, there came another noise, further away and nearer to where the box had been buried. It was barely audible but sounded like a dead branch breaking – as if someone had stood on it. At the sound of this, Adam picked up the pace, though remaining in the trees and desperately trying to make as little noise as possible.

As the tarmac road came into sight and they could see the outline of their car, Adam slowed his pace, continually looking all around, the gun held at the ready. Rebecca's heart was pounding as she kept close to him. Moments later, they were on the tarmac road walking back to the car. Adam opened it, quickly throwing the box and book onto the back seat as he said, 'Jump in!'

Having done so, a whole host of birds took flight deeper in the forest, clearly disturbed by something. Adam started the engine and reversed the car into the track to turn around, back towards Nauendorf. He revved the engine, and the car spun out of the muddy surface, before finding grip on the tarmac as he raced down the road. Taking the first bend, he slowed down, lowering his window as he did so. Rebecca followed his gaze and saw a Blue Mercedes tucked off the road behind some trees. Adam quickly aimed the gun out through the window and fired. One of the car's front tyres exploded as Adam accelerated away.

The noise of the shot had been deafening and had badly shaken Rebecca, who had not expected it. When she had gathered her thoughts, she turned to him and said, 'What did you do that for?'

'I'm just taking precautions. That car had not been there when we first came, and it is not the kind of vehicle a forestry worker would use. It also seems peculiar, that it should be parked some distance away from the track and partially hidden.'

Rebecca said nothing to this, and Adam continued, 'The people who are after us are ruthless and are clearly very resourceful. We must take great care. Whatever is in that box is extremely important to them. I'm going to dump this car, and we can go by train for the next part of our journey.'

Rebecca did not respond, preferring to look out of the window, lost in her own thoughts.

Stefan and Kaspar had entered the forest with Leopold, but they had returned once they eventually found the spot that had been disturbed by Adam, leaving Leopold to excavate it. They had raced back to their car, only to hear the pistol shot and to see Adam's car disappearing down the road amid clouds of dust, just as they came out of the trees.

Chapter Forty-one

KRÜGER WAS PASSED THE receiver by Karl. He answered with a curt, 'Hallo?'

'It's Kaspar, sir.'

Kaspar continued, 'Herr Krüger, we tracked them to a forest near to Arnstadt. The man and woman entered the forest with a shovel, and so we followed them. Some way in, they seem to have dug a hole near some rocks and then filled it back in, before leaving.'

Crouched down by the side of the road and beside Kaspar, Stefan was busily trying to change the wheel of the car, as fast as he could.

Hearing a sound behind him, Kaspar turned to see Leopold running through the forest towards him. He was filthy, covered in mud, twigs and dead leaves having had to dig the hole out by hand as he couldn't find the shovel.

'Sir, a moment please,' Kaspar said.

Turning to Leopold, who arrived panting heavily and who looked quite irritated, he said, 'Well?'

'There's nothing there Kaspar, except some old rags, but they look like they are German military issue from the war.'

'Herr Krüger, it appears that they have retrieved something, which was buried in the forest which may date back to the war.'

'What was it?' Krüger said, trying to contain his excitement.

'I'm not sure, sir. We only saw them from a distance, but it looked like a box of some sort.'

Kaspar swallowed hard as he went on, 'I think they may suspect we were following them, as they shot out one of our tyres. We are trying to fix ...'

'What!' Krüger yelled, watched intently by Müller.

'Herr Krüger, it could be that they were just cautious. Anyway, Leopold put a tracking device on their car last night, so as long as we are able to get going quickly, we can keep on after them. Stefan has nearly changed the tyre already.'

Herr Krüger said in a profoundly menacing voice, 'No more mistakes!'

'Sir!' Kaspar replied in the affirmative.

On hearing of the awful turn of events, Herr Müller flew into a tirade, which only subsided ten minutes later when Krüger received another call from Kaspar to say that they were in pursuit once more and that the tracker was performing well.

Herr Müller sat in contemplation for a short while and then turned to Krüger saying, 'Inform the men that if they do get a clear and safe chance to get what belongs to us, then they may take the opportunity. They *must* be absolutely sure that the items are with these two individuals and that they can safely obtain them. I do not care what they must do to complete their task. I cannot risk the chance of these individuals escaping.'

Krüger replied, 'Yes, sir.'

CHAPTER FORTY-TWO

Steigenberger Grandhotel Handelshof, Leipzig, Saxony, Germany

ADAM DROVE ON IN THE direction of Bad Berka, as they then headed, onwards, towards Leipzig. He stopped briefly in Naumberg to pick up some tools from a hardware shop and shortly after leaving the town, turned into a quiet country road where he pulled the car over. He used a cold chisel and a club hammer and began to break open the box. The joints had weakened over time, and it was relatively easy to work. Opening the lid, Rebecca and Adam saw a black leather case which, when opened, contained various files with documents inside.

Adam discarded the metal box and the tools in the roadside undergrowth and threw the leather case into the car before heading off for Leipzig. They left the car, parked in a side street in a less affluent suburb of the city, with the key in the ignition and the doors unlocked, before taking a bus into the centre. Adam made a booking at the impressive Steigenberger Grandhotel Handelshof, as it was relatively close to the train station. They went to their separate rooms, where they freshened up before Rebecca joined Adam. Later Adam telephoned down for room service, ordering dinner, and after it had been delivered, they opened the briefcase and began to look through the papers while they ate.

The documents were in code, and they tried to make sense of them. But it was impossible, and it appeared that the meaning was indecipherable.

Adam pondered, 'I have a friend who used to be a Navy Seal. He met his wife in the military before she began to work for the NSA. She's now heading up the corporate security team for an American conglomerate.'

Rebecca said, 'NSA?'

'The American National Security Agency. I could try her, she might be able to help, or to put us in touch with someone who may know more.'

'Sure, whatever you think.'

Adam called a number in New York, and after four rings, a sleepy voice said, 'Uh ...Yeah?'

'Abe, its Adam.'

'Huh, Adam ...uh ...why are you calling so early?'

'Sorry, but I'm in Germany at the moment and was hoping you, or actually, Emily could help me with something.'

'Well, sure ...hang on a minute ...' He suddenly went on, 'Are you ok buddy?'

'Yes, fine thanks.'

A moment later, Emily's soft tones, in stark contrast to Abe's gruffness, sang out with, 'Hey, Adam ...how's it going?'

'Fine thanks. I'm sorry to call, but I was hoping that you could tell me which codes the Nazis used during the Second World War to encrypt secrets? ...And how to break them?'

'Woah!' Emily laughed, 'I haven't even had breakfast yet. What on earth are you up to?'

'I'm sorry, Emily, I really can't say at the moment.'

'You've intrigued me now?' she laughed and continued, 'Well, let me see. I studied them, of course, during my training, but it was a while ago.'

She was quiet for a moment, collecting her thoughts, 'Well, they could have been using any number of codes. Often the Enigma machine was used, though the Nazis began to have suspicions, towards the end of the war, that it had been compromised. That's the most legendary one. Others might be ...teleprinter stream cyphers, possibly the Lorenz cypher ...maybe a Book code or Cipher, or the Geheimfernschreiber ... the Reservehandverfahren ...'

'Wait!' Adam said, looking at the copy of Mein Kampf which lay on his bed, 'What do you mean by a book code?'

'Well, a book code gives references to a page, a line and a word in a book. If the words are more specialist and may not appear in the book, then a book cypher is preferred, where the reference in the book is to a letter or number in a particular book rather than a word. It is more laborious to encrypt and decipher, but ...'

Adam butted in, 'What book needs to be used?'

Emily was slightly taken aback by his abruptness, saying, 'Well ...that's the joy of this type of code, it can be any book. If both parties, sender and receiver, have the same book with the same edition of it, then it is relatively straightforward. Spies liked it because if the book in their possession was not unusual, then they were difficult to entrap. Also, if ...'

'Can you tell me how they work?' Adam cut in.

It began to cross Emily's mind that he had been drinking. 'Well ...yes, sure I can. Let me see, well a book code ...' She then went on at length to discuss the way book codes and cyphers were encrypted and cracked.

When she had finished, Adam said, 'Thanks Emily, you've been great!' after a few brief pleasantries, Adam rang off.

Emily took the phone, with the dead tone, from her ear and stared at it.

Turning to Abe and smiling, she said, 'Your friends are just plain weird!'

Abe laughed and pulled her close as they cuddled up under the bedclothes again enjoying each other's warmth.

Adam and Rebecca began to try to decipher

the codes. It was terribly slow going, but it started to yield results.

By the next morning, they knew precisely where they were going and why.

While Rebecca showered, Adam took the opportunity and telephoned Castle Zbiroh and booked them a room.

Kaspar found their parked car with the tracker but did not go near it for over an hour until he saw two rough-looking youths eying it up. It was clear that they were about to steal it, and as they climbed into the unlocked car, Kaspar stepped out of the doorway he was hiding in. He levelled his gun at the boy who fancied himself as the driver. The child froze solid, as did the other individual.

Kaspar waved his head in a gesture of – Get lost! The two terrified lads did not need another invitation as they disappeared off, into a nearby park.

Walking past the car, Kaspar noticed that the keys had been left in the ignition and he instantly realised why.

He ran back to his own car and said to Leopold and Stefan, 'They've dumped the car. Let's get to the train station and the car hire. After that, we can try the hotels.'

Chapter Forty-three

Leipzig Hauptbahnhof, Leipzig, Saxony, Germany

REBECCA AND ADAM HAD gone to sleep, and by the time they awoke, they had missed breakfast in the hotel, so they checked out. Adam paid the invoice in cash and glancing at the itemised bill, he noticed that a phone call had been made the previous night from Rebecca's room to a UK mobile and that it had lasted for four minutes. Thoughtful, he memorised the number and dropped the sheet into a rubbish bin.

They went for a short stroll, taking their luggage with them. Walking around the town centre to get some fresh air they stopped at the historic Zills Tunnel restaurant. They decided to eat a light snack there, before walking to the train station.

There was a short queue for tickets, and Adam continually surveyed the surroundings, while they waited. He was scanning the area for anything which seemed untoward, but he saw nothing to concern him. Rebecca looked up at the lofty ceilings of the magnificent Leipzig Hauptbahnhof, which she understood to be the largest train station in the world. She had become used to Adam's constant surveillance of everyone and everything and was now less concerned by it. She thought to herself how elegant and cavernous the building was, with its tall ceilings and the classy shopping malls below.

After buying their tickets, they had little time left and had to hurry to the platform. They were catching the 11:31 to Dresden-Neustadt, where they were to change trains before taking the 13:02 to Prague.

Rebecca and Adam boarded and sat down together, keeping their luggage bags and the leather briefcase with them. There was also a steady stream of other people rushing for the train. Though Adam viewed some with suspicion, none particularly caught his attention. Some, however, were worthy of more attention, unknown to Adam.

The trip passed by uneventfully and they spent the time in silence, looking out of the windows at the countryside, lost in their own thoughts. Under an hour later they arrived in Dresden and alighted the train.

CHAPTER FORTY-FOUR

Bahnhof Dresden-Neustadt, Dresden, Saxony,
Germany

IT HAD TAKEN THE NEO-NAZI'S more than four hours of methodical searching and bribes before they tracked the couple down to their hotel and then on to the train station. After that, it was just a matter of waiting and watching, while, between them, they tried to get some rest.

Along with the other passengers and Rebecca and Adam, the Germans alighted the train. They had headed out towards the main concourse with its throngs of people and bought coffees at the cafeteria.

There was just over half an hour to wait, and the neo-Nazis surreptitiously kept watch while Adam scanned the area. With only fifteen minutes to go until the next train arrived, Rebecca said, 'I'm just popping to the loo.'

Adam responded, 'Fine, I'll come with you.'

They walked over together, and once Adam had seen her enter the ladies, he disappeared into the men's lavatory. The facility was spotless, and from the strong smell of cleaning fluid, it seemed as if it had just been cleaned. There was no one else in the toilet until just before he was about to leave. Adam had washed his hands and was drying them when two men entered together. He recognised them from the Leipzig train, though, he remembered, they had joined it separately. They glared at Adam and walked straight towards him, as they began pulling guns from their shoulder holsters. The first man started to say, 'Hände hoch ...'

Adam violently swept his arm across the front of the leading man's body, catching his gun hand as he did so and putting it out of harm's way. He then swiftly brought his right fist up, smashing his knuckles cruelly into the neo-Nazis jaw. As he fell back, the man knocked into the other German, pushing him sideways. However, the second German recovered quickly and began to raise his gun towards Adam before he had time to react.

Adam stopped still, aware of the danger of his predicament. As he rapidly considered his options, he became aware of a slight trickle of blood running down his hand.

Suddenly, Adam saw another two men silently enter the doorway behind the two Germans. They were dressed as businessmen, and both wore glasses. Adam's heart sank, as he realised that the odds against him, were now too high.

The second German had levelled his gun at Adam and was smiling, looking as if he were about to fire when Adam heard the sound of two soft 'cracks'. They were the unmistakable sounds of a silenced handgun being fired. The German's head jolted sideways and smashed against the wall, as his hand and body sagged in tandem, his gun making a clatter as it fell to the ground. As quickly as they had appeared, the second pair of men had disappeared.

Adam stood looking, in amazement, at the two Germans who lay in a heap. The first had a bullet wound through his temple, the second, a shot fired through the base of his skull. Adam grabbed one of their guns and stepping over them looked out onto the concourse, just in time to see the other two individuals walking in single file out of a side entrance. The man ahead was clearly shielding the shooter, while he unscrewed the SAK suppressor from the barrel of the Walther P22 before he tucked them inside his overcoat.

Adam was utterly mystified. He went back into the toilet and quickly dragged the two lifeless bodies into one of the cubicles. Adam then locked the cubicle door from the inside and climbed back out. Quickly grabbing some toilet paper, he cleaned the blood from the floor, before throwing it into a waste bin.

As he left, he looked towards the ladies' toilet, just as Rebecca appeared.

'Let's go! ...or we'll miss the train,' he called, trying his best to smile.

As she came to him, Adam grabbed her hand, and they both walked swiftly to the platform where the train waited.

Rebecca thought that Adam was looking about him, more than usual. She wondered why but felt that he was just more cautious as there were so many people milling around in the station.

They showed their ticket to the railway clerk and joined the melee of other passengers catching the 13:02 bound for Prague. The train was reasonably full and within minutes of them sitting down it began to pull out of the station. Adam looked over at the entrance to the toilet and just caught sight of three men in business suits entering the gents in a group. Two of them were pulling oversized suitcases on wheels. Rebecca was beginning to become unnerved by Adam, who was clearly more on edge than usual.

'What is it, Adam? You're frightening me!' she murmured.

'Nothing! Don't worry, I just like to be careful, particularly in crowded places,' he replied.

She accepted his response, though she still felt tense. Rebecca was tired, and it was not long before she fell into a deep sleep with her head gently wedged between the window and the seatback.

Adam did not sleep. He kept a constant watch, while he tried to unravel and make sense of the events which had occurred at the

Dresden-Neustadt station. Someone else was interested in their quest, and he knew not who or why!

Chapter Forty-five

Interpol headquarters, Quai Charles de Gaulle, Lyon, France

JULIETTE LIGHTLY KNOCKED ON Eirik's marginally open door and walked in as he said, 'Come in!'

She said, 'We've had reports in from the British and the German's. Scotland Yard tracked the couple to a hotel in East Anglia via the use of their credit cards. The hotel had the number of the car they were using, as it was in their private car park. It belonged to the dead man in Cleobury Mortimer, the vehicle has since disappeared. The Brits have not had any further information. The German Bundeskriminalamt has tracked the use of their cards from northern Germany, then south-east to Leipzig and more specifically the Zill's Tunnel restaurant. The police also think that the individuals had stayed at the Steigenberger Grandhotel Handelshof. But by the time the police had attended, the individuals had left over an hour previously.'

She paused, catching her breath and continued, 'The hotel staff were questioned about the individuals, but they gave the police little to go on. The reception staff did say, however, that they had been questioned and offered large bribes, by two unsavoury Germans. The men were after information about the couple which they did not divulge, and they made it clear that they had declined the money. The men had attended within minutes of the couple leaving. They had asked to see their room, but this was also declined. The staff said that they were very menacing and only left when the manager intimated that he would call the police about them. The men did not say which organisation they represented, though we can guess.'

Eirik Jensen said thoughtfully, 'I would not like to be in their position with neo-Nazis tracking me! I wonder why these people are so important to the Germans?'

Juliette responded, 'It must be a high priority as the Germans are throwing everything at it,' she continued, 'Unfortunately, the trail has gone cold again!'

Eirik considered the train of events and said, 'Right, well keep on it. You'd better let your contact at the Bundeskriminalamt know everything we have on this and offer them full cooperation. I'll speak to Chief Superintendent O'Connor myself to keep him appraised of the situation.'

CHAPTER FORTY-SIX

K RÜGER WAS PASSED THE receiver by Karl.

'Herr Krüger, its Kaspar. The couple have just boarded a train heading south towards Prague. We didn't get anyone on the train.'

'What!'

'Sir, Stefan and Leopold have disappeared.'

'What do you mean disappeared?' Krüger barked.

The men in the room all stared silently at Krüger as he spoke, while Müller had a look on his face, which was impossible to read.

'The station is very crowded. They were following the couple, while I waited by the main entrance and watched the concourse. When the pair reappeared, Stefan and Leopold were not following them. The couple then ran for the train and were some of the last to get on it. I have searched the train station, but I cannot find any trace of either of our men.'

Krüger said, 'Do you think this man is to blame for their disappearance or have the police or security forces picked them up?'

'I don't know, I can't understand it,' Kaspar said despondently.

'Right, I will get other assets to Prague. Keep a lookout for our men and then make your own way to Prague on the next train,' Krüger barked, as he killed the call and gave the phone back to Karl.

Krüger glanced over at Müller and said, while the others listened, 'As you will have gathered, Stefan and Leopold have disappeared. Kaspar does not know if the couple had a hand in it or if other forces are coming in to play. These people appear to be making for Prague. We will intercept them there.'

Everyone looked at Müller. He had a face like thunder but said nothing: the only sound, the crackling of the burning wood in the fireplace.

CHAPTER FORTY-SEVEN

Collections Department, Mossad headquarters, Tel Aviv, Israel

THE CALL FROM THE EMBASSY in Bern was patched through to Ariel Mandler's phone, 'Yes Ezra!' he said.

'Hello sir, I just wanted to inform you of a development. The neo-Nazis made a move on the man they have been tracking, but our agents neutralised two of them before they could kill him.'

'Good, well done! Were they seen?' Ariel questioned.

'Only briefly by the quarry, but by no one else. The man and the woman have now boarded a train heading south. I have another of our teams tracking the couple now.'

'What about the bodies? I don't want the German authorities getting wind of this.'

'My team have retrieved the bodies, and they

are currently in-transit to a landfill site outside the city. The corpses will never be found.'

'Excellent ...Let me know of any further updates as they occur.'

Ariel slowly dropped the phone back into its cradle as he pondered the matter.

CHAPTER FORTY-EIGHT

Great Falls, Virginia, USA

MURPHY OPENED THE BACK door of his home and walked down the garden slope to the summer house on the edge of the wood which neighboured his property on one side.

On entering, he found Miller waiting for him. They had decided that it might be best for his former subordinate to park his car some way off and to approach the house through the trees, meeting in the small building. Murphy made a mental note to have the building checked by his handyman as he felt there was a distinct smell of damp inside.

Murphy was glad to see Miller, 'Thank you for coming to see me Tom', he said.

'It's my pleasure, sir,' he replied.

'Well, have you anything new to report?'

'Yes, sir. The new Director, Paul Shultz, is

seeing an awful lot of the President for some reason. It's not just the number of meetings, but also the peculiar duration.'

'What do these meetings concern?' Murphy enquired.

'No one seems to know, or at least it is nothing obvious, even though it is out of the ordinary. There has been no further mention of the killings in England, and there have been no investigations ordered into it. If anything, it is a no-go area for our office.'

Miller continued, 'I have also heard a rumour that President Brown may be heading to Russia in the next month or so, for a meeting with the Russian President, Ivanov. It's a rush job, and the purpose of the meeting seems to be unspecified.'

Murphy looked puzzled and said, 'How strange, there had never been any hint of that previously.'

'No, and I always thought that the two leader's relationship, if anything, was rather frosty.'

'Quite!' Murphy said.

Miller replied, 'I have cajoled some of my contacts in Europe and within Langley. It appears that the old man who was killed in England was a former Major in the SS. He was given a false identity, for an undetermined reason, by the British and was passing himself off as a Swiss National. He must have been in some danger as he had guards, who were all ex-military.'

Miller paused and then continued, 'The British believe that one of his guards could be in league with the Germans or may even have abducted the dead man's granddaughter.'

'Anything else?' Murphy enquired.

'Yes, the Israelis are involved. They have active teams in the UK and in Germany working on this matter. They are putting a lot of resources into it. Whatever it is, it's big!'

Murphy looked pensive, 'The Israelis, hey?' He looked out of the window into the garden and without turning to face Miller he said, 'Any idea what the link is between these various strands?'

'No, not yet, sir, but I am certain that there is a link.'

'Yes. So am I Tom! So am I!'

He stood in silence for an age, looking down towards the river and then turned to Tom saying, 'Thank you, Tom. We will speak again.'

Murphy left the garden room and returned to the house. Miller watched him go and waited for twenty minutes. He then departed through the hidden backdoor where he had first entered. It led into dense scrub followed by a moderate stroll back through the trees to his car, accompanied by the happy chatter of finches and the occasional haunting call of a crow.

Murphy walked into his laundry room. Pressing a wooden panel on the wall, it popped open. Revealed, in an alcove, was an old-fashioned telephone with the handset attached to the base by a spiral wire cord. Unseen, behind the wall, the telephone line disappeared below Murphy's house to an incoming point in his neighbour's house.

His neighbour, a retired colonel in the Marines, was an old friend and golfing partner. No questions asked, he had allowed Murphy, years before, to have the secret line installed. It was billed as one of the colonel's phone lines, while Murphy paid his golf club membership in recompense.

Murphy used this secure line to phone a number in Italy, which he had been given years before. And then he waited.

CHAPTER FORTY-NINE

Praha-Holešovice Railway Station, Prague, Czech
Republic

THE TRAIN PULLED INTO PRAGUE station later that afternoon, and Rebecca
woke with a start as the train jolted to a
stop.

'Wake up sleepy head!' Adam mocked; in the
cheeriest voice, he could muster.

Rebecca sat up and arched back as she yawned
out and looked around, 'Have we arrived?'

'Yes, we're in Prague.'

'Come on, let's go,' he said, smiling.

She thought to herself how warm and pleasant he could be when he just relaxed. But Adam
was far from relaxed, he just tried to hide his inner thoughts more carefully.

Rebecca, still tired, was slow to get up from
her seat and also to prepare to leave. Adam
glanced about him, while she readied herself,

content that they were likely to be reasonably safe in the crowded station.

Eventually, they stepped down off the train and walked along the platform lost amid the other passengers, who had also alighted the train.

'Where are we going now, Adam?' Rebecca said.

'We need to hire a car and then we will head out of the city as soon as possible. There is no reason to hang about here.'

They walked over to the tourist information office and spoke to the lady behind the counter. Adam asked her about the history of the station and pretended to look about the building as she gave him a quick synopsis. He could not see anyone who obviously gave him cause for concern. However, he also knew that a real professional would be difficult to spot among the throng of people.

When the lady had finished, she pointed them in the direction of the Sixt car hire firm, which was just opposite the entrance to the railway station.

They walked the short distance to the office and then waited while the man behind the counter served the customer ahead of them. Rebecca took the opportunity to sit down again and to rest. Adam looked out of the windows paying particular attention to anyone who was looking in their direction.

The customer ahead of him finished his business and Adam booked a car. As he finalised the paperwork, the vehicle arrived, and the driver came into the office, passing the keys to Adam.

Shortly after they left the car rental office, they were on their way out of the bustling city heading for Zbiroh. Unseen amidst the masses of people, a man left the train station and climbed into a car which had just pulled up by the pavement. He had been watching the pair since they had arrived in Prague. The man continued to follow Rebecca and Adam at a safe distance as they passed out through the suburbs.

Chapter Fifty

Collections Department, Mossad headquarters, Tel Aviv, Israel

THE UNTRACEABLE CALL WAS patched through, from the clandestine Israeli installation in Italy, to Mossad headquarters, Tel Aviv, Israel.

'Ariel, how are you, my old friend?' Murphy asked.

'John, how lovely to hear from you. Yes, I am very well, thank you. Though I was sorry to be informed of your difficulties. Most unfortunate and most unwelcome.'

Murphy did not dwell on this, preferring to break the ice by asking about Mandler's family and other such pleasantries, before getting down to the real reason for the call.

Eventually, Murphy, to Mandler's amusement, said, 'Now, you are probably wondering why I would be calling you so unexpectedly?'

'Well ...' Mandler said, thinking that he had an idea what the call was about.

'May I speak candidly, Ariel?' Murphy butted in.

'Yes, yes ... please do,' Mandler retorted.

'You will know of my sudden departure as Director, and you will almost certainly know, that I was forced out.'

'Yes, that is my understanding.'

'I have been trying to investigate what prompted my removal, and I believe that it may have a great deal to do with a recent murder in England? One that your office is keeping close tabs on.'

'My dear John,' Mandler said with genuine affection, for he had always liked and trusted Murphy, 'please take care what you say, there may be those in your own country who would like nothing better than to finish you off with a treason charge.'

'Thank you for the advice, Ariel. I know that it is well-meant. However, events are moving on, and my personal safety is no longer of importance.'

Mandler's eyebrows raised up, and he was silent for a moment, before saying, 'You are correct, we are investigating certain events in England. They have links to a neo-Nazi group which we have monitored for a very long time. The matter in hand appears to be of major significance to these fascists and could well have worldwide significance.'

'Can you tell me anything else?' Murphy asked.

'At present,' Mandler mused, 'I'm sorry but ...no.'

Mandler continued, 'Can *you* give me any information, John?'

Murphy thought for a moment and then broke the habit of a lifetime, 'Yes ...yes, I think I can.'

He paused and then continued, 'My demise followed swiftly on the heels of the President finding out about the killings in England. I believe that Brown, though he tries to hide it, is extremely interested in this and subsequent events. My replacement, Shultz, is a strange choice and an unpopular one. Once in place, Shultz was also absorbed by this matter, but not so interested it seems that he wanted to start a formal investigation. If anything, it appears that he wished to prevent one. Now I understand that there is a rush meeting being arranged with Ivanov, the Russian President. I feel, strongly, that there is a common thread which runs through these matters. You may also have heard reports that the Russians seem to be interfering with elections in various countries, with, as yet no clearly definable agenda.'

Mandler considered Murphy's response. He was plainly shocked that Murphy, who had always played his cards close to his chest, should be so candid at this point.

'John,' Mandler said with great compassion and sincerity, 'I know this call must have been tough for you to make. But I believe that it is one which will benefit both of our countries in the long term. We, in Israel, are very troubled by the general trends. The rise of the far-right in Europe, particularly in Germany, Austria and the Scandinavian countries and the role Russia was playing. Thank you for the information which you have given to me. I will look into these matters, and when I have anything that may assist you, I will be in contact.'

They said goodbye, each with a better appreciation of their opposite number.

Mandler thought for a moment and then asked Daniel to come into his room. There were matters which needed to be set in motion.

Chapter Fifty-One

Hotel Continental, Pilsen, Western Bohemia, Czech Republic

HERR MÜLLER AND HIS ENTOURAGE had left the Harz Mountains and made their way to the city of Pilsen in the Czech Republic, which was relatively close to Zbiroh.

Leaving early in the morning in several cars, they had lunch in the spa town of Bad Lobenstein before continuing onwards to Pilsen. The journey was uneventful, and the group arrived in the mid-afternoon just as a light drizzle had begun to fall.

They checked into the Hotel Continental, which retained a glorious, old-world charm, something which Müller appreciated.

Müller had left Krüger and Karl at the hunting lodge, deep in the Harz forest. They were crucial and would remain the centre of operations.

Herr Müller's group had booked four suites

and rested themselves before preparations were to be begun for the drive to Zbiroh.

Two hours later, Kaspar arrived at the Hotel Continental with Emil and Nagel, who had been drafted in to help. He asked for Herr Müller's room at the reception, only to be told that he and his 'friends' had gone across the street to a bar for a drink.

The three men left the hotel and walked across the busy road before entering the bar. The rain had just begun to subside, leaving glossy dampness on the pavement.

Kaspar saw the Germans huddled in a corner and made his way over to them. As he did so, they stopped talking, and all turned to look at him. 'Good afternoon Herr Müller,' he said, ignoring the other men.

Müller did not reply; instead, he just gave Kaspar a withering look.

'Sir, may I ask if anything has been heard about Stefan and Leopold?'

Sneeringly Müller said, 'I think it is pretty clear that we will not be hearing from them again. Not in this world!'

Müller glared at Kaspar, before snapping, 'Sit down!'

Kaspar sat down immediately, as did the others who had arrived with him. He felt sick to his stomach.

They then, in unison, listened intently as the plans were laid out concerning the Zbiroh matter. Müller emphasised that the man they were following had proved himself to be very resourceful and extremely dangerous. He had passed a cruel look towards Kaspar, as he mentioned this final warning.

Chapter Fifty-two

THE OTHERS HAD BEEN GONE FOR many hours.

Krüger stood alone in the room listening to the violent crackling of the fire, as the three dogs lay on the rug, fast asleep. Earlier, he had taken them for a long walk to help clear his mind and to exhaust them. He felt invigorated by the exercise, the cheery sounds of the birds and most of all by the damp forest smells.

He was holding a glass of whiskey, though he had not drunk any of its contents. Walking over to the window, he looked out into the darkening forest. His mind was preoccupied. Unseen, the lynx watched him from the undergrowth as a chill wind swirled through the branches.

Krüger was unhappy that he had been left behind, though he appreciated that Müller had wanted someone left at the lodge who he could trust. He also knew that there was no way that Müller would have missed this moment of discovery.

After some time, Krüger turned and walked back to the fire.

The lynx lost interest, blinked and softly made his way further into the forest, brushing past the scrub. It was killing time once more.

The wild cat had not been alone in watching Krüger. However, the other eyes, which monitored the lodge, were human. Unlike the creature, they did not lose interest.

CHAPTER FIFTY-THREE

Collections Department, Mossad headquarters, Tel Aviv, Israel

DANIEL CAME INTO MANDLER'S office without knocking.

Mandler said thoughtfully, 'Daniel, I have another task for you. It is related to the matter in hand.'

Mandler took a deep breath before continuing, 'I want you to get on to our agents in the Kremlin and find out whatever you can about the meeting which is being proposed between Ivanov and the American President. Also, I need you to investigate Ivanov, President Brown and Paul Shultz, the new Director of the CIA. Find out if there is any possible link between them and if any of them might have a connection to this neo-Nazi matter?'

Daniel stood, stupefied, staring at Mandler.

'Well, get on with it!' Mandler barked, impatient with the delay.

'Yes ...yes, sir,' Daniel stuttered before leaving the room.

As he walked along the corridor and back to his room, he tried to make sense of what he had just been asked. He could not think, on any basis, what those disparate elements could possibly have in common.

CHAPTER FIFTY-FOUR

REBECCA AND ADAM HEADED south-west of Prague and onwards towards Zbiroh. On the way, in the suburbs of the city, Adam had stopped at several specialist stores and had bought some more tools, scuba equipment and climbing gear.

Unseen, and several cars back the neo-Nazi's who followed had been joined by another vehicle, allowing them to alternate, making it more challenging to spot them. The fascists were not overly concerned if they lost their quarry as they were, by then, quite sure where they were going.

CHAPTER FIFTY-FIVE

Castle Zbiroh, Křivoklát and Brdy Forest, Western Bohemia, Czech Republic

THE LIGHT WAS JUST BEGINNING to fade by the time they reached the magnificent castle resplendent in its Neo-Renaissance architecture. It was a glorious sight, rising, as it did, above the vast and charming Křivoklátské and Brdy Forests of Western Bohemia.

Zbiroh Chateau had a rich history and a host of secrets, which she refused to give up, easily. Many of these myths had their beginning during World War II. The intriguing castle had been occupied, for part of the war, by a clandestine SS division. No one in the locality was sure what they had been doing, but one of their tasks seemed to be to monitor radio communications across the world.

The mystique of the castle had abounded

and had drawn conspiracy theorists, right-wing groups, historians and a whole host of treasure hunters ever since the end of the war. Many of the theories had at their centre, the well and talked of secret passages and rooms hidden deep underground. Experts had searched the well repeatedly, finding weapons, jewels and documents sealed in boxes which had been thrown in at the end of the war. The contents of the documents had never been revealed.

But always the investigations were hampered by the fear that the well and other hidden parts of the castle had been heavily mined with explosives by the SS, ready to blow up unwanted intruders.

Adam drove through the middle of three arches, which formed the stone entrance gate, slowing down as he passed between two high columns, fashioned in the style of the Tuscan order. From there, he drove up the winding track until he came to a couple of larger than life, bronze lions standing sentinel, on tall stone plinths, before the gates of the castle. He pulled the car off the track and parked up. As the sound of the engine died, Adam sat momentarily, looking up at the awe-inspiring walls before they alighted, taking their luggage with them. Adam left the tools and the other equipment in the car. He would return for the scuba gear once they had checked in and had located their rooms.

They passed between the imposing lions and through a grand stone archway flanked by two impressive Corinthian columns. The majestic entrance cut through the less austere, creamy yellow, of the painted castle walls. Going through those walls, the pair came out into a large courtyard. It was surrounded on three sides by the lofty edifice of Zbiroh and on the fourth, by a walkway with an ornate, low wall. This gave on to a dreamy view of the forests, mountains and plains beyond and far below.

A large, stone fountain in the centre of the courtyard gave forth a low, bubbling spout of water which softly echoed in the semi-enclosed space. Suddenly a waitress rushed from a restaurant which was set into the castle's ground-floor wall, opposite the walkway.

In passable English, she said, 'Sir, Madam. Please, how may I help you?'

Adam wondered how she had known to speak English and responded, 'We have booked three nights at Zbiroh, from tonight.'

'Please, sir, may I have your name?'

Adam said, 'Mr & Mrs Goldman.'

Rebecca stifled a laugh.

'Please, sir, follow me. May I help you with your luggage?'

'No thank you,' they said in unison.

They accompanied the woman, walking back under the interior arch. Then, passing through a large wooden door, they ascended an ancient, stone staircase within the walls of the castle themselves. At the first floor, they were led, in silence, along a long, dark corridor, to another wooden door at the end. The young lady opened it with an enormous key, which had the appearance of something that was better suited to a collection in a museum, rather than a room key in a hotel.

The door swung open, and as Adam and Rebecca walked into the room, they were both taken aback by the beguiling view of the landscape through the vast windows. The room itself was large and pleasantly furnished and very much, had the sense of great age, as indeed it had.

Leaving two sets of keys on a side table, the lady walked to the door and turning, said, 'Please, if I can be of any further help, let me know.'

Adam leant forward and passing a few coins to her, said, 'No that will be all, thank you.'

'Thank you, sir!' the lady said, smiling at him, a bit too sweetly, he thought, as she turned and left, shutting the door as she went.

As the sound of the young woman's echoing footsteps began to fade. Rebecca screamed, 'Goldman!' bursting out in pent up laughter, as she did so, 'And Mr and Mrs ...you 'are' a little presumptuous, aren't you!'

Adam looked at her, temporarily lost in his thoughts. She felt, fleetingly, that she could detect an almost imperceptible sense of sadness pass over him.

Then suddenly he smiled widely and said, 'I had hoped, you would like my sense of humour.'

They both laughed as they dropped their luggage onto the floor. Adam saw her glance at the double bed, and he said, 'It was the only room they had left, I'm sorry. But I will sleep on the floor.'

Rebecca blushed slightly and looked away, saying nothing.

Quickly, changing the topic, Adam blurted out, 'Right, I'll go down to the car and get the equipment. I'll be back in a few minutes.'

He left without waiting to receive a response.

As Adam came through the arch and walked back outside, between the great lions, he noticed ahead of him, two men walking off down the track. They had come from the direction where his car was parked, and as they disappeared around the bend, one of them appeared to surreptitiously glance back. They were both casually dressed and rather stocky. Adam felt a twinge of suspicion having watched them, though he brushed this off as a faint touch of paranoia. He opened the trunk of the car and pulled out the two, bulky heavy-duty nylon bags which contained his kit. He locked the car again, leaving only the five 12 litre scuba cylinders containing the air for diving.

Darkness began to fall, and he made his way back to the room, marvelling at the castle as he went and pondering that it would be the perfect place for a honeymoon. He laughed involuntarily to himself, wondering where that thought had magically come from.

Returning, he dropped the luggage in the empty room. Hearing the shower flowing at full pelt behind the locked bathroom door. He slipped his hand into Rebecca's bag and retrieved the phone, feelingly quite unsavoury as he did so. The messages had been wiped, as had the recent calls, on what looked to him like a cheap burner phone. Not what he would have expected her to use ordinarily. However, when he checked the contacts section, there was only one name – Fitzgibbon. Adam tapped the name, and the number which was displayed was instantly recognisable as the one she had called in the hotel in Leipzig. Concerned, he replaced the phone.

The name Fitzgibbon was known to him.

Adam slid the bags under the bed and then carelessly picked up a notepad and pencil which lay on the side-table. He wrote a few lines to Rebecca, saying that he would be down in the restaurant having an aperitif and asked that she joined him when she was ready.

Adam descended to the courtyard and walked over towards the restaurant. Seeing the place devoid of people, he decided to reconnoitre the area. Adam continued past the few empty outdoor, tables walking towards another impressive entrance through the castle walls, again supported by classical columns. He climbed the steep, spartan, but impressive stone steps within, before passing through glazed wooden doors and entering another, this time irregularly shaped inner courtyard. A high tower jutted out of the small, sombre, enclosed space from atop of a natural rock obtrusion. Seeing no one Adam crossed the cobbled courtyard slowly, taking careful stock of the environment. Everywhere, evidence of the ancient rocks, bursting through the architecture, which had been built respect-fully, around it. The gloomy enclosure, the moss on the stones, cobbles and on the walls and the deafening silence leant an eerie, almost tactile sense of foreboding to the place.

Following much of the circumference of the walls, an empty, galleried walkway looked down on Adam. Ahead of him, as he passed a glazed wooden staircase set into the castle wall, he saw what he had come for, dropping down into the bowels of the rock – the entrance to, what was said to be, the deepest well in Europe.

Adam retraced his steps, descending the grand staircase back into the courtyard. Looking across at the restaurant, he could now see a young couple sitting outside enjoying a drink together, utterly engrossed in each other. He walked past them and going inside, as the early evening was beginning to chill, he was immedi-ately struck by the darkness of the environment, to the extent that it was almost oppressive. As the large wooden door gently but firmly closed behind him, Adam saw a waiter rushing towards him, 'Please, sir. Will you be dining alone?'

Adam said lazily, 'No, I am expecting a friend.'

'Certainly sir. Please follow me!'

Adam was led to a small table against the far wall by an open fire, which had the appearance of having recently been lit and where the logs were just igniting and beginning to violently crackle. The increasing mellow light helped enhance the atmosphere, as did the lighting, by the waiter, of the candle in the centre of the table.

'Please sir, could I get you an aperitif, while you wait?'

'Yes, do you have Aperol?'

'Certainly, sir,' the waiter said as he disappeared off.

People began to enter the restaurant with increasing regularity, until he saw the door open once more, only to display the enquiring face of Rebecca. She glanced around the darkened room and on noticing Adam broke into a broad smile and walked over to sit with him. Just then, the waiter delivered the drink. She looked tired and had a dishevelled elegance about her, which Adam found enthralling.

Adam was utterly awestruck by her radiant, natural beauty, and for a moment, was almost lost for words.

The waiter asked, 'Please Madam, can I get you an aperitif?'

'Um, yes,' she said, biting her bottom lip ever so gently, 'that looks fun, I'll have one of those,' she said, pointing at Adams glass.

'Madam, yes, I shall bring you an Aperol,' the waiter responded before disappearing again.

Adam said, trying to appear nonchalant, 'You look lovely.'

Rebecca smiled coyly, 'Thank you.'

She looked at Adam quizzically and tried to discern his inner feelings, but frustratingly unable to, she continued, 'Do you know, it's a funny thing ...being here. I can't stop thinking of my grandfather and how I am walking, where he walked, a lifetime ago when he was in his youth. It's so beautiful now and calm, but back then with those SS monsters here, it must have been a scary place.'

'I know, similar thoughts crossed my mind earlier.'

The waiter returned with Rebecca's aperitif, and they took the opportunity to make their food order. She much enjoyed the unusual smell and taste of the drink and relaxed back into her chair, transfixed by the brilliance of its orange-red colour.

Rebecca was very animated and chatty throughout the evening and was, Adam thought, such warm company. He found her easy to listen to and to engage with, and he felt the time slipping by imperceptibly. Occasionally, Adam would glance around the room, keeping track of the comings and goings and subtly assessing the individuals and groups to determine if they might pose a threat.

The place was filled mainly with couples, but two sets were with children and what looked like an au pair or nanny in tow. Adam had more interest in the groups of men. There were several of them, ranging between two to five individuals, all seemed to be separate and all, it appeared, were speaking German. His grasp of the language was not good enough to tell if they were Swiss, Austrian, German or something else and he did not want to ask Rebecca in case it worried her. They were all well dressed, physically fit and ranged between the early twenties to mid-seventies in age. They showed no interest in Rebecca or Adam, and for all he could tell, they were hikers or climbers of whom there were many in the region.

Suddenly the door to the restaurant opened once more and the fading light of the night sky illuminated an excessively thin woman who appeared to be on her own. She was not tall and had a sullen look on her face which was framed with a cheap, bleached, short-cut hairstyle which did not suit her.

Nobody but Adam paid her much attention. She looked about and then walked in and seated herself at a table in the back of the restaurant tucked away in a darkened corner.

The waitress promptly came to take her order, and as she did so, the humourless customer slowly looked her up and down in an unfamiliar and belligerent manner. She snapped that she wanted a coffee, and the waitress left somewhat faster than she had come and looked as if her eyes were beginning to moisten, Adam thought.

The thin woman looked about and on seeing Rebecca glared purposely at her with a glint in her eye. Seeing Adam staring straight back at her, the woman held his gaze somewhat longer than he would have expected and then turned away.

Rebecca had not noticed the woman, which Adam was glad about. Sometime later, the waiter delivered the coffee to the customer, putting it on the table rather abruptly.

Adam did not care for that woman, though he was unconvinced that she was any part of the broader picture.

'I had a look around before you came down,' Adam said to Rebecca.

'I've found the well, it's in a room in a small courtyard just beyond this restaurant.'

'My, but you've been busy,' Rebecca laughingly chided him.

Then she inquired, 'Is it difficult to get to?'

'No, it's a short walk from this courtyard. I think we should wait until the early hours of the morning and then we can start to investigate it.'

Rebecca felt a chill run down her spine, 'Is it safe?'

'Sure, it will be fine,' Adam said, smiling. He could see the concern in Rebecca's face and quickly changed the topic to lighten her mood.

'So, what do you want to do when you grow up?' he said mockingly.

'What a cheek,' she laughed, picking up a bread roll from the basket in front of her and threatening to throw it at him.

'Ok, ok ...I surrender!' Adam smiled.

She grinned across at him as she gently dropped the roll and he was transfixed by the sparkling of her eyes in the candlelight. She looked directly at him in a profoundly intimate manner and said nothing for a moment.

Eventually, she looked away and then returning to his gaze said, 'I don't really know. I used to have all sorts of ideas, but now I feel ...well, a bit mixed up.'

She looked away, with what he felt was a touch of embarrassment. Adam said nothing, there was nothing to say. He just wished the evening could go on forever.

They were interrupted by the waiter who said to Adam, 'Please sir, may I get you a dessert?'

'No not for me,' he said, looking at Rebecca who gently shook her head. He continued, 'Just the bill please.'

They sat in silence until the waiter returned, and then Adam signed off the bill to be added to their room. Leaving a tip, Adam stood up and said, 'Shall we go? We have a long night ahead of us.'

Rebecca stood up and left ahead of Adam. He could see sadness in her eyes now, which consumed his thoughts as he followed her. If he had been more observant at that point, then he might have noticed one of the men in the group of five, carefully watching his exit.

As they crossed the courtyard and came to the stairs up to their apartment, Adam said, 'Why don't you go up and I will just have a short stroll before I go to sleep. I'll wake you at 2.00 a.m.'

Rebecca smiled softly and then turning abruptly, she was gone. Adam walked a circuit of the castle and then followed her to the room.

On opening the door, Adam saw that Rebecca had made a makeshift sleeping bag with a large blanket and was lying on the floor, fast asleep, by the side of the bed. He smiled and went over to the bed, turning down the bedclothes. He then leant down to Rebecca and peeling back the blanket, gently lifted her on to the bed, covering her with the duvet. She hardly stirred, exhausted from the recent events. The touch of her skin and the smell of her perfume were captivating.

Adam then lay down on the floor where Rebecca had been and pulled the blanket, still warm from her body heat, close around him. Setting the alarm on his watch, he slipped off into a deep sleep.

His contentment was not to last.

CHAPTER FIFTY-SIX

Collections Department, Mossad Headquarters, Tel
Aviv, Israel

MANDLER WAS HAVING A NAP when
he awoke to a knock on the door. As he
began to rise from the temporary bed,
he said sleepily, 'Yes, come in.'

The door opened slowly, and as Mandler
stood upright, before rubbing his eyes and walking towards his desk, Daniel walked in with a
troubled look on his face. Mandler was himself,
bemused by this, as he usually found Daniel to
be overconfident, to the point of arrogance.

Mandler pulled his chair back, and as he sat
down, he said more kindly than usual, 'Yes,
Daniel, you have some news for me?'

'I think so, sir ...Yes, I do sir.'

'Go on,' Mandler said lightly.

'Our agents in America and Russia have been
looking into the matter we previously discussed.

They have found certain anomalies, which we did not expect.'

Daniel sighed deeply, almost with a sense of regret, before continuing, 'It would appear that President Brown's grandfather and several members of his family at the time were ardent supporters of fascism even up to the end of the war when the Axis powers were in disarray. The family were never overtly vocal about their views, but both the CIA and the FBI had an interest in them. Then in the mid-1940s and just 'before' the war in Europe had ended they performed a volte-face. There was never again another mention of those extreme right-wing views, amongst that group or any of their descendants. There does appear to have been a concerted effort, understandably, within the family to whitewash their past. We have been able to find links to Germany in his family history. They were mostly German, Welsh and Scots, with a couple of Scandinavians several generations back.'

'Interesting!' Mandler mused to himself.

Daniel drew breath and continued, 'As to the new CIA Director, Paul Shultz, he did have a strong link to both Austria and Germany in his genealogy, not that that, in itself, made him a National Socialist. However, several members of his family certainly were Nazi's. He had two great-uncles who were in the SS and another who worked within the German military intelligence, the Abwehr. One of his great-aunts was particularly notorious. She was also in the SS and worked as a guard at Ravensbrück concentration camp.'

Mandler, incredulous, asked, 'What happened to that revolting bunch?'

Daniel continued, 'Of the two great-uncles in the SS, one died in October 1944 on the Eastern Front. His whole unit was wiped out by the Russians in the battle for Ukraine. It was a common occurrence in that conflict. The other one was captured by partisans in Poland in January 1945. It is understood that he was beaten to death. The Abwehr man is believed to have been killed during the Battle of Berlin in late April 1945. He had been wounded and was listed as captured by the Russians. I think we can guess what happened to him in the end. As to his great-aunt, she was a particularly unpleasant individual. She was hanged by the authorities after the war in a town called Hamelin in Germany.'

Daniel paused for breath and continued, 'But there is something strange about them and other members of the extended family?'

'What is strange?' Mandler questioned.

'Starting in early 1945, there was a concerted and meticulous effort, by the Nazi's to destroy a great deal of the incriminatory information or even the more general information about the whole family. Several departments of the Nazi machine were involved in the process at a remarkably high level, and many of the records disappeared. However, the chaos at the close of the war and the Nazi propensity to document everything, often in triplicate, meant that the task was not fully completed. Shultz's family then emigrated to the States in the early 1950s and have been, on the face of it, exemplary US citizens ever since. Many are churchgoers and have also been in the armed forces, attaining notable ranks. Again, there has been a very real and a successful effort, by the family, to expunge the past. Once more, some might say, understandably.'

Mandler laughed morbidly, 'And Ivanov? Are you going to tell me that he is descended from Adolf Hitler himself?'

Daniel smiled grimly, 'Who knows?' his cryptic words stifled Mandler's mockery before Daniel continued, 'President Ivanov has been more difficult to investigate, as you might well imagine. His grandparents were said to have come from a small village in the hills west of Smolensk in European Russia. The village was destroyed by men from the Nazi Einsatzgruppen in 1943. There was nothing unusual in that, given the history of those brutes. Most of the villagers were summarily shot or sent to concentration camps. Ivanov's grandparents and other relatives were, apparently, killed at that time while Ivanov's father, again apparently, escaped and joined the partisans. While fighting with them, he was severely injured by shrapnel which meant his face was disfigured, and he lost his right eye. In late 1944 the Nazis sent a directive ordering the immediate putting to death of anyone, still alive in their concentration camps, who had come from that village and the closest surrounding villages. The order was methodically carried out.'

'Now that is very peculiar!' Mandler said under his breath.

'After the war, Ivanov's father married a teacher from a Moscow junior school, and they had just one child, Ivanov. His mother died in childbirth, and the father never remarried. His father, who had settled in Moscow on becoming married, worked as a translator for the government. He died nearly ten years ago. Ivanov was said to have been quite close to him, and the two of them regularly went on hunting trips together. The boy became a man, and eventually, he joined the KGB soon after leaving university, where he had studied politics and psychology. It was said of him, by classmates and colleagues, that he was a loner who was ruthless and totally focussed. Ivanov eventually left the security agency and went into politics and the rest, as they say, is history.'

'So, a rather hazy past. How convenient!'

'Sir, there is more. Ivanov's father was sometimes mocked for his accent. He claimed it was because he came from the country, but others from the same region, as he came from, said that it just sounded a bit odd. Some even called him 'little Adolf' for fun because of the accent which they noted sounded slightly Germanic. They suddenly stopped saying it once Ivanov joined the KGB. The father was also said to have been fluent in German, as is Ivanov.'

'Strange that someone from a rural Russian

village should be fluent in German. Are there any more people from his community who survived the war?'

'There were,' Daniel replied.

'Were?' Mandler intoned.

'Yes, that's right *'were'*. Only a few survived, but as far as we can ascertain those people have all died from unnatural deaths, many years ago. Motor accidents, suicide, robberies which went wrong, one house fire ...the list goes on.'

Mandler sat deep in thought as Daniel just blankly looked at him. Daniel trying to read Mandler's thoughts, Mandler ruminated, trying to make sense of his own.

'We have here the pieces of a jigsaw puzzle.' Mandler said.

He continued, 'Well, there certainly appears to be a hidden link between these distinct pieces. Keep digging Daniel. I have a feeling that I may know where this is all going.'

Daniel hoped that Mandler would elucidate, but he did not, and so he left the file with his findings, thus far, on the desk. He turned and left the room and his boss, who was buried in contemplation.

Mandler thought for some time about the recent revelations, trying to piece together the unlikely parts.

He picked up the brown file and read through it before putting a call through to Murphy. As he did so, he sighed very deeply.

The telephonist in Italy had to hold for several minutes while the line rang out. Eventually, there was a click, and a deep American sounding voice boomed, 'Yes!'

The telephonist said, 'Sir, I have a call for you, please hold the line.'

Seconds later the call was patched through to Tel Aviv, and Mandler responded, 'John?'

'Hello, Ariel,' Murphy responded warmly.

'May we talk openly?' Mandler asked.

'Yes, I'm in my ...private office,' Mandler smiled to himself, remembering that Murphy had once told him that his 'private office' was a small laundry room without the space to swing a dead cat.

'Good,' Ariel continued, '...since our recent conversation, my men have been digging. I believe we have found a common link.'

He paused for a moment, more for dramatic effect than for breath before continuing to lay bare his findings.

Murphy listened intently, half incredulous, half knowingly.

When Ariel had finished Murphy said, after a moment's reflection, 'Well Ariel, there's a thing! I think your country and mine may have a severe problem on our hands.'

'Yes, I agree. But we need more information to fill in all the gaps, and we also need proof. We are doing what we can, but are there any resources which you can still call on John?'

'As you know, my hands are tied, to an extent, though I do have some trusted friends and colleagues who may help me.'

They were silent for a short while before

Murphy said, 'I will see if there is any way that I can get some sort of monitoring of Shultz and Brown's phones, computers and offices. It may now be difficult, but I will do what I can. Shall we speak in a week from now unless something is particularly pressing?'

They agreed and said their farewells.

Murphy was better than his word, he had his personal contacts in the NSA help him put together a small team of specialist military operatives and techies who were sworn to the highest level of secrecy.

They could not breach the Oval office or Shultz's office, but they did hack their phones and computers. They did not, however, stop there. They also tapped into the electronics of their extended families. And that is where they struck gold.

CHAPTER FIFTY-SEVEN

Castle Zbiroh, Křivoklát and Brdy Forest, Western Bohemia, Czech Republic

THE ALARM ON ADAM'S WATCH began to beep softly, dragging him from his slumber as he turned it off. He lay half-awake for a moment listening to the still of the night, broken only occasionally, by the ominous hooting of the ubiquitous tawny owl hidden deep in the darkened forest below.

He slowly rose, feeling a rush of cold air as he did so. Dressing, he silently grabbed the two bags with his kit, which he had pushed under the bed and quietly left the room. He slipped noiselessly along the corridor and downstairs where he waited for a moment surveying the calm of the courtyard ahead of him. Still hearing, only the owls call, he stole effortlessly across the cobbles, keeping to the cover of the shadows where possible. He reached the other archway and seeing his way clear disappeared into the dark of the stairwell. He returned five minutes later without the bags, which he had left in the room housing the deep well. This time, once he had crossed the central courtyard, he continued outside the castle to his car where he retrieved one of his air bottles. As he shut the boot of the car, he leant down and grabbed a handful of the tiny pieces of stone which made up the gravelled parking area. Placing them in his trouser pocket, he waited by the car, under the tree canopy, surveying the castle walls and the windows, but saw no movement. He could not say why, but he felt a sense of unease as if he was being watched. With nothing to substantiate it, he retraced his steps back to the well where he had deposited the cylinder, before returning to the bedroom.

Rebecca remained deep in sleep, and he stared at her, entranced, for a while, almost sad to have to wake her. He looked at his watch, the luminous dial of which read 2.10 a.m.

He gently shook her arm, and she slowly opened her eyes, remaining half asleep. Upon seeing Adam, she smiled and lay there momentarily looking at him. Suddenly, she realised that she was not still dreaming, and she sat up pulling the bedclothes to her chin.

'It's time to go. I have all of the equipment in place,' Adam said quietly, 'I will wait outside the door while you dress.'

He slipped outside and waited in the hallway for Rebecca. She appeared surprisingly quickly, in a pair of faded jeans, a loose-fitting, purple sweatshirt and trainers. She had clearly 'made an effort' with her hair, but it still looked tousled, which, Adam thought, made her look all the more vulnerable and real.

As they walked down the corridor, unspeaking, she slipped on a light blue windcheater which she carried.

Adam, once more, stopped as he came to the courtyard and monitored the area. He no longer heard the sound of the owl, though, in the castle, all was still. He walked close to the castle walls, keeping in the shadows as he made his way to the steps which led to the inner courtyard. He was followed like a shadow by Rebecca.

They climbed up in unison and once more, stopped on reaching the inner courtyard. Finding that all was peaceful, they crossed to the unpretentious door and dropping down a few steps, entered the room with the well, gently closing the door behind them as they did so.

Adam grabbed the gravel from his pocket and placed it in a pile on the low wall which surrounded the wellhead. Turning to Rebecca, he said, 'If anything happens while I am in the well, then you can warn me by pushing these stones over the side. Even if I am underwater, I will see them sinking to the bottom.'

'Do you think something will happen?' she said, looking alarmed.

'No, don't worry, it's just a precaution.'

Adam then began to busy himself with his equipment. Opening the first bag, he grabbed various harnesses, ropes, pulleys and rock-climbing gear. Adam also took out a short steel pole which he set across the wall surrounding the well. He tied this off securely, to use it as an anchor point. From there Adam set up various lines, one of which was tied to the pole and then the rest of its length was dropped into the well falling until it snapped taut and vertical.

Next turning his attention to the other bag, he retrieved a wetsuit from it and began to strip down to his boxer shorts. Rebecca tried to appear as if she were averting her eyes, though she couldn't help sneaking an occasional look at Adam's taut muscles as he wriggled into the neoprene. He busied himself expertly, putting together the BCD, the buoyancy control device and attaching the air bottle. He checked the regulator for airflow and then put a little air into the BCD to help it float when it was in the water. These were clipped to the end of one of the ropes which had not been dropped into the well. Then a mask, snorkel, crowbar and a short set of fins were put in a net bag and were again attached by carabiner to the rope.

Strapping a dive knife to his lower leg, Adam then lifted the diving gear to the top of the well and took up the slack on the rope with the pulley system. He then swiftly lowered the equipment into the well, tying it off, only when it had reached the water.

Pulling on a Black Diamond climbing harness, Adam attached a carabiner to the front. He then took a metal figure of eight which he fed the rope into before attaching the metal ring to the carabiner which he then locked off. He slipped a headlamp on, adjusting the straps as he did so.

Taking a small nylon rucksack from one of the bags, he filled it with various bits of climbing gear, before slinging it over his shoulder. Climbing up onto the wall, he looked down at Rebecca. He said, 'I may be down there for some time, don't worry – it's more laborious than dangerous.' With that he suddenly fell back into the harness into mid-air, holding himself with the rope's friction on the figure of eight. He laughed as he saw the sudden horror on Rebecca's face as she thought he had fallen into the abyss.

'You swine!' she said grinning once she had caught her composure.

He smiled back at Rebecca and then, his face full of concentration once more, began to release the pressure on the rope, and he gently commenced abseiling down into the bowels of the earth. Adam was rapidly enveloped in darkness until she saw a sudden illumination as he turned on the headlamp. It was an unearthly sight as he slipped, suspended, into the depths surrounded by a halo of light, becoming more obscure with each passing second.

She noticed as he came closer to the water that he kept stopping and spinning around on the rope studying the walls of the well until eventually, he had descended to the surface. It was difficult for her to make out what was going on as the well was so deep, but he seemed to have unclipped himself from the rope and had begun kitting up with the scuba gear.

Eventually, he slipped effortlessly into the depths amid an explosion of air bubbles and the light, though still there, took on an ethereal quality.

She watched transfixed by the repetitive sound of the spent air fizzing as it broke the surface echoing softly up the length of the well, unaware that other eyes were also transfixed on her.

Rebecca felt very alone in the darkness, but oddly the sound of Adam's air bubbles below did not leave her feeling lonely.

Thirty-five minutes had passed, and as she continued to watch below, she suddenly became aware of a cold breeze against the back of her legs. It had not been there before, and as she turned; she saw the shape of a man framed in shadow in the half-open doorway. In his hand, he held a pistol which was pointed at her.

Rebecca bit her lip in horror, but then remembering Adam below she slid her hand, unnoticed, along the edge of the wall dislodging the little pile of gravel.

She heard the faintest of sounds of it falling and then it was gone.

The man stepped forward, raising his gun in a gesture for her to raise her hands, which she did. Far below Adam who had been working his way around the face of the well looking for the entrance he sought, saw grains and small pebbles falling like a dust shower before his eyes as he studied a particularly unusual piece of the stonework. He stopped momentarily, unsure of what to do. He did not want to alert anyone above that he knew they were there if indeed that was what the signal indicated. Therefore, he desperately tried to keep his breathing, with its consequent exhaust gases, regular.

Rebecca thought she heard a minute change in the rhythmic sound of the bubbles, which gave her the sense that Adam had received her signal.

The man in the entrance moved inside, followed closely by two others who also carried guns, the last of whom shut the door behind him.

Adam stopped to collect his thoughts. He was hanging, suspended in the icy water just over ten feet below the surface. Adam did not know the nature of the problem above, but he feared that their pursuers might have found them. Though Adam racked his brain as to how they could have been tracked to the castle, he knew that any answer would not help them now. Adam believed that both Rebecca and he would be safe 'until' they had found the gold, but after that, they would be surplus to requirements.

He turned back to the wall and looked more closely at what appeared to be an anomaly in the stonework. Pulling his divers knife out of his leg scabbard, he began to scrape at the joints of the dressed stone. In the corner of one section, where several of the blocks met, the stonework seemed to have different colouration, as if it had been repaired. Adam dug into it watching as it easily crumbled away, filling the water with a milky cloud of dust. Suddenly, a whole lump fell off, rapidly dropping into the darkness below, revealing a large metal ring which looked rusted, but, nonetheless, in general, good order. He pulled hard and yanked on it with little effect. He then braced his legs against the wall and pulled again with as much strength as he could muster. As he did so, a whole section of the blocks pulled out into the well itself, remaining suspended in the void and held by massive metal hinges, which became visible on opening. The water had clouded dramatically with all the detritus of over half a century, and Adam remained where he was, holding the metal ring while he waited for the particles to dissipate.

As the water began to clear, Adam saw a black hole revealed, where the door had previously been. Alive to the fact that there may be watchers above who would be monitoring his progress, he slowly dimmed the headlamp until it shut off and then entered the opening. The recess was the size of a small wardrobe with a floor and now with three sides. As Adam looked up, he could see that it had no roof as the air bubbles were breaking about ten feet above him within the hidden chamber. Adam gradually began to ascend the chimney-like structure, bumping as he did into a set of steel rods which had been set into the far wall and were fashioned into a rudimentary ladder. Adam surfaced and turned his lamp on again. The ladder within the chamber rose for another fifteen feet and then seemed to give on to a larger space. He gently removed his regulator and began to breathe, finding the air quite safe, though damp and with a musty smell. Adam loosened the BCD and clipped it with a carabiner to one of the metal rungs. Removing his flippers, Adam pressed them inside another bar to hold them and began to climb.

On reaching the top of the ladder, he stepped up onto a steel platform and then looked out into a cavern, dimly illuminated by his light, the size of a large church.

It was packed with crates of varying sizes most of which carried the mark of the German eagle atop the Nazi swastika, or the SS runes.

Adam stood in awe, possibly much the same as Howard Carter must have felt in Tutankhamun's tomb as he also looked upon a long-lost creation of mankind. Taking in the vast room and its contents, he stepped down onto the rock floor and began to walk through the corridors created by towers of boxes.

He found piles of documents, both loose and in sealed crates, again with the *SS* stamp on the outside. There were many stolen artefacts and in sealed cases, which Adam pried open, famous paintings by the likes of Van Gogh, Raphael and Metzinger among others. The looted master-pieces had been missing ever since the end of the Second World War when the Nazis had hidden them.

Near the wall at the end of one of these corridors, he found five skeletons, each body had a single bullet-hole through the skull, and the decaying rags which hung from their remains were the striped pyjamas of concentration camp inmates. Each also bore a yellow star, denoting them as Jews.

Adam looked, in horror, at the sorrowful and pathetic sight and was reminded of the fortunate escape of his mother's family.

Turning away, he walked over to one of the crates with rope handles attached to the ends and which bore the SS markings stencilled on top in black paint. Taking the crowbar from his knapsack, he levered the lid off. As the wood splintered and fell away, he saw, revealed before him, golden ingots with the German eagle stamped across the centre, where once, in all likelihood, the Belgian emblem would have been embossed. The gold shone through the gloom, untarnished by the passage of time, its glimmer and purity, incongruous in the otherwise murky surroundings.

Adam continued his search of the room, finding discarded weapons, grenades and tools. There were also some old SS uniform jackets and hats hanging from pegs on the wall as if they had only just been left there, though the layers of dust covering them told a different story.

He marvelled at the ingenuity which created the void and the vast hoard it contained.

Adam studied an area of wall at the rear, around a natural crevice. It seemed wrong, given the overall rockface. Adam looked closely, noticing peeling paint, which had been used to camouflage a false wall. He ran his hand over the surface until he found what he was looking for. A small lever tucked in behind a notch in the man-made wall, released the hidden door, much the same as the one in the well. He pulled the door open to reveal, what appeared to be, a natural fissure in the rock which formed a tunnel which in turn meandered through the bedrock. It looked as if it had been used to some extent long ago and it still had a string of cables and lights running its length, which would, once, have illuminated the passage.

He walked along the tunnel which gently sloped downwards before, turning a sharp corner, after which it came to a dead end. This time the crevice and false wall were clearly visible as, from the inside, there was no need to hide its existence. He pulled the lever which stood proud of the surface and using a large metal handle on the door, pulled it open towards him. As he did, moonlight flooded the crack through the bushes and undergrowth which shielded the crevice, on the outside, from prying eyes. A welcome gust of cold fresh air raced past him. He pushed his way out and thirty feet below him, down a gentle slope, he saw a rough track, which was clearly, occasionally used for vehicular access, probably to enter the forest below. By the road, a large limb from an ancient beech tree lay, where it had fallen, several months before - a silent testament to the lightning bolt which had ripped it from its host.

Adam considered his options. He could try to leave by this exit and return to the wellhead. However, he was in a damp wetsuit, and his neoprene boots would not make the going easy. If the Neo-Nazis were there, then they would have men watching the whole area. Once they found that he had gone into the well and then come out of the castle by another route, then they would know that he had found what he was looking for. They would also be able to approach the cavern from the forest, which would mean that they had no more need of him.

Adam felt that on balance, it would be better to return via the well and to hide the fact that he had found the gold for the moment. Once he understood what he was dealing with, then he could combat them more effectively.

He closed the false door once more and retreated down the tunnel, before closing the second door.

He walked over to the weapons, which he had seen earlier and found that most were in a poor state of repair. Looking up at the hanging SS tunics he took them from the hook and found under one of them a black leather belt with a leather holster attached. He undid the buckle on the holster and pulled out a Luger, with a full clip of bullets inserted into the handle. A further full clip was held in a separate, though attached, compartment of the holster.

Though the holster itself was showing signs of age and mould, the quality of the workmanship and its complete encasing of the weapon had left the Luger and the spare clip in pristine condition.

He took the gun and hid it, along with the spare clip, in a small cut in the rock beside the platform he had first stepped out onto. He then took a slab of rock from the floor of the chamber and descended the ladder once more. Kitting up, he dropped back down the ladder and into the well. Before shutting the large stone door, he took his dive knife and placed it in the corner of the opening, placing the piece of rock over it to disguise its presence. He then unclipped the scabbard and let it fall into the depths. He braced himself against the wall of the well and pushed the great door shut once more.

Slowly turning on his light again, to give the impression of ascending from depth, he gradually finned towards the surface. Looking up, he saw nothing but the wellhead, with no sound to be heard.

He unclipped his BCD and clipped it and his fins to one of the spare ropes, leaving them floating at the surface. Taking his rucksack off he retrieved two Jumars, some carabiners, a couple of slings and two étriers, ladders made from a high strength nylon webbing.

He first attached the Jumar ascenders to his harness using carabiners and slings and then attached each Jumar to the rope. To each of the Jumars, he attached an étrier. Then he began to ascend the line, with some trepidation as to what awaited him above.

He slid one Jumar up the rope and then used its étrier to step up. Next, he slid the other Jumar up and put his weight into that one's étrier. It was a slow and laborious process, not least because of the depth of the well, but it was efficient.

As he neared the top, he stopped for a moment to catch his breath. He was panting heavily and had a chill layer of sweat all over his body. As he hung in the dark, he listened and heard only his own breathing. He then continued up the rope, and on reaching the rim of the wall that surrounded the well, he swung himself over and clambered up onto the lip. Looking around quickly, he could see nothing in the darkness. Unclipping the harness, he jumped down from the wall, and as he regained his footing, a man stepped out of the shadows, with a gun levelled at him.

The man said in a coarse, Germanic voice, 'Hände hoch!'

As he put his hands up, the door opened, and Rebecca was marched in, held before the other two men who also had pistols at the ready.

'Oh Adam, I'm so sorry,' she said, breaking free and running to him. As she embraced him, she burst into tears.

Adam lowered his hands and placed them around Rebecca and said, 'Don't worry, it will all be simply fine!'

Adam recognised two of the men, the one who had spoken and one of the two who had just entered. They were the ones who had been walking away from the car the evening before. The third, an older man, had, he was sure, been in the group of five men in the restaurant on the previous night. He was, possibly, in his late seventies, but maybe older, though still having the appearance of one who was powerfully built, having the air of an ex-military man. He appeared to be in charge.

The older man then spoke in clear English with a strong German accent, 'So Adam, at last, we meet. My name is Müller.'

He continued in a self-assured and self-satisfied manner, 'You retrieved something which was buried in the forest near Arnstadt. Where is it and what, exactly, is it?'

'It was a metal box, and it had a document in it which told of the location of a hidden chamber in the well of the castle. Once I had read it, I destroyed it, as your men were after us,' Adam said bluntly.

He saw no reason to hide the truth, or at least most of it, as he was sure that they probably had much of the picture already.

'Yes, it has the ring of truth, but maybe we will return to this topic over the coming days.'

He continued, 'So you will know the whereabouts of certain *property* which belongs to us, which I believe will be in this chamber. Now, if you wish to help us to find it, then you and your young lady friend will be left to go on your way, unmolested. However, if you chose to be unco-operative, then I cannot vouch for your safety.'

Adam said, 'Well, Müller, that sounds like an offer I can't refuse.'

'It's Herr Müller to you,' Müller said with a haughty snarl, continuing, 'Good. I am glad that we see eye to eye. Now, tell me what you have found?'

Adam looked at the three men, thinking that he did not relish his chances with any of them. He now knew that there were at least seven of them, the five at the table and the other two. What he did not know was if that was the extent of their personnel.

'Nothing yet, I searched the walls above the waterline and down to about twenty feet below the surface, but it is slow going, as it is very murky down there.'

'I want you to go down there again, but this time with two of my men.'

'I can't, I have been down there too long already, and I don't want to get the bends. I need to rest overnight, and then I can re-start tomorrow night.'

The senior German turned and looked questioningly to one of the men, who nodded.

'Well, we shall wait until tomorrow then. But for insurance, one of my men will guard your young friend in her room, until our work is done. You need not worry yourself; she will be perfectly safe in our care. We have another room that you can use.'

'Have your men scuba-dived or abseiled before?' Adam asked.

'Yes, they have enough experience for a dive such as this, and they have a high degree of skill with high alpine climbing, so any ropework will not be a problem.'

Adam thought that the answer might reveal

a particular weakness in the men's abilities underwater.

'I only have enough kit for myself!'

The German laughed and said, 'Not to worry, my men checked your car yesterday, and they have sourced a similar level of equipment to yours ...Will there be anything else ...Adam?'

'No, that was all, Müller.'

Müller was silent for a moment, but the disdain on his face was palpable as Adam, once more showed disrespect without using the form of address, 'Herr'.

'Just one last thing, before my men show you to your room. If you had any thoughts of double-crossing us, then that would not be advisable,' the German said this, with such menace that he left Adam with little doubt as to the consequences of such a course of action. Though Adam knew that double cross or not, there would be only one outcome for Rebecca and for him, when this was over if they still found themselves in the neo-Nazi's hands.

Rebecca and Adam were both led away. Rebecca back to her room, but not before she stole one last tearful glance towards Adam. He, on the other hand, was taken to another part of the castle and shown into a guest room. One of the Germans sat on a chair outside.

Adam was exhausted from his efforts. He thought, how glad he was that he had secreted the leather case, documents and the copy of Mein Kampf under the spare wheel in the depression in the boot. If the neo-Nazis had found

it already, then they would probably be dead by
now.

He lay on the bed and thought of his predicament and considered the options, before slipping into a deep sleep.

CHAPTER FIFTY-EIGHT

Collections Department, Mossad headquarters, Tel Aviv, Israel

THE PHONE RANG JUST ONCE before Mandler picked it up, 'Mandler!' he said curtly.

'Sir, we have a call from John Murphy.'

'Yes, yes, put him through.'

There was a soft click, and then Mandler said, 'John, how are you?' Murphy had called before their arranged date, and Mandler was excited to know why.

Murphy ignored the pleasantries and launched straight in, 'Ariel, my men have had a breakthrough. They had been monitoring Brown and Shultz but got little or nothing of use to us. However, they also kept tabs on some of their relatives, and it was while listening to a call between one of Shultz's cousins and a man named Manfred Schwartz in Buenos Aires that things began to become clearer. His cousin is the owner of the Texas Petrochemical giant Callox Telson. The man he was speaking to runs a shadowy company called La Araña.'

'The Spider?' Mandler questioned.

'Yes, that's correct. The call involved future dealings between Russia and Callox Telson International. So, we did some further digging about Schwartz. His former name was Manfred Auer, and he was spirited out of Berlin shortly before the end of the war and reappeared in Argentina under his new identity where he opened the company which he still heads. He had worked in the Abwehr in Berlin ...'

'Wait ...Can you hold for a moment?' Mandler interjected.

'Yes. What is it, Ariel?'

Mandler had thought that the name Manfred Auer had rung a bell for him, but the mention of the Abwehr clinched it. He picked up the file that Daniel had left with him earlier and flicked through the pages. Then Mandler stopped suddenly. There it was, he thought!

'John, this man Manfred Auer was the direct boss, in the Abwehr, of one of Shultz's great-uncles. The one who is said to have died in Berlin at the end of the war.'

'Well, well ...that is more than just a passing coincidence,' Murphy said.

Ariel continued, 'There is something else.'

Murphy waited expectantly.

Ariel breathed deeply and said, 'The Abwehr files indicate that great-uncle Horst was fluent in Russian. He had, among other wartime theatres, been posted to the Eastern Front. A considerable period of that time was spent based in Smolensk. Earlier in the war, in 1942, he was lucky to have survived a grenade attack. He was left with scars to the face, and he lost an eye.'

'The right eye?' Murphy slowly questioned.

'Yes, the right eye!'

'Goddammit! Ivanov's father!' Murphy yelled.

'Yes, it certainly fits!' Mandler said with a heavy heart and a deep sense of concern.

The two men were silent for a while, trying to fully take in the enormity of what they had discovered. Mandler thought privately that La Araña was a misnomer. They would have better used the name El Cangrejo, the crab, as these fascists undoubtedly had the state of Israel and the whole world in a pincer movement, which no one had seen coming.

CHAPTER FIFTY-NINE

EIRIK RANG THROUGH TO Juliette and asked, 'Anything new in this neo-Nazi thing?'

'Not really, the trail has gone dead with the couple. The Bundeskriminalamt were tracking the neo-Nazis, as a large body of them left their headquarters in the Harz Mountains and then crossed into the Czech Republic. I had alerted the Czech police who took over the pursuit. The Germans were ensconced in a hotel in Pilsen where other individuals met up with them. However, I've just received a call from Prague. They gave the Czech's the slip, and we don't know where they have gone.'

'What!' Eirik, yelled.

Juliette was shocked as the gentlemanly Norwegian was usually very restrained.

'Right,' Eirik continued, 'get on to all of the neighbouring countries and warn them that these people are on the move and that they are probably armed and extremely dangerous. Get back to the Czech's and impress on them that they need to have this matter dealt with as a top priority.'

He paused for a moment and said ominously, 'There is something afoot. I keep getting reports of Russian subterfuge. Then there is the increasing violence and mobilisation of the far-right across Europe generally. I fear for the future – for all of us!'

He dropped the receiver without waiting for a reply. None was necessary.

CHAPTER SIXTY

Collections Department, Mossad headquarters, Tel Aviv, Israel

MANDLER AND MURPHY BOTH knew the enormity of what they had uncovered. They also knew that to defeat it - if defeat was even an option, then they would have to work very quickly.

They spoke for over an hour discussing and honing their plans.

When they were finished, they wished each other, '*Godspeed*'.

CHAPTER SIXTY-ONE

Castle Zbiroh, Křivoklát Forest, Western Bohemia, Czech Republic

ADAM SLEPT, SURPRISINGLY well through what was left of the night. He woke suddenly at 9.25 a.m. on hearing a delivery truck coming to a screeching halt in front of the castle gates. He rose and looking out of his window saw a man opening the back of a frozen food truck, as he made his morning food delivery. The cloud of dust which had been kicked up by the vehicle hung around in the air and then drifted off towards the distant forest, carried on faint gusts of wind.

Adam looked out into the distance at the vast expanse of trees casting a swathe of green across the landscape, opening the window as he did so. The air was fresh and had the faint, resinous smell of pine. The rustling sound of the breeze running through the tree canopy would, ordinarily, have given the scene a remarkable effect. However, this morning, his thoughts were lost in the events of last night and in his concern for Rebecca.

Turning away from the window, he walked to the door and slowly opened it. Outside in the short corridor, a gruff looking man sat in a chair, his steely gaze fixed on Adam. 'Good Morning,' Adam said. He received no response and indeed, no recognition of any sort from the brut.

He closed the door once more and thought of his predicament. It was one thing to make his escape, but quite another to ensure that Rebecca could also be saved.

Adam showered and headed off for breakfast to the restaurant. Just before he left his room, he grabbed a pair of his training shoes and wrapped them tightly in a brown pillowcase from the bed. Adam then slipped them into the waistband of his trousers under his jacket. He had decided to return to the well that night, as he felt that this was the only way in which he could keep Rebecca safe. He descended the stairs followed, as if a shadow, by the guard who had remained at his door. The man had said nothing, but Adam heard his steps marking time with his own as they walked across to the courtyard. Adam glanced around before entering the restaurant, seeing only his escort in view. He walked in and sat down at a table on the far side, carefully looking, as he went, at all the people who sat inside. Adam could see many of those who had been there on the previous night.

Though there were a few exceptions, most notably he did not see anyone whom he felt might be a member of the neo-Nazi group, apart from his guard. He sat two tables away, frequently looking over at Adam.

Five minutes passed before one of the men, Emil, who Adam had met, the night before, when he exited the well, entered the restaurant. A waiter served him, and he sat quietly drinking, what appeared to be coffee, and he paid no attention whatsoever, on the face of it, to Adam.

The waitress burst through the door, which led from the kitchens, entering the restaurant carrying a couple of plates of food, which she promptly placed down before two of the diners. Looking over at Adam and the German who sat near to him, the waitress came over and asked the neo-Nazi, in German, what he would like, and the man replied too softly for Adam to hear. The waitress then came to Adam's table and asked, in English, what he wished to order. Adam asked for a coffee, orange juice and toast, with a side order of fried eggs. As with his previous request, she did not write it down before disappearing off through the door, back into the kitchen.

A few moments later, she returned with two coffees, one for Adam and one for the German, who stared at him. Adam slowly drank his coffee. The waitress re-appeared five minutes later with his orange juice, eggs and toast with a large slice of butter on a side plate. Taking the opportunity, Adam ordered another cup of coffee. It was a strange situation that he found himself in, but he knew that it was one that had dire consequences if he misjudged the Germans or his own response to them.

Adam took his time with breakfast and on finishing called the waitress over and put the bill on his new room number, winking at the German as he did so. He then left. As Adam entered the courtyard, once more, he glanced over at the stairs that lead to the wellhead. He then crossed the quad and looked out from the viewing platform at the forest below. Adam tried to appear as if he was just passing the time and looking at the view. But as Adam looked, he took care to note the track below, which he could see shaded by the great trees. Always watched over by the guard, he waited ten minutes before turning and exiting the square through the arch and across the bridge to the castle's exterior.

As he crossed the bridge, Adam saw ahead of him, near the parked cars, two of the Germans who stood chatting to each other. On seeing him, they stopped talking and tried to appear uninterested. Adam turned and walked down the slope, along the path which eventually took a shallow turn to the right onto the trail. He strode along giving the appearance, to anyone watching, that he did not have a care in the world and that he was purely out for a woodland stroll. Adam glanced back over his shoulder, knowing that he was being followed, having occasionally heard footsteps in the leaves or the breaking of twigs being crushed underfoot. He saw, twenty yards behind him, the lone German who had been with him all morning. A further thirty yards back, one of the two neo-Nazis who he had seen stood by the cars also followed him. Both men kept to the same pace as Adam and gave no outward appearance of having any interest in him. The carnival of three carried on their route as they walked the circuit of the castle.

Unseen, or at least unnoticed by the Germans, Adam paid particular attention to the area above the broken tree branch that he had seen from the crevice the night before. He slipped the pillowcase out of his waistband and glancing back saw that he was shielded momentarily from their sight by the curve of the path and some bushy undergrowth. He dropped the bundle just behind the fallen limb. It was hidden from view by the branch and because the brown pillowcase mimicked the decaying forest floor. He marvelled at the ingenuity of the Nazis who had designed that vast cavern whose secret exit was invisible from the exterior. He carried on, rising, as he continued, coming out near the grand terrace. Adam glanced at his watch, giving the impression of a man who had time on his hands and no particular way of helping it pass. He stopped temporarily, glancing around and below him, at the track, he had taken, back to the main entrance of the castle.

Emerging from the woods along the track, Adam saw his two neo-Nazi watchers who were by then walking side-by-side. They were chatting to each other and looking at him. He turned to see the other German, they had left behind, still stood by the cars, and he also stared intently at Adam. Turning, he slowly walked down the road to the main entrance of the castle, which adjoined the highway, stopping again as he reached the arched entrance gateway. Once more, he glanced around and then made another show of looking at his watch.

Then he turned to the right and walked along the road, continually followed by the two men who looked intensely angry. He walked on for more than a mile, and at one point he was passed by a large, black Mercedes. As it cruised by, he noticed one of the Germans, from the night before, was driving.

The man drove on for eight hundred yards more and then pulled onto the grass verge. There he waited while Adam continued his walk. When Adam came near to the car, the German then drove off a further eight hundred yards and parked once more and waited. Adam passed by what he had been looking for - the woodland track's exit, which gave onto the main public highway. Adam tried to show no interest in the trail and carried on for a further three hundred yards before turning back along the road, returning to the castle. As he did so, the same two men passed him by, within half a yard saying nothing, but glancing at him as they went. 'If looks could kill', he thought to himself.

After walking a few yards, Adam heard them turn around. He could also hear the car making a turn in the road, though it did not follow him.

As Adam advanced on his way, they continued to follow him once more. He slowly walked for another four hundred yards, before stopping once more and looking at his watch again. Adam looked around as if bored and then carried on towards the entrance archway. On reaching it, he turned back towards the castle. As he walked up the entrance road followed by his shadows, he was watched from the castle car park by the German who had remained. Without giving him a glance, Adam continued to cross the bridge and headed back towards his room. He turned into the stairwell, which gave on to his apartment, he glanced back and saw that his original guard had stayed by the cars with other one of the Germans and the other one had begun to follow him. Adam slowly walked back to his room, and as he turned and shut the door, he saw the German relax back into the chair a few feet away. Adam lay down on the bed, collecting his thoughts and resting. He knew that he would need all his strength and all his guile in the night ahead and taking the opportunity, he dozed off for two hours.

He was intent on keeping the Germans busy or on their toes for as much time as possible. Unlike him, some of them, at least, would have to be on guard all the time, whereas he could rest when he chose to. Adam woke up just after one and once more went for a stroll. This time he wandered around the interior of the castle so that he could get a better understanding of his environment. At all points, he was followed.

He looked from one of the windows on the second floor into the quadrant, seeing a German leaving the restaurant with a tray and a plate of food and drink. He walked across the square, under the arch heading towards the bedroom that he and Rebecca had occupied initially. He presumed that the food was for Rebecca and that they had no intention of allowing her out of the room until this matter was ended. If that was the case, then that suited him. Adam thought to himself, how foolish of them. They had indeed left her in the same room, where he knew to find her.

That meant that they would have to leave at least one guard and maybe more, watching over her while the others would have to monitor him and his whereabouts. If he did manage to escape, then finding Rebecca might well be more straightforward than he had expected. Adam had lunch and then went for another walk to waste more rest time for the Germans and to keep them on edge. He continued this disruptive pattern until he went down for his evening meal at seven o'clock. On leaving his room, once again, Adam was followed by the German who had sat outside his door.

He saw that several of the neo-Nazis were eating together in the restaurant when he arrived. They ignored his entrance, all apart from, what appeared to be the most senior German who momentarily glanced up at Adam and smiled as if one guest was silently saying to another, good evening.

Adam finished his meal watched by his shadow who sat, drinking a coffee, at a table nearby. Then he noticed one of the Germans at the main table get up part-way through his meal as the waitress came towards him with a tray full of food and drinks. Taking it from her, the man then walked to the door and left. Adam let a few moments go by and then, he exited the restaurant quickly, followed equally swiftly by his guard. The other neo-Nazis gave him a furtive look and stopped eating. Adam was in no rush. He just wanted to further unnerve and frustrate the Germans. As Adam entered the square, he saw the German with the tray disappearing up the stairs in the direction of his original room, which further confirmed to him, the probable location of Rebecca.

Adam made haste and walked at pace back down the road to the main entrance gate and out onto the pavement, which bordered the highway. He glanced back and saw that he had been followed by, not only his guard but also three of the men who had still been eating. He carried on down the road, heading this time to the left for a couple of miles. He was tailed by the four on foot and once again the Mercedes. Adam then stopped, checked his watch, looked around once more and then abruptly turned back towards the castle.

As he passed by the four Germans, they made no pretence of ignoring him. Each member of the team watched him intently and with venom. He was glad to be getting under their skin and to be taking power away from them. He returned to the castle swiftly at a brisk walking pace and then went back to his room for twenty minutes, where he lay on the bed relaxing. Afterwards, he got up once more departed the room followed by the guard who had the blackest of looks. As he descended the stairs, he noticed the guard on his mobile phone, speaking softly and animatedly in German. He could not determine the words, but Adam had no doubt that he was warning his comrades.

Adam went downstairs and once again left the castle heading across the bridge and descended into the woods below, ambling along one of the walking tracks. The light was beginning to fail, and in the woods, the former beauty had given way to an intense gloominess. Adam was followed on his path once more by his guard and five other Germans, who had clearly been in a rush to catch up. They all looked so angry that they could spit blood, though none of them talked. One of them was hurriedly eating half a bread roll from the restaurant, where, no doubt, he had been disturbed once more. There was an air of apprehension about them Adam thought as if they expected him to bolt and probably hoped that he would try. He kept up a steady pace through the woods taking meandering routes, doubling back, then walking at pace on straight parts of the paths. When Adam occasionally caught sight of the Germans, they were never far behind. He could see that they were genuinely irritated by him. Adam returned once more, and by the time he had reached the castle, darkness had fallen.

On arriving at the castle, Adam came face to face with the neo-Nazi who appeared to be in overall charge, Herr Müller. As Adam approached, the man forced a smile, but the smile was more of a grimace.

He said to Adam, 'I hope that you fully understand that your actions may have severe consequences if you choose to conduct yourself in a way, which is ...' he paused momentarily, '...contrary to my wishes. You will not leave your room again tonight, until three a.m. At that time, you will make your way downstairs, and you will return to the wellhead, where I will be waiting.'

The words *where I will be waiting* were said with such an air of menace that Adam could palpably feel a chill run down his spine. Adam sincerely hoped that he would get the opportunity to permanently settle scores with that individual.

Adam smiled nonchalantly and said, 'But I will need to get my equipment?'

Müller replied through gritted teeth, 'You need not worry yourself about that. The equipment you require will be at the wellhead when you arrive. Make sure you do not let me down!'

Adam lied as convincingly and amiably as he could muster, 'Look I just want to get this over with, as much as you do. It's in both of our best interests.'

Müller gave him a quizzical look, almost unbelieving, but not really sure. After a long pause, he said in a mildly more pleasant tone, 'Well I will see you tonight then.'

Adam smiled and walked on, returning to his room, followed by a new German, one he had not seen before. That meant there were at least eight Germans, Adam thought.

As he closed his door, he looked at the neo-Nazi who went to sit down in the chair nearby. Adam noted that as the man did so, he dropped heavily into the chair. The German was tired and terribly angry. The man would not get much rest for the rest of the night waiting and expecting Adam to reappear at any point before the three-a.m. appointment. Adam, on the other hand, had an excellent sleep. While he had walked around reconnoitring the castle and the surrounding area, he had hatched a plan. He now waited with anticipation for three o'clock so that he could put it into operation.

Adam felt rested and reinvigorated when he woke at 2:45. He got ready silently, not giving the neo-Nazi any indication that he had awoken. Adam waited and listened at the door for the German, eventually hearing approaching footsteps. At the first knock on the door, Adam wrenched it open as fast as he could, startling the man who looked as if he were going to have a heart attack. He had fallen back a few paces as he fumbled to reach his gun inside his jacket in the shoulder holster. Adam said in English, 'Right, let's go!'

He walked past the neo-Nazi, marching off down the corridor at a considerable pace. The

German took his hand off the butt of the pistol and followed as he composed himself. His face was seething red with anger, as he followed Adam close behind. The guard was much closer to Adam than was safe for him to be. It gave Adam, if he had wished for it, the opportunity to suddenly launch a lethal attack.

Clearly, their professionalism was beginning to slip. Adam smiled to himself as he walked, thinking to himself, 'There is time enough for any action, my friend.'

Adam strode downstairs, seeing another German waiting for him as he reached the ground floor. Walking into the courtyard, he glanced back as if looking at the two Germans who were now close behind him. But Adam was not only looking at them; instead, Adam glanced past them to see if anyone stood within sight outside the castle wall. He had seen the shape of two men standing under a tree, near the cars, partly illuminated by lights near the bridge.

'Right,' he thought, 'that makes four Germans so far, including the two following me. Then one, possibly two with Rebecca ...actually, there will probably be two with her, as they would need to leave one at her door if the other needed to go to the toilet or to pass messages. Then that would leave, by my calculation three to four more Germans waiting for me at the wellhead and two of those would enter the water with me. Yes, that's the key!' he thought.

Having crossed the central courtyard, Adam climbed the stairs and walked across the smaller inner enclosure where he saw one of the neo-Nazis standing outside the wellhead room. When Adam arrived, the guard stepped aside and held his palm out in a show of guiding his way to the well. He remained outside the door, while Adam and the two following him entered the small room. It was quite crowded. Müller was there with the two men from the night before and also Emil and Kaspar. They had kitted up and had large amounts of equipment strewn everywhere. Adam thought to himself, 'That seems to be all of the neo-Nazis accounted for!'

He thought there must be just one more alone guarding Rebecca. That appeared to make sense as far as they were concerned as she posed little threat to them, and they were purely her gaolers.

'Gut!' said the boss smiling grimly, 'I'm glad you appear to have seen sense. Emil and Kaspar, will descend into the well with you. They have orders to slaughter you if there is the slightest provocation, so make sure that you do exactly as you are required to, and all will be well.'

'Slaughter', Adam pondered, '...what an unusual, animalistic word to use, possibly disclosing the monster's baser self.'

Adam looked at him and then at the two men who he thought, look tired. Both of them fixed him with a steely gaze as if they prayed that he would give them the chance to turn words into actions. He suspected that any death, at the hands of these men, would be gruesome.

Adam said in a matter-of-fact way, 'Right well

let's just get this over with so that all of us can get on with our lives!'

He then walked over to his bag of kit to get ready for the dive. As Adam did so, he saw Emil and Kaspar pass surreptitious glances at each other, giving each other a half-smile. Adam was confident that, both Rebecca and he - getting on with their lives - was certainly not part of their plan. Adam knew that the moment the neo-Nazis had what they wanted, Rebecca, and he would be mincemeat.

Adam busied himself inspecting the equipment and assembling it, before kitting up. The Germans checked the ropes and the other gear watched over by their boss. They seemed happier and less concerned now that they were involved in the task at hand. Adam closely observed them as they prepared their equipment and pulled it on. They were clearly highly proficient with the climbing and abseiling equipment. On the other hand, he could see that neither one of them was particularly at ease with the diving gear, which showed their inexperience. Kaspar did seem the more experienced of the two.

Once they were prepared, they donned the climbing harnesses and began lowering the three diving BCDs into the water. Both Germans held large diving knives with serrated edges, which made working with their hands quite awkward. Kaspar then continued, attaching himself to the rope before abseiling expertly down to the water surface where he unclipped and began pulling on his BCD. Adam realised that their boss had spoken truthfully about his team who were clearly mountain men who had some experience of diving. Adam felt fortunate that this was their weakness, for it was underwater that they would be out of sight and most vulnerable. The second German, Emil, then pointed to the wellhead urging Adam to descend after his colleague. He abseiled down the rope and was swiftly followed by Emil. Once they had reached the water, they too put on their diving kit, and all three turned their head-torches on.

It was a large well, but with the three of them and the equipment, it had left little free space. Kaspar said, 'I will go ahead of you at all times, and Emil will go behind. No tricks, Englishman!'

'I'm American!' Adam replied, just before putting his demand valve into his mouth. The other two gave each other a harsh, knowing look and then did the same.

Adam realised that he needed to act swiftly, as he would need time to help Rebecca before the others began to suspect that something was wrong. Therefore, with Kaspar going below first, he descended with the Germans, directly to the point at which the underwater door was located. On reaching it, Adam stopped them and then pointed towards the section of stone which held it. Initially, they seemed lost, not understanding what he meant, as Adam had previously given the appearance that he had not found what he was looking for, yet. He could see both of their eyes framed in their face masks in the eerie light of the head-torches. They both had eyes that stared out into the darkness of the water, visibly expressing to Adam that they were ill at ease in that environment, or possibly even scared.

Adam pushed his hand forward and grasped the metal ring twisting and pulling it to release the door. As he did so, he glanced at the two Germans, Adam could see in their eyes through the facemasks, anger and caution as they realised now, that he was up to something. It was unclear to them whether he had just decided to give up the prize or whether it was a trap. As the door opened, Adam hoped that just as before the clouds of material would severely muddy the waters, which would give him his chance to attack. Unfortunately, though the area became moderately grit filled, much of the material which had built up over the years had effectively dispersed on the night before.

The Germans looked at the open door with great caution. Adam went to enter the water-filled cavern but was held back by Kaspar. The neo-Nazi entered ahead of him and looking back, he then quickly began to ascend the metal ladder. Emil then directed Adam to enter the chamber. As Adam did so, he turned his head-torch off and he surreptitiously slipped his hand under the rock which he had placed in the corner of the opening earlier and removed his dive knife. Adam turned swiftly using his legs to push off the wall violently, back into the well directly at Emil. The German had been closely following Adam and had both hands gripping the sides of the entrance which held him solidly in the water.

Adam sunk his knife deep into the neoprene and straight through the Germans' heart. Emil had a look of sheer horror in his eyes, and his body wrenched violently. Then as his hands slipped their grip, his body twitched momentarily. Emil feebly grasped at Adam who watched his eyes and saw the life disappearing out of him. He left the knife buried in the German's chest to reduce the amount of blood which came out. Adam then released the last of the air in the Germans BCD reducing his buoyancy, before letting go of the lifeless body. Adam grabbed the rock from the opening, which had previously covered his knife and stuffed it inside the German's wetsuit. The added weight and the lack of buoyancy swiftly sent the corpse disappearing into the depths below framed by the light of his lamp as it faded, the deeper he went.

Adam thought that those above might believe that the three divers had descended much deeper than they actually had on seeing the disappearing light.

Adam turned and made his way back into the opening and climbed up the ladder.

As his head came out of the water, he released the demand valve and pulled his face mask off, dropping it into the water. Kaspar, who was standing above him, held his dive knife in his hand and was looking directly at Adam, his head-torch illuminating the scene. He had a look of sheer delight on his face.

'Come up Englishman, don't be scared!'

Adam had a nasty feeling that Kaspar had

every intention of killing him at that point. He continued to climb up the metal ladder until he came to the same height as the platform. Thrusting his arm outwards Adam grabbed one of Kaspar's feet, still wet from the dive. Yanking it, the German lost his footing, slipped and fell onto the rock floor below. He recovered surprisingly quickly, though clearly shaken. Adam clambered up, as fast as he could go and jumped out onto the platform. As he did so, he saw Kaspar quickly regain his footing and spin-flip the dagger around in his hand, ready to throw it at Adam. He had the upper hand on Adam momentarily, relaxing as he saw Adam above him unarmed.

The German looked down at the top of the ladder, sensing that something was wrong. Adam saw in his eyes the questioning, as to the whereabouts of Emil. Realising suddenly that his comrade would never be appearing, the anger showed in his face as he pulled his arm back to throw the knife. As Kaspar did so, Adam lunged for the Luger, grabbing it from its hiding place. Turning the gun quickly and crouching as he did so, he fired a bullet straight through the left side of Kaspar's jaw. As the bone exploded, the knife flew at Adam but clattered harmlessly against the rock wall beside him. Kaspar staggered back and turning his head as he fell, displayed to Adam a large exit wound just below the hairline. Kaspar lay on the floor moaning softly though gurgling breath.

Adam looked down at him and said, 'I told you already, I'm American!'

He slowly took aim and fired another shot, straight through the neo-Nazi's temple.

Kaspar lay motionless.

CHAPTER SIXTY-TWO

YEVGENY KERIMOV PICKED UP his phone as it rang, 'Yevgeny, its Ivanov! You have done well, my friend!'

Kerimov said, 'Sir, it is a pleasure!'

'I particularly liked your work in discrediting the Director of the CIA.'

Ivanov continued, 'You must keep up your efforts. It will not be long now until we have accomplished our goal.'

'I only wish to serve Mother Russia, sir!' Kerimov said.

There was an uncomfortable silence on the phone, and then Ivanov muttered, 'Once we have achieved dominance, I promise you, Kerimov, you will get your due!'

Kerimov said nervously, 'Thank you, sir!'

As the line went dead, Kerimov sat in deathly

silence in his upper-floor office in the Online Marketing Bureau's headquarters.

He thought about Ivanov's last words and his unusual, glacial, use of his surname instead of his first name. A cold chill ran down his spine as he wondered what his 'due' would be.

CHAPTER SIXTY-THREE

Castle Zbiroh, Křivoklát Forest, Western Bohemia, Czech Republic

ADAM TURNED HIS HEAD TORCH back on and jumped down from the platform on to the rock floor. He grabbed a pickaxe which lay against the wall and then returned to the waters of the entrance. Pulling the underwater door shut, he wedged the pickaxe shaft through the handle, to prevent the lock being opened again from the well itself.

He knew that he had little time before the Germans above, began to become suspicious. He wanted as many of them to remain at the wellhead, in anticipation, as possible as it gave him less of them to deal with at one time.

Returning to the main chamber, he pushed one of the upper wooden boxes off a pile, and as it hit the ground, the echoing noise was like an earthquake. The wood had splintered, and the crate collapsed into pieces, strewing bars of gold across the floor. Adam scoured the chamber until he found what he needed, two old canvas bags, similar to those used by plumbers in times gone by. He also picked up a small axe which he dropped in the bag along with Kaspar's dive knife, the Luger and the spare clip.

Putting a gold bar in each bag, he went to the back of the cavern, struggling under the weight of them. He opened the concealed portal and then carried the bags down to the end of the tunnel, dropping them near the second door. He turned his head torch off and pushed the lever of the secret gateway, which led to the outside. Using the large metal handle on the door's inner face, he pulled it open towards him, letting moonlight flood into the tunnel. He pushed out through the opening and then past the scrub that surrounded it, dragging the bags as he did so. Turning back, he pulled the door shut again and pushed the undergrowth back into place.

He quietly made his way down the gentle forest slope towards the limb of the beech tree. Though the neoprene of his wetsuit had protected him from the thorny scrub, the neoprene boots that he wore made walking difficult and he slipped several times. As he reached the track, he walked more slowly and cautiously. Seeing nothing, he lowered the bags to the ground and finding the pillowcase he had dropped earlier he took the diving boots off and put the trainers on, which made walking much more straightforward. He shoved the dive boots and the pillowcase into one of the bags and set off along the track as fast and as silently as he could go, given the weight of the gold which he was carrying.

As he came to the path which led up to the car park by the castle's bridge, he dropped the two bags behind a large tree. Taking the dive knife, the axe and the Luger he carried on, more cautiously up towards the cars where he heard the two Germans furtively talking. He crawled very carefully up the slope to within three yards of them. They were both smoking and leaning against one of the cars with their backs towards him. Then, Adam stood deadly still. They had both pulled away from the vehicle, said a few words to each other and one of them had set off towards the front gate. Adam waited until he was out of sight and until the other neo-Nazi had settled back against the car. He then stealthily crept closer to the German. He was within a couple of yards of him when a small twig cracked under Adam's feet. It was enough to make the German turn towards him. Adam lunged forward lashing out with the axe as he did so. The stunned German, taken utterly by surprise, looked as though he was going to call out. Before he could the axe sliced deeply, right through his forehead. A low moan of expelling air came from his lungs as his head and body fell away, lifeless.

Adam searched his pockets and took the Mercedes car key, which he found. He then tried the first of the two Mercedes in the parking area with the key, and it unlocked. Leaving the car open, Adam grabbed the dead man's feet and dragged the body down the path and deep into the undergrowth at the side. He piled decaying leaves and twigs from the forest floor over the body to disguise it. Hearing the other guard returning in the distance, he ran back up the slope and picked up the axe and the smouldering cigarette, which the dead man had dropped by the car. Adam moved into the shadows by the cars leaning against one of the tree trunks with his back to the other man. He gave a few puffs on the cigarette to keep it alight and then waited, listening to the sound of the footsteps coming, ever closer.

Adam heard the rhythmic sound of the steps becoming louder and louder as he puffed out a cloud of smoke. Then the man's steps faltered, and he said in a questioning voice, 'Herman, Was ist ...'

The man, sensing something was wrong, had reached for his holstered gun. Adam spun around letting loose the axe which he had held ready in his hand.

The axe amputated two fingers, embedding deep into the man's chest. The impact made a dull, thudding, crunching sound as the ribs broke. Adam ran forward as the neo-Nazi toppled backwards. The German was severely wounded but not dead. Adam grabbed the man's gun as the neo-Nazi tried to fumble for it with his tortured hand. He attempted to cry out for help. Throwing the weapon into the bushes, Adam throttled the life out of the neo-Nazi. Once he was dead, he was deposited in the forest beside his friend.

Adam raced into the castle and up towards the corridor, leading to the room where Rebecca was being held. He looked around the corner and saw that there was only one guard on duty. He had leant his chair back against the wall and was sitting in it, asleep. Adam crept along the corridor and placing his hand over the man's mouth, buried the knife into his chest at the point where his heart lay. The man's eyes burst open, and his hands went to his chest. Adam held the neo-Nazi in a bear hug as he struggled and died. He then carefully removed the knife.

The key was still in the door lock, and Adam turned it, but it did not move. The lock was not on! He silently turned the handle and entered the room. He looked in horror as he saw Rebecca, who was tied to the top of the bed. She was naked, bruised and spread-eagled. Her mouth was gagged and her face, which had turned to him, was terror struck. Her flushed cheeks were wet with streaked mascara and tears.

She spoke with her terrified eyes which directed Adam to the open bathroom door. He could hear that someone was in there. Every atom of him ignited with a total sense of purpose, a base abhorrence and a sense of duty and finality. Just as he began to stalk towards the door like a wild cat, with the knife firmly held in his grip, the blond woman from the restaurant appeared.

As she did so she was sneering to Rebecca, 'Jetzt meine Kleine ...'

On seeing Adam, the evil smirk she had displayed suddenly went blank in shock. Frau Vogt held a small scalpel in one hand and a large bottle of liquid in the other. Her expression abruptly turned to a look of pure hatred as she raised her arm to throw the bottle at Adam, just as he threw his knife at her. The weapon was thrown with such hostile force that the blade embedded deep into her shoulder, protruding through her back. Frau Vogt staggered back into the bathroom, slamming into the wall behind as she dropped the bottle from her grasp. The liquid contained within emptied out onto her chest, stomach and legs as her eyes looked down in abject fear.

The woman slid down the wall as the tip of the blade, peering through her back, made an ugly screeching sound while it dragged down the bathroom tiles. Slowly descended to the floor, the pathetic creature let out a blood-curdling scream as she watched in agonizing, paralysing horror. At the same time, the acid gave off fumes, burning deeper through her clothing and bubbling skin.

Frau Vogt had begun to froth at the mouth, and her body was contorting as the acid relentlessly ate through her flesh. Adam walked over to her, brutally wrenching the knife from her body as she glared at him in unimaginable torment. He looked into her cruel eyes with a cold stare and then buried the blade up to the hilt into her left eye socket. Her body went limp, and she was silent.

The foul, sweet smell which emanated from the still dissolving corpse was overpowering, making Adam feel as if he would retch.

Adam had killed before, and he would kill again, though he took no pleasure in it. However, his look of pure loathing as he glared at the dead woman betrayed a deep sense of conviction that she was someone truly evil, who deserved nothing better.

Adam grabbed a dressing gown from a hook in the bathroom, took the scalpel from the corpse's hand and then shut the door. He covered Rebecca's body with the garment and then used the knife to cut her bonds and the gag around her mouth. Rebecca threw her arms around him, sobbing uncontrollably and babbling hysterically.

Adam did his best to comfort her. Eventually, she said through tears, 'That monster was going to do the most awful things to me!'

Adam said, 'Don't worry, she is dead now, and she will never hurt anyone again.'

He whispered, with a great sense of relief to have her safe and in his arms once more, 'Quick, get dressed. We are getting out of here. Fast!'

He went to leave the room to give Rebecca privacy, and she said almost frenziedly, 'No, don't go! Don't leave me alone!'

So, he turned and looked out of the window while she got ready, hearing her softly weeping as she did so.

When she was ready, he ushered her into the hall. Rebecca winced as she saw the other dead neo-Nazi. Adam dragged the German's body into the room and pushed it, out of sight, under the bed. He then took a towel from the side table and cleaned the blood from the floor. It was also flung under the bed.

He turned and locked the door, putting the key in his pocket.

'Please take me away from this place, Adam!' she begged. He ignored her and grabbed her arm, half dragging her along the corridor down the stairs and then to his own room. Once there, Adam changed and picked up a few things himself while Rebecca tidied herself up in the bathroom. The two of them then left for the car park.

The place was deadly silent as they reached the Mercedes. Rebecca climbed in, while Adam quietly opened the boot of their own car. He retrieved the items from under the spare wheel and then locked the car before throwing the keys into the forest. Adam then ran down the path and retrieved the two bags with the gold. Returning to the Mercedes, he put the bags into the boot. Adam jumped into the driver's seat and started the car. He reversed quietly from the parking space and drove down the entrance road and out of the property.

As they headed to Pilsen, Rebecca's mind was in turmoil.

CHAPTER SIXTY-FOUR

Israeli Embassy, Badeniho 2, Prague, Czech Republic

MANDLER WAS PUT THROUGH to the Mossad agent in their Embassy in Prague.

'Fishel?'

'Yes sir, how can I be of assistance?' Fishel Rubenstein said officiously. Rubenstein had joined Mossad four years earlier. He had never met Ariel Mandler previously, but he, like many others, knew of his powerful reputation.

'I want two people to disappear permanently.'

Unfazed, Fishel said, 'Certainly sir, may I ask their names.'

'Rebecca and Adam will do for now. I will have one of my team, Daniel, call you to work out the niceties.'

'Yes, sir, I will await his call.'

'And Fishel ...' Mandler said with menace, 'Remember ...Permanently!'

'Yes sir!' Fishel replied, a sense of unease wafting over him.

CHAPTER SIXTY-FIVE

Along the Forested Road to Pilsen, Western Bohemia, Czech Republic

THERE WAS LITTLE TRAFFIC ON THE road, and Adam kept up a determined pace. The night was dry, and it was still very dark, made more so by the encroaching forest trees: the only punctuation, the blinding lights of the occasional passing vehicle.

Adam had his window down, hoping that the refreshing night air might cleanse his soul and keep him alert. His mind was awash with a tumult of emotions.

Neither spoke of what was done or was going to be done by Frau Vogt. Nor did they speak of that monster's fate.

Rebecca had pushed her seat back, ostensibly to help her to sleep. She took the opportunity, however, to watch Adam, to study him unnoticed. She still wept. But more privately. The uncontrollable fear of moments before still reverberating through her body.

She was trying to make sense of her turbulent emotions. Rebecca looked at him as he drove - his robust features, muscled body and self-assuredness. His kindness, his cruelty, his warmth, his coldness. A killer. A cold-blooded killer. She mused, 'How could she love him? How?'

But she did! She could hardly restrain herself from lunging forth to hold him close.

Rebecca had always had the upper hand in relationships and enjoyed the sense of power in playing hard to get. But no longer! She wanted him much more than anyone she had ever known – she wanted him forever time.

Her mind raced – the past, the future, happiness, sadness ... She looked out at the passing forests and smelled the intoxicating pine. Awash with mental exhaustion, she slipped into a deep, coma-like sleep.

Unawares, Adam continued to the Plzeň hlavní nádraží, the Pilsen Central train station where he found a public phone. He put a call through to Interpol in Lyon and left an anonymous message about the neo-Nazis and the gold. Adam then placed a telephone call to a number in Ingolstadt, a small city on the Danube, north of Munich. Dumping the Mercedes in a side street, he hired a new car before heading southwest towards the German border.

CHAPTER SIXTY-SIX

ADAM PULLED OFF THE AUTOBAHN and headed to the outskirts of Ingolstadt. He had not told Rebecca where they were going or why, but eventually he pulled into the driveway of a small house, on the edge of a vast forest.

Adam got out of the car as a tall, muscular man emerged from the front door. The man shouted out to Adam, in French, as they both hugged each other like long lost friends.

Rebecca stepped from the car, and the man immediately came to her and shook her hand very firmly. The skin on his hands was surprisingly soft, she noticed.

'I am Baptiste,' he said in heavily accented English with a hint of garlic on his breath. The

415

name was French, but the accent was strongly Germanic, she thought to herself.

Adam said, 'Baptiste, is another old friend from the Legion. He is going to assist us.'

'Thank you, Baptiste,' Rebecca said, 'It is a pleasure to meet you.'

'Well let's get started shall we.'

Rebecca wondered what he meant, but very shortly afterwards, it became evident.

Baptiste, so she found out, as he talked incessantly, had deserted from the Legion after four years and had found it necessary to obtain a false identity as a result. He then went into the business himself, helping other Legionnaires in a similar predicament, or indeed anyone who paid.

He had already prepared two British passports and driving licences in readiness, having received the call from Adam. He shot the necessary photographs in his studio in the garage. Baptiste was meticulous. He had, different sets of clothes for them both and made them change their hairstyles slightly to give the appearance that the photos were taken months apart. He had advised Rebecca to redo her make-up for the driving license and to her horror had given her a particularly tarty shade of lipstick to put on. The end results were incredible.

As a final touch, after the photos were taken, he took a pair of clippers and shortened Adam's hair appreciably.

They stayed the night and had a pleasant meal with Baptiste and his Spanish wife, Magdalena.

By the morning, the documents were ready and saying their goodbyes, they went on their way.

Adam drove to Munich and dumped the car. They both then walked across town to another car hire company and hired a different car in his new name. To keep matters simple, Baptiste had used the same forenames and had given them false passports with different surnames.

CHAPTER SIXTY-SEVEN

Village of Balzers, the Alps, Southern Liechtenstein

THE LIGHT HAD FADED QUICKLY, that evening as storm clouds closed in covering the mountain peaks, swiftly racing down through the valleys. The air felt suddenly fresh, and the rain had begun to lightly fall, a precursor to the thunder and lightning that was yet to come.

It happened in a quiet country road on the edge of the village of Balzers in Liechtenstein. Nobody had witnessed the crash. But it was believed that the banker, who first discovered it, had come upon it shortly after it had occurred. He was unable to help the passengers as the fire was too intense, so he called the police immediately.

By the time the emergency services had arrived, the car was wholly aflame, and the petrol tank had already exploded. The two bodies were burnt beyond recognition, but they were quickly identified by the car rental agreement, passports and other documents in their luggage which were thrown clear in the crash.

It appeared to the local police that the two occupants were killed when their car went off the road just north of the village. It was a scene they had witnessed many times before and had, to some extent, become emotionally immune to. Both the policemen, who had initially attended the crash, had been suspicious of the banker as his conduct was verging on peculiar and was undoubtedly unhelpful. It soon became apparent that he had just left his girlfriend's home shortly before and was on his way home to his family. He was desperately uneasy at the thought of his wife finding out that he had been miles from either his bank or his home. It would be challenging to explain to his wife why he was in the area of the crash at that particular time. The police took a short statement and sent him on his way, laughing at his predicament as the banker drove home.

The officers did a search on the burning BMW's plates. It was a Czech registered car, and it was a long way from home. Therefore, the policemen questioned staff at the heliport, which was nearby. It appeared from their investigation that the occupants had chartered a helicopter flight from Balzers to Interlaken in Switzerland for that afternoon. They were nearly an hour late by the time of the crash, and the officers surmised that they had been speeding to make the flight, which formed a toxic mix with a road surface that was becoming wet. Ironically, the pilots would have shied away from a journey through the mountains in the twilight, during stormy weather.

The car lay off the road, in a field, on its roof. It was left in situ until the next day when a tow truck and a crane were scheduled to clear it during daylight hours. The bodies were removed from the car, that evening, shortly after the firemen had doused the flames. The firemen had worked meticulously, dealing with the devastation they had seen many times before, though they never got used to the smell of burning flesh. An ambulance took them to the mortuary, and an autopsy was scheduled later in the week to confirm the cause of death and their identity.

Chapter Sixty-eight

Embassy of Israel, Alpenstrasse 32, Bern, Switzerland

EZRA GOLDMANN WAS SAT at his desk when the call came through.

'Sir, I have Mr Mandler on the phone for you,' the receptionist said as he replied, 'Yes, thank you.'

Unknowingly he sat up a little straighter in his chair, and his breathing quickened and became louder as the call came through.

'Ezra, I need you to *liquidate* those people in the Harz!'

'What, all of them?' Ezra said, shocked by his request.

'Yes, all of them and as soon as possible.'

'Shouldn't our German team deal with that?'

'No, I want to use outside assets. They are being sent to Germany as we speak. You will co-ordinate the operation.'

'Well, yes, certainly, sir.'

'It would be helpful if it was an accident. You know how prickly the European press can be!'

'Yes, you can leave it to me, sir.'

'Ezra, this is of the utmost importance.'

'I understand,' Ezra said, even though he did not truly fully understand.

Several days later the press was awash with details of a fire in a large, secluded home in the Harz Mountains. The police provided few details only saying that the blaze occurred during the night and that everyone had died in their sleep. In total, eleven people had perished. The remains of three dogs had also been found. It was presumed the blaze was started by an ember from the open fire and that the occupants had died of smoke inhalation.

Once it became known that the occupants all had links with neo-Nazis the press went into a frenzy of speculation. Over time this dissipated for want of evidence and as the initial reports were roundly ridiculed, as fanciful conspiracy theories.

The lynx had seen the fire, and he had viewed the silent watchers who had set it. He had looked with interest as the Israelis left, satisfied with their night's work. Then the creature turned back towards the forest, taking his leave to embark on his own killing spree.

One moonless night, several days later, three men stood, obscured by trees, near to where the lynx had lain. They stared in silence at the burnt outbuilding. The smell of smoke from the fire still hung heavy in the air. The older man pulled a cigarette from the packet of Eckstein No5s he had slowly drawn from his pocket. He lit up with the same gold lighter that he had held on the beach many decades before while he had waited in desperation for the U-Boat. He remembered back to that period when he had also felt close to despair. He slowly caressed the lighter in his hand while surveying the scene.

Former SS-Oberführer Gartmann felt an incredible sense of anger. The loss of so many men was a significant inconvenience, but the deaths of his dogs pained him deeply. Though 'nothing' compared with his sense of loss at the damage that had been done to Das Spinnennetz. Gartmann had been fortunate that he had not been found among the bodies in the fire.

The Shadow, 'Der Schatten' smiled a grim smile as he said to himself, 'This is not over, I will rebuild again.'

Hearing a police siren in the distance, one of his men whispered, 'Herr Müller, we should go, sir! The police still have officers in the area.'

The man's use of his long-time alias brought Gartmann back to the present.

Herr Müller was silent for a time before taking a long drag on the cigarette. He slowly exhaled the smoke into the cold night air, watching it billow away into the darkness.

He was about to say something but stopped himself.

Müller turned and walked past his men, who promptly followed him.

The lynx who lay nearby, unseen in the

undergrowth, watching and waiting, gave a low growl and angrily bared its fangs as they departed. The forest was his once more.

CHAPTER SIXTY-NINE

Interpol headquarters, Quai Charles de Gaulle, Lyon, France

'SIR, I'VE HEARD BACK FROM our investigator in Liechtenstein who arrived this morning,' Juliette said before continuing, 'He's discussed the 'accident' with the local police. They have taken the view that it was a tragic crash caused by an anxious driver using excess speed in rapidly deteriorating conditions on a road he did not know.'

'Amazing, an open and shut case then!' said Eirik Jensen sarcastically. 'What did the autopsy reveal?'

'Nothing,' responded Juliette.

'Nothing!' exclaimed Eirik.

'It never took place. The bodies were cremated before the procedure was performed. 'Apparently' it was a clerical error or some sort of misunderstanding. They seemed a little embarrassed by it.'

'Embarrassed! That goes way beyond, incompetence!' barked Eirik.

'It's been impossible to get a straight answer from anyone there, as we have been stonewalled. The Principality has its own peculiar ways of doing things, they like their privacy, and they do not like outside interference.'

'They did ask where we wanted the ashes shipped and if we felt we could settle the, not inconsiderable, costs?'

Juliette's boss, incredulous, raised an eyebrow and said, 'How thoughtful! Don't even bother to respond!'

'Well, I expect we will, now, be unable to determine the true identities of the occupants of that car. I cannot help but feel that whatever the documents show and whatever the police officers in Liechtenstein have 'determined', they were not who we expected. Who those bodies were and what ever became of the real Rebecca and Adam, we will probably never know!'

'Do you really think the cremation was a clerical error, sir?' Juliette questioned.

'Of course not, I passionately believe that it was a carefully determined course of action by those persons, whoever they are and who wish to hide the truth.'

Juliette said, 'It crossed my mind that the anonymous tip-off about the neo-Nazis in Zbiroh, may have come from the same people. The call was traced to Pilsen, where the car was hired. The timings between the call and the travelling time by car until the crash does work.'

'Yes, Juliette. The same thought came to me.'

'The Czech police have reported that they have found several bodies at and in the grounds of Zbiroh. They believe that they are all German nationals. They sent some of their divers into the well.'

Juliette stopped momentarily, and Eirik said, 'What did they find?'

'A secret cavern with an entrance underwater within the well.'

'And ...'

'And ...Nothing! Well, almost nothing. There was a body of a diver in the cavern with another at the bottom of the well. There were some empty boxes and old tools and German uniforms lying around, but apart from that, it was empty. The Czech's did say that the place had been cleared out in the very recent past. It also had a hidden exit which led to a track in the forest below. They questioned local residents who said that there had been a lot of activity in the forest before the police arrived. They had believed that the coming and goings of all the trucks had been to do with logging. The Czech's have their men searching for the convoy but have found nothing so far.'

Eirik said, 'How very disappointing – we may never know what was there!'

'We have an idea,' she continued as Eirik, encouraged, looked up, 'One of the officers found a solid gold ingot in the undergrowth near the track. It had a Nazi eagle stamped on it.'

Eirik said nothing in reply. He just shook his head slowly as he stared at the floor. Juliette waited a moment and then left him.

She called through to Scotland Yard and the German Bundeskriminalamt and gave them, what was to be her final update.

CHAPTER SEVENTY

THE CALL CAME THROUGH IN THE early morning from Prague.

'Yes, Fishel?' Mandler enquired.

Rubenstein said coldly, 'Rebecca and Adam died in an automobile accident in Liechtenstein, sir.'

'Good! And their bodies?'

'They were burnt beyond recognition in the crash and the subsequent fire. The bodies have since been cremated. Our friends in Liechtenstein have been most accommodating. No one will ever know.'

'That is excellent news. Is there any question as to the identities of the cadavers?'

'No, sir. Our forging team in Bern made accurate duplicates of their identity and car hire documents which were found near the vehicle.

We obtained the actual car which they had hired in Prague, from the Munich car hire company, for a substantial fee. All records of its return to Munich have been erased.'

'And where did the cadavers come from, out of interest?'

'Again, the Liechtenstein authorities were most helpful. I believe the bodies were of two unknown drug abusers who had died in Switzerland earlier in the year. The two countries have a close relationship, and the local morgue was happy to have them claimed so that they could close their books.'

'And the real Rebecca and Adam?' Mandler enquired.

'They are currently in the south of France living under assumed names.'

'Right, that just leaves them to deal with now!' Mandler said.

CHAPTER SEVENTY-ONE

THE PRIME MINISTER HAD been briefed the night before on his schedule for the coming day. Through the night he had pondered the reason behind his 10.00am meeting with the Israeli Ambassador. He questioned his private secretary, but he, Valentin, had said that it had been made at the request of the Israeli Embassy a week before and had been scheduled for thirty minutes. The only reason given for the meeting was that it concerned 'inter-cultural friendship'.

The Prime Minister was at his desk when the Ambassador was shown in. He was accompanied by a colleague of his, who carried an ornate wooden box, which he seemed to be struggling to hold.

'Good Morning Ambassador.'

'Good Morning Prime Minister,' said the Ambassador amiably.

'It is always a pleasure to see you, Ambassador, but might I ask what the purpose of today's meeting is?' the Prime Minister enquired.

'Well, my government instructed me to deliver a gift to you from the Israeli people to the people of Belgium.'

As he spoke these words, the Ambassador held out his open hand indicating the wooden box, which was being held, with some difficulty, by his Embassy man.

'How kind and how unexpected. Please place it down on my desk.'

The man slowly walked forward and gently lowered it to the desktop.

The Prime Minister intrigued, walked over and slowly lifted the lid. As he did so, all four sides of the box lowered away, revealing a large, golden Leo Belgicus. It was the Belgian Lion which adorned the Belgian coat of arms.

The Prime Minister looked in wonder at it. The detail of the rampant lion was incredible and the exquisite craftsmanship of the statue, striking. He studied it for a few moments and then walked over and picked it up. It was surprisingly weighty, and the Prime Minister lowered it, quickly, back to the desk with a soft clunking sound.

Turning to the Ambassador, he said, 'It is incredible! Magnificent! By the weight of it, I suspect that it is solid gold?' he gently questioned.

'Yes, Prime Minister. It is.'

The Prime Minister was dumbfounded.

He had been in politics for far too long to real-ise that there was no such thing as 'a free lunch'.

Turning to the Ambassador, he said, 'May I ask the meaning of this wonderful gift?'

Expecting a thunderbolt, the Prime Minister waited, as the Ambassador smiled gently before saying, 'It is purely a tangible show of my coun-tries affection for the people of Belgium and our shared past.'

The Prime Minister thought to himself, 'What an unusual turn of phrase, remembrance of times past? What could he possibly be alluding to?'

But before he could question the Ambassador about what he really meant, he said, 'Prime Minister, I have used up too much of your time already. Thank you for taking the time to see me.'

He then shook hands with the Prime Minister who spluttered out, 'Ah ...yes ...thank you ...on behalf of the people of Belgium for this most touching show of appreciation ...I can assure you that it will be put on display in a prominent place.'

Then they both said, 'Good Day'.

The Ambassador and his aide left both the room and a very perplexed and curious Prime Minister.

Once they had gone, his private secretary returned, 'Well, Valentin, I really do not know what all that was about. It is most curious. But we are now the proud recipients of this.'

Valentin looked at the impressive statue, 'Sir. It is incredible, it must be worth a fortune.'

'Yes, that is what I thought!'

Valentin continued, 'What do they want?'

'Yes, that is also what I thought!' the Prime Minister said, half smiling.

He continued, 'But incredibly, this 'does' appear to be a free lunch!'

Valentin was bemused by the words but put it down to one of the Prime Ministers idiosyncratic expressions which he had picked up at Lancing College. As a child, he had been privately schooled there in West Sussex in England, before entering the Belgian military and then politics.

Two weeks later, amid some media attention, the lion was installed, in a specially constructed cabinet in the main hall of the Prime Minister's Office.

Unseen, on the base of the statue read the inscription, in Latin, 'In remembrance of times past.' Underneath the words the date 1939, was written in Roman numerals.

It was the date the Belgians had sent their precious gold to, what they saw as, 'safety' during the Second World War.

Though the Belgians had long since received compensation for the stolen gold, the Israelis felt that they were still due some sort of recognition of the find that had been made, however, surreptitiously that credit was made.

CHAPTER SEVENTY-TWO

Near the Western Wall, Old City of Jerusalem, Israel

FOUR SOLDIERS STOOD AT the entrance to the Western Wall Tunnel in Jerusalem's Old City. It was late in the evening, and the light was beginning to fade, though the air was still pleasantly warm. Three of the soldiers stood in a loose, relaxed huddle chatting, though nevertheless alert. The fourth leant against the weathered stone wall, solitary and nervously looking about him. There were very few people in the area and those who remained or were passing through, elicited a mild interest.

The tunnel was closed to the public at that time, though it was not empty. One hundred and fifty feet into the passage, a lone man stood in the dim light that flickered from a candle that had been placed on the floor. The man was dressed in a dark suit and looked to be in his sixties. He was Ariel Mandler, and he was deep in prayer facing an ancient sealed up archway. Known as 'Warren's' Gate it was the closest place a Jewish person could get to the 'Holiest of Holies'. His head bowed down repeatedly as he performed the prayer for the dead, Kaddish. It was a solemn, contemplative prayer for his own family and for the many Jews who died in the camps.

He was an Ashkenazi Jew. His mother, Helena, had come to, what was then, Palestine as an orphan after the Second World War once she had been released from Buchenwald concentration camp by the American army. Helena's family had been part of the Jewish diaspora which had settled in Germany centuries before.

Helena had lost every member of her family to the Nazi slaughter and had begun a new life in the young state of Israel.

She had married his father, Yaakov, a few years after arriving. His family had left Holland just before the war and had settled in the United States. He had gone on to fight in the American infantry all the way through Italy, Austria and into Germany. After the war, he had returned to the US for a short time before deciding to go to join the nascent Israeli state. Ariel had been brought up with German and Yiddish which were spoken at home, while at school, he learnt Hebrew and English.

Helena had died young. He always felt that she had just suffered too much, and the toll on her had been too high. He was brought up by his father in Haifa, an ancient city which lies on the Mediterranean coast. Once he was old enough, he had joined the army, rapidly rising to the rank of Captain before transferring into the Special Forces unit, Sayeret Matkal. After three years with them, he was sent to work with Mossad, where he had remained ever since.

The Mossad boss had finished his prayers though he remained silent, facing the wall for more than ten minutes. Standing there, alone, his thoughts turned to the five skeletons which had been carefully recovered by his agents from Zbiroh. His team had worked tirelessly, with the use of DNA analysis, to trace any of the relatives of those poor unfortunates. Those relatives who were found were invited to attend a private funeral in Jerusalem. The victims were buried together and in the same order that they were found. They were given full military honours and the only other attendees were Mandler and the Israeli Prime Minister. Mandler sighed heavily and then bowed and crouched down to pick up the candle. He then slowly retraced his steps back along the tunnel and out into the evening once more. As he emerged, the soldiers stopped speaking and loosely stood to attention, looking at him. Then they followed his gaze as he looked towards a man of middle eastern appearance who was making towards them with a calm determination. Even at this distance, they could see the bulge of a pistol under his jacket. The soldiers began to turn to fully face him, raising their weapons as they did so, when Ariel said, 'Stop, it's alright, he is one of us.' With that, the soldiers relaxed.

The man wore jeans, trainers and a yellow t-shirt with a black bomber jacket and he walked with immense assurance. When he walked up to the group, he ignored the soldiers and said to Ariel, 'Good evening, sir.'

Ariel said, holding his outstretched arm out, 'Come, walk with me, Seth.'

They began their stroll, followed at a distance by the group of soldiers.

'You have been appraised of matters?'

'Yes', said Seth.

'Then you know we have some loose ends to tidy up. Rebecca and Adam need dealing with first and then there is the matter of our friends in the Harz Mountains. We need to deal with all of their contacts.'

'I understand, sir.'

'You and your 'colleagues' will take an El Al flight tomorrow from Tel Aviv direct to Marseille, and from there it is a short journey along the coast. Here are your orders and your tickets. The flight leaves Ben Gurion at 18:00 tomorrow.' As he said this, he handed Seth a large brown envelope which he took from his coat pocket.

'Good luck,' Ariel continued as they shook hands.

'Thank you, sir,' Seth said as he turned and walked away.

CHAPTER SEVENTY-THREE

THEY, REBECCA AND ADAM, sat at a table on the terrace of the Eden-Roc restaurant. Shortly before, they had finished their lunch and were now relaxing. Rebecca sipped on a Kir Royal, a subtle mix of Champagne and Créme de Cassis and a firm favourite with the French. Adam drank an ice-cold beer, a Blue Moon Belgian White - popular with the Americans. He was enjoying the sight of the condensation as it ran, slowly, down the outside of the glass. There was a gentle breeze blowing, which cooled them in the summer sun.

As they looked out across the Mediterranean towards the Lérins Islands, a heat haze gave the island group an almost mirage-like quality. Rebecca and Adam spoke intermittently but, for the most part, they just enjoyed the ambience and being in the company of each other. The

439

floor of the terrace was made of a sun-bleached wooden decking which in turn was surrounded by white, metal railings topped with a gleaming mahogany handrail giving the overall effect of a luxury liner's deck. This was further enhanced by the gentle lapping of the waves below and the constant passage of expensive yachts and cruisers.

They had been honeymooning in the Hotel du Cap-Eden-Roc on Boulevard JF Kennedy, in fashionable Antibes. It was one of those places 'to be seen in' on the French Riviera, and the hotel oozed elegance and old-world charm, and for now, it was perfect.

Earlier that day, Adam had read the Times newspaper while he waited for Rebecca. It, along with many of the other leading world newspapers, was available, daily, to their international clientele. He was mystified to read of their own deaths in a road accident months before in Liechtenstein. Equally puzzling was the ensuing diplomatic wrangle involving Britain and America over the conduct of the subsequent investigation into the deaths of their citizens.

Though the deaths were very convenient, he was deeply troubled by the article. He felt that it was not something to bring to the attention of Rebecca.

As the sun began to slowly sink and they slipped further into the afternoon Rebecca said, 'Adam, shall we take a walk down to the Pointe de l'Ilette and walk some of this decadence off?'

'Sure,' Adam said.

They got up from the table, and Rebecca arranged a light cotton shawl around her shoulders. She had bought it in the town from a very jolly North African street-trader. It had wildly vibrant colours in stark contrast to the plain, white cotton dress and white sandals that she wore. It was ideal for keeping the sun away from her shoulders.

Adam left a substantial tip, the bill itself would be automatically charged to their room.

As they left, the waiter re-entered the restaurant with a silver platter holding a magnificent pair of lobsters bound for another table of guests. They nodded their thanks as they passed him and left on their short excursion.

It was still hot, as they strolled, Adam's arm encapsulating Rebecca's shoulders. They could feel the lightest of breezes brushing their faces as they walked, giving some relief from the heat.

It was the most beautiful of evenings, and they felt utterly at one with each other. The smell of pine on the air was magical.

They leisurely walked on down the quiet, winding 'Le Chemin de la Mosquée' road.

On a remote bend in the avenue, surrounded by trees, a man stepped out, from behind a stone pillar.

He was only five or six feet away, and he said in perfect French, 'Hello, Adam. My name is Seth.'

They both stopped and looked at the man. He was smartly dressed in a tropical, cream suit with an open neck azure shirt and tan loafers. Adam looked over his shoulder as he heard an almost imperceptible noise, only to see two other men standing ten feet back from them, one on either side of the road. All three of them looked like they could handle themselves, and Adam could see the outline of what looked like shoulder holsters under their jackets. They were all in their early thirties, and each had a Mediterranean complexion.

Adam said nothing.

'You must be Rebecca,' the man said smiling, 'it's an honour to finally meet you.'

Rebecca did not respond. Instead, she turned to look at Adam, who gave a cold stare to the man.

'Well, I expect you are not interested in pleasantries, are you. Let's just get down to business.'

With that, Rebecca turned to look in horror at the softly spoken man. Had the Nazis caught up with them, she thought. Her body began to tremble as she felt Adam's body, tense against her. The man put his right hand inside his jacket pocket and seeing Adam's face change, he raised a flattened left hand and said, 'Stop, you have nothing to fear!'

He continued, though more slowly, to put his right hand inside his jacket and then pulled out a sealed envelope.

'We work for Mossad, Adam. I have been asked to give you these documents.'

He slowly stepped forward and handed the envelope to Adam, who released Rebecca from his grasp.

'How did you find us?' Adam asked.

With the hint of a smile, he said, 'I really couldn't say, Adam! However, you should know that no one can ever truly hide from us.'

He raised his arm and pointed at the envelope, which Adam still held and then went on to say, 'It's just as well that we tracked you down, Adam. The letter contains details of your finder's fee, for certain ...how should I say ... 'lost property' which you both were instrumental in finding.'

Adam looked down at the letter as the Mossad agent went on to say, 'It is from certain European governments and comes with a hefty bonus from the Israeli people.'

He shook hands with Adam saying, 'I was asked to convey their sincere gratitude for your efforts in this matter,' he then took Rebecca's hand and kissed it, to her pleasant surprise.

Adam said, 'I should inform you that we retained two gold bars that we found.'

'Yes, well, you've informed me now. Thank you. Let's just call it ...spending money.'

'Now, I must not intrude any further on your romantic evening.'

Stepping aside, he began to walk back up towards the other agents as Adam and Rebecca looked at each other and set off on their way.

'Oh,' the agent quipped looking back as Adam and Rebecca turned to face him, 'there 'is' one more thing ...if either of you finds yourselves in 'difficulties' and are ever in need of 'friends', then please feel free to contact us.'

As the agent turned away, Adam thought he recognised the features of the shooter in Dresden-Neustadt train station. His glasses gone, his hair colour different, though indeed it was the same man.

Continuing down to the Pointe de l'Ilette, they sat on a rock, side by side just as the sun began to sink towards the horizon, turning the sky a brilliant golden orange. Rebecca, unable to control her inquisitiveness any longer said, 'Well, aren't you going to open it?'

'I thought I'd leave it until later,' he said, smiling as she laughingly made a lunge for it.

'Ok, ok, ...give me a moment!' he laughed.

Adam opened the envelope and held the letter before them, as they began to read. The document was very matter of fact and gave details of two Swiss accounts, one in each of their names and details of how they could access them. The letter then went on to say that $20 million had been deposited in each account. They turned to each other, and Rebecca threw her arms around Adam and kissed him full on the lips.

They were deeply in love and decided to stay in the south of France for a few months.

Adam contacted an old friend who he had met in the Foreign Legion called, Ricardo. After serving his time in the Legion, Ricardo had gone on to work in the management and security of gold mines in Africa, and he knew how to turn gold, very privately, into liquid cash. He took the bars and for a 'small' fee paid them out in dollars. Rebecca did not want to keep the money from the sale of them.

On a frosty, January morning an elderly nun called Sister Maria Seraphine, sitting in the CAFOD headquarters in London, was slowly working her way through the incoming post. CAFOD was a Christian charity which worked in many of the more unfortunate parts of the world to aid development. She enjoyed her work, there was not too much stress, and she loved talking to the other younger ladies in the office and feeling that even now, despite her advancing years, she could still be of value.

Sister Maria Seraphine opened one of the envelopes with their donations or applications to set up direct debits to the charity. She noticed that it had some interesting French stamps which she saved to sell on to collectors to add to the fund. On opening the contents, she found an anonymous gift letter accompanied by a substantial bankers' draft as a donation to their charity to help the poor of the world. In fact, it was to be by far, the largest single donation that she or anyone else in the office had ever seen.

Turning to her friends, she said, still white with shock though trying to feign a sense of certainty as she held up the donation, 'There I told you our prayers would be answered!'

As Sister Maria Seraphine went to throw what was left of the envelope into the rubbish bin, she stopped herself. Suddenly she broke into a broad smile, and her eyes began to fill with tears. On the back of the envelope was a neatly drawn letter R surrounded by a circle. She had seen that notation previously.

Years before, a young girl had come to work at the office during her summer holidays while she was studying. She was a lovely girl, and they had got on very well despite their vast differences in years. On the day that young girl, Rebecca, was leaving the old nun had bought her a small box of chocolates to thank her for her help. Rebecca was very touched and had, some weeks later, sent a 'thank you' card with a modest donation for the charity. The card had been signed with a letter R inside a circle.

CHAPTER SEVENTY-FOUR

SIR RUPERT FITZGIBBON'S TAXI pulled up at the main gate of the RAF base in South Ruislip, stopping abruptly at the barrier. An RAF policeman in a white-topped peaked cap left the guardroom as Sir Rupert exited the taxi and paid the fare.

As the MI6 chief turned, the Corporal said, 'How can I help you, sir?'

Sir Rupert replied in an unnecessarily supercilious tone, 'I am expected, the code word is 'Raven'.'

'Yes sir,' the corporal waved to a colleague in the guardroom. The policeman watched the barrier rise and noticed that the sky had darkened appreciably. At the same time a Land Rover, which had been parked nearby pulled up, and the driver opened the door to allow Fitzgibbon to climb in. As the vehicle pulled away, the corporal walked back to the guardroom muttering something rather ugly about dear old Sir Rupert, a latrine and a red-hot poker. Suddenly the rain began to fall.

The Land Rover drove through the airbase, before gently turning in a wide arc until it came to a stop at the steps leading up to the Voyager air transport plane. Fitzgibbon got out without thanking the airman and walked up the steps. As he did so, thunder rumbled in the distance, and fat raindrops exploded on his balding head. He was shown to his seat, and within minutes the Voyager had begun to taxi to the runway.

He had arranged the flight to Washington D.C. in the strictest secrecy leaving no record of it or of him to be found in the future.

He thought of the last text he had received from Rebecca. He was genuinely concerned with its contents, though it also offered him a great opportunity. He now knew the threat that he faced, and he had the means to dispose of that threat, permanently. 'Poor Rebecca,' he thought, grinning to himself as he did so, 'She really is far too trusting.'

Now that he knew what Adam was going to do with the documents and the point that they would be delivered, he only had to 'intervene'. He smiled to himself as he looked out at the airfield and the pouring rain, and he began to dream of his imminent retirement.

The Voyager was quickly cleared on to the runway by the control tower. Outside the rain had become torrential, but the wind was still surprisingly light as the aeroplane took off. The crew were unfazed by the mysterious passenger and the secrecy of the mission. They had become accustomed to these types of flights since they had been based at Northolt.

Sir Rupert slept throughout most of the journey, only to be awoken by one of the female crew shortly before landing. After disembarking, he passed through security alongside the aircrew, using false identity documents.

After that, he disappeared.

CHAPTER SEVENTY-FIVE

ADAM HAD WATCHED THE house for half an hour before he began to creep through the gardens. As he prised open the rear garage door with a crowbar, he made out a footstep behind him in the gravel and heard someone say in a very snooty voice, 'How nice to finally meet you, Adam.'

Turning around slowly, he saw a grinning, balding man in his late fifties holding a gun which was pointed directly at Adam. He was dressed as if he was on his way to do a day's work at the local bank. Adam noted that the gun had a silencer.

'Sir Rupert, I presume?' Adam said politely.

Fitzgibbon's smile faltered at this, and his look became questioning.

'How do you know who I am?' he asked.

Adam had the sense that Sir Rupert was

unnerved, so he added, 'I'm glad that you accepted my invitation!'

'What invitation?' Sir Rupert barked back, clearly rattled.

'I had concerns for some time about the texts and calls being made by Rebecca. So, eventually, I asked her outright, and she was very forthcoming. You see, despite you telling her that I may have been secretly acting against her grandfather's and her best interests, she had begun to trust me.' Adam had wanted to add 'and to love me', but he felt it was best not to.

Adam continued, 'I'm glad that you received her last text. I felt sure that you would turn up, like a bad penny.'

Fitzgibbon, who now looked decidedly wrong-footed, put a brave face on it. He ignored Adam's last quip and continued, 'Yes, I thought that was quite a shrewd move. It's a shame that she didn't continue to question your motives, it would have been of assistance to me. However, this has brought us to this current situation which I now need to deal with. By the way, where is Rebecca?'

'She is where she should be,' Adam replied unhelpfully.

'No matter, Adam, I shall deal with her after I have killed you.'

'How did you begin to suspect that things were not as they seemed concerning my involvement?' Sir Rupert asked.

'I was surprised that the Major had been found after so many years in hiding. Then there were the texts and the phone calls, as I said. Also, although I was protecting Rebecca, I felt that she was, at times, untrusting of me. But the clincher was seeing your family name on a list.'

Sir Rupert looked down at the documents which lay at Adam's feet, 'Ah yes. Most unhelpful. But now, thanks to your help, that problem can be finally resolved, and I can quietly retire to a happy and very prosperous life in the British Virgin Islands.'

'So, what's the plan?' Adam said, feigning fear.

Fitzgibbon revelled in his power over this dangerous man, and he smiled, saying, 'Murphy will be found, dead, in his house. Killed by you. The police and the FBI will never get to the bottom of the matter, but they will assume that you were, in turn, killed by an accomplice. As to Rebecca, I'm afraid that she will just have to disappear. Maybe an unmarked grave deep in the woods nearby. Then there is one final matter I must deal with in Berlin. One of my people at the Embassy, Hopkins, who is an accommodating young man, has now become superfluous to requirements. I will relieve him of the considerable sum of money that he has recently acquired, and then I will dispose of him. I intend to leave no loose ends, you see!'

Adam smiled broadly.

'What's so funny?' Sir Rupert said as a shadow of fear passed over his face.

'Did you really think that I would have come here alone?' Adam replied as he glanced over Sir

Rupert's shoulder at an imaginary partner, saying as he did so, 'Kill him, Paul!'

Sir Rupert, who had never been in the field, turned in a state of panic to look over his shoulder. Seeing nobody there and suddenly realising his fatal mistake, he swiftly spun back to face Adam.

He never saw the crowbar, though he should have done. Adam had thrown it directly at Fitzgibbons' face. Fortuitously the point had entered just under the jawbone with considerable force travelling upwards into his skull.

Fitzgibbon staggered back falling against a hedge, dropping the gun as he did so. He slipped to the floor in a near sitting position. His face was contorted in excruciating agony while his whole body seemed to be trembling uncontrollably.

Adam walked over towards the dying man and picked up his silenced gun. He stood before Sir Rupert, as he glared disbelievingly at his killer.

Fitzgibbon spluttered out in a low voice, 'Ple ... ple...please ...'

Adam advised, 'You really should have made me drop my weapon!'

Adam looked at him and raised the gun up until it pointed towards the dying man's forehead, saying, 'I hope you enjoy your retirement, Fitzgibbon.'

The sound of the shot was just loud enough to startle a bird which had been searching for worms on the lawn, but otherwise, it went unheard.

Murphy had returned to his home after a day spent in Washington DC meeting some of his former colleagues. He often felt a sense of sadness, over the last three years since his wife had passed away, coming home to an empty house.

He had entered and had thrown his keys on the hall stand, before making his way to the kitchen. As he walked in, he had a sense that something was not as it should be. He looked over to the right, at the kitchen table and saw a sheaf of papers with a tattered, old book placed on top of them. The place was in silence.

Murphy was concerned, his cleaner did not come until the next day, and he never varied her. He grabbed a pistol from its hiding place above a cupboard and softly paced around the house, but there were no visible signs of entry, and he was alone. Murphy made his way to the kitchen table and looked down at the items on its surface. The books cover was indiscernible, and so he flicked it open. He recognised a piece of his own lined notepaper inside which he kept hanging on the fridge to note down any items for the weekly shop. The page had been neatly ripped out, and a handwritten note on it said, 'This may be of assistance to you. Semper fi!'

Murphy stared at the words, 'Semper fi'. It was the Marine Corps Latin motto, 'Semper Fidelis' - 'always faithful'.

Murphy dropped the note and leant forward opening the books cover. He was shocked to see before him, the signature of Adolf Hitler scrawled across the front page of, what was, by the looks of it, an early edition of Mein Kampf.

He picked the book up and flicked through it, seeing bits of dust and specs of degraded paper falling away on to the documents below. Seeing nothing particularly noteworthy with the book, except for the obvious – Hitler's signature, he dropped it on the table and picked up the papers. There were two distinct bundles, one set was typed, and the paper had partially faded and yellowed with age. A typewriter had clearly been used as opposed to a modern computer and printer. On each of the pages, the seal of a Nazi Eagle had been stamped. The discernible text appeared to be written in German, the rest, seemingly, being written in some sort of code. Scrawled across the front of this bundle was the title, Das Spinnennetz. He did see a clearly visible signature scrawled in ink at the bottom of one of the pages, H. Himmler. On seeing it, he slowly shook his head in unbelieving contemplation.

The second bundle of papers were crisp and brilliant white and were also typed. They seemed to follow a similar format to the first set of documents and were, indeed, a translation and deciphering of them. These had been prepared with the use of a modern printer. The title page stated simply, the Spider's Web.

An explanatory note, presumably from whoever left the items with Murphy, revealed that a homophonic substitution book cypher had been used to encrypt the documents. It continued that the Mein Kampf copy left on the table as a memento was the key to the code.

Murphy read the file with disbelieving horror and a growing sense of certainty. The document revealed the names and addresses of people who had been Nazi sympathisers during the War. They were to be part of a large ongoing organisation after the inevitable Nazi defeat in 1945. It also set out the funds, much of it in stolen gold and looted artwork, which was to be used in the furtherance of the Nazi goals.

As he had turned one of the pages, he found the UK driving licence of Sir Rupert Fitzgibbon. It had fresh blood on it. He had noticed the surname, Fitzgibbon, within the list of names.

Murphy knew many of these names and families who were in the most powerful positions. Two names on the list finally gave him his answer as to why he had been removed from his position as Director.

He looked up from the file, poured himself a large glass of his favourite French chateau's Chablis. Murphy walked out into the garden and finding an Adirondack chair, sat down to survey the sloping lawn giving on to the great river below. He always felt, whenever he looked out at the view, how very privileged he was to live in such an enchanting place. He savoured the coldness of the wine glass and the aroma of the wine and took a long slow sip.

He tried to gather his thoughts, taking in the scent-laden, fresh air as he did so, when he noticed a small yacht passing downriver towards the sea. It was a reasonably commonplace sight on the river. The boat and its two occupants, a man and a woman, were rather ordinary, but the American Ensign which fluttered in the breeze from the stern was extra-ordinary. As Murphy rose to his feet, he could clearly see that it was hung the wrong way up, the sign of dire distress. Murphy had never actually seen this in peace-time and had only ever seen it once, at a forward base, when serving in Vietnam. As he watched, the yachtsman turned away from the helm, stood to attention looking up towards Murphy and saluted. The young woman also looked to-wards Murphy, giving him a lazy wave as she did so.

'Semper fi?' Murphy thought to himself. The former Director stood loosely to attention, lost in his thoughts and saluted back. Then as the yachtsman turned away, he raised his glass in a toast and said softly to himself, 'Thank you, my friends, whoever you are.'

Murphy watched as the 'See Glass' made its way down the Potomac, disappearing around a bend on its meandering passage out to sea.

Murphy had not noticed the large bundle in the cockpit of the yacht. The mortal remains of Sir Rupert Fitzgibbon lay there under a dirty tarpaulin, awaiting burial at sea.

CHAPTER SEVENTY-SIX

B Y THE EDGE OF A PATH BORDERED by a wealth of Japanese cherry trees and close to the Thomas Jefferson Memorial, a man stood waiting. It was a chilly morning, and there were few others in the park. He had arrived a few moments before and was soon joined by two other men. To anyone passing by, they would have appeared no different than any other businessmen in the teeming city.

One of the newcomers said, 'Mr Murphy, it is a great pleasure to meet you.'

'Likewise,' Murphy said.

They shook hands and the agent, unseen, palmed the small memory stick, slipping it into his pocket.

'Please give my regards to Ariel when you next see him,' Murphy said.

458

'I certainly will,' the man replied as they said their goodbyes. Murphy watched the two Mossad agents as they walked away past the memorial before, turning and heading off in the direction of downtown.

'I wonder what use they will make of that list of names?' he thought to himself.

He did not have to wait long to find out.

CHAPTER SEVENTY-SEVEN

TWO WEEKS LATER CARL BROWN, the President of the United States, was visiting Keesler Air Force Base. Brown was keen to display his support for and association with the military, who he knew he would need on his side in the coming months and years.

His Presidential motorcade had been waved through the front gate, while an air force band played the 'Stars & Stripes' and an honour guard smartly came to attention.

Shortly afterwards the vehicles came to a halt near a large hangar. President Brown had just left his car and was being greeted by the Commanding Officer of the 53rd Weather Reconnaissance Squadron. The Squadron, who flew the Lockheed WC-130J, were also known as the 'Hurricane Hunters' for their work collating data about tropical storms. Suddenly the back of the President's head exploded loudly as a single, high-spec bullet, a Hornady A-MAX .50 (.50 BMG), hit him just behind the left ear, exiting through the Occipital lobe at the back.

A sergeant, attached to the USAF 81st Security Forces Squadron, who was helping to guard the President, also received a superficial wound to his neck, from the bullet, as it exited the President's head before burying itself into a concrete wall.

The Secret Service agents immediately created a protective cordon around the President and like the Security Forces desperately tried to ascertain the threat and the condition of the President. Unknown by agents at that time, the sniper, who had taken that one fatal shot and had been hidden in trees nearly 3000 yards from them, was already making his getaway.

The agents lifted the President back into the limousine and tried to cover the open wound with bandages as the car raced to another pre-arranged part of the airbase. There was blood everywhere. Contingency arrangements had been made for such an event, which was standard Presidential procedure.

The vehicle screeched to a halt beside a waiting Sikorsky HH-60G Pave Hawk helicopter which had started its rotors, in preparation, when the President had initially entered the airbase. Onboard was a highly experienced Aeromedical Evacuation team from the 43d Aeromedical Evacuation Squadron, who were based at Pope Army Airfield, North Carolina.

Two of the team members raced towards the car with their equipment, and the President was gently taken from the vehicle and put on to the stretcher they carried and almost instantly he was lifted by four agents who shoved him into the helicopter. At the same time, the medics continually worked on him. A ring of agents and members of the Security Forces Squadron, who had followed, created a protective perimeter around the car and the helicopter.

The air force base and the surrounding police forces, once informed, were in a state of pandemonium as they hunted ruthlessly for the assassin. The manhunt was tireless. However, it was only weeks later when the experts managed to determine the sniper's likely position that they realised that he would have had sufficient time to make his escape. No evidence was found at the presumed site, and all agreed that the killer had to be military trained, to the highest degree.

The crew took off with the medical team and two of the agents on board. It was swiftly followed by another helicopter which carried a further five Secret Service agents. The noise of their departure was thundering. Both flew at top speed the short distance to the military hospital. The President died as the aircraft began to take off, but the medical team continued to frantically work on him in a vain hope that there was some slim chance.

Brown was officially pronounced dead soon after, by one of the senior military surgeons who examined him in theatre.

CHAPTER SEVENTY-EIGHT

THE VICE PRESIDENT, MARCO Cruz, was in Washington when he heard of the attack on the President and his subsequent death. He wished to go to Mississippi to pay his respects and to accompany the dead President back to Washington.

Cruz was immediately driven to Ronald Reagan Washington National Airport, by his Secret Service detail. As his limousine came to a halt beside the Boeing C-32, Air Force Two, Cruz could see all the frantic activity around the plane. Among the crowd was a New York State Judge, John Franklin, who was in Washington visiting colleagues and who had been heading home. Franklin had answered a loudspeaker call requesting that any Judges in the terminal should make themselves known to airport staff.

Surprised and unsure of the reasoning, he had done so. Franklin was quickly ushered towards the Vice President's plane by Security Staff.

As Vice President Cruz boarded the plane, he was followed by a motley assortment of Security Service agents, aides, administrative staff, members of the CIA and FBI, the Judge, a peppering of high-ranking military personnel and an official photographer. The crew were already aboard, and they looked particularly sombre as they greeted the passengers and rapidly made ready.

Air Force Two was given priority and taxied out onto the runway the moment the last person was aboard, and the doors had been sealed. Fifteen minutes after take-off, Cruz was sworn in as President in an impromptu ceremony, by Judge Franklin who looked quite shell shocked. It had been just 1 hour and 45 minutes since President Brown had been assassinated.

Cruz swore the oath of office of the President of the United States on his mother's bible. He had always taken it with him since her death years before from lung cancer. As he lay his palm on the worn leather cover, he felt a surge of emotion and duty wash over him.

It was a particularly momentous time made even more pivotal as, once sworn in, Cruz became the first American President, from a Hispanic background.

Shortly after the ceremony, President Cruz had a private meeting with several members of the Secret Service, CIA, FBI and two senior members of the military.

He looked at each of the meeting's participants, saying, 'Well, does anyone know who is responsible for these events?'

The various members began to put forward their views. Discussing, then arguing, then considering. At all times they gave everything from white supremacists to home-grown religious fanatics, to crackpots, to international terrorists as possible culprits. A Lieutenant General, named Clarke, interjected saying, 'We are certain that the shot was taken from a great distance outside the base perimeter. The actual shooter was almost certainly someone with an exceedingly high degree of training as a sniper. Without doubt, military-trained, whether by the US or by a foreign power.'

This was the one thing that they all seemed to agree on, President Cruz realised as he looked at the thoughtful, nodding heads of his colleagues.

The one person who had remained silent, during what had been, at times, a rather heated debate, was the CIA representative. During his briefing, President Cruz had been told that the Company Man was a rising star in the CIA and was highly regarded. 'By chance' Miller had been close to the airport as events unfolded.

During a lull in the conversation, President Cruz looked directly at Miller and said, 'Tom, isn't it?'

'Yes, Mr President.'

'What ideas do the CIA have about this awful matter?'

Miller said softly, 'We have some lines of enquiry which we are looking at, but nothing concrete, as of yet, Mr President.'

Cruz looked at him, thoughtfully. What was going on here, he wondered? Not only was the statement lame, giving up no information or suppositions, but it was also accompanied by something odd. Momentarily before he spoke, Miller gave an almost imperceptible glance with his eyes to the right and left. Cruz read it as a furtive look, which was unnoticeable to the others who were beside him, but which was clear to Cruz as he faced Miller directly.

President Cruz said nothing, though he did see the FBI representative raise an eyebrow in disdain at the weak answer from the CIA man. The conversation continued for another fifteen minutes, and it was resolved that they would all keep in close contact with the President and their colleagues and that a further meeting would be arranged within the next few hours.

The meeting adjourned, and the members began to make their way out into the main cabin. As they did, Cruz said, 'Tom, please wait behind a moment.'

'Yes, Mr President.'

As the last of the people left the room, President Cruz considered that Tom had seemed unfazed by the fact that he had been asked to wait behind, almost as if he expected it.

The door closed and President Cruz said, 'I

get the impression that there was something else that you wished to say ...privately. Am I correct, Tom?'

'Respectfully, yes, there is Mr President.'

Cruz waited as Tom began, 'Mr President, just before Paul Shultz was put in place as Director of the CIA, I was tasked by his predecessor John Murphy, to commence an investigation. I was told that it was top-secret and was not to be discussed, even with other colleagues at Langley. It was an investigation into a spate of recent murders in England. Primarily into a particular old man's death. He had previously been a Major in the SS during the war. The focus of the investigation was to concern itself with any possible links between this person and President Brown.'

Cruz kept his demeanour but internally was dumbfounded. 'Go on,' he said with his best poker face showing.

'Sir, there is a link. Not only between these deaths, a worldwide Nazi organisation going back to the end of WW2 and to President Brown ...but also to Paul Shultz.'

This was too much for Cruz to continue to conceal his thoughts, 'What! Are you sure?'

'Mr President. Yes, sir, I am absolutely sure.'

Cruz was shocked, though he had, along with other colleagues, questioned both the removal of John Murphy and the appointment of Paul Shultz. Both matters had created much speculation in the corridors of power that something was amiss.

Miller waited a moment while the President took in the enormity of what he had been told.

Continuing, he explained, 'Mr President, I believe that there has been collusion on a worldwide scale, at the highest of levels, among like-minded individuals in positions of great power, with fascist sympathies, to subvert the world order. These people are at the top of their fields in commerce, politics, the military ...in fact, every facet of life where power can be exerted to the benefit of Das Spinnennetz, as it is known. The Spider's Web. It is a Nazi organisation which was the dream-child of, and orchestrated by, Heinrich Himmler the head of the SS during the closing months of the Second World War. There were only two people I knew for sure that I could trust. One of them was John Murphy.'

The President, who had begun to wonder if this was all a nightmare and he was still actually asleep, said sharply, 'And the other?'

'You, Mr President.'

President Cruz looked at him for a brief moment and then laughed out loud, saying, 'Clearly!'

CHAPTER SEVENTY-NINE

James S. Brady Press Briefing Room, West Wing, White House, Washington D.C, USA

THE WHITE HOUSE PRESS Secretary, Julia Davenport, walked into the Press Briefing Room and efficiently placed herself before the podium laying a few sheets of paper down before her. There was a hushed murmur among members of the media, who were in attendance in the packed room.

Davenport said, jokingly as she looked at them, 'A full house I see!' she then continued, 'I will not be taking any questions today. Good afternoon ladies and gentlemen. The President has asked me to share with you, certain information which has come to light relating to the assassination of President Brown. Following exhaustive investigations, the killer of President Brown is widely 'believed' to have entered the mainland US sometime before the killing, arriving on a flight, it is believed, from the Far East. The source of this information and some aspects of that information are classified.'

Stopping momentarily, she cleared her throat and continued, 'Paul Shultz has been removed as CIA director. He is to be replaced with his former boss, John Murphy.'

The room had a wild electricity buzzing through it with the disclosure of this unexpected news.

'The plot to kill the President has been investigated. We now have the name of the individual behind it. Our 'investigations' have uncovered 'evidence' about the assassination by, as yet unknown foreign nationals. It was masterminded, by Paul Shultz.'

With that, the room went wild with questions, and it took a while to calm things down.

Davenport said, 'Please can I continue,' she paused while people sat back down and the noise subsided, continuing, 'Mr Shultz has now been arrested and will face trial at a later date.'

The noise and general confusion arose again, and this time, she continued above the melee in a higher tone, 'And with that, I will end for today. Thanks so much, guys.'

The press went frantic, with questions flying everywhere, but Julia ignored them all walking as elegantly and nonchalantly out of the room as when she had arrived.

The media went wild with speculation, supposition and downright fantasy.

CHAPTER EIGHTY

N O U.S. VICE-PRESIDENTIAL candidate had received an Electoral College majority, and so, the Senate had selected the Vice President. In a surprise move, a little-known senator was named as the next Vice President of the United States.

With his hand on his grandmother's Jewish Torah, the young Californian Senator David Weiss made a pledge before God to defend the Constitution of the United States of America.

Hundreds of thousands of people stood in a slight, mist-like rain to watch him take the oath on Capitol Hill. The swearing-in ceremony took place on the west front terrace of the Capitol and was a seminal moment for the people of America. They watched as the first Vice President, from the Jewish faith, was sworn in.

By Vice President Weiss's side were his wife,

Hannah, who worked in New York as a commercial lawyer and his two daughters, Sara and Jessica

Shortly after Weiss was sworn in an article appeared regarding the new Vice President in the New York Times, which followed an in-depth interview with one of its journalists.

As part of the interview, it became apparent that Weiss's ancestors had come from humble beginnings. His Jewish grandmother, Rebecca, had been a nanny in a small town called Stolp, in what was then Prussia. She had been saved from the Nazi concentration camps by a brave, aristocratic German family.

Chapter Eighty-one

Buenos Aires, Argentina

IN THE LATE AUTUMN, SOME of the world's broadsheets carried the news of a massive gas explosion in Argentina, with its consequent loss of life. Witnesses had reported hearing an enormous bang and of seeing a great fireball followed by a huge dust-cloud rising into the sky, where an office block had once stood. The shock wave had blown out windows many streets away. One of the local residents had said that she thought she had seen the gas company's engineers working near the building a few days before. This was denied by the company, and subsequently, the witness was roundly denigrated by the local media. The small office block lay in the suburbs of Buenos Aires and following the disaster, most of the occupants had died instantaneously.

The few who survived the explosion and who

were dragged from the rubble had horrific injuries and substantial burns. They all died of their injuries either on their way to the hospital or shortly after reaching the trauma unit. The articles went on to say that the building had been the headquarters of a relatively nondescript, international logistics company called 'La Araña', 'The Spider'.

The deceased were not named by the press, save for the Director of the firm, Herr Schwartz. He was among those pulled from the rubble, already dead.

The subsequent inquiry into the disaster, barely made the tabloid press outside of Argentina as it made no startling revelations and took years to complete.

CHAPTER EIGHTY-TWO

Keesler Air Force Base, Mississippi, USA

THE PUBLIC OUTCRY ABOUT Shultz was vociferous. A swift trial was convened in Mississippi, ostensibly to heal the wounds in the country. However, the hearing was never to take place.

A top-secret meeting had been quickly convened of the most influential political, military and intelligence individuals in the country. No records were taken of who attended that meeting, of what was discussed, or indeed what was fully decided.

What was clear was that Shultz was never to stand trial. He had been sentenced to death by firing squad.

It was deemed fitting that the sentence was to be carried out at Keesler Air Force Base. There were 'some' muffled complaints in the meeting, about whether due process was followed and the overall speed of the decision. However, the general outrage that followed the Presidents having been shot by one of his most trusted advisors at the highest level killed any support for complaint of any kind. In the shadows, a powerful force, deep within the US Intelligence and Security establishments had Shultz in its crosshairs, and the outcome was a *fait accompli*.

The sentence was carried out in a quiet part of the airbase, where a shooting range was situated. The number of people present was strictly regulated for national security reasons. Most were unaware of the true identity of the condemned man. Apart from the firing squad, there was a small contingent of senior military men, a doctor and two CIA representatives. Shultz was led to a wooden post which had been sunk into the ground, for the purpose. It was at the end, just in front of the range targets. A chain with manacles was attached to the post, halfway up and was to be used to restrain Shultz's arms, though the shackles were rather lengthy. The former Director was led to the post by a Sergeant and a Master Sergeant. His handcuffs were removed, and he was about to be chained up when he asked if, as a last request, his arms could be unchained and then Shultz also said that he wished to face the firing squad without a hood over his face.

The Captain was slightly nonplussed and glanced back towards the CIA men, who stood close by. The more senior one shook his head. On being told no by the Captain, Shultz, unseen, gave the briefest of smiles. The Captain then read out the charge and the sentence. He asked if Shultz had any last words, but Shultz just ignored him. The Captain, along with the Sergeants and the CIA men retired behind the line of the firing squad. It was an overcast day, and it had called for heavy rain, but none had yet come, though a constant cooling breeze did drive straight down the firing range.

The officer headed over to the CIA men, had a brief discussion and then walked to the side of the firing squad. He called out the commands, and the men came to attention and subsequently assuming the position as they raised their rifles to fire.

Suddenly, at that point, Shultz came smartly to attention and performing a perfect Nazi salute crying out, 'Sieg Heil!'

All, barring the CIA men, were shocked, but none so much as the Captain, who faltered slightly and as he cried out, 'Fire!' found that his voice, to his embarrassment, broke.

As the bullets found their mark, Shultz was thrown back with great force against the post and fell, slumped below it. The rifle cracks were deafening, and as they began to subside, they revealed the wild cawing of a judicious murder of American crows, moved to flight to escape the din. The Captain looked at the lifeless body of Shultz, and then as the sounds began to diminish, he walked over to the body. His forehead was moist with sweat, and a bead also ran down the centre of his back. He looked down at Shultz in wonderment and pulled his pistol from the holster to perform the *coup de grâce*. The body before him was peppered with bullet holes and blood. The Captains finger trembled as he found the trigger. Then, steeling himself, he fired one shot through Shultz's temple and saw the body jerk with the hit. He had never shot a man before, and he felt sick to his stomach, even though the prisoner had almost certainly been dead already.

The Captain continued to look, transfixed, at the lifeless body of Shultz. The hood had partially come away, giving enough of a view of the face to make it clear who lay there. Then he was disturbed, by the sound of the Sergeant escorting the doctor to the body to confirm the death. The Captain grabbed the hood and pulled it back across the face. He stepped back as the doctor checked the body and then turned and nodded to the CIA men as the other two departed. At that point released from his momentary torpor, the officer, replacing his gun in its holster, turned smartly and marched back to the firing squad. All present were told, by the senior CIA man, that they were never to make mention, to anyone, of the final act by the executed man or of the execution generally as the whole proceedings were classified 'Top Secret'. Though the words, in a sense were rather anodyne, the manner they were conveyed by the Senior Agent, left all with a sense of dread, if they were ever to spring a leak.

Once everyone had left, leaving only the two

CIA men, a black GMC Savana van with darkened windows, drove up. Two further CIA operatives got out with a stretcher and retrieved the body, placing it in the back of the vehicle, and then all four of them departed with the corpse.

Medical, autopsy and prison records were altered or fabricated. The family and the media were told that Shultz had died of a sudden heart attack while awaiting trial.

Shultz's body was cremated by the CIA, and his ashes were then returned to his family.

It was clear to them that it was not advisable to ask questions.

CHAPTER EIGHTY-THREE

A MONTH LATER, A SUKHOI Superjet 100 aeroplane crashed shortly after take-off from Chkalovsky military airport, northeast of Moscow. The plane was part of the Russian presidential fleet and was carrying Viktor Ivanov, among others. The Russian President had been heading to Sevastopol with members of his government. They were to meet with a delegation from India. The aim was to increase trade links and also to foster more significant interaction between their respective militaries.

The plane came down in the densely wooded Khimki Forest, without any Mayday being broadcast by the pilots. In the ensuing fireball, there were no survivors. The explosion had been heard more than ten miles away. Along with the President, many members of the government also perished. Initially, China was suspected, as it was clear that the increasingly closer ties, between Russia and India, were of grave concern to them. Their involvement was soon discounted and terrorism, though never proved, became the generally accepted theory in the ensuing months. A day of national mourning was called.

Yevgeny Kerimov heard the news of the death of Ivanov on the radio. He was sat in his office in the Online Marketing Bureau's headquarters. He smiled – a broad smile of relief more than anything, saying out loud to himself, 'Rot in hell Ivanov!'

Yevgeny felt as if heavy weights had lifted from his shoulders. He then ordered his team to spread malicious gossip, as a matter of urgency, about Ivanov to discredit his memory and anyone who still supported him.

Yevgeny had, for some time, sweated over what Ivanov had meant by being given his 'due' when Ivanov's goal was achieved. A week before the fatal crash, two CIA agents under the direct instruction of the Director of the CIA, John Murphy, had visited the offices of the Online Marketing Bureau. They had left Yevgeny under no illusions as to what he and his family were going to suffer as payment for his loyalty to Ivanov, had he survived.

Having set the balls in motion, Yevgeny poured himself an ice-cold, double vodka and flopped down into a chair behind his desk. He looked longingly at the glass and let out a heavy sigh, feeling a deep sense of relief.

Lifting the glass to the sky, Yevgeny said in heavily accented English and with a wry smile on his face, 'Thank you, America!'

He then downed the vodka in one gulp, enjoying the burning sensation in his throat.

The subsequent investigation into the crash, which took many months to finalise, could not come to a firm conclusion as to the cause and finally settled on pilot error as most likely. The pilot's family's protests, as to the lack of evidence for this outcome, were initially ignored and eventually hushed up.

Over the coming months, the media were in a frenzy as, worldwide, one public official after another committed suicide, was killed in an 'accident', was assassinated or died of 'natural,' though unexpected, causes at a premature age. Eventually, as the deaths began to subside, to the chagrin of the busy reporters, the organisation, which had been known as Das Spinnennetz, gradually disintegrated.

Overshadowed, in the media, by the Russian story, a footnote in much of the press, was an article concerning Thomas Hopkins death. The attaché seconded to the British Embassy in Berlin.

Hopkins had been found by a lady walking her Rottweiler in the Grunewald Forest to the West of Berlin. By all accounts, the woman was slightly built. Apparently, there were those who on occasion would see them out, who would say that the powerful dog actually took her for a walk. The canine had, unusually, run off the path into a nature reserve which was off-limits and would not return when called. She had presumed that some scent in the forest floor, covered in decaying leaves as it was, had attracted the dog. When she went to find 'Bruno' she was horrified to find him barking at the body of a man, who was hanging by a noose from the branch of an aged birch tree.

Unsurprisingly, no mention was ever made of the fact that Hopkins was a member of MI6. However, a note on the deceased's body lead investigators to understand that he had committed suicide, after having had an acrimonious divorce and subsequent money problems.

Ariel Mandler was reading the article, in his copy of The Times newspaper, over breakfast. As he did so, he methodically sliced his buttered toast into thin regular strips. Mandler thought it strange that the reporter should be at pains to mention the dog's breed and its name, Bruno, but gave no mention of the name of the person who found the body. What a peculiar people the British really were, he thought to himself, as he dipped one of the newly cut soldiers into the top of his soft-boiled egg.

Just as Mandler turned the page to read a further article about the Khimki Forest disaster, four members of the Israeli hit squad he had sent to Germany were boarding a plane bound for Rome. Their circuitous route would then take them via Istanbul and Athens before finally heading back to Israel's, Ben Gurion International Airport close by Tel Aviv.

He leisurely finished his breakfast and

thought no more about the British agent hanging in the tree. But for some unknown reason, he could not stop thinking about Bruno and the twist in fate which had brought him such unaccustomed fame.

CHAPTER EIGHTY-FOUR

O N A BLUSTERY AUTUMN DAY, on the banks of the Potomac and close by Great Falls, a small crowd had gathered from the nearby communities along with the local Scout Troop. It was to be a low key, ceremony which was to take place. The event was to mark the unveiling of a life-size bronze statue in honour of 'The American Spirit'. A reporter and a photographer had been sent from the local newspaper, the weekly Fairfax County Times. Once it was over, they were to head to the Lake Braddock Secondary School, which was close-by, to interview the new Lacrosse coach.

Brett, the reporter, was milling around the crowd asking for people's comments and trying to find out who was going to do the unveiling, which seemed to be unknown to all present.

Clayton, the photographer, had taken a few

shots already but was now saving himself for the main event before he snapped any more.

It was 11:30, and the ceremony was due to take place at midday, but to Brett's consternation, there still seemed to be no officials in attendance.

Then as he began to walk back to his car to get his hat, he saw a line of cars and an army truck passing along the road leading towards them. They were slightly obscured by the trees, but there was no mistaking the entourage. His heart missed a beat as he thought, 'It just can't be!'

He ran back towards Clayton, at full pace and the sound that he made moved the waiting crowd to turn, intrigued by the sudden kerfuffle. Then as Brett passed by, their gaze was held by the road and what they also now saw.

Clayton, who had been leaning against a tree relaxing, suddenly stepped forward towards Brett, who looked like he was about to have a panic attack, 'Whoa! It's the President! Come on, Clayton.'

Clayton, stunned for a moment, began to race after Brett. Moments later, the line of limousines stopped on the road, and the truck drove over the grass parking near to the statue. There was hushed anticipation among the crowd. They saw the Marines begin to dismount from the lorry with their polished rifles in hand. The soldiers gradually formed into line, a Sergeant quickly bringing them to attention before ordering 'at ease'. The Secret Service agents had also left their vehicles and had taken up their positions, as President Cruz and the Director of the CIA, John Murphy alighted. The crowd burst into spontaneous applause and cheering.

The noise began to subside, and the Sergeant brought the Marines to attention once more and marched them to one side of the plinth.

Several local dignitaries who had arrived with the entourage walked forward and formally greeted the President and Murphy, after which they all walked to the statue which was covered in a blue, silk fabric with a long gold cord and tassel hanging from it.

Scout Troop 673 quickly formed up, proudly at attention as the President passed by. Clayton was snapping for all he was worth, with his heart pounding, to a dramatic beat, while Brett's pencil busied itself in his notebook as he wrote furiously.

Following formalities, the President stood, with Murphy at his side, at a small podium which had been erected that morning.

'Good Morning, ladies and gentlemen,' he began, to the echo of, 'Good Morning Mr President,' from the beaming crowd.

'Today, we are gathered here to pay homage to the 'American Spirit', by unveiling this statue in honour of our gallant men and women in the military. Liberty is one of the bedrocks of our society, and it is hard-won, by those among us who bravely step forward to protect our country and our ideals.'

The President continued, 'Many of those brave individuals are known to us and are rightly honoured by their nation, often with medals and commendations, for their great deeds. However, many others serve our great country, and their contribution may have been previously disregarded, overlooked or even unknown. It is for those unknown men and women who we are, today, gathered here to honour. They are a part of the whole, and we owe them much more than we will ever know.'

His eyes suddenly darted towards Murphy.

'Now before we are blown into the Potomac ...' he finished as the crowd laughed. President Cruz stepped towards the statue and grasping the tassel said, 'I dedicate this statue to all of the unacknowledged American Military men and women and to their acts of heroism.'

Suddenly the Sergeant yelled out to the Marines, 'Port Arms!' followed by the command, 'Ready, Unlock!'

Then as the President pulled the cord releasing the statues cover, the Sergeant gave the command, 'Aim, fire!' three times.

The bronze statue of a life-size cast of a man and a woman in uniform, both standing confidently to attention, saluting with their eyes. They looked upwards, towards the top of the valley.

The inscription below, read, 'The American Spirit of the Unknown Soldier.'

The river valley echoed with the sound of the rifle cracks and the frantic calls of birds, flushed from their roosts. Then as the Sergeant called out, 'Cease-Fire!' the men were brought back to attention, a corporal who had stood off to one side by the flagpole, unfurled the Stars and Stripes and ran them up, before tying the flag off.

The flag fluttered proudly in the breeze and showed no sign of distress.

As the soldiers were dismissed, the President and Murphy stepped forward towards the onlookers and spoke briefly to members of the enthralled crowd. President Cruz then walked over to the Scouts who remained at attention and said smiling, 'At ease, men!' and as they began to excitedly gather around him, spoke to them of his own Scouting days and of the activities of their Troop.

Then as he went to leave, Brett stepped forward, pressing his hand down his crumpled corduroy jacket in a vain effort to look more respectable. He said in his most official and mildly pompous voice, 'Mr President, Brett Anderson and Clayton Lee of the Fairfax County Times. May we have a few words for our readership?'

The President smiled kindly and said, 'Why certainly, I am always happy to speak to the Press. How about a photo too?'

With that, the President gathered the Scouts around him, in front of the statue and Clayton took more photos than he had done, at any one time, in years, while Brett asked the President a few choice questions.

Both Brett and Clayton would remember that moment for the rest of their lives.

The President was giving of his time but then

had to depart. As he walked to the limousine, flanked by Secret Service men, he left in his wake a, still, astonished crowd of onlookers. He turned to Murphy and said, 'Do you think we will ever know who he was?'

Murphy smiled and said, 'I'm not sure that he wants us to know!' as he said so, a strong gust of wind blew a host of leaves rustling across their path.

CHAPTER EIGHTY-FIVE

Gaston Faure Literary Agency, Rue Gît-le-coeur,
Paris, France

I T WAS A LATE AUTUMN DAY IN Paris. The
light was beginning to fade as the man readily turned into the narrow, rue Gît-le-Coeur,
happy to be protected, somewhat, from the driving rain he had experienced on his walk.

Sometime before, he had received a telephone
call from Gaston Faure his literary agent to say
that a package had arrived by hand, for the novelist. Faure had mentioned that it was heavy
and that he had been told, by the man who had
dropped it off, to be sure that only the addressee
should open it. The man had been quite insistent. Faure had said, that he felt that it was most
peculiar.

Soon afterwards, the novelist, intrigued, had
kissed his wife and daughter goodbye and had
left his flat in the fashionable Parisian, Marais

district and had headed off to meet the literary agent. He had bought the apartment six months before as his fortunes had improved.

On the walk to the office, his thoughts were occupied with deciphering the meaning of the mysterious package, crossing the Île Saint-Louis, the Île de la Cité and then the Seine as he did so. Just as he turned to walk along the side of Notre-Dame de Paris, what had been a pleasant, though blustery late afternoon, had been soured by a sudden downpour and he had inevitably increased his pace.

The rue Gît-le-Coeur was chic and rather short, which he gave thanks for as he ducked into the office and out of the penetrating rain.

Faure laughed to see him, 'But my friend, you are drenched. Why didn't you take a taxi?'

The novelist smiled, saying, 'I fancied a swim!'

They had become good friends, ever since their initial meeting two years before, when Faure had first been offered his novel to promote. The books runaway success had only served to further cement their relationship.

'Well, I don't know what to say. It seems quite strange. I hope it's not a bomb,' Faure said laughingly, though his face displayed some small sense of concern, as though he seriously thought that it might be a possibility.

He pointed to the package, which lay on his secretary's desk. She had gone home shortly before it was delivered and they were, therefore, alone in the office.

The novelist picked up a pair of scissors and

began to open the package. Faure walked to-wards the window and looked outside at the passers-by, to give him some privacy.

Then on hearing a gasp from the novelist, he turned suddenly, saying, 'What is it, Franck?'

Standing there transfixed, Franck, just stared at Faure, the half-opened package before him and a small card in his hand.

Faure, increasingly concerned, said, 'What's wrong, Franck?'

Franck held out the card, which Faure took. It was cream coloured, and the handwriting was in royal blue ink. Softly, he read it aloud to himself, 'Au revoir, mon ami et bonne chance'.

'Franck, what does it mean?'

Franck looked down at the parcel and Faure, nervously, stepped forward to see what he was looking at.

He too let out a gasp and slowly looked up at Franck. Silently they stared at each other, trying to take in the enormity of what lay before them.

Then they both looked back at the package, and at the gold ingot, it held, with the Nazi eagle emblazoned across it.

Franck could almost sense a warm Andalusian breeze brush across his face carrying with it the scent of a grand old Bougainvillea.

He turned to Faure and with a face full of sentiment said, 'It means my friend, that an old comrade did not forget me.'

Epilogue

Yachting off Tuckernuck Island, Massachusetts, USA

I T WAS A WARM DAY; THE SKY WAS clear
and deep blue in colour. Only a few incon-
sequential clouds bounced along the horizon
to remind the world of their very existence. A
cool breeze raced across the sea, creating low,
bubbling whitecaps as it passed by. The yacht
cut through the pristine waters with effortless
grace, leaving its passing wake as the only im-
permanent mark of its passage.

Nestled in the stern, the young woman lent
back, with the tilt of the yacht, into its guide rails.
The wind gently caressed her hair and made it
dance, while her eyes softly closed intermittently against the sun's glare and the sharply, racing
air. Rebecca lazily glanced around at the sea, the
sky and the few clouds and from time to time, at
Adam. He stood at the wheel. She looked at him

with a comfortable complacency, and when she did so, she unconsciously gave a soft smile.

Standing tall and bold against the elements, he had an intense look on his face as he concentrated on the task at hand and at the waves before him. Adam was all she had ever wanted, even before she knew what she would one day want. She was happy now, happier than she had ever been before. She could taste the salt in the air and on her lips, and it made her feel truly alive. Every now and then, a gentle spray would touch her face and would remind her of where they were. They had been sailing for several hours, and without a word, Adam began to slowly manoeuvre the yacht into a long sandy bay. It was remote and for all appearances, had never seen the hand or foot of mankind. Beyond the sand, coarse grasses defended the land from the encroaching sea. Rebecca smiled, 'I can never remember being so contented, as I feel now,' she thought.

As the yacht began to turn and to slow, while it passed into the shallows, Adam called out to Rebecca saying, 'Darling, can you take the helm?'

With careless ease, she stood and steadied herself and took the wheel from Adam as he began to lower the sails and then weaved his way to the bow. Adam dropped the anchor feeling it gently dig into the sandy bottom. The yacht started to turn with the wind, as it gradually went to sleep.

Adam clambered back to the cockpit peeling off his tattered cotton T-shirt as he went. It had once been brilliant blue but was now a washed-out cornflower.

As he reached Rebecca, he said, 'Come on, sleepyhead! Scared of the water?' he smiled, a childlike smile, as he undid his baggy shorts which, being made of heavy khaki canvas, hit the deck of the yacht with a thump. The bright yellow swimming shorts that he wore underneath gleamed in the sunlight just before they plunged with their owner into the blue waters. Rebecca watched as his feet disappeared beneath the waves and waited and waited and waited. Their Labrador who lay on the deck enjoying the sun lifted his head lazily and then went back to sleep.

As Adam did not reappear quickly, she felt a growing unease, a sickness in the stomach, a quickening of the heart. And then, he was there, twenty feet away bursting through the surface like a dolphin.

'Come on, I'm lonely!' he laughingly called. Rebecca smiled back at him, the happiest of smiles and slipped out of her floral cotton summer dress revealing a classic halter-neck, black swimsuit. With the grace of a ballerina, she flicked her red sandals to the side and disappeared seamlessly into the deep.

The waters were still cold but profoundly refreshing, and the sensation made them feel energised. Briefly, they swam together and then each, Rebecca first and then Adam, headed for the shore.

The sand was surprisingly warm as they lay side by side, hand in hand. Rebecca, her heart racing, ran her arm across Adam's chest and embraced him as they kissed tenderly and then more fervently. Unspeaking, at one with each other, each with their own thoughts, each with their own feelings for the other. The sun burned through the breeze and kept them warm as they dozed.

From time to time, the silence of this lonely place, broken only by the sound of the waves, would be breached by a gust of air ripping through the coarse grass beyond. Along with the strengthening wind, the sand began to come. And with one sudden blast of sand, Rebecca lent up and pressing Adam's chest she said, 'Let's go! It's beginning to get cold.'

He laughed and said, 'But it's positively balmy!'

She stood, grabbing his arm and pulled him up. As he was about to rise, she let go, letting him fall back. Giggling, she turned and ran to the sea, throwing up clouds of sand into the air from her feet. Rebecca heard him racing after her as she laughingly shrieked, running through the shallows before diving into the dynamic waters.

Moments later, she felt powerful strokes thrusting through the waves close by and then passing her as Adam swam towards the yacht. He clambered on deck calling back to her, 'Last one aboard, makes dinner!'

She stopped in the water and called out, mockingly pouting as she did so, 'That's just not fair!'

He replied, 'All is fair in love and war, and anyway, I'm the captain!'

Rebecca tried to form a grouchy face but could only laugh through it. She then carried on at a slower pace as she began to make for the short ladder at the rear of the boat. Stopping momentarily, she looked up at the name of the yacht emblazoned across the stern - rocking, lifelessly, with the gentle movements of the sea.

'See Glass', she mused as she looked at the lazy script of the signwriter's hand.

But it wasn't the 'See Glass' at all. The real name they had chosen was too crass for an elegant yacht and so, being a lover of word games and crosswords, she had played with it. The 'See Glass' was so much more refined. Rebecca looked up and saw Adam busying himself preparing the sails, and she suddenly made a couple of short strokes and grabbing the ladder climbed aboard.

She took the wheel while Adam, who was by then in his shorts, hauled up the anchor and set the sails. Within minutes Adam had re-taken the wheel, and she had begun drying herself and putting on fresh clothes. The small yacht edged its way out of the bay and into the somewhat more turbulent open waters.

As the sails suddenly filled, the yacht began to pick up speed, cutting through the whitecaps with a gentle rocking motion. Rebecca turned on the small radio which she had brought with her and as she did so, Acker Bilk's haunting instrumental, 'Pescadores', began to intersperse with the sound of the breeze.

Rebecca sat back, looking ahead and out to sea, gently swaying with the motion of the boat, her lengthy hair fluttering wildly. Occasionally, she would look across at Adam, feeling the warmth of the sun on her face as she did so. Theirs was an attraction, so very deep. Adam would glance over at her, his face filled with concentration, but on seeing Rebecca, softening into a heartfelt smile. Looking into each other's eyes into their souls beyond, punctuated, interrupted, only by the low barking of their happy Labrador. The evocative clarinet permeating all, in tune with the rhythm of the wind and of the waves

The yacht 'See Glass' or more appropriately its anagram, 'SS Eagles', effortlessly sliced through the waves. Those golden eagles had been the source of their previous misfortune but had become the basis of their ongoing good fortune.

AFTERWORD

Thank you for taking the time to read my book. I hope that you enjoyed it.

I'm self-published and therefore I do not have a publishing house promoting my work. You can greatly help me and potential new readers by leaving a review about See Glass? As long or as short a review as you wish would be great.

I read all reviews and greatly appreciate the time and effort that my readers go to in leaving them.

If you wish to join my mailing list to be among the first to hear about forthcoming books and deals then please sign up at www.idograf.com

About the Author

Ido Graf grew up in the Mediterranean and in the United Kingdom, predominantly in London.

After studying for a bachelor's degree, Ido went on to study for a masters, before taking other specialist qualifications.

He spent considerable time in military bases in Europe and the Middle East and comes from a police & military background.

Ido has travelled extensively in North & South America, Europe, Africa, the Far East, Russia and the former Eastern bloc countries.

He was questioned at length in Guinea by the Presidential Guard on spying allegations relating to the Presidential Palace and in Sierra Leone by agents of the state concerning alleged diamond smuggling.

Ido and a friend of his once engaged in a shooting competition in the Củ Chi district of Ho Chi Minh City, with John F. Kennedy while Jr. Daryl Hannah watched the three of them as they fired

AK-47s. It was an extraordinary, chance encounter when they were travelling in Vietnam in the 1990s.

Ido is a fully qualified scuba diver and skydiver. He is a proficient snowboarder, skier (both downhill and cross-country) and a highly experienced alpinist.

He has worked in various sectors for both government departments and private concerns in a variety of sensitive fields in the UK and North America.

Ido Graf is a writer of mystery and suspense thrillers. His works, which he is now publishing, are derived from his own experiences and from meticulous research. He visits all of the locations that he writes about to maintain the highest standards of realism within his novels.

Though much of his output is contemporary in nature, it frequently has a historical basis at its core.

The main focus of his books is in the political, corporate espionage, thriller and adventure categories.

He hopes that you enjoy his novels. Please follow Ido Graf on his blog:

https://www.idograf.com

Acknowledgements

It is no easy task to write a novel. Each of these people or groups have had an impact on my writing and on my will to write.

On some occasions, they may have felt that their contribution was minimal, but their impact was tremendous and at some moments, crucial.

Special thanks for their support, critical appraisal, guidance and encouragement:

Family and friends including

My darling wife and my sons

Helen & Louis

My extended family

Paul & family, Andy, Mark, David & Kerri, Ian, K.W., Mark & family, Mark & family, Nathalie & family and Michael & Maggie.

Gerlinde – German language and cultural expertise

S.A.S. & Ana – Spanish language & cultural expertise

Isabelle - French language & cultural expertise

John - North American political and Eastern European expertise

Frank - U.S. Naval & Military expertise

Tiffany & the team at Grammarly software

For their time, kindness and advice

R. Barnett, Washington D.C

M. Hamilton, New York

INSPIRATIONS

A lifetime ago, though their inspiration still resonates through me – Mr Brennan, Mr Pocock, Sister Christine and Miss Janota, among many other wonderful teachers. I remember you all with great fondness.

The many authors and craftsmen and women of the art of fiction which I have read including, among others, such greats as Graham Greene, John le Carré, Frederick Forsyth, Nelson DeMille, Robert Harris, John Grisham, Jack Higgins, Mark Dawson, Thomas Hardy, Evelyn Waugh, Desmond Bagley, Hammond Innes, Helen MacInnes, Alistair MacLean, Robert Wilson, Randy Wayne White

and most of all the works and inspiring life journey of

Lee Child.

The kindness, encouragement and tutoring of novelists: Frederick E. Smith and Rosemary Aitken.

Also

Special thanks go to those people, some I may never even have known or met, throughout my life who have extended to me - kindness, support and assistance even though, on occasion, there was no reason to have expected it.

Any successes in my writing are built on the shoulders of those mentioned above, any faults solely my own.

Made in the USA
Columbia, SC
03 August 2022

64531923R00309